ADVANCE PRAISE FOR
MORAG MCKENDRICK PIPPIN AND
BLOOD MOON OVER BENGAL!

FAIR WARNING

Elizabeth slowly stood. There wasn't quite an inch of space separating them, and she tingled with the electricity that sparked off their bodies. Tipping her head back, she looked Nigel in the eye. His searing gaze settled on her now trembling lips.

"You're an intuitive girl, Elizabeth. You ought to run for the door—now, while you can."

Not taking her eyes from his, she replied breathlessly, "You would let me go if it was what I truly wished."

"I'm but flesh and blood, and I want you more than I've wanted anything in this life."

Blood Moon Over Bengal

MORAG McKENDRICK PIPPIN

LEISURE BOOKS   NEW YORK CITY

*This book is dedicated to my husband, Loren,
who said I could do it—and for his love
and support while I did.*

A LEISURE BOOK®

October 2004

Published by

Dorchester Publishing Co., Inc.
200 Madison Avenue
New York, NY 10016

ISBN 0-8439-5452-3

Printed in the United States of America.

Visit us on the web at www.dorchesterpub.com.

ACKNOWLEDGMENTS

A special thank-you to my mother, Cicely Tolhurst McKendrick, for her meticulous proofreading, critiquing, and listening.

Blood Moon Over Bengal

Chapter One

Calcutta, State of Bengal
1932

"They just bloody dropped dead!" The young major's voice trembled in anger as he faced his commanding officer. Electric punkas whirred sluggishly overhead, barely stirring the stifling air in the spacious office and doing nothing to dry the sweat pouring off his body.

The Colonel leaned back comfortably in his cushioned chair, lighting his pipe. "Yes, well, they were Indians weren't they, Major? It's not like they were British officers."

"They were *men!* Sir! They were not disposable because they were not British. Sir!"

Colonel Mainwarring lifted his grey eyebrows, raking the soldier before him with a contemptuous glance. "The entire regiment is aware of your singular opinion on that subject, Major Covington-Singh. However, it doesn't change the fact that the British Indian Army—especially the soldiers of the

1st Rangpur Foot—must at all times be ready. We do not mollycoddle our men because it happens to be rather warm."

"Sir, I appreciate that we are not here to enjoy the niceties of a tea party, but it was 120 degrees when those men died from heat exhaustion. More than one day is needed to recover from such a march before departing on manoeuvres again."

The Colonel leaned forward to deposit his pipe in an ashtray and reach for a legal-size envelope from a corner of his massive desk. "Nonsense. Any soldier worth his salt will do whatever is required of him. In a few short weeks the summer will end and the monsoons will start. Outbreaks of cholera and malaria will soon follow. Much more efficient to get done what we can now. You can start by studying this lot," he said, handing the Major the thick brown envelope. "Another murder while you were on manoeuvres. Nasty business, and normally not our concern to muck about in civilian matters, but several"—he gave Major Covington-Singh a sharp look—"highly placed Indians have caused a palava with the Commissioner and now he's dumped it in our laps. Or more precisely yours, since you are Security Officer, Major."

"Another Brahmin woman, I see, sir. That makes two now." Major Covington-Singh frowned, flipping through the pages. "If we don't count the prostitutes in the Bustees."

"You are aware, Major, anything that may happen in the Bustees is pure conjecture. It is a no-man's land. No bloody use imposing law and order in that hellish warren. No, we need only worry about the Brahmins. Find the wog responsible and arrest him. Can't think why the civils cocked it up. Likely too busy chatting up these passive-resistance berks."

"And if it isn't an Indian, Colonel?" the Major asked, his voice tight.

"Are you implying an Englishman may be culpable, Major? Don't be ridiculous! Of course it's a bloody Indian. It's a simple situation, Major. Take care of it." He reached for his pipe and tobacco pouch. "Dismissed."

Nigel Covington-Singh saluted and performed a smart about-face before departing the office. He paused a moment, shading his eyes from the unrelenting glare of the Indian sun. He'd accomplished absolutely nothing by bearding the Colonel in the den the old man so rarely left, in an attempt to stall manoeuvres until the mercury fell below the 120-degree mark. No wonder the Colonel remained in ignorance of how "warm" it truly was. Nigel wiped his forehead with a handkerchief and headed for the Officers' Mess. A pint of English lager was what he needed.

The lounge was dark after the brightness outside, and with several fans operating, blessedly cool. A native server dressed in a white dhoti and tunic with matching turban approached when Nigel took a seat at the bar.

The server bowed, his face impassive. "Sahib, your pleasure, please?"

Nigel answered him and turned, hearing the stool next to him scrape the floor. A man of medium height, with brown hair and captain's epaulettes sat down and nodded to the bartender.

"I say, old chap, bloody hot out! Do pour me a large gin and tonic, there's a good man." Turning to Nigel, he announced, "Just posted here two days ago. Don't know if I'll ever get used to this heat. Doesn't get like this in Ireland—or in America. Spent three years there. Do you know those ridiculous Yanks have outlawed liquor! Can't go to one's club for a quiet smoke and a civilised drink. One is required to patronise an illegal 'speakeasy.' Rowdy places they are, too. And if the proper palms haven't been greased the bobbies break in and haul everyone off to the nick!" He paused to drink deeply from his sweaty glass. "I say, haven't introduced m'self yet. Harry Woodford at your service, Major—?"

"Nigel Covington-Singh."

"Heard you just lost five men on manoeuvres. Bad luck, old man!" Woodford reached in his pocket for his Woodbines and politely offered one to the Major. After lighting both cigarettes, the Captain looked Nigel in the eye and remarked, "Damned lucky it wasn't any more in this heat."

Not wishing to discuss the sore subject, Nigel simply replied, "Quite." Taking a sip of his beer, he enquired, "What took you to America?"

"My fortune, of course. I am, unfortunately, one of those sorry creatures—a second son. Always handy to have a spare tucked away—until of course the heir grows up healthy and produces an heir of his own. Makes one quite superfluous. M'father, the Earl of Tillinghurst, you know, sent me off to America to make my start." He gazed at the dregs in his glass forlornly before continuing. "Only trouble was I arrived a mere three months before the Crash. Lost everything, of course. Men were blowing their heads off right and centre, doncha know. Tried to make the most of it, but in the end I had to ask m'father for help. He arranged a commission, and here I am ready to cut a swath through the jungle."

Nigel smiled and ordered another round of drinks. "Instead of picking your way through the headless bodies and getting jostled about in one of your speakeasies, you'll be contending with mosquitoes the size of finches, cholera, malaria, snakes the length of this bar, and once the monsoons start, unending rain with mud everyplace you now see dust." He crushed out his cigarette and took possession of his new lager. "The heat is at its worst now summer is almost over."

The Captain shook his head. "Funny thing for summer to end in June." He pushed his empty glass out of the way and stirred his new one before sipping at it.

"I say, one can't help hearing things, and even in the short time I've been here I've heard a few about you. Isn't your father a bigwig up north somewhere?"

"You could say that, yes. He's the Maharaja of Kashmir."

Captain Woodford's eyes grew large and he opened his mouth to speak, but his words were lost by the low drone of an engine overhead. Very close overhead. It sputtered, coughed, quit and started again in a high-pitched whine. In accord, both men rushed to the doorway to witness an old Bristol fighter more fall than land on the dusty parade ground several hundred yards distant.

Black smoke issued from its engine as the old flyer came to a halt. Three machine-gun mountings from the Great War era swung loosely, and something from the tail fell heavily into the dirt. Already the fire lorry was on the way, sirens blaring. Men poured from the surrounding regimental offices.

Approaching the growing pandemonium, Nigel could see what he had thought were bombs under the wings was in actuality luggage. He watched two slender figures emerge onto the wings from the cockpits. An officer stepped forward to assist them.

Once the fliers were safely on the ground, they reached to pull off their aviation caps and held their audience spellbound. One revealed golden finger-waved tresses and the other, short red curls.

Chapter Two

Elizabeth slid off the wing with the help of a wide-eyed young lieutenant. It had been a long journey with many discomforts: storms at sea, delays caused by train derailments, and now by far the worst—a near plane crash. Adrenaline still fizzed in her veins. Next to her, Fiona was busy brushing the dust off her flying suit and combing her fingers through her hopelessly knotted bright red hair. Elizabeth knew she didn't look her best either, and she was in no mood to face a battalion of swarming men and a screaming fire engine.

The lieutenant enquired as to any injuries and was assured that they were only a bit rattled. An older officer strode through the gathering crowd.

How exotic-looking, Elizabeth thought, and suddenly she wished she wasn't so dishevelled. He had a tall, muscled physique with very broad shoulders, and he was deeply tanned. Wavy black hair and a mustache graced features that seemed carved from stone. His high cheekbones and aquiline nose conveyed a slightly Asiatic impression that was curiously belied by angry blue eyes.

"Have you lost any sense you might have been born with? The airstrip is twelve miles due north. This is a military parade ground, not your private landing strip. Any number of my men could have been killed."

Instead of shrinking from his anger, Elizabeth lifted her chin, answering his challenge. "But they weren't, because the ground was empty. I chose it for that reason. Not that I was presented much choice, Major"—she caught sight of the name badge attached to his khaki uniform shirt—"Covington-Singh. The engine cut out and Miss McKay and I were lucky to find anywhere to land safely. And aside from the harrowing experience of falling out of the sky, it's rather convenient as this is our destination. We've come to visit my father. Colonel Mainwarring."

Nigel felt his stomach clench. This lovely, delicate blonde was the daughter of the commanding officer of the regiment? He mentally shrugged his shoulders. Not that he'd be allowed near her anyway.

Stepping forward, the redhead said, "Perhaps some of your men could unstrap our baggage, Major, and escort us to the Colonel's bungalow. We're quite tired and not at our best at the moment. Our aeroplane must be towed, of course. I'm sure a mechanic must be somewhere about to right the engine. Then you shan't have to worry about us—"

"Buggering up your precious parade ground again," finished Elizabeth with a twist of her lips.

"Ladies, I should be happy—with your permission of course, Major—to accompany you to the Colonel's quarters. Newly commissioned Captain Harry Woodford at your service."

"They're all yours, Captain." Nigel turned and began organising the clearing of the ground.

Harry held out an arm for each girl. "Pay no attention to

him Miss Mainwarring, Miss McKay, he's endured a particularly trying week."

Elizabeth noticed the good Captain gazing at her friend's
generous chest. Men did that. Fiona was very small, barely
five feet, in fact, and slender—except for what Fiona termed
her "oversized bust." The poor girl was quite self-conscious
and did what she could to hide it, but it was really quite impossible. Already she was blushing hotly.

Elizabeth unrepentantly interrupted the Captain's musing.
"One would hope he's not such a boor every day. I do hope
Father received my letter. With all the delays encountered in
travelling I'd not be surprised to find we had beaten it here
because of our little airborne shortcut."

"He couldn't fail to be overjoyed at such lovely visitors.
And please do call me Harry," he said, giving Fiona an especially warm look. He arranged a staff car for transportation
and apologised for his lack of talent as a tour guide once
they were on their way.

"Just arrived m'self, you see. However, I know enough to
point out this area of the cantonment as the family sector.
Bachelor officers live on the other side of the regimental
buildings in smaller bungalows."

The avenue was wide and paved, unlike the smaller hard-
packed dirt side roads. A few tamarind and palm trees bor-
dered the road and the mostly one-story houses were set well
back from them on generous fenced lots. It was really quite
beautiful in a foreign sort of way.

Arriving at their destination, Harry excused himself and
drove off in a cloud of dust.

Elizabeth stood looking at her father's imposing stone
bungalow, with its steep eaves and large immaculately kept
garden. Blooming tropical flowers and roses shared equal
space, and plenty of shade was provided by palm, citrus, and
banana trees. It hadn't changed. But she'd been only a child

when she'd seen it last. She brushed her suddenly moist palms on her flight suit.

"Oh, Fi, have we done the right thing? I haven't seen him since I was twelve. It's been nine years and I barely know him. I'm not sure I *want* to know him. He was always so authoritarian, no room for any opinion save his own. It's no wonder Mum left him."

"You never would have forgiven yourself if you simply sailed on to New Zealand without giving your relationship a chance. He could be different now that you're an adult. He certainly can't tell you what to do anymore."

Elizabeth smiled and headed for the garden gate. "He always made fun of Uncle Charlie for dirtying his hands on a filthy sheep station. Yes, Uncle dirtied his hands all right. Right into black gold. It's just too bad neither he nor Mum lived very long to enjoy it."

"But *you* can." Fi followed her up the verandah stair.

The doorbell was rung and they were let in by a turbaned butler. He expressed no surprise at the unexpected arrival, merely informed them the *Sahib* had not arrived home for the evening, and offered to show them to guest rooms and provide refreshment.

The girls revived themselves with tea and biscuits while their baths were drawn. By the time they finished bathing, their baggage arrived and they were shaking out the creases of their clothing. Elizabeth chose a shimmery gold bias-cut dinner frock and her mother's pearls. After applying powder, mascara, lip rouge, and a touch of her favourite Arpège perfume, she met her friend in the drawing room.

Fi was studying a collection of ivory carvings on the mantelpiece. Surveying the room, Elizabeth shook off the clinging feeling of déjà vu. Bronze statues of Indian deities resided on carved dark wood tables, and Oriental carpets she remembered from before covered the teak floor. The room was smaller through adult eyes. Elizabeth made straight for the drinks table and poured two sherries.

"Do let's fortify ourselves before the dragon arrives breathing fire, old girl."

"I think you're making too much of it. He'll be overjoyed to see you, I'm sure. You are his daughter, after all." Fi sipped from her crystal glass and made herself comfortable on the settee.

"I'm not so sure. Mum never admitted to leaving him, but blamed the recurrent malaria for sending her home to Devon. She maintained she couldn't survive another season in India, and England *did* do wonders for her health. Father only visited once, nine years ago. They got on horribly and he left early. He may think me disloyal as well."

"That's ridiculous! You were a child! Besides, you were sent home for your schooling. You couldn't very well trot back to India on holidays."

Elizabeth poured herself a second sherry. "Yes, well, I have mentioned that Father has rather peculiar ideas. Doesn't he keep anything stronger than sherry?"

"And what might you prefer instead, Daughter? The infamous pink gin that sends more British soldiers home in a box than malaria? Or perhaps you'd like the direction of the nearest opium den?"

Chapter Three

A tall, thin man with a receding hairline stood framed in the doorway. His hair was greyer, and more frown lines surrounded his sharp green eyes than she remembered. The khaki uniform he wore was dusty and wrinkled, and he tapped his swagger stick against his thigh. He never had been an affectionate parent, but she had been his little girl once. An eon ago. Continue as you mean to go on, Elizabeth reminded herself, looking him straight in the eye.

"It seems jubilant greetings and a joyful reunion are not fashionable this year. I'll try to keep my elated emotions under tight control, Father. An opium den isn't necessary. A simple scotch will do nicely."

"Six million pounds hasn't depraved you quite that much I take it." Colonel Mainwarring sent his daughter a sideways look as he made his way to a carved cabinet beside the drinks table. He fished a key out of his pocket, inserted it into the lock and brought out a half-full bottle of Loch

Dubh. He poured two fingers and handed it to her saying, "Not too plebeian for the new heiress, I presume?"

Elizabeth raised her eyebrows at his dog-in-the-manger attitude. "It will have to do in a pinch, won't it?" She sat in a leather wing chair and took a deep breath to settle her nerves.

"Father, I haven't seen you since I was a child, and even then infrequently. After that last visit, you never came back or returned my letters. Mum and I lived modestly on the stipend you sent until Uncle Charlie left us his fortune so recently. I'm on my way to the sheep station." She paused briefly, taking careful note of his blank features. "I stopped here, invading your privacy because I needed to find out whether there is a relationship between us to salvage. I've lost one parent. I was hoping I'd still have another." There— she had done it. Poured out her heart to him. So much for stiff-backed pride. Now he would tell her she meant no more to him than one of the tropical mosquitoes. Just wave the pesky things away and forget about them.

Her father sighed, sipped his scotch, and walked to the window overlooking the lush garden. He continued to gaze out at the feathery tamarinds and the banana trees heavy with fruit. The roses were wilting in the heat, but the bougainvillaea thrived, decorating the garden like a multi-coloured garland. A sweeper was clearing the walk, and a flock of crows flew by squawking. Finally he turned back to her.

"I'm not a man to show my emotions, but the defection of your mother hurt me deeply. My pride stung as well. It was easier to let my man of business handle the financial functions, bury myself in regimental affairs, and forget the pain of losing my wife and daughter." He cleared his throat and sampled his scotch again. "Probably not the best way to deal with such a situation, but there you have it."

Elizabeth closed her eyes in relief. At least he had not outright rejected her. With an effort, might this hint of vulnerability she witnessed grow, and possibly crack the authoritarian facade? Opening her eyes and smiling gently, she assured him, "You didn't lose me, Daddy. I've always been your daughter. Perhaps now we may become acquainted with one another. Fiona and I would love to see some of India now we're here."

Fiona turned from her discreet study of a dull hunting scene. "Very much so. One hears the most extraordinary stories: man-eating lions and tigers, a religious sect bent on murdering for pleasure, wives throwing themselves on their husbands' funeral pyres. Why, I've even heard of a snake that can devour a man whole! I think I should like to purchase one of those creatures whose sole purpose in life is to kill snakes. What are they called?"

"It is a mongoose," the Colonel answered dryly. "I don't believe you will encounter any trouble with the local animals or the worshippers of Kali if you avoid strolling in the jungle. Take a bearer with you, keep to the British sector and you will be just tickety boo. And suttee has long been outlawed, so you won't witness any faithful wives burning themselves alive."

Elizabeth smiled at her friend's deflated expression. "I'm sure we'll find some danger and adventure, although I would have thought our rough landing this afternoon might have cured your penchant for thrills for a day or two, at least. Shall we see if supper is ready?"

There was certainly a long way to go in bridging the gap with her father, Elizabeth thought as she led the way to the dining room, but it appeared the first pontoon at least had been erected.

Supper proved a spicy affair for the newly arrived pair. Curried shrimp from the Bay of Bengal and jasmine-flavoured rice were adventures for their untried palates. More water was consumed with the meal than wine. Ice cream, served

on the verandah, was a welcome treat. Excusing himself
early, the Colonel withdrew to read through recent dispatches in his study.

Elizabeth took the last bite of her melting dessert and
leaned back in her cane chair sipping crème de menthe.
Closing her eyes, she enjoyed the lazily drifting scents released by the heated flowers.

"We must find the bazaar tomorrow and indulge in simply
scads of shopping. Those saris must be wonderfully cool."

Fiona looked doubtful. "I wonder if they are quite the
thing. We haven't seen British women wearing them."

Elizabeth was musing that they could jolly well make
their own fashion when a sporty two-seater roared to a halt
at the gate. A well-dressed woman with a filmy scarf wound
round her head and throat exited the car and mounted the
short flight of stairs.

"My dears," she said, peeling off her scarf with a dramatic
flair, revealing a blond finger-wave 'do similar to Elizabeth's
but with black roots. "I simply had to be the first to welcome
you to Calcutta. I'm Beryl Tate. My husband is the Deputy
Commissioner of Bengal," she finished in an important tone.

Introductions completed, Elizabeth offered liqueur. "I'm
sorry my father isn't present to welcome you, but business
called him to his study."

Beryl settled into her chair and pasted on a bright smile.
"It's quite all right—I came to see you two. We must get you
out to the club and introduce you around. Caused quite the
sensation, you did, nearly crashing your aeroplane on the parade ground! Then the news comes tearing about that one of
you is the Colonel's long-lost daughter—and an heiress to
boot! Everybody is just dying to meet you, especially the
handsome young officers. You simply *must* come to the
weekly Wednesday dance tomorrow night at the Mohd Bagh
Club." She leaned forward in a confidential manner, taking
for granted her request would not be denied. "Now, do tell

how you learned to pilot an aircraft. I'm sure I'd be much too frightened to fly as a passenger let alone drive the thing. Canby—my husband, you know— wouldn't allow it! Why, he thinks I can't competently drive our Aston Martin! I'm quite brilliant when it comes to driving. Everybody says so. Now, you must tell me how Colonel Mainwarring's daughter came to inherit millions of—" Distracted by the sound of an engine, she abruptly broke off, swivelling in the direction of the road. A dark cabriolet pulled up behind her motorcar and, apparently recognising the handsome driver, Beryl hurriedly pulled out her compact to freshen her bright red lip rouge.

Elizabeth glanced at her guest in some amusement and reached into the carved wooden box on the table to extract a cigarette. She fitted it into a holder as Major Covington-Singh gained the verandah. He bent to light it, regarding her steadily over the flame of his lighter. Quite unexpectedly, Elizabeth felt a rush of awareness of him as a male and her heart sped up.

"Playing the welcome wagon, Beryl?" he asked sardonically, lighting his own cigarette.

"I might ask you the same, Nigel." She stared at him with heavy-lidded eyes and raised her hands to her hair, fluffing it. The action pulled her dress tightly over her bosom.

"Enjoy your role. I'm here on business with the Colonel—not that it isn't a pleasure to see you two ladies again," he said, nodding to Elizabeth and Fiona.

Looking up at him, Elizabeth took a deliberate draw on her cigarette and exhaled slowly. "I trust your parade ground is in working order again, Major? Miss McKay and I are quite recovered from our ordeal and would hate to discover we had contributed to any lasting inconvenience. You will let me know the whereabouts of my aeroplane and the repairs needed?"

"It belongs on the rubbish heap, but if you like we can

summon a mechanic from the airstrip to look at it. Whomever you bought it from took you for a ride, Miss Mainwarring."

"And a rather frightening one at that. However, at the time it was a godsend. We didn't fancy being stranded in the middle of nowhere by a train derailment. We were lucky in obtaining a lift to the nearest town. I rather trusted my own piloting skills over those of a strange, hired driver."

He looked her over thoroughly, studying her shining gold hair, delicate bone structure, bee-stung lips, and the long graceful column of her neck. His roving eyes lingered on her form-fitting satin gown, imagining her breasts overflowing his cupped hands, admiring her narrow waist, nicely rounded hips, long, long legs, and dainty feet encased in very high-heeled gold leather sandals. He forced the picture of them both naked and writhing together on his bed out of his head.

"Very intelligent after all, Miss Mainwarring. The slave trade is alive and well in this part of the world. You and Miss McKay might have been a valuable commodity. Now excuse me." He indicated the folder he held. "Your father is waiting for these dispatches."

Fiona took a gulp of her liqueur. "Good Lord! Slavery! In this day and age! I've never been so glad of your flying lessons, Elizabeth. Elizabeth?"

Elizabeth mentally shook herself. The Major's heated gaze had turned her knees to liquid and her blood to lava. Nothing quite like this ever had happened to her. She possessed any number of male friends, but none positively melted her with a mere look. She had a feeling that like Caro Lamb's Lord Byron, Nigel Covington-Singh was *mad, bad, and dangerous to know.*

"I'm sure he exaggerates, Fi. For goodness sake, it's 1932! He *was* only funning, wasn't he, Mrs. Tate?"

Mrs. Tate's mouth tightened, accenting the lines of dissipation around her lips. She hadn't missed the looks passed between Elizabeth and the man she had marked as her next lover. "I'm afraid not. Much goes on under the polite surface in the East. This is a land of mystery and intrigue, my dears. You have much to learn of Asia!"

"So we were discussing before you arrived," Fiona mentioned. "We thought to visit the bazaar tomorrow, perhaps to purchase a sari or two. Such an exotic garment, and it's much too hot for European clothes, anyway."

"And several of those darling enamelled bronze bowls and incense burners," added Elizabeth. "They will remind me of an adventurous holiday in India when I'm rusticating on my rural sheep station in New Zealand."

"You may purchase the saris, but you must never wear them outside your bedrooms." Mrs. Tate shook her head vehemently. "No, it is simply *not* done. One of the rules you must learn, my dears, is the definite demarcation between Indians and us. We do not mix socially. It is only acceptable to do so when attending functions where Indian royalty or highly placed civils are present. Unfortunately, there are more and more of them these days. As a result they are getting above themselves with this 'India for Indians' propaganda."

"But it is their country," Fiona ventured. "Surely it must be difficult to totally avoid them."

Elizabeth leaned forward. "Are you saying no Indians attend the club dance tomorrow night?"

"Of course not. They throw their own parties and dances. Besides, they would be as uncomfortable as we should be if they were to appear. It is difficult enough now there are so many, it seems, in local government. Why, even the Deputy District Magistrate, Deputy Superintendent of Police, and our local Superintendent of Transportation are either wogs or cheechees, who are just as bad." Mrs. Tate refreshed herself from her glass once more.

Elizabeth and Fiona exchanged glances before the former spoke. "I am aware that 'wog' is a derogatory term for Indian, but what on earth is a 'cheechee'?"

"A cheechee, Miss Mainwarring, is an Anglo-Indian," said Major Covington-Singh, who stood just behind her in the doorway. "A Eurasian. Or, in the vernacular preferred by some British"—he cast Mrs. Tate an icy glare—"a blacky-white or an eight-anna. Nicely brought up British ladies have nothing to do with them. Their reputations are forever tarnished. Their skins may even turn darker just by association." His piercing blue gaze abruptly switched to Elizabeth. "Never be caught alone with one. But I'm sure your father will provide a complete education on the subject. Goodnight, ladies. Goodnight, Mrs. Tate." He strode across the verandah, down the stairs, and, jumping over the door of the motorcar, took off into the gathering gloom.

Mrs. Tate, flustered and blushing, half rose from her chair, gave up, and sat back down.

"That wasn't at all well done, I'm afraid. My wretched tongue! How very inconvenient for him to be near just then."

"I take it the Major is in the minority in his opinions of the Indians," Elizabeth commented.

Her guest's eyes widened. "Of course. I mean he would, wouldn't he? After all, he *is* an Indian!"

Chapter Four

The Mohd Bagh Club embodied the spirit of India with its great carved mahogany columns, teak floors, murals depicting scenes of Imperial India, and the gigantic Bengal tiger skin hanging over the empty fireplace on the opposite wall. An orchestra played a lively tune on the raised stage in the centre of the room, and there were already a few dancers whirling on the polished floor beneath them. Behind the dancers, comfortable-looking leather chairs and settees reposed on the scattered Kashmiri carpets.

The scene wasn't as glittering as it might have been a few years ago, for the dreary depression invaded even India. Several of the ladies' evening frocks dated back a few years and bore signs of makeovers, but there were many of the newer frilled chiffon, bias-cut gowns as well. And the current fashions were observed in longer hair, vermillion lip rouge, painted fingernails, and pencil-thin eyebrows. Men sported the Prince of Wales style of wide-legged trousers fitting snugly around the hips, white waistcoats under their dinner jackets, and the required slicked-back hair.

Elizabeth had chosen a floor-length turquoise lamé gown, with a fashionable halter neck exposing her entire back. She wore coordinating sling-back Ferragamos with very high heels. Fiona's slinky white satin gown contrasted nicely with her carrot curls, which were already escaping from the liberally applied styling pomade.

Catching sight of them, Captain Woodford hurried to greet them.

"The two loveliest ladies attending the dance! I was hoping our newest visitors might grace us tonight." He gazed warmly at Fiona—or rather at her bosom. "I should like to claim several dances with you—both of you, of course," he added quickly. "But first, refreshment." He raised his arm, signalling to a waiter.

The orders taken, a plump woman in perhaps her mid-sixties approached and introduced herself as Mrs. Emily Stanton. Although she owned a tea plantation in Ceylon, she always considered her home to be in the more cosmopolitan Calcutta, she informed them.

"Come, let us find a suitable table so we may acquaint ourselves with one another. Do go away, Captain, while we ladies enjoy a nice coze. The evening is early yet, and you young people will find plenty of opportunity to dance the night away when this old widow retires in about an hour. Here, this will do nicely." She indicated a table at the edge of the room between two potted palms. "So very convenient to point out people while remaining unobserved oneself. Except by the servers, of course."

The waiter found them and, placing the gin and tonics before them, retreated into invisibility as so many of the Indian servants did. Captain Woodford, looking somewhat nonplussed at his summary dismissal, apparently decided he was *de trop* and promptly took himself off.

"You are quite the celebrities in our small colonial community. Most of us had forgotten the Colonel even had a wife, let alone a daughter with six million pounds! You'll find fortune hunters aplenty in Calcutta. Are you an heiress as well, Fiona?"

"Goodness no! I'm only Elizabeth's companion—albeit a very well compensated one."

"Only a technicality. Fiona and I were always the closest of friends in school. Shortly after the completion of our studies, her parents were killed in an automobile crash. She was forced to procure a living immediately, and as I desperately needed help caring for my mother in her final illness, it seemed the ideal situation. She passed away less than a year ago, just after I was named my uncle's heir." Elizabeth felt tears forming, but continued anyway. "Mum was so happy for Charlie. As the black sheep, everyone predicted he'd come to no good."

Mrs. Stanton patted Elizabeth's hand sympathetically. "We shan't have any sadness tonight. Look there now." She directed their attention to a stout, balding middle-aged man standing at the edge of the dance floor drinking from a tall, sweaty glass. "That is our Deputy District Commissioner, Canby Tate. He's probably keeping an eye on his frequently erring wife. I understand you made her acquaintance last evening. Quite an honour, I'm sure. She considers herself, as the wife of the second-ranking civil, to be the local Lady Jersey. Being the Colonel's daughter levels the playing field, and she'd usually have waited a few days before calling to let you know she considered you her social inferior. Could it be your fortune, my dear?" Mrs. Stanton paused to sip from her crystal glass. "Ah, she's managed to elude her slightly better half yet again, and is all but sprinting to the bar where her mark innocently awaits." The weathered skin around Emily Stanton's eyes crinkled as she smiled widely and leaned back in her chair. "Here's drama indeed. The handsome young man she has all but draped herself over is Major—"

"Covington-Singh," supplied Elizabeth. Her gaze narrowed on the couple, who appeared oblivious to their surroundings. The Major pulled Mrs. Tate toward him and settled her against the bar. Elizabeth turned back to her companions with pursed lips. "We had the dubious pleasure of meeting yesterday afternoon. He seemed to think I should have crashed my aeroplane rather than land safely on a perfectly deserted parade ground."

Mrs. Stanton frowned before understanding dawned. "Ah, yes, I see," she murmured. "Nigel can be somewhat overbearing occasionally. As he is now." She nodded toward the bar.

Turning, Elizabeth saw Mrs. Tate leaning on the bar, but instead of embracing her, Nigel held her at arm's length, and deducing from the thunderous expression he wore, was giving her a blistering tirade. Suddenly he dropped his arms and stalked to the French doors leading to the dark garden. Patting her hair, Mrs. Tate pushed from the bar, her eyes glued greedily to his retreating back. Before she took two steps however, her husband reached her and seized her elbow, hustling her from the room.

"Nigel wants nothing to do with her, of course. Canby usually turns Nelson's eye to her, um, indiscretions, but he is enough of a bigot not to stand cuckold by a half-caste—even if that half-caste is royal."

Chapter Five

"Royal?" Elizabeth's eyes widened. "How is that, Mrs. Stanton?"

"Oh, do call me Emily, my dear. Why, he is the youngest of the Maharaja of Kashmir's three sons." She paused to savour the explosion of her little bombshell, looking innocently at one, then the other of her companions. "Do one of you girls happen to carry cigarettes? I seem to have left mine somewhere."

Fiona reached inside her satin evening bag, extracting a silver cigarette case. She passed it and the twin lighter around the table. "Please, dear Emily, don't keep us in suspense any longer. What on earth is a maharaja's son doing *here?*"

Exhaling deeply, Emily once more leaned back, enjoying herself immensely. "It appears, my dears, that Nigel suffers from ambition. He is determined to attain rank with nothing other than his own hard work and perseverance."

"How extraordinary!" Against her will Elizabeth was impressed.

"Yes," agreed Emily. "He could be any number of things if his father had his way: a major-general, administrator of his own extensive land holdings, or perhaps an ambassador."

Tapping her cigarette ash in the enamelled metal tray, Elizabeth leaned closer. "Why then did he choose the British Indian Army? It seems the hardest course open to him. Even arriving just yesterday, I am aware of the dislike and suspiciousness the British here feel for both the Indian and the half-caste."

The older woman nodded and raised her voice slightly to be heard over the melodic notes of a Strauss waltz, which beckoned flocks of dancers to the floor. "Despite wealth and royalty, life has not been easy for Nigel." She took one last draw from her cigarette and crushed it out before launching into her story.

"Ranjit had only recently ascended the throne when he welcomed the Duke of Avesbury to his court. The Duke's only daughter, Lady Vanessa, accompanied him on his diplomatic mission. The two young people fell instantly in love and brooked no interference on the matter of race. His Grace spoiled his daughter and could deny her nothing, especially after the new Maharaja made a public declaration he'd take but one wife.

"The progressive couple soon married in the Hindu fashion, followed with a Christian ceremony to soothe the Covingtons' sensibilities. Gulab is the heir. Dhalip, the second son, is lifetime chief advisor to the throne. Worried about a secure future for her third son, particularly if the first two procured several wives, Lady Vanessa planned a British upbringing for Nigel. Accordingly, he was graduated from Eton and Oxford, as were his brothers, but he spent more holidays with the Covingtons and moved extensively in British social circles. Alas, even in that social stratosphere, he remains Indian. Oh nothing disrespectful to his face, of course, but no one let their daughters near him. Ironically, in private life in India he is viewed as a half-caste—a target of suspiciousness from both races."

Confused, Elizabeth asked, "His royalty doesn't prevent this?"

Emily shrugged. "Perhaps not by the Indians if he were not, well, quite so British, but the damage, if indeed it is damage, is already done. In the Indian Army the British are officers and the natives, sepoys—enlisted soldiers. Nigel allowed his father the favour of one small intervention: the arrangement of a commission as a lieutenant several years ago. Otherwise, Nigel was destined to stagnate as a 'native officer.' They rank below British officers, you know. He'd have spent his entire career to rise only to subdar-major. Not quite as high as a second lieutenant. Every one of his promotions has been hard-earned. He's his own man in the army."

Fiona swallowed the last of her gin and tonic and shook her head. "I doubt I'll ever straighten out the social strata in India."

Elizabeth leaned back in her cane chair, regarding Emily Stanton thoughtfully. "He *does* seem a determined, complex man. Tell me, how do you know so much about his private life?"

Emily chuckled. "In a week you will know everything about everybody in our small community. And everyone will know *your* next move before you yourself know. We absolutely thrive on gossip. Ah, here comes the faithful Captain Woodford to insist upon a dance with Fiona." Glancing at her small wristwatch she declared, "It is past my bedtime, my dears, so goodnight and have fun dancing the night away!"

Neither of the girls lacked for partners, and if Elizabeth noticed the omission of the handsome Major Covington-

Singh to take a turn, she made no sign. After several numbers she made her way to the powder room to refresh her lip rouge, and on her way back to the ballroom spied a side door ajar. Thinking of a welcome breath of fresh air, she stepped out into the muggy night and found herself in a small alcove surrounded by bougainvillaea, bamboo shrubs, and several bushy, exotic flowering plants unfamiliar to her. Feeling shut off from the world, she leaned against a palm tree and closed her eyes, breathing in the tropical scents of mimosa and night-blooming jasmine. The strains of a popular song reached her, and she hummed "Blue Moon" in tune with the orchestra:

> *You left me standing alone,*
> *Without a dream in my heart . . .*

The rasp of a match striking its sulfur pad broke the spell, and opening her eyes Elizabeth discovered the large form of Major Covington-Singh looming in the semi-darkness. He exhaled a cloud of smoke from his newly lit cigarette. He did not offer her one. Boldly looking her over from head to toe, he puffed once more before speaking.

"You shouldn't be out here, you know. I believe I informed you last night the danger to your reputation that time alone with a cheechee might cause. At worst the high sticklers will have you ruined. At best you'll be eaten alive by mosquitoes."

Elizabeth felt herself run cold, then hot as the implication of his words hit home. Images flitted through her mind of how they might occupy "time alone." Flustered she retorted, "They don't seem to bother you!"

"Who? The high sticklers—such as your father—or the mosquitoes? Never mind. I ignore both." Nigel regarded her through narrowed eyes, taking in the way the soft material of her gown clung to her slender but curvaceous figure. A cool breeze wafted by, pebbling her nipples. Unconsciously she arched her neck, enjoying the feel of the cool air caressing her heated skin. Fire flowed in his veins. Exhilaration raced through him as he imagined spanning her waist with his brown Indian hands, pulling her against his hard, aching body and carrying her to his bungalow where they could take their pleasure of each other all night in the tangled sheets of his bed. Royal blood be damned, he'd likely find himself ambushed in the jungle and killed for fixing his interest on her, and still he was hard and straining at the seams of his uniform trousers. To hell with it.

Elizabeth watched the conflicting emotions chase themselves across Nigel's face. He seemed to come to a decision and crushed his cigarette under his heel. With the grace of a panther he approached.

She sucked in her breath as he came close and reached out, gently grazing her neck. That slight touch sent shivers tingling out to her fingertips and down to her toes. His fingers blazed fire along her shoulder and up to settle under her chin, raising her face to his. She was intensely aware of his male smell mixed with a spicy patchouli cologne, and of the rough tree trunk digging into her back as his heavy-lidded gaze bored into her.

"So much for the mosquitoes," he murmured and lowered his head. He met her lips with his own, coaxing them open before gliding and curling his tongue around hers.

Heat pooled low in Elizabeth's belly as the world spun out of control, and gasping softly she reached up and wrapped her arms around his neck.

Nigel couldn't stop his savage growl of triumph, and losing his last vestige of control, he deepened the kiss, angling his mouth first one way and then another. Blood hammered through his body and he pressed her even closer, molding her body to his.

Elizabeth's breasts swelled, her tongue fighting deliciously with Nigel's. Trembling, she pressed herself closer to the solid, unyielding planes of his chest. She'd never imagined sharing such intimacy with a man fully clothed. Then, he moved so she could feel his hardness, and she knew she was out of her depth.

With a mastery she didn't know she possessed, she pushed at his chest until reluctantly he lifted his mouth from hers.

She leaned weakly back against the palm tree, shaking. Never had she felt thus or experienced such a reaction to a man. Never lacking for dates or escorts, she'd been kissed by several men, but not like this. She'd not have allowed it. But Nigel was definitely different. A more appealing man— or more infuriating—she'd never met.

A woman's voice abruptly crashed through Elizabeth's fog of desire, forcing her to her senses. Suddenly she was appalled by her behaviour. To permit a man she barely knew to maul her was mortifying enough, but others' observation of such a performance was insupportable. She refused to admit that she had enjoyed every minute.

Panting now as much from alarm as arousal, she pushed frantically at Nigel. "No. Please."

Breathing heavily himself, Nigel's burning gaze bored into her, questioning the abrupt change from ardent lover to frightened girl. And then he heard it, too, the high trilling voice calling his name.

"Bloody hell," he swore as he released her and watched her run into the building.

Nigel rounded on Beryl, his eyes glinting with fury. At first he'd regarded her pursuit of him as amusing: the District Commissioner's wife hot after a man she considered her social inferior. Eager for the novelty of bedding her own blacky-white and so confident he would jump at the chance to make love to a white woman. A woman past her prime and bulging at the seams of her green chiffon evening gown.

It seemed the kindness he'd shown her in this very alcove

had been mistaken for attraction on her part. Or, perhaps, an effort to erase the scene of two weeks past so he would see her as other that the pathetic town tart weeping inconsolably. In truth it must be a miserable life she led. She hated India, and she despised her husband. To relieve her mean existence she bedded almost every white man in Calcutta, then played them against each other for amusement. Until he'd placed his arm around her shoulders to comfort her, she hadn't seen him as a potential lover. Not a half-caste. Now she considered him her new mission. And Beryl rarely gave up.

After drinking steadily all evening, the woman wove rather than walked toward him. Melted mascara left dark smudges beneath her eyes, powder caked and streaked her face, and her bleached hair stood on end, giving the impression she'd already indulged in a good shag. Oblivious to Nigel's anger, she smiled, holding aloft a bottle in one hand and two crystal flutes in the other.

"Champers, darling?" Setting the bottle down on a small table nearby, she poured out two glasses. "It's only a '26, a perfectly ghastly year of course, but one gets used to the perfectly ghastly after years at the outer reaches of the Empire."

Nigel ignored the proffered glass. His voice dripping contempt and chest still heaving from the bonfire of sexual hunger she'd intruded upon, he turned on her. "Madam, I find your attentions tiresome in the extreme. I have no interest in a married woman who acts the whore and whose only attraction to me is to sample a forbidden fruit she'll never afterward acknowledge." He strode off, disappearing into the dusk.

Beryl gazed after him in some surprise, then shrugged and tossed back her champagne. At least, she reflected fuzzily, he hadn't called her a middle-aged whore.

Elizabeth's trembling fingers scrabbled trying to open the latch on the small window in the powder room. Finally the rusty hinges yielded and a steady breeze blew softly on her heated skin. Good Lord, how could she have behaved in such a loose fashion? Glancing in the mirror, she was dismayed by her dishevelled appearance: lips swollen, hair in disarray, and slumberous eyes. Why, she looked as if she'd just risen from bed! Nigel's bed. Her face flushed and her heart raced at the conjured images. She shook herself and began repairing the damage to her face and hair. Smoothing the fluff from her gold compact over her nose, she reflected that Major Covington-Singh obviously considered her an easy mark. Well, why wouldn't he, for goodness sake? She'd permitted him to stroke, fondle, and kiss where no man before dared touch! And denial hadn't even entered her mind. No, her traitorous body had been too busy brimming with new and intoxicating sensations. Well, he'd soon find she wasn't any common scrapper to come running at the crook of his little finger. No doubt he possessed a veritable stable of willing women. Or, perhaps being an Indian, seraglio was a more appropriate word.

The fact that Nigel was half Indian bothered Elizabeth not at all. Patricia Mainwarring had been as free a thinker as her husband was biased and narrow-minded, and she had infused her daughter with liberal beliefs. Elizabeth didn't regard race as a barrier to her attraction to Nigel—no, it was his dictatorial, imperious, arrogant attitude, not to mention his apparent assumption that she possessed so low a standard as to let him have his way with her merely because they happened to occupy the same secluded bower.

Composed at last, Elizabeth slipped her cosmetics into her bag and turned to leave, then stumbled awkwardly back when the powder room door crashed open.

"Here you are! We're frantic, trying to find you!" Fiona's voice held a tinge of hysteria. "Isn't it frightful? Everybody is quite shocked, and of course it is agreed upon that she had no business sneaking about the native bazaar after nightfall.

Goodness! Shouldn't have been anywhere but her own bed so late at the age of sixteen. We—that is Harry, Captain Woodford"—she flushed crimson—"thought you may have met the same fate!"

"Steady on, old girl. Here, sit on this silly excuse for a chair." Elizabeth pulled forward a wicker stool. "You look in dire need of a large gin and tonic. Hmm. Perhaps we can dispense with the tonic. I'll just pop out to scare one up for you."

Fiona seized Elizabeth's arm as she headed for the door. "No! You mustn't wander off alone! It's not safe. In fact, Captain Woodford is waiting for me just outside this door. The bar is closed. The ballroom is in chaos." She stared at her friend as comprehension dawned. "Good God, you haven't heard! Rose Durrow, the Transportation Deputy Commissioner's sixteen-year-old daughter was found *murdered* just outside the native bazaar tonight!"

Elizabeth leaned against the wall and stared wide-eyed at her friend. "Good Lord, Fi! What kind of monster commits such a gruesome deed? And why?" She closed her eyes momentarily, suddenly thankful for the Major's assiduous attentions. Who knew what might have occurred to a lone woman near midnight in a deserted and shadowed garden?

"The police are predictably tight-lipped. All they are saying is the poor girl was discovered just before midnight." Fiona glanced at the dress Longines on her wrist. "About forty minutes ago. There's one more thing. Apparently, Calcutta has played host to a series of grisly murders in recent months. This is the first British victim. My details are sketchy, but the native population believes the murderer is an Englishman, and it appears the persistent protests lodged by the Indian Congress are met by silence from our authorities. Speculation raced wildly about the club tonight that the murderer has changed venue!"

"This intrigue thickens too much for my liking, Fiona, I—"

A discreet knock interrupted her, and Captain Woodford peeked around the door. "I say, ladies, the management is locking the building. We really ought to 'scram,' as the Yanks say."

Elizabeth shivered as they made their way through the empty, darkened building, silent except for their breathing and the sharp staccato cracks of their heels on the teak floor. Suddenly, a white-turbaned Indian materialised before them, driving her heart into her throat.

But instead of wielding a kukri in a homicidal rage as she somehow feared, he merely touched folded inward hands to his forehead, making the sign of Namaste, and bowed before unlocking the doors.

Chapter Six

A red-gold light burned through Elizabeth's eyelids, forcing them open. A golden glow gilded the unfamiliar cane furniture and glinted off the dressing mirror on the other side of the mosquito netting. Fear clawed down her spine momentarily at the foreignness of her surroundings; then she remembered and relaxed on the pillows once again. Of course. Her bedroom in her father's house in India. Shaking her head to clear it of the cobwebs of a restless night, she sat up, wearily pushing aside the netting. But she couldn't as easily shake away the memories of the dreams laced with confused images of Nigel kissing her, or horrifying scenes of a faceless murderer on a bloodthirsty rampage. No wonder her mind wanted to wake in the accustomed surroundings of her old bedroom in Devon!

The day was already warm and the birds well into their morning symphony. She'd best hurry if she intended to catch her father before he left for his office. He was sure to possess some answers to her many questions. Attending briefly to her ablutions, she headed for the breakfast room to find him drinking his tea and reading the paper.

Glancing at her above the top of the morning edition, he greeted her by saying, "If you are looking for your companion, she is queening it over several of the local female gossips on the verandah. To hear her tell it, you two barely escaped with your lives and virtue intact last night."

"Good morning to you, too, Father." Elizabeth helped herself to some still-warm porridge from the sideboard. "Aside from being rather frightened, nothing untoward befell us, so there's absolutely no need for your solicitous concern." Smiling good-naturedly, she sat across from him at the highly buffed walnut table. Pouring a cup of tea, she added, "We're quite recovered, thank you. However, it seems a panic is in the offing about a blood-crazed killer hunting not only Indian women now, but British ladies as well. Perhaps you can inform me of the details? Those which aren't secret, of course."

Colonel Mainwarring set down his paper, reached for his pipe and tobacco pouch, and leaned back in his chair. He went about filling his pipe with a certain precision while pondering exactly what he should make known to her. Wouldn't do to tell her everything, of course. Silly female would blow the gaff to all and sundry. Finally lighting his pipe, he began a carefully edited version.

"Six months ago Indian women began, er, popping up dead, so to speak. All in the city of Calcutta proper. As the first two were of low caste, not much notice was taken. However, the following two victims were of the Brahmin Caste— the equivalent to our aristocracy—which has the native population, not to mention the local Congress, in an uproar. Apparently, they are nourishing some idiotic notion the perpetrator is British! Out of the question, of course. Now rumours are spreading, blaming earlier murders in the Bustees on the same individual, but there's no foundation because the Bustee murders are just that—rumour."

"Where and what are the Bustees, Father?" Now finished with breakfast, Elizabeth pushed her bowl aside.

"The most appalling slums in the world, my dear. No sane person ventures in voluntarily. A wretched stew of poverty, slavery, and prostitution unsurpassed anywhere on Earth. It isn't the sort of place murders are reported. So you see, any earlier leads cannot be proven." He drew heavily on his pipe and exhaled a cloud of smoke.

"But why is the Indian population insisting an Englishman is behind the murders? And what about poor Miss Durrow? Was she . . . was she killed in the same manner?"

Colonel Mainwarring snorted. "The girl has nothing whatever to do with the others. Undoubtedly some wog killed her in a similar fashion in an attempt to make us think it was related." His eyes were chips of green ice. "We've taken notice, by God. My officer in charge of security is working closely with the Police Commissioner. Bloody hell, there'll be no more British girls assaulted and murdered by those damned, filthy—"

"Assaulted, Father? Do you mean those unfortunate women were . . . were *intimately* assaulted before death?" Elizabeth swallowed and cleared her throat. "Just what was the method of . . . termination?"

The Colonel sat forward, tapped the bowl of his pipe empty in the cut-crystal ashtray with slightly more force than necessary. Then he stood, fitting his uniform cap on his grey hair before answering.

"Yes," he said tightly. "They were all viciously raped, beaten, and strangled."

Chapter Seven

Dazed at the graphic description in her father's parting shot, Elizabeth thoughtfully made her way to the verandah to join Fiona. Her disturbing reflections, however, were jolted from her mind in a flash as she stepped outside. The morning heat engulfed her, almost swallowing her with heavy humid air. The large wilted leaves of the banana trees in the garden were utterly still, and the branches of the banyan didn't waver. A couple of crows cawed as they fought over one of many ripe oranges fallen from the citrus trees along the side of the bungalow. Only the dark pink bougainvillaea seemed energetic as the bright garlands climbed the verandah pillars and trailed along the eaves creating a tropical lace border.

A murmur of conversation drew her attention to the shady end of the verandah where Fi entertained several ladies, most of whom were leaning back in their cane chairs waving fans desultorily over shiny faces. Elizabeth joined the group, and Fi made the introductions.

Harriet Compton, wife of the major in charge of operations in the regiment, was slender to the point of emaciation and hardly resembled her voluptuous eighteen-year-old brunette daughter, Diana. Major Wight's wife Marjorie, attractive, perhaps in her late thirties, was accompanied by her younger cousin, Georgina Smythe, visiting from England, who nodded, smiling; and last, the familiar face of Emily Stanton.

Mrs. Wight leaned forward, almost causing her tan beret, which was set at a precarious angle on wavy coffee-brown locks, to fall into the jug of lemonade in the centre of the table. "My dear, what an opinion you must have developed of our small community! Not your second day in Calcutta and a horrid murder in our very own backyard!" She shuddered delicately and re-adjusted her beret. "Why, the next thing you know it will be the Mutiny all over again, and we'll all be murdered in our beds!"

"Nonsense," interjected Mrs. Compton impatiently. "Hysteria solves nothing and sends the wrong impression to the Indians. Obviously they are labouring under the false notion we can be cowed into releasing that upstart Gandhi by murdering helpless women." She pounded the cane table for emphasis, shaking the crystal glasses. "Mark my words, it's the native rebels of the Indian Congress behind this outrage!"

Emily calmly sipped her lemonade. "Do you really think so, my dear? Mohandas Gandhi persuaded the National Congress years ago to pursue Home Rule through nonviolent means. I hardly think these Indians have suddenly abandoned their principles and are sneaking about in the dead of night murdering defenseless women. And even if one of the militant sects were behind these grisly crimes, why would they kill their own women?"

Mrs. Compton's colourless eyes narrowed in her sunken face. Her pointed chin jutted forward and several greying tendrils fell from her old-fashioned bun. Sweeping the errant hair aside in agitation, she continued in her former vein. "A crazed maniac killed poor Rose Durrow. Cowards, the lot of them. And what *would* occur if we left, I ask you? Anarchy. Permanent anarchy. We'd be back cleaning up their mess for them just as we've been doing for nearly three hundred years. Where would they be without our railroads? Our schools, telephone wires, roads, or motor vehicles? Back to long caravans slowly trekking over vast tracts of desert and jungle, only to fall victim to the murdering followers of the goddess Kali; penury even more devastating than today, and slavery caused by the power-hungry maharajas; constant religious wars; hundreds of thousands of women burned alive on their husbands' funeral pyres! They ought to be on their hands and knees thanking us!"

Diana, far from startled by her mother's outburst, as everyone else seemed to be, looked as if she wanted to curl up and disappear. Taking a sip of lemonade, Elizabeth watched Emily's small conciliatory smile over the rim of her glass.

"I do beg to differ, Harriet dear. The Indians are *not* children and it *is* their country. The time is coming for Home Rule. More Indians every day are appointed to high civil positions. The government could outlaw the National Congress, but it hasn't seen fit to do so—another indication HMG isn't intending to hold on forever.

"And really, if one of the splinter groups not following Gandhi's passive resistance movement were at fault for poor Rose's murder, don't you think it likely they would glory in claiming responsibility? Besides, Prasad is President of Congress this year, so the passivists are the ruling power at the moment." Turning to Elizabeth, she said, "Do offer me one of your cigarettes, my dear, I'm always forgetting mine."

Mrs. Wight's brittle laugh rang as she sat forward to light Emily's borrowed cigarette. "You *never* carry your own fags, darling, that's why you are always mooching."

The atmosphere lightened considerably; however, Mrs.

Compton pursed her thin lips and crossed her spindly legs as if reluctant to let go of her pet subject.

"Mrs. Wight," Diana shyly ventured, "Under the circumstances, is your picnic party to the Maidan still on? After Rose's—well, I'm sure everyone will understand . . ."

"Gracious me!" Mrs. Wight gasped and fluttered her hands. "I'd forgotten. Oh, dear, it's too late to cancel—Cook has prepared most of the food and several of the officers have gone to the trouble of acquiring a special furlough to attend. The Durrows weren't coming in any event. I suppose it may appear callous, but we must remember that there is life amidst death—or is it the other way round? Oh well, it simply must go on. We shall all need cheering at any rate."

Miss Smythe patted her cousin's hand, her long vermillion nails flashing in a stray sunbeam. "Of course you mustn't cancel, dear Marjorie. We desperately need an outing to shake us out of these doldrums. A refreshing excursion to the Hooghly River, good food and wine, not to mention a handsome officer to escort one on a tour of the Botanic Gardens afterward. Why, it's just the thing."

"I don't think it's at all the thing," Mrs. Compton began.

"Don't say so, Mother!" Diana scooted to the edge of her seat, seizing her mother's arm with both her hands. "Why, all my friends are attending, including Lieutenant Toppenham." Realising the scene she was creating, she lowered her hands to her lap and sat back. Keeping her eyes down, she muttered, "Papa does so like Freddy. He's related to the Devonshires, don't forget. Several times removed, but the connection still exists. Who knows what conversation might pop up while enjoying a romantic stroll in the gardens."

"Well," relented Mrs. Compton, relaxing a bit. "I suppose it's a good idea to get out before the monsoons start. Which is any time now—the hotter it gets, the closer the rains are to deluging us."

Miss Smythe smoothed her fingertips over her shining

cap of chestnut hair and shot Mrs. Compton a wicked smile. "Husband-hunting is such a calculating business, isn't it? One must be ever vigilant of just the right opportunities to bag the very choicest prize while appearing not in the least desperate. A game of wit and chance, to be sure. Now, don't make a fuss, Harriet," she said when the older woman glared and opened her mouth to speak. "I'm scouting myself. Goodness, it's why I'm in Calcutta." Addressing Elizabeth and Fiona, she said, "Marjorie's party is perfect for meeting the most eligible young men. Do say you will come. It will be a lovely time."

Elizabeth laughed. "Put like that, who could resist? Fiona and I are looking forward to meeting Calcutta society." Her eyes twinkled. "And beaux are never amiss."

Just then an early model Daimler coughed to a stop in front of the bungalow and Captain Woodford and another officer stepped out.

"Oh dear, I forgot!" Fiona frowned, disconcerted. "Before the confusion broke out last night Harry and Captain Langley volunteered to escort us to the Chitpore shopping district."

Elizabeth smiled at the new visitors, remembering the handsome captain of medium height and sleek blond hair from the previous evening. His light blue eyes lit with pleasure as he wished her a good morning.

"Run along and have a good time, darlings." Emily rose from the table. "It's far too hot for me. I think I'll just return home to sit in front of my new electric fan."

The other ladies gathered their fans and handbags, expressing their farewells. Mrs. Wight called over her shoulder as she left, "Whatever you do, you *mustn't* pay the asking price! And don't forget my party on Saturday!"

"Excuse us while we fetch our bonnets, Captain Woodford, Captain Langley," Elizabeth murmured.

"Please, call me Marcus." Captain Langley grinned, holding open the screen door for her.

He is gorgeous, thought Elizabeth a moment later as she adjusted a floppy hat Garbo-style on her gold finger-waves. One eye peeked flirtatiously out from under her hat and bright red lips curved in a secret smile as she regarded her image in the mirror. It was too bad the spark of attraction was absent. She was afraid *that* was reserved for the exotic and infuriating Nigel Covington-Singh. Hmm, perhaps a whole day in the handsome Captain's company might change that if she worked on it.

Humming to herself, she slipped a few gold bangles on her slender wrist, smoothed the light green silk of her belted frock, straightened the seam in her cream stockings, and slid into a pair of like-coloured high-heel sandals. Minutes later, a pleasant breeze caressing her face, she was flying down the road in an open Daimler.

Chapter Eight

The marketplace at Chitpore proved a potpourri of exotic sights, sounds, and smells. Elizabeth's nose twitched at the pungency of strong spices warring with the musky odour of raw silk and stench of cow excrement that dotted the dirt road. All humanity, it seemed, was represented: soldiers and officers of the 1st Rangpur Foot, Eurasians, Sikhs, Mohammedans, Africans in flowing robes, Indian ladies in colourful saris, and lepers in filthy rags begging for bread.

Vendors hawked their wares in English, Urdu, and Hindi. Each promised the best value at the very lowest price for the choicest brass incense burners, exquisitely wrought silver jewelry, elegant enamelled bowls, the finest silk and cotton garments, precious gems and the most luxurious Kashmiri carpets.

Mesmerised cobras rose from reed baskets, swaying to seductive tunes played by crouching snake charmers. Flamboyantly dressed monkeys chattered and wove through the crowd, some begging and others nipping at merchandise.

The Daimler jockeyed for space among bullock carts, tongas, horse-drawn drays, and the sacred humpbacked cows. It was at one of these cows Harry blew his horn.

"Blasted beasts are everywhere! Not a damned thing one can do about them either. You there!" he shouted to the Indian nearest the animal. "Get that bloody cow out of the road!"

The Indian responded with rude hand gestures and a spate of incomprehensible Hindi. The cow took its time plodding its bulk out of the Daimler's path.

"Not quite the thing, old man," Marcus remarked. "You haven't been here long enough to appreciate just how the natives revere their cows. Those beasts are gods on Earth to these Hindus, and woe to the man who disrespects the smelly old things. As incongruous as it may seem, there is actually a majority of Mohammedans here in Bengal, although the Hindus are the ruling party." He paused to chuckle. "Now, down in Hyderabad it's just the opposite. You think the damn cows are a nuisance here? One can't make a move down there without stepping in the—er, ahem, ladies—the er, waste product." He subsided into an uncomfortable silence.

"Cow shit everywhere, I presume," supplied Fiona cheerfully.

Marcus smiled. "Er, quite."

"What say we stop for something long and cold?" Harry suggested, manoeuvring the vehicle to the side of the road in a space that passed as a parking slot. "Something to eat as well. We'll need all the sustenance we can manage for a gruelling day of shopping." He tossed a grin over his shoulder to the girls in the backseat. "I've heard marvellous endorsements for the House of Bengal." He set the hand brake, hopped over the side and opened the back door for Elizabeth and Fiona.

"The food is excellent, but I don't think it's quite the at-

mosphere for the ladies." Marcus sounded embarrassed.
"Perhaps the Mahal Calcutta instead. It's just a block farther
down the road."

"Nonsense." Elizabeth raised her chin and took Marcus's
proffered arm as she started walking. "Ladies nowadays are
more adventurous than our predecessors. A little 'atmosphere' sounds quite intriguing. We shan't swoon, I assure
you gentlemen. Why, we even indulge in such shocking behaviour as smoking cigarettes and piloting aeroplanes." Her
eyes widened innocently and she added in a confidential
manner, "Our skirts even are worn above our ankles."

"Point taken." Marcus laughed and steered them into a respectable enough looking building.

Soon they were settled on the shaded upstairs lanai, enjoying a cold locally brewed beer and a tasty lamb masala
with a delicately spiced rice.

Midway through the meal Elizabeth spotted the reason for
Marcus's hesitation in eating at this particular establishment. It appeared a bordello enjoyed a brisk business a few
doors down and across the street! She nudged Fiona's knee,
discreetly directing her gaze toward a lanai crowded with
several beautiful women, their eyes rimmed darkly in kohl
and dripping a king's ransom in jewelry. The sun shot sparks
off the diamond studs in their noses and glinted in their long,
flowing dark hair as they chatted and called gaily to the men
passing below. Strange henna designs decorated their graceful, gesturing hands and continued past their wrists, disappearing into their luxurious silk saris.

An aggressive-looking dark-skinned man stood below,
opening the door with rapid regularity for customers coming
and going. Under their fascinated stare a familiar figure exited the enterprising house of ill repute. Deputy Commissioner Tate stood in the doorway hitching his trousers up his

thick middle and adjusting his topi before sauntering a bit unsteadily down the road in the opposite direction.

Both Elizabeth and Fiona let loose a crack of laughter, which they tried unsuccessfully to turn into coughs. Their hands bumped reaching for their beers and they surrendered, convulsing in giggles.

Harry followed their gazes and turned in horror to Marcus. "Quite see I should've listened to you, old chap." He dabbed his perspiring forehead with his linen napkin. "My apologies, ladies. Inexcusable to expose you to such, er—"

"Real life?" provided Elizabeth. Recovered now from her mirth, she pushed her empty plate aside and reached into her chic Schiaparelli bakelite handbag for her Dunhills. Fitting one into a holder, she held it out for Marcus to light. Drawing deeply, she leaned back comfortably in her chair, eyes twinkling merrily.

"Yes, do relax Harry." Fiona similarly held a cigarette for him to light, which he did with something approaching his normal aplomb.

"Most ladies would be quite insulted witnessing the leading brothel and opium den in full action." Marcus signalled the waiter for another round of refreshment.

Fiona's eyes widened. "So *that's* why some of them stumble out. Is opium smoking quite accepted here, then?"

"It's perfectly legal." Marcus chose his words with care. "And most every officer partakes at least once for the experience—but should it become a frequent pastime, it most definitely is frowned upon."

"We *are* quite adventurous." Elizabeth looked mischievously from Fiona to the dawning horror on the faces of their male companions. "But we shan't ask you to escort us to an opium den . . . today."

"Should think not," huffed Harry. "Why, haven't even been to one m'self . . . yet." Then, realising the humourous prank played on him, played along. "Be glad to tell you about it when I do, though."

Fiona, suddenly uncomfortable that there might be a brothel attached to the opium den Harry sampled, abruptly turned to Marcus. "The ladies you found us with this morning were debating Indian politics. We were abysmally ignorant and had absolutely no idea what they were talking about. Perhaps you could explain the National Congress and this Gandhi fellow."

"Ah, we might be here for days, so I'll give you a condensed version. You may have sussed that the natives are striving for Home Rule. The Congress is a political party founded back in '85 and originally advocated limited democratic reforms under our rule. However, twenty years later it began calling for self-government and in 1920 adopted the strategy of nonviolent resistance devised by Mohandas Gandhi. Gandhi is known among the natives as a social and religious reformer. He is also a lawyer who was educated in London. He is pushing for a boycott of British commodities, courts, and educational institutions. Unfortunately, his passivist rallies have often ended in violence and mass arrests. It seems every time he is arrested, the tide of Indian Nationalism rises. The whole country is a bloody mess, and some fear another mutiny." He took a long sip of his lager.

"Now, that is something I'm familiar with." Elizabeth turned to Fiona. "In 1857 the sepoys mutinied, massacring thousands of Europeans. It went on almost two years, but finally the East India Company gained the upper hand. As a result, Parliament transferred the administration from the John Company, as it was also known, to the Crown."

"Boiled down, but accurate." Marcus smiled. "Every year Congress elects a new president, and although Gandhi has never served in that office, a number of his fellow passivists have, including a fellow named Rajendra Prasad, who is doing duty this year. Last year we weren't quite so lucky. Jawa-

haral Nehru stood, and he likes to stir things up. Not that
Gandhi can't do that as well. Two years ago, in fact, he led
the Salt March to the Gulf of Khambat on the western coast.
The natives must buy their salt from us, you see. He violated
that monopoly by boiling seawater to produce salt. Similar
actions occurred throughout India, and when Gandhi was arrested yet again riots broke out everywhere. Trains were
stoned, telegraph wires cut, and several government officials
assassinated. And just in case you think this isn't quite
enough excitement, last year the Muslim League, fearing
Hindu domination, demanded special privileges in an
Indian-proposed dominion government. This continues to
result in even more rioting, this time between Hindus and
Muslims. You certainly chose a turbulent period to stay in
India," he finished dryly.

Elizabeth's lips twitched. "I don't suppose India is ever
dull. How long have you served in the Indian Army, Marcus?"

"Since '25 when I graduated Cambridge, although I was
born in Lucknow. My family's lived here since just after the
Mutiny. . . ."

The conversation became nothing more than a soft buzz
in Elizabeth's ears and her blood froze in her veins despite
the heat and perspiration trickling between her breasts, when
glancing in the direction of the bordello, she spied another
familiar figure. Not squiffy, this one. He was just as attractive as ever in his khaki uniform and confident military bearing, bending his head to speak to the doorman.

So Nigel frequented whorehouses. Is that what he had
thought her to be when she'd succumbed so easily to his caresses the night before? Straight from her kisses to a prostitute. All cats must indeed be grey in the dark. Her knuckles
whitened, gripping her slippery glass as an exquisitely lovely
native woman rushed onto the lanai and called down a
farewell. He waved to the beautiful prostitute before starting
down the road. Passing the House of Bengal, he looked di-

rectly up at her. His eyes narrowed and his lips tightened when he noticed Marcus, but he quickly tossed her a mocking smile, and touching his cap in salute, continued on his way.

Abruptly Elizabeth stood, almost knocking over her chair, and murmured an excuse about visiting the powder room. She admitted ironically to herself—leaning on the vanity, her blood pounding in her temples and breathing deeply to steady herself—that encounters with Nigel had the disturbing habit of sending her to the loo. Not quite the effect he was used to producing in a woman, she was sure.

"What's this?" Fiona bustled in. "Curried vegetables a bit too strong for you, love? It does take getting used to, doesn't it? I must say, the sun doesn't seem quite as warm after eating one of these spicy Indian dishes, though. One must certainly drink quite more than one's share of gin and tonics or lager to survive a native meal. Do you suppose the food will be as foreign in New Zealand?"

Elizabeth straightened and regarded Fiona's concerned countenance in the mirror before them. "Oh, I imagine we can rustle up a pot of cock-a-leekie soup, or perhaps a nice juicy joint." Reaching for her gold compact, she tried to smile, but the traditional stiff upper lip failed her.

"No, Fi, it's not the food that's aggravated me so. I truly wish it were. Oh, botheration!" she blurted as the American Beauty lip rouge she was applying broke and the tip fell into the sink. She wondered briefly if the currently popular Max Factor sold his line in India or New Zealand. It didn't matter. She was wealthy now, she reminded herself, and could ruddy well mail order just about anything. It was really too bad one couldn't do the same and just order up the perfect man. Sighing regretfully, she bundled the rest of her cosmetics into her handbag.

"It's no good. Marcus is very appealing, not to mention just the proper sort of gentleman one might bring home to meet one's family. The sort with whom one may enjoy an easygoing relationship, with no particular high or low points. A nice-looking, comfortable man."

Fiona turned on a tap and held her comb under the stream of water, flicked off the excess and attempted to drag it through her fuzzy curls. "You make a perfectly gorgeous man sound frightfully dull, darling." She patted her hair carefully, and putting her comb away sent her friend a sideways look. "Which means you've someone else in mind."

"A very unsuitable someone else, who makes me feel more alive than I have ever felt." Elizabeth sighed. "Unfortunately, the sparks are flying down a one-way road. I assumed otherwise, but I have been shown quite clearly such is not the case. Disappointing, almost devastating in fact, to find one means nothing more than a passing amusement."

"Ahh, you mean of course the handsome Kashmiri prince," Fiona's lips quirked in an impish smile. "The tall, dark, imposing major who objected to us landing on his empty parade ground. Not a politic choice if you are wanting a reconciliation with your father, I'm afraid. He seems to believe anyone with Indian blood is inferior. And he makes no secret of it. At any rate, I doubt you have to worry about your 'sparks.' He couldn't keep his eyes off you last night."

"No, you are mistaken, Fi. He just emerged from th-that posh whorehouse a minute ago! Keeping time with a bit of all right at midday!" Elizabeth paused, taking a deep calming breath. "It's just as well, really. It would anger Father like billy-oh. He'd be horribly humiliated and likely disown me. Then I will have lost both parents," she finished miserably.

"If he disowns you, he loves himself more than you! What game is he playing—if he can't control you, he won't love you? Ballocks! Perhaps you are better off without him after all." Fiona took hold of Elizabeth's shoulders and looked her in the eyes. "Your mother wouldn't play. That's why you grew up without him. You mustn't let him rule your decisions in this, or in any other matter. If you want your major, don't let your father ruin it. It's obvious to anyone who bothers to look, Major Covington-Singh is crazy for you. I am positive there is some perfectly legitimate reason for him to . . . be where he was." She shrugged her shoulders. "Give him the benefit of the doubt. Now"—she opened the door—"let's have a jolly time and spend absolutely scads of money!"

Nigel exited the silver shop and paused to one side of the door to light one of his Woodbines. He blew out a cloud of smoke, carefully observing the jostling throng in the marketplace. His informant should be showing himself anytime. The sun beat down unmercifully, and no hint of breeze stirred the heavy air. He could smell his own perspiration, mixed with the stench of opium and the clinging scent of perfume from the dozen or more brothels and opium dens he'd visited that day. It was a filthy job, and not one he could trust to a subordinate.

It was a bloody dicey position: investigating the brutal rape/murder of a white woman while ignoring the Indian victims—especially now with the National Congress claiming an Englishman was the culprit and clamouring for justice. He must answer to a British population enraged that an Indian failed to be arrested immediately for Rose Durrow's murder.

Nigel did know one thing: The murders were perpetrated by the same person. And he had a sinking suspicion the malefactor was British. The murders bore a startling resemblance to a series of killings committed in Singapore in '22 and Kenya in '27. The hallmarks were identical: a crude carving of *whore* into the victims' stomachs. The information had not been made public, but state authorities insisted it was leaked, and therefore any number of people knew it. Even if he were to uncover the solid evidence he sought, Colonel Mainwarring was unlikely to pay credence to it.

One didn't blame an Englishman when one could nick a convenient native. As if race relations weren't already near to boiling.

And these weren't normal murders at all. No. Scotland Yard coined them "sequential murders." Apparently they required a special expertise. Just his luck. Sod's law.

During his junket through Calcutta's scummy underside, he hadn't much luck in uncovering pertinent leads. Whorehouses didn't generally ask clients' names, and men with a propensity toward violence were seldom admitted again to the establishment—bruises marred the merchandise and injury prevented a full workload. There were, of course, the sort of decadent enterprises that specialised in torture. As a rule, those repugnant institutions were found in the Bustees. And Nigel's tattle knew every corner of that God-awful stew.

Of course, he could go over the Colonel's head directly to the Commissioner with the proof, once he'd obtained it, but the resulting ill feeling would make for an even rockier relationship with Mainwarring than already existed. Nigel grimaced, took a last pull on his cigarette and threw it on the pavement, crushing it under his toe. Rocky would be the least of it, if he got wind of Nigel's pursuing his daughter.

From the looks of the intimate party at the best table in the House of Bengal, perhaps it was a moot situation. Did the good Colonel's daughter delight in playing one man against another? Nigel wondered cynically. Did she get jollies from kissing him passionately last night and flirting outrageously with another today? Some women did. Especially spoilt, wealthy women. Well, he didn't play games—even for her.

He couldn't recall feeling such an all-consuming passion for a woman since his first infatuation at the age of fifteen. His expression lightened as he remembered Marina, his mother's secretary. A short liaison, as they were soon dis-

covered. It seemed he possessed a penchant for unsuitable
females.

As if thinking of Elizabeth could conjure her, he spied her
graceful form across the road. She was fashionably garbed
in a slender green silk walking dress and high-heel sandals.
Most women in India wore sensible, sturdy shoes. Not Elizabeth. The extra height added glamour and a sumptuous
swing to her elegant stride.

As Nigel watched, she glanced flirtatiously up at Langley
around the floppy brim of her hat and, laughing, tapped his
arm before stepping to a table overflowing with handmade
carpets. Removing her gloves, she ran her hands over the
rugs, sensuous, caressing, as if touching a lover's body.
Langley's eyes flared in response. Hell, Nigel was responding himself, imagining those slender fingers trailing down
his chest and lower still.

Abruptly Nigel shook himself, throwing off the aura of
carnality. Temper quickly took its place. It wasn't just her,
he told himself, it was the fact he hadn't enjoyed a woman in
a very long time. That would have to be remedied, and soon.
Woodford called to the couple from inside the carpet shop
and Langley answered, holding out his arm for Elizabeth.

Nigel turned to re-enter the silver shop, and did not see
Elizabeth shake her head at Langley, waving him on while
she continued to study the rugs.

Left alone on the pavement, Elizabeth moved from table to
table admiring the exquisite workmanship. She soon found
herself in the shop next door, where the carpets were not
only exhibited on tables, but also hung from the ceiling. It
was just as well she owned plenty of lolly, she thought, as
she couldn't decide which to purchase; they were all so
beautiful. Deep reds splashed boldly, while the lighter hues
of pink, aqua, and yellow provided the intricate details. She
touched the luxurious, tightly woven wool of rug after rug

until she came upon a gauze curtain dividing the shop into two sections.

"Hello?" she called, sweeping the drape aside. "Is anybody there? I wish to make several purchases."

Why, they were hiding the best in the back of the shop! Slipping behind the curtain, she moved even farther into the shadowy interior, toward a truly magnificent specimen hanging from a beam in the ceiling. The Taj Mahal, brilliantly white, with gold accents, a colourful garden, and a dazzling sapphire sky. Why hide such magnificence out of customers' sight? It seemed she must shout down the proprietor if she intended to acquire this jewel today. She turned to hurry out to the front entrance—and immediately slammed into a hard, broad chest.

Chapter Nine

Elizabeth opened her mouth to scream as strong hands fastened to her upper arms, steadying her. Her head fell back and suddenly her startled gaze collided with the angry features of Nigel Covington-Singh. Abruptly she shut her mouth. She shivered in reaction to his closeness, and goose bumps appeared on the delicate skin where he touched her. Her breathing quickened and tingles of sexual awareness rippled down her spine as she realised they were alone, behind the curtain, cut off from the rest of the shop.

Her trembling and vulnerability melted Nigel's wrath like butter sizzling in the hot sun. The cacophony of the market outside dimmed, and in the silence behind the curtain, he heard their deepening breathing and the beating of his heart. She smelled of sweet Arpège and a womanly muskiness. They were so close her soft breasts were crushed against his chest. The blood pounded in his temples. Unable to resist, he took a deep breath and dipped his mouth to her parted lips.

Forgetting her determination to teach this man she was

no tramp for a playboy to toy with, Elizabeth actually found herself reaching to meet his mouth—until she caught a whiff of incense-like perfume mixed with some other, unidentifiable scent. The horrible scene played again in her mind: Nigel leaving the cathouse and the beautiful young woman waving farewell. She wrenched herself away from him.

"I think not, Major!" Blushing hotly, and ashamed of her inability to master her own lascivious emotions, Elizabeth busied herself brushing at her clothing as if to rid them of some loathsome, foreign material. When she felt able to look at him with a measure of composure, she found him staring at her, his gaze hooded.

Still panting from his intense response to her, Nigel watched as Elizabeth almost desperately tried to wipe any possible evidence of him from her garment. As if his touch in some way sullied her pristineness. Her actions made everything clear. She wasn't playing the spoilt, rich-girl game of "bounce one man against the other" after all. His face twisted at the sudden bitter taste on his tongue. She had seemed, from the first moment of their meeting when she climbed down from the cockpit of that flying piece of rubbish, fresh, original, and nonconformist. But this lemon fell close to its tree after all.

He'd known eventually she would discover the local taboo against Indians and Brits forming romantic relationships. Perhaps taboo was too strong a word. It was done, but discouraged. The participants generally made their own society, and were of necessity thick skinned, as powerful prejudices existed on both sides of the racial fence.

Apparently she wasn't about to disgrace her precious person with a repulsive eight-anna. Sadness and resentment rushed like bile through his veins. That this so disheartened him, showed how quickly and just how far she'd managed to creep under his skin. Time to remove her. To set her firmly out of his sphere.

He bowed mockingly. "My most humble apologies, Miss Mainwarring, for any insult offered. I should have realised your eager response to my insulting behaviour last night was the direct result of, shall we say, several too many gin and Frenches. You may be sure I shall not repeat such an indiscretion—unless of course, you come toddling in my direction again after tippling heavily on blue ruin."

"Too many—! Tippling! Why, you scoundrel. I most certainly *was not* drinking heavily last night. I never have been drunk in my life! How dare you accuse me of such low moral fibre. It was *you* taking advantage of *me* in an isolated garden." She was so cross, she actually stamped her foot. Why, he had nearly kissed her after being with a prostitute! And fool that she was, she'd almost fallen into his lecherous arms again. Now he implied she was loose *and* an inebriate. Stung out of all patience, she declared, "You are unfit for your title of officer and a gentleman!"

"Ah, yes, I remember now." Nigel looked down his aquiline nose at one of the most desirable women he'd ever had the misfortune to meet. Elizabeth's eyes glittered with violent emotion and twin spots of brilliant pink rode high in her fair cheeks. He could almost see the steam shooting out her ears. "You absolutely overpowered me with protestations of maidenly modesty. And, like the wolf I am, I devoured you until Providence in the unlikely form of Beryl Tate happened along." He chuckled sourly. "You ran so fast, all you were missing was a red cape and hood."

Enough was enough. Elizabeth refused to dignify his taunt with a reply. If he was no gentleman, at least *she* was a lady. She lifted her chin.

"I believe nothing more remains to be said between us, Major. Do please allow me to pass," Elizabeth requested with exaggerated politeness.

Nigel blocked her exit. "I'm afraid there is, Miss Mainwarring." All mockery absent, his voice was hard and his eyes flat as he looked down at her. "Did our conversation on white slavery the night of your arrival fall on deaf ears? Or is your memory of limited capacity? *Never* separate yourself from your companions outside the British sector. Do you not realise how easy it would be to strike you over the head and smuggle you out the back door? Blondes are especially tempting in an area of the world where dark beauties dominate."

Strangely, the enjoyment he had expected to derive from this lecture didn't materialise, even with the dawning horror widening her clear blue eyes. He continued ruthlessly.

"Don't make the mistake of believing your wealth is a deterrent. It's not worth a slaver's life to release you on your own ransom. You'd know too much. Before you knew it, you would be languishing in a seraglio in sexual bondage to some corpulent, rich, rat-faced man anywhere from Afghanistan to China to Indonesia. Who knows where his tastes may run? He might lend you to his friends or delight in inflicting pain. Eventually you would contract a venereal disease. And when your looks desert you—which would not be long under those conditions—likely your only escape from such a life would be a slashed throat with your body thrown on a refuse heap."

Elizabeth stared at him in frozen shock. Her hand fluttered near the region of her heart before she resolutely lowered it to her side. Good God! What had she been thinking! Taking a deep calming breath she said, "How considerate of you, Major, to remind me of what may befall an innocent young woman when she strays from the proper path." Her eyes bored sharply into his. "You may be sure I shall, in the future, not wander far from an appropriate companion. Now if you will excuse me, I intend to follow your advice in seeking my friends. Good day." She swept past him, she thought, with a credible hauteur.

Chapter Ten

Several days passed in an oppressive haze of heat. In every direction the distance blurred and waved under the ardour of the sun. Neither the citrus nor the tamarind trees so much as waved a leafy branch in the sultry stillness engulfing Calcutta. Each day surpassed the last in sweltering intensity. Tempers flared and a restiveness pervaded an atmosphere already fraught with tension and anticipation of the impending monsoons.

Riots broke out in the native bazaar between Hindus and the more numerous Muhammadans. Natives demanding the apprehension of the madman responsible for the murders of their women initiated still more violence at the edge of the British sector. The Army suppressed the savagery without loss of life to itself. However, the civilian Indians were not so lucky. Many funeral pyres burned, turning the air even thicker and almost too heavy to breathe, thus forcing the rescheduling of several social functions, including Mrs. Wight's picnic.

It did not, however, keep the soldiers from their daily manoeuvres on the black tarmac parade ground. Every day at
least one man dropped from heat exhaustion, yet the men ad-
hered rigorously to training. And more often than not, it was
Major Covington-Singh leading the march.

Elizabeth watched, shaking her head in pity at the soldiers
carrying rifles and heavy packs, while she and Fiona flew
past in the backseat of a chauffeured staff car, on their way to
join Captain Woodford for luncheon at the Mohd Bagh Club.
Hot as it was, it was surprisingly refreshing to be outdoors
after several days of being cooped inside the bungalow, as
her father insisted it was unsafe to step outside. After Nigel's
lecture, she was inclined to listen to her father's advice.

Now that most of the smoke had finally cleared and an apparent pause appeared in the hostilities, she was looking forward to attending a polo game late that afternoon. How
pleasant to mingle in society again. Perhaps her father might
even escort her.

Elizabeth knew her father had much with which to con-
tend, especially with these worrying disturbances, but it occurred to her that he might make *some* effort to become
acquainted. It seemed all the endeavour was on her part.
Could it be her imagination, or might her father not wish a
reconciliation? She frowned, troubled by the notion. No, she
thought resolutely, she could not believe that. Would not believe it. Not after travelling all this way. Not wanting it as
badly as she suddenly realised she did.

She was very used to carrying the weight of life on her
young shoulders, spending most of her years nursing her
mother through frequent bouts of malaria. She'd learned
adult responsibilities early.

Being the strong one of the household left her in desperate need of a shoulder to lean on. She'd always envied her
schoolmates their fathers, and occasionally accompanied her
friends on their family outings. That practice, however, was

short-lived, as it was too painful to experience what she acutely missed. So she pretended she did not miss a father's love and guidance. The longings, buried so deep in her psyche so long ago, were just now emerging.

Elizabeth caught herself grinning at the fantasy of her father actually taking a personal interest in her life: advising her on business investments, beaming down at her as he escorted her to the altar where her faceless but eager bridegroom awaited. Bouncing her babies on his knee. The grin dissolved. Unless she worked at bringing him around, she might as well continue existing as just another form of furniture in his bungalow.

Well, she thought, seizing her floppy hat as the staff auto whipped into the club's randall, tenacity was a quality much to be admired—and she possessed it in spades!

Captain Woodford stepped forward to open the car door for Elizabeth and Fiona once the vehicle came to what was very nearly a screaming halt. Uniform cap in hand and Cheshire grin dominating his handsome features, he assisted them onto the curb.

"I say, jammy thing you modern girls fly." He chuckled and greeted Elizabeth politely, but directed an especially fond glance to Fiona—and her generous bosom. Fiona, in turn, played the coquette by fluttering her eyelashes. Elizabeth stifled a laugh, thinking of all the flirting, blushing, and sly touches under the table she was chaperoning this afternoon. It appeared at least *some* true love did, indeed, run smooth.

Colonel Mainwarring did escort Elizabeth to the polo game that afternoon. Indeed, he declared, he felt it his duty to accompany such scandalously clad young women for their own safety. Raising his eyebrows, he surveyed Elizabeth and Fiona in askance.

"What is the world coming to that women must dress as men or display so much skin? The polo players are like to fall off their ponies or slam into each other gawking at the spectacle you provide," he grumbled as they piled into his shiny red Stutz Phaeton.

Elizabeth smiled at his fussing. Although they weren't yet worn at Wimbledon, shorts were fast becoming popular with the younger sporting set. She wore a pair of whites ending at mid-thigh. A sleeveless white blouse and matching high-heeled mules completed her outfit. Fiona was not quite as daring in wide-legged beige trousers and a pale yellow sleeveless blouse. When they arrived at the polo field they did indeed receive a number of stares. Apparently, in Calcutta, women in trousers were still considered a bit fast—not to mention women in shorts!

Elizabeth adjusted her hat Garbo-style and slipped on a pair of tortoiseshell sunglasses as she, Fiona, and the Colonel made their way to a table where they could observe the action. Spectators milled about socialising; small families crowded together on blankets on the ground enjoying picnic suppers, while others hosted sizeable parties taking up several tables.

In passing, she heard some of the tabbies whispering behind their hands at such a shocking display of leg, and tut-tutting on the unfortunate colour of her skin. Elizabeth, however, was quite proud of the honey hue her skin had acquired. She delighted in the new fad of sunbathing, and had luxuriated for many hours in her bathing costume upon a lounge on the deck of the ship that had brought her to India.

Once seated and orders for refreshment taken, she and Fiona sat back to relax. The sun was sinking, but the mosquitoes were lazy as yet, and for once a pleasant breeze stirred. On the whole it appeared they could look forward to a diverting evening.

* * *

Nigel blinked, blinded momentarily by the bright orange ball hanging low in the western sky. He was emerging from the stable adjacent to the playing field, leading his best polo pony. It was too bloody hot to play and he would have to change ponies often; but, he conceded to himself, a distraction was badly needed to alleviate the laden atmosphere.

Arriving at the field, his eyes swept the onlookers, resting appreciatively on a woman in white shorts strolling confidently through the crowd. Apparently she was unconcerned by the stares she garnered as she showed off long, tanned, and delicately muscled legs. The sunglasses did little to hide her identity. He certainly didn't need to see the Colonel or Fiona taking seats beside her to know who she was. Only Elizabeth Mainwarring possessed the nerve—the innate flamboyance—and the figure to pull off such a gambit.

A hot tide of anger and possessiveness suddenly overwhelmed him. Every man here must be imagining those long legs wrapped around his waist, her urging him to thrust faster, slower, deeper. Sweat popped out on his forehead. Jesus, he needed a woman. And she'd made it insultingly clear she wasn't interested. He snorted in disgust. No, he must find his Nirvana elsewhere.

The pony, sensing Nigel's turbulent emotions, whinnied and pranced in impatience. Nigel immediately ran a soothing hand down the animal's back.

"Hold on, Shiva, old man, you'll get your run shortly." He gave the pony a final pat, and turning toward the field, came face to face with Beryl Tate.

"Nigel, darling, how wonderful to see you! You look quite recovered from your little temper tantrum of the other night." She smiled and sauntered closer. Her generous breasts strained to break free of her ivory frock. Regrettably, her hips followed the tendency. Seeking to show off her profile, she angled her face to the light, but the unforgiving glare of the sun revealed cosmetics applied with a heavy hand—and a faint bluish bruise along her jaw line.

He wondered idly if she liked it rough, or if her husband had attempted to mend her straying tendencies by putting his fist down. He dismissed the thought—he didn't care and it wasn't any of his business.

"I don't indulge in temper tantrums, Beryl," he answered in a hard voice. "I simply informed you I wasn't interested. Nothing has changed. Go back to your husband."

"Canby? Oh don't be silly, darling. He ceased to amuse years ago. No, my tastes are running more exotic of late. I usually get what I want, darling, and right now I want you." Beryl sucked the scarlet-tipped nail of her middle finger between her lips, slowly drew it out and trailed it diagonally across Nigel's chest as she walked around his body. She came to a halt just behind him. Pressing her breasts into his hard, muscled back, she stretched on her toes to reach his ear, and whispered, "I have the use of a secluded bungalow tonight, Nigel darling. Meet me here after the tournament and I'll take you there. I'll wear something black and filmy, and do absolutely *anything* you like."

Her tongue darted out to taste his salty flesh, but she suddenly froze as she followed Nigel's gaze. Elizabeth Mainwarring's table was square in her vision as she peered over Nigel's shoulder. Her stomach clenched in jealousy.

"You needn't look in that direction, Nigel dear. She'll not have anything to do with you, you know. She's as rich as Midas and likely to look to an *English* title to marry. And I really don't believe she has the imagination to even consider anything too sporting outside of marriage. Besides, like father, like daughter." She came to stand in front of him.

"Shut up, Beryl."

Ignoring him, she continued, "And speaking of the good Colonel, I believe he's been busy judging the way that silly Wight tart has been blushing and rubbing against him every time she thinks no one is looking. Hmmm, the prodigal daughter must have hammered quite a dent in his style." She smirked and tossed her brassy hair. "Marjorie is wasting her time, really. But then, I suppose one has only to look at her husband." She laughed as if she knew something he didn't.

Nigel sighed, annoyed. "Beryl, try not to be more tedious than you can help, and for once take no for an answer." And then, feeling an urge to needle her because of his own frustration: "I detect sour grapes. Colonel Mainwarring must have refused you as well."

"Why no, darling." She smiled widely. "He was panting after me. He owned some impressive *equipment*, indeed, but his stamina was sadly lacking." She eyed Nigel from head to toe as if he were a piece of chocolate cake and she just off a two-week reducing diet. "You darling, being such a *vigorous* male animal, wouldn't find it a problem thrusting that magnificent *weapon* into a snug and willing portal all night long!" Her brown eyes twinkling she added archly, "I'm positively drenched in both imagination and a repertoire that would only leave Miss Priss gaping in horror—if she were aware of its existence."

With that Beryl gave a final smug smile and left, sashaying to the bar. A very large celebratory gin and French with at least two olives was called for. She didn't doubt for a moment Nigel would fail to meet her.

Elizabeth felt the blood drain from her face watching the scene between Nigel and Beryl Tate. Butterflies fluttered in her stomach, and her fingers tingled as she reached for her glass of lemonade. Nigel stood tall in jodhpurs and riding boots, his white polo jersey stretched to hug his broad shoulders, black hair tousled as if caressing fingers had just tunnelled through it. His expression was hidden by shadow as Beryl all but rubbed her body on him before stepping away with a voluptuous sway in the direction of the outdoor bar.

How could Elizabeth be so foolish as to let the very sight of him wreak havoc with her senses? It appeared she possessed the uncanny knack of discovering him in compromising positions with women of questionable character. Clearly he was used to a diverse assortment of women. It was highly unlikely she represented anything other than a momentary diversion. Well, she had no intention of developing round heels for anybody. It was past time to take herself in hand. But chemistry had a mind of its own, it seemed.

A timely distraction arrived in the form of Harry and Marcus, relieving her of the dilemma. Chairs were produced and room made for them. Soon Elizabeth's attention was directed entirely to the spectacle of the swift and exciting polo game. The rival team, officers of the Bankura Rifles stationed east of Calcutta on the Burma border, were worthy opponents.

Marcus made a charming companion: lighting Elizabeth's cigarettes, ensuring her glass remained full, and even though his chair was a trifle closer to hers than strictly necessary, always the gentleman. He gazed at her with an adoring gleam, but with an esteem and regard she found gratifying. Not the dark blue eyes glinting hot and carnal with erotic thoughts of sweaty, naked bodies fusing together on tangled sheets. She found herself blushing, and for lack of anything else, used her gold cigarette case as a fan. Respect, she told herself, was far more important.

"Yes, Miss Mainwarring, isn't it just too hot to *breathe?*" Mrs. Wight asked, patting her wavy brown hair a bit nervously as she stopped by Elizabeth's father's chair. "You must purchase a fan from one of the roaming vendors. Nuisances they are mostly, but occasionally one finds a use for them.

"Anyway, I simply had to stop by to remind you of my picnic tomorrow." She touched Colonel Mainwarring lightly on the shoulder. "I shan't take no for an answer. The Maidan will be delightfully cool, you know. Lots of trees for shade and a refreshing breeze off the Hooghly. Plenty of entertainment, too. We usually pack our Victrola, so please feel free to bring your favourite records. For those who don't care to dance to the latest hits"—her eyes slid to the Colonel— "older pastimes are also available, such as croquet, charades . . . and the like." Her voice became more brisk and she looked up, including the whole party in her gaze. "It's quite the best party of the year."

"Yes, Marjorie dear, you are just the one to teach Andrew the *older* pastimes, aren't you?" Beryl came to stand on the opposite side of the Colonel. Her full gin and French sloshed over the rim of the glass as she surveyed Mrs. Wight from hooded eyes. "Hmm, will Andrew be 'up' for the lessons, do you think? But then it may not matter because you haven't been practising much have you?" She chuckled, then took a large sip of her drink.

Mrs. Wight rather resembled a fish, staring at Beryl with shocked wide eyes and a gaping mouth. Colonel Mainwarring flushed an unbecoming shade of puce and snapped, "You're drunk, Beryl. Go home. I won't say 'to your husband' because I wouldn't wish you on the poor sod. You may make your apologies to my daughter, Miss McKay, and Mrs. Wight at a later date. Preferably when you are sober—if such an occasion exists." He stood and, pivoting toward Mrs. Wight, he offered her a bow. "Of course we shall attend tomorrow, my dear. Nothing would give us more pleasure than to help make your party a success. Isn't that so, Elizabeth, Fiona?"

Startled out of her attentiveness to the fascinating undercurrents, Elizabeth rallied, replying in a cheery tone, "We have been eagerly anticipating what we have been told is *the* social event of the summer, Mrs. Wight."

Looking hugely relieved, Mrs. Wight murmured her thanks and moved on, sending an uncertain glance toward Beryl as she left.

Colonel Mainwarring resumed his seat and, without glancing up, said, "You are *de trop*, Beryl. Superfluous. Redundant. Unnecessary."

Unimpressed, Beryl replied, "Really, Andrew, you must watch yourself or you'll come perilously close to apoplexy." Fishing an olive-laden toothpick out of her v-shaped glass, she bit into the succulent green orb with startlingly white teeth and nibbled it slowly, sensuously. Finally hooking the forbidden lover she'd lusted after for weeks, she was feeling cheeky and full of herself. Noting Marcus's proximity to Elizabeth, she flipped him a mischievous smile. Such easy pickings tonight.

"My, but you are looking amazingly erect and vigorous this evening, Marcus, dear boy. Did the girls at the House of Vasana not complete the job properly this afternoon? Or did the young stallion miss his regular appointment?" Finished with her olives, Beryl stirred her libation with a finger and then licked it thoroughly, regarding him with a sly twinkle. "Found another filly more to your liking, have you, darling? Or is it just that your pockets are severely to let again? Naughty boy. You must learn when to step away from the gaming tables, or one day one of those nasty Indian money-lenders will take offense at your often substantial debt and we'll see you floating facedown in the Hooghly. What a waste, darling. I implore you to give it up while you're ahead." Her tone became insinuating. "Perhaps Miss Mainwarring might help you out of your difficulties—for a price of course!"

Marcus's face became increasingly ugly with each insulting innuendo, and now he stood, leaning over the table, directing a deadly stare at Beryl.

"How dare you presume to take me to task, madam? You can only spend considerable time in the lurid underworld of Calcutta to be cognizant of the gambling and prostitution marinating in that salacious stew. Therefore, you must also be aware only the young and very beautiful qualify for positions in the type of establishments to which you refer. As you are endowed with neither attribute, I can only think you have hunted such depraved sport when men fail to entertain—"

"That is quite enough, Captain!" Colonel Mainwarring stood so abruptly his chair tumbled to the ground. "You forget yourself, sir! Your conduct is ungentlemanly. You are confined to your bungalow until further notice. Get out of my sight!"

Marcus straightened to attention at once, saluted with a shaking hand to his mottled forehead, whipped about and stalked through the milling crowd.

The Colonel then rounded on Beryl, his face dark with temper. He slapped his swagger stick against his right thigh as if he were imagining hitting her with it.

"As for you, madam, you may do likewise. Immediately."

"I apologise most sincerely, Andrew." Beryl widened her eyes in a mock attempt at innocence. "Certainly didn't mean to cause offense, of course. My poor endeavour to lighten up a bit of a dull crowd. Such long faces you all had! Really, such a fuss. Well, ta-ta, I'm off." She sauntered toward the bar, well pleased with the turmoil she'd left in her wake.

Colonel Mainwarring watched the woman until she was out of sight and then spoke curtly to his daughter, Fiona, and Harry.

"I apologise for the disturbance. If you will excuse me, I will return shortly."

"What a disgusting creature!" Fiona affected a dramatic shudder. "I must say, I thought she was a wee bit toady when she called on the evening of our arrival. Isn't her husband the Deputy Commissioner? Where is he? Why doesn't he keep her firmly in hand?"

"Only man hereabout who can't, I hear." Harry cleared his throat. "Er, sorry ladies, afraid that's the way of it. Why don't I retrieve something a bit stronger from the bar—say a large gin and tonic all around? We'll be cookin' with gas as the Yanks say. Back in a jiff."

"Let's stretch our legs while Harry is gone, Fi. I quite feel as though I've landed in one of those old-fashioned bogs dug in the back garden. I need a breath of fresh air. Why don't we visit the polo ponies' stable? Animals provide such a calming effect. Things will slot back into perspective by the time we return."

Stopping occasionally to greet acquaintances, they left the spectator area and, following the gravel path through a small stand of coral and teak trees, soon arrived at the bustling stable. Indian stablehands were briskly brushing down animals just off the field, and many players now in the game break were readying fresh ponies for play. Stopping at one stall to admire a gleaming chestnut, Elizabeth reached out to pat the pony's nose. A large brown hand fastened around her wrist, arresting her movement.

"Shiva here has a nasty habit, Miss Mainwarring," Nigel informed her. "He bites."

Elizabeth's heart sped up and she grew warm all over, especially where he still held her wrist.

"Thank you for your timely intervention, Major. You may release my hand now, if you don't mind."

"Of course." He nodded politely to Fiona. "Are you enjoying the game, ladies? Not too hot for you, I hope."

"Oh, we're bearing up quite tolerably," Fiona answered. "We look forward to cooling off a bit tomorrow at the Maidan. I understand Mrs. Wight's picnic is the event of the summer. You *are* attending, Major?" At Nigel's nod she continued, carefully avoiding glancing at Elizabeth. "Perhaps if you are not engaged, you might be so kind as to escort us. We're left without our previous escort at the eleventh hour."

Blindsided by Fiona's defection, it was a moment too late when Elizabeth spoke. "Really Fiona, I'm sure the Major—"

"I'd be delighted, Miss McKay, to perform a needed service for two such lovely ladies. However, it will be a tight squeeze in my two-seater."

"Nonsense, Major. Your motorcar is equipped with a rumble seat, is it not, as are most roadsters? Why, we'll just toss a coin to see who wins it." She smiled coquettishly. "A gentleman might even volunteer to occupy it while allowing the ladies in front. After all, how could a lady driver make a courageous soldier such as yourself nervous?"

"Touché, Miss McKay. I will call for you both at ten o'clock. Until then." Nigel nodded farewell.

Elizabeth spun on her heel, heading for the stable doors, stunned not only by the rapidity, but the very fact that Fiona had manipulated the situation to satisfy romantic notions. Her vision blurred around the edges and suddenly walking took extraordinary effort, as if she were moving underwater. *Blast* Fiona! She did not wish to spend a day with that skirt-chasing rogue, even with Fi as a buffer. Ha! Buffer indeed! Fiona planned on melting away as soon as was decent.

That Fiona was falling in love with Harry was obvious to anyone who cared to look. As happy as she was, Fi couldn't conceive of the baser cravings or habits of men less honourable than her newfound love. For the first time in memory, Elizabeth was truly irritated with her dearest friend. She was working on a suitable reprimand when her thoughts were interrupted by the Major's deep voice calling her name. As if by magic, her perception was again clear and sharp.

Nigel appraised her long firm legs before slowly meeting her gaze. His eyes were dilated, almost black. "Although your present ensemble is very attractive indeed, Miss Mainwarring, you must be sure to dress in something . . . more protective tomorrow. The gentle draft off the Hooghly can be deceiving and the unwary find themselves severely burned."

Elizabeth felt her face—and her legs—go hot as if the sun had indeed touched them unkindly. The audacity of the man!

To speak to her in such a vulgar manner and to treat her as if she were a brainless ninny! Well, she'd be damned if she let him see how he aggravated her.

Smiling, she replied in a sugary voice, "Why, Major, not only will I endeavour to be on time, I even think I can find a suitable garment that will not cause inconvenience to either of us. Good day."

She simmered in silence until they were out of earshot of the stables, then faced Fiona.

"How could you, Fiona? He's nothing but a cad and a playboy. He makes advances on respectable women, then patronises whorehouses, for goodness sake. Did you see him with Beryl Tate earlier? Clearly they were arranging an assignation. The man is a bed-hopper!" Pausing to catch her breath, she continued in a calmer manner. "The insinuation in his voice just now was insulting. He is no gentleman, of that you may be sure." Recalling her friend's almost constant companion of the last few days, she added, "What about Harry? He will be hurt and disappointed not escorting you."

"Harry is too certain of himself by far." Fiona tipped her chin up a notch. "Perhaps I have been a little too accessible these last days. A little distance might lessen his cocky attitude." Returning to the subject at hand, she reminded Elizabeth, "I mentioned that Nigel must have excellent reason for visiting that bordello, and I still believe it. My intuition is seldom wrong—my Scots blood, you know. Nigel is a man of integrity. It's as plain as the sun in the sky he's drawn to you, and wishes Beryl to the moon. Advances, indeed! More likely he kissed you until your toes curled." Noting Elizabeth's flushing cheeks, Fi nodded in satisfaction and continued. "You've just never been this attracted to a man before, and now you feel like the rug's been pulled from beneath you. Embrace it, darling, don't run from it." Turning serious, she said, "I told myself I was silly, but there was something dicky about

Marcus. One couldn't take exception to him. He's quite proper and polite, not to mention gorgeous. Almost the ideal man. Perhaps that was it—too good to be true. At least we may be thankful to Beryl for bursting that bubble!"

Elizabeth agreed. "Still, my imagination is having trouble picturing such an apparently refined and sophisticated man embroiled in such unsavoury pursuits. I suppose the golden, angelic surface misleads a number of women. At least I shall no longer feel guilty preferring a rogue to the polished courtier."

The hurried crunch of footsteps to the rear alerted them that they were no longer alone; and making way on the gravel path, they recognised Lieutenant Toppenham, Diana Compton's beau. The young man of medium height nodded somewhat distractedly as he passed. Elizabeth returned the silent greeting politely, but raised her eyebrows after he walked briskly by, at the rumpled way his uniform hung on his slender build. How strange, she thought, that an officer should show himself thus in public. When he disappeared around the bend in the path, Elizabeth continued the discussion with Fiona.

"I'm not sure you are entirely correct in your assessment of the Major. Indeed—"

Screaming suddenly shattered the calm evening air, drowning her last words.

Chapter Eleven

Elizabeth froze, staring at Fiona in horror. Trembling, they both made a lightning-quick survey, expecting a killer to materialise in the underbrush waving a knife in a bloody frenzy. Thankfully the bamboo shrubs and ferns bordering the path remained innocuously still. But only for a heartbeat, as another scream shrilled, and another.

"It's coming from the stables," Elizabeth cried.

As one, they wheeled toward the sound, running as if the devil's disciple were on their heels. Emerging from the wooded path, they observed a gathering of Indians and polo players from both teams fanning out behind the long, low building.

Nigel's voice boomed, ordering the dispersal of the throng and demanding a doctor be fetched immediately. Through the thinning cluster Nigel caught sight of the girls.

"Miss Mainwarring, Miss McKay! A word if you please!" They arrived out of breath and stopped short at the sight of a figure huddled against the stable wall in a fetal position. The poor girl, wild in her sobbing, skittered farther along the wall each time Nigel attempted to approach her.

"Miss McKay, if you would be so good as to fetch a horse blanket from inside." He raked his hair back with impatient fingers. "Miss Mainwarring, please stay with her while I hurry the doctor. *Now*, ladies, if you please!" he added when both women remained still as statues from the shock.

"Of course, Major, at once," Fiona managed through stiff lips, before leaving on her errand.

Suddenly the dishevelled victim looked up. It was Diana Compton. Her normally neat dark brown bob stuck out in tufts. Tears, joined by brown mascara and green eyeshadow ran down her cheeks in a muddy waterfall.

"It was a filthy Indian did it." Swollen, red eyes spit defiance at Nigel. "It *was!* Damned wogs!" She collapsed into sobs once more.

Nigel spared her no more than a sharp glance before departing.

"Now then, Miss Compton—Diana, everything is going to be just fine. Nigel has just gone for the doctor." Elizabeth nearly cringed at her own words. Everything was *not* fine. Might never again be fine for Diana. She felt an overwhelming uselessness in the face of such disaster, but nonetheless knelt, taking Diana in her arms and rocking her in a soothing rhythm, crooning and making nonsense conversation. It took several moments, but finally her charge quieted, only hiccupping sounds escaping her raw mouth. Deeming it safe to do so, Elizabeth set about straightening Diana out to assess the extent of the damage.

The girl's dress was torn, and several ladders marred her stockings, but Elizabeth jolted upright in dismay at the blood smearing Diana's thighs and her underwear dangling from her left ankle.

"Dear God!" Fiona returned with a coarse blanket and

hurriedly covered the injured girl with it. "Who did this, dear? Did you see? You must tell us!"

"Damned bloody wog, that's who! I-I was taking a-a walk. He jumped me. H-he r-*raped* me!" She ended on another sob. "Oh God! What shall I tell Mummy and Father?" Her fingers closed around Elizabeth's wrist with surprising strength. "You *mustn't* tell my parents. You mustn't! They will send me away in disgrace. I'll never marry! Oh God, who will marry me now?"

She whipped herself into a new fit of hysterics, which both Elizabeth and Fiona struggled to contain. At last, cried out and exhausted, Diana sat in a piteous huddle, sniffling.

Abruptly, Elizabeth remembered a rumpled Lieutenant Toppenham passing them on the path. He was barely mindful of his surroundings. Could it be . . . ? No, Diana insisted it was an Indian. But, she would, wouldn't she? If an officer actually raped her, it would be exceedingly difficult, if even possible, to prove. An officer at all times treated a lady with honour, unless invited to do otherwise—which would mean, of course, Diana was no lady. Only the worst sort of slag enticed a gentleman only to cry rape upon receiving the asked-for intentions. It was, of course, invariably the woman's fault. Indeed, it was universally known that men possessed no self-control when tempted by a female. Elizabeth nearly snorted aloud at the absurdity of *that* notion.

On the other hand, in accusing a native, all sympathy remained with Diana. Everyone knew Indians were an unprincipled race and lusted after women with delicate white skin. Still, Diana was quite ruined. Society expected the victim to whisk herself off, out of sight and mind, so the vagaries of life did not intrude upon those worthies' nicely ordered world.

Indian or officer, a scandal of profound proportions was ready to explode. And not only scandal.

A "guilty" Indian was bound to be found and made an example of, and perhaps even blamed for the recent murders. The tenuous cords of social tension already were drawn tightly between natives and British, but now they were unravelling in a speed-dive.

What sort of violence might erupt if a native were charged with the rape of a British girl?

"Are you positive it was a native, Diana?" Elizabeth's voice was low and urgent.

Diana's tears stopped instantly. "You doubt my word, Miss Mainwarring," she replied indignantly. "I have said it was an Indian, and so I maintain. How could you *think* a white man would do this!"

Before Elizabeth could reply, a florid-faced, white-haired man carrying a black satchel arrived with Nigel and two Indian orderlies carrying a stretcher.

"Thank you, ladies. I'll take over now," the doctor said curtly, hunkering down beside Diana. He promptly opened his bag, retrieving a hypodermic needle, which he tested before inserting into his patient's arm. She whimpered at the prick, and looking up, took notice of the orderlies. Immediately terror-stricken, she screamed and whipped her head about seeking an escape route.

"No, no *no*. Get them away from me," she demanded, attempting to crawl away.

One of the Indians stared at Diana in dislike; the other schooled his features in a bland expression and merely waited, holding the stretcher.

The doctor clasped Diana's shoulders in a firm grip. "Now then, my girl, calm yourself. No one is going to hurt you. No one. These chaps are here to take care of you. No harm will come to you, do you understand?"

Diana's eyes glazed as the powerful sedative took effect, and slowly she turned to the doctor, slumping against his chest.

Observing the rapid onslaught of the drug, Nigel spoke softly. "Have another of those ready for the mother, Dr. Stafford. I thought it best her parents wait for her at their home."

Dr. Stafford looked up from settling his patient on the stretcher. "Just as well. Hysterical parents at a scene such as this? Not at all the thing. A circus, indeed. And hard enough on them without exposing themselves to the public and garnering more attention for their poor daughter." He shook his head sadly. "An Indian, she claims? Ah, well, she's ruined at any rate. I imagine she will be bundled off to England as soon as may be, while her father seeks a post elsewhere." He picked up his valise and spoke to the bearers. "Now then, chaps. Go gently but swiftly, we stop for no one. And no chattering to your mates about what you've seen and heard here," he reminded them in a sharp tone.

"Good God!" Harry exclaimed. He stood motionless on the path leading from the spectator grounds, then leaped out of the way of the passing retinue and strode to Fiona. Capturing her elbows in his large hands, he quickly scrutinised her for possible injury. Finding none, he self-consciously stepped back to a more circumspect distance. A drop of perspiration rolled down his cheek, but he ignored it and tunnelled distracted fingers through his short locks.

"For a moment I thought—well, it was loudly rumoured a girl suffered a vicious attack at the stables and you were gone when I returned with the drinks. Stupid of me, of course. I'm relieved to find you unharmed, Fiona—you too, of course, Miss Mainwarring. There's a great palava over to the grounds and guards are posted at the other end of the path. Bally jammy I managed through. You must allow me to escort you home without delay. Once you are settled and fortified by a good stiff gin, you might inform me of the particulars of how you landed in the middle of this appalling situation." Gripping Fiona's arm in a proprietary style, he guided her down the dirt path, apparently forgetting Elizabeth and Nigel.

Harry's anxiety about Fiona's safety was palpable, and reluctant to intrude upon their privacy, Elizabeth hung back several moments before slowly following them. By unspoken agreement, Nigel fell into step with her. Nothing was left to be done and only a few polo players remained, seeing to their horses in the stable.

The sun disappeared below the horizon leaving behind layers of orange, pink, and turquoise gauze streaking the sky. A royal-blue blanket, dusted with the spangles of the coming night, waited impatiently for full due. Dusk lasted a matter of minutes in the tropics. Already the crickets were in full song, a firefly darted between the branches above their heads followed by a swooping bat. The early night smelled of sun, mimosa, and dust.

Suddenly the coral and teak tree leaves clattered in the strong breeze sweeping through the wood. Elizabeth felt goose bumps ripple along every inch of her exposed skin. She resisted the urge to move closer to Nigel. There was absolutely nothing to be frightened of, but just the same she couldn't help glancing over her shoulder. Was that the crack of a branch in the woods? She stopped abruptly and peered into the gathering dusk. She couldn't shake the notion there was something or someone out there, watching.

Nigel turned, frowning. Elizabeth's face was as white as her shorts, and she was staring into the trees. He couldn't blame her, after all that had occurred since she arrived in Calcutta, if she expected a raving maniac to burst forth from the bush. Still, the last thing he needed was another woman with the screaming abdabs.

"Come along, Miss Mainwarring. No bogeyman is about to attack you when a soldier armed with a kukri is escorting you." He tapped the wicked, curved blade sheathed at his hip for emphasis.

Elizabeth's eyes snapped to Nigel's shadowed face and then to the path ahead. They had almost reached the halfway point. Fiona and Harry were nowhere in sight. She'd be damned if she showed her momentary panic. Straightening her spine, she forced the chilling feeling of being watched to a dark corner of her brain. This was as good a time as any to tell him of her suspicions concerning Diana.

"Major Covington-Singh. Miss Compton accused an Indian of her assault; however, it may not be so."

Nigel's eyebrows rose and he stepped closer, studying Elizabeth intently. "Just what do you think occurred, Miss Mainwarring?"

Elizabeth stepped back, hesitating. He was so close she could feel the heat radiating from him, see the individual hairs of the stubble darkening the planes of his face. His intense blue eyes pierced the very depths of her soul. There was no going back.

Clearing her throat, she said, "Moments before Miss Compton screamed, Lieutenant Toppenham, whom I understand to be her beau, brushed by Miss McKay and myself on this path in the most brusque manner. I was disconcerted at the time to note the frightful disarray of his uniform. Dust and grass clung to the fabric, his shirttail hung loosely outside his trousers, and . . . a scratch on the side of his neck dripped blood on his collar."

For a full minute Nigel was silent. Then, "You do realise the seriousness of this accusation, Miss Mainwarring?"

"It is no accusation, Major. Merely a statement of what Miss McKay and I witnessed immediately before Miss Compton screamed."

Nigel finally looked away and sighed. Sodding hell. Which was worse: a native or an officer? Either way, it promised an epic scandal. And because of his heritage he'd be caught in the middle. Again.

He rubbed his suddenly aching neck. "Please say nothing

to anyone yet. The last detail this investigation needs is—what the . . . ?" He spun toward the wood. A loud and obscene grunting rose—and died just as quickly to a barely discernable whimper.

Nigel shot in front of Elizabeth, his kukri half out of its scabbard, but relaxed, pushing the deadly weapon back home upon the sound of low feminine laughter and a triumphant and familiar male voice.

"Was that hard and forceful enough for you, Beryl? Fancy *that'll* keep you until I can give you another hearty shag tomorrow."

The voice came from their left and maybe ten yards into the wood. The man was breathing heavily, as if from prolonged exertion.

Blood pumped a dull red in Elizabeth's face, but curiosity and something else warred with embarrassment as she stood in the shelter of Nigel's body. She could still feel his heat and smell the musky male scent of him. A strange warmth swirled deep in her belly and her skin tingled, responding to his closeness and the episode of carnality to which they played unwilling witness.

Beryl's laughter trickled through the tropical vines and branches. "I'll admit screwing against a tree is rather raw and primitive even for me, but don't flatter yourself, Phillip. All you've done, darling, is prime me for a night-long marathon with a truly young and *vital* lover! Really, Phillip dear, when *was* the last time you had it off all night? Poor disillusioned Marjorie believes you are so out of training she's taken to panting after your commanding officer. A fine pair they make too, as she doesn't expect much and he can't follow through." She giggled. "Perhaps he'll be so pleased with her, you will make Lt. Colonel in record time!"

A vicious crack rent the soft evening air.

"Bastard!"

"By God, Beryl," came the savage reply. "One of these

days you'll go too far and a little slap on the cheek will be the least of your worries. But then, you might just enjoy that."

Elizabeth's lassitude fizzled at the mention of her father, and now the outbreak of violence doused it as efficiently as a jug of ice water. There was a crashing through the underbrush, and rising to her toes she peered over Nigel's shoulder in time to see the man emerging from the wood onto the path several feet in front of them.

Major Wight did not look in their direction but immediately turned to his left, intent on returning to the playing field area.

Nigel swore roundly under his breath and, without bothering to apologise, seized Elizabeth's wrist to tug her in the same direction.

"Right, then, Miss Mainwarring," he said with determination. "Let's not muck about. It's been a bloody difficult day, with much still to do, and I'm not keen on dealing with Beryl Tate as the crowning point of my evening. Make haste before she comes tripping out of the trees."

Elizabeth blinked in surprise and shut her gaping mouth with a snap. Good God! Surely the woman wasn't normal? Did she attempt to bed every man in sight? Had Beryl really engaged in an affair with her father? No—*that* was none of her business, she reminded herself.

But who was her young and vital lover? Nigel? Had he arranged an assignation earlier with Beryl? No wonder he was in a hurry to leave. Running into his evening's entertainment with Elizabeth in tow might indeed prove a sticky situation for him. She recognised the hot flush in her veins for the jealousy it was. And what right did she have to be jealous? None. Never had she experienced the force of attraction that she felt for Nigel, but he was not for her. A maharaja's son wouldn't look to her, a mere millionairess, for a legitimate relationship. He would marry for his family. Certainly it was dog in the manger, but it was easier to think of him meeting Beryl than admitting to herself she wasn't up to snuff.

He practically dragged her over the dirt track. Instinctively, she wanted to dig her heels into the rough ground and snatch her wrist out of his grip, away from his touch, away from *him*. She resisted the urge because stopping meant the possibility of a confrontation with Beryl.

With every meeting she felt her resolve and control disintegrating as far as Nigel was concerned. One of these days she might actually give in and become Nigel's plaything. And that wouldn't do at all. Because she didn't think she'd ever be able to forget him as easily as he might forget her.

Chapter Twelve

"Elizabeth? There you are, old thing! We're just off, but the Major is due in a few minutes, so you won't be long behind us." Fiona tossed her friend a sunny smile from the end of the bright corridor and turned to leave.

Just outside her bedroom, Elizabeth looked up, startled, from the cream lace gloves she smoothed over her fingers. "Fiona! What are you talking about? The Major is escorting both of us."

Fiona had the grace to look sheepish as she pivoted back to her friend. Her leather-shod toe played with the fringe attached to the light pink and blue Kashmiri runner, and she peeked at Elizabeth through rusty eyelashes, stalling the inevitable. She looked perfectly lovely in a butter yellow linen dress with a string of large carved ivory buttons down the side. A wide-brimmed straw hat covered her usually unmanageable carrot curls.

"Actually, Harry is taking me after all. He was so concerned for me last night, I couldn't say no when he insisted I not step out of his sight today." She blushed. "It's for the best. It will be so much easier for the gentlemen to keep an eye on just one lady apiece instead of two, you know. And Nigel will positively be glued to you today! Your dress is charming, love. It's the new Adrian, isn't it? He truly outdid himself with—"

"Very clever, Fiona! Don't think I'm forgetting anytime soon that you have left me alone with a . . . a masher!"

"Rubbish! I would have one of my feelings, love. The only danger you'll be in is savouring the time of your life with a man dazzling enough to masquerade as one of those gorgeous Hollywood film stars!" Outside, a car horn hooted in several sharp staccato bursts. "Oh, by the way, your father is coming with us. He didn't specifically enquire the identity of your escort, so I didn't enlighten him. Ta-ta, love!" She winked and hurried for the door.

Elizabeth stood rigid for a moment, her lips pressed into a tight, flat line. Of all the treacherous, double dealing, perfidious—oh! There were not words black enough for Fiona's disloyalty! She headed for the dining room, feeling an idiotic and juvenile urge to fling her silk purse across the room. Instead, with controlled, deliberate movements, she placed the bag on the table and poured herself a cup of strong black Darjeeling. Concentrating on not trembling, she took a long bracing sip of the hot tea and paced to the window.

She was a big girl and could deal with her renegade emotions without company! The Maidan was a large area, and nearly the whole British community was to be in attendance, so she needn't see Nigel once she arrived. She'd make sure they kept a safe distance.

Feeling calmer, Elizabeth let her eyes refocus on the colourful garden outside. Several gardeners squatted, pulling weeds from the dry beds of hibiscus, jasmine, and orchids. Even in the shade of the eaves, the orange Armistice roses were wilting sadly. A labourer pushed a barrel-bladed mower, fol-

lowed by the Bhisti spraying water everywhere from the
leather bag strapped to his back. He looked up just then,
staring at her with a strange blankness as if he really didn't
see her, then returned his brown craggy countenance to his
task, a weary flag to his step.

Already the heat waves shimmered in the distance. The
lightweight French blue chiffon frock Elizabeth wore boasted
sheer flounces for sleeves with another row adorning the
mid-shin hem. The river breeze would ruffle them sufficiently to keep her cool, she was sure.

Finished with her tea, Elizabeth set her cup back in its
saucer just as a bright yellow Alfa Romeo cabriolet roared to
a stop in front of the bungalow. Nigel hopped over the low
door of his sporty motorcar and opened the boot. Walking
around to the passenger side, he lifted out a boxlike object
the size of a portmanteau and carried it back to the boot, settling it carefully inside.

A moment later he was shown into the dining room, looking cool and crisp in white trousers and a white linen shirt,
the sleeves rolled up to the elbows to expose his darkly
tanned forearms. His kukri rested in a battered leather scabbard against his thigh.

He leaned against the door jamb, hands in his pockets,
studying her with lazy cobalt eyes. They sparked in appreciation of her wavy, golden hair and the sexy high-heel sandals that matched her frilly dress. The blue-lavender
coloured her eyes a sparkling jade and brought out a becoming flush in her skin, while the dress itself clung in the most
enticing places.

"You took my advice admirably, Miss Mainwarring. You
are stunning this morning." He came into the room, removed
his topi and tucked it under his arm. It left his thick black
hair tousled. But it did not serve to make him look boyish.
To the contrary. His almond-shaped eyes boldly appraised
her and his trimmed mustache accented his sensuously

moulded lips. As a rule, Elizabeth didn't care for mustaches. It seemed men either affected an effeminate pencil line or grew a great bushy thing more in keeping with a gorilla. Nigel's was neither. It covered his upper lip without engulfing it, and it was parted just a tiny bit in the middle. Oh yes, Fiona was spot on. He most certainly might pass for a matinee idol.

Elizabeth found herself blushing despite her conviction that his preference in female companions was related directly to the speed in which they dropped their knickers. Still, he appeared intent on charming her today. Well, she could be charming, too—and distant.

"Good morning, Major. May I offer you a cup of tea?" At his nod she prepared him a cup, and as she replenished her own, remarked, "You must be looking forward to a small holiday this afternoon after such a disagreeable evening. Please tell me how the Comptons are holding up."

Nigel raised his eyebrows when she did not join him at the table, but took her cup to stand beside the window. He regarded her silently and remained standing, stirring his tea. Finally he set his spoon on the saucer.

"The Comptons are faring as well as expected. The Major is on furlough for several days. He and his wife are suffering from shock, bewilderment, and, of course, anger. Fortunately, Diana will not endure any lasting physical injuries. Several serious cuts bear watching to see they don't turn septic, and Dr. Stafford recommends a few days of sedation. Understandably, Major and Mrs. Compton are eager for the culprit to be caught and punished."

"Poor Diana. How heartbreaking."

"Most certainly." He pushed away his untouched tea as if impatient or tired of the subject. "Is Miss McKay ready yet?"

Elizabeth set her cup and saucer on the sideboard. "Due to the current unrest, Captain Woodford was unable to bear

Fiona out of his sight. And acting as knight in shining armour, he whisked her off in a trusty motorised steed with my father acting as chaperon. It appears we must make do with one another."

The tremendous weight of the murder and rape enquiries burdening Nigel's shoulders now lightened immeasurably at the prospect of actually having Elizabeth all to himself. Warmth rushed through his veins, right down to the soles of his feet. In bittersweet resignation he finally acknowledged to himself that he'd lost the fight. He knew with a sudden conviction he'd take her any way he could have her—including engaging in the type of secret affair he found demeaning and sordid. The abyss—infinite in possibilities and dangers—opened, beckoning. He leapt.

"Shall we go then?"

He waited for her to precede him through the door, and as she did so, touched the base of her spine in a conspicuous caress, guiding her out.

His fingers burned through Elizabeth's frock like a branding iron and didn't lift even as she stopped at the hall mirror to cover her face with the netting from her ridiculously tiny hat. She shivered at the hunger she saw blazing in Nigel's eyes, but did not step away.

By the time he opened the low passenger door to the cabriolet for her, his fingers had curved possessively around her hip. He vaulted over his own door, turned the ignition, and they were thundering down the road, dust billowing behind them.

The bonnet was long, but the seating space small enough that Elizabeth felt the dark hair on Nigel's arm rub hers every time he shifted gears. So much for distance! Her heart raced, and she felt warm in spite of the rushing wind. Needing to cool her responses and keep some semblance of perspective, she cast about for something to take her mind off his closeness. Remembering the box he'd placed in the boot, she asked him about it.

"That," he replied, "is a communications wireless. It works something like a telephone. It is powered by a battery and allows soldiers to communicate in the field."

"How extraordinary! I've never heard of such a thing. Imagine actually speaking to someone in civilisation when one is north of Watford! How does it work? Will you demonstrate its use?" Elizabeth turned to Nigel, genuinely intrigued.

He removed his eyes from the road momentarily to give her an amused smile. "I suppose you would like to acquire one immediately so you may exchange juicy bits of gossip wherever you choose to travel? I'm afraid it isn't possible yet. Perhaps never. This is a relatively new use for the wireless, and not many frequencies are available. The few useable ones are for military use only."

Elizabeth frowned. "How vexing. I was thinking how expedient it might prove on my sheep station in New Zealand. Consider the valuable time saved in a medical emergency or the inconvenience of a motorcar problem solved without waiting for hours in the dark or inclement weather."

"However beneficial its employment, it is, unfortunately, by no means perfect. It may only be used in open spaces, as the signal is line of sight only. It is not capable of travelling around corners, and a stormy climate inhibits communication. Even in optimum conditions the sound quality cannot compare to the telephone."

"You make it sound as if this new wireless is quite unreliable. Why then are you bothering with it?" Elizabeth held tight to the car's small door as Nigel abruptly stopped to allow several bleating sheep to cross the road. A herder followed the skinny animals, shouting encouragement in Hindi.

One large brown hand gripped the steering wheel while his other rested on the side of the vehicle. "Unreliable or not, it is the only means of mobile communication available to us currently. It's a damn sight better than nothing."

"Why not use telegrams or the telephone then?"

Nigel transferred his gaze from the sheep to her. "Out in the field this instrument acts as a telephone." He grinned. "Faster than messenger service or carrier pigeons. And on manoeuvres one does not have the luxury of sending or receiving telegrams." He released the clutch and the brake as the last of the animals crossed, and accelerated to an alarming speed.

Elizabeth clamped her hands to her hat and hit the back of the seat with a jolt. "Of course, how silly of me." After a moment or two, she closed her eyes and lifted her face to the sky, luxuriating in the velocity. "Do you always drive this fast, Major?"

The Alfa Romeo hugged the road as Nigel negotiated a corner. "There's no point in owning a machine such as this if one isn't prepared to put it through its paces." He turned to admire how the force of the wind molded her chiffon gown to her breasts, even accentuating the V of her thighs, and thought of a few erotic paces he'd like to show her. "It's one of life's pleasures."

Elizabeth slowly opened her eyes at Nigel's intimate tone, and quivered as his pupils dilated and his hot gaze raked her body.

"One of many for you, I'm sure," she murmured dryly, before facing the road. The distance she'd promised herself was rapidly slipping and, angered by it, she lashed out mindlessly. "Tell me, Major, are you bringing your wireless to the picnic as a party favour, or are you expecting an important transmission from one of your subordinates slaving somewhere out in the broiling sun?"

Her goal was achieved admirably. The seductive mood shattered like glass into nasty sharp little fragments.

Nigel's mouth tightened. "Show and tell, Miss Mainwarring, ceased its charm before I was out of short pants. The Commissioner of Bengal is very concerned about this string of murders. So much so in fact, he has ordered the Army to take over the investigation from the civil authorities. It would be unwise to be left without a means of immediate communication in light of the current state of affairs. Indeed, the incident last night is an unfortunate example."

Stricken at her own unthinking jibe, Elizabeth cursed her rash tongue and wished she could call back her words. "Of course, Major, how thoughtless of me," she said, gripping her door again as Nigel hit the brake and swung his roadster into a dirt-packed car park. "One can hope your wireless is but an unneeded safety measure today." And now the subject was at hand, she finally brought up the question burning in her mind all morning, "Did you speak to Lieutenant Toppenham?"

Nigel brought the motorcar to a halt at the farthest point from the entrance to the Maidan, clicked off the ignition, and set the hand brake.

"Toppenham is not talking, except to deny all charges. He is confined to his quarters for now on my suspicions and your statement alone. But there is not much I can do if Diana Compton continues to deny him as her rapist." His gaze narrowed. "It *is* only circumstantial. Are you or Miss McKay willing to give evidence in a court of law?"

"Without question, and I know I may speak for Fiona."

"You realise, of course, the British community will likely turn its collective back on you for your action? You will be maligned and defamed for testifying against your own kind when a native may easily be condemned and the whole incident forgotten."

"Not so easily for those involved, I dare say, Major. And I've never particularly cared what others thought of me. To do so severely limits one's potential. What I think of myself is far more important."

Nigel nodded, satisfied. "Cross your fingers it needn't go to that extent," he said, and exited the car.

When he opened the door for her, Elizabeth commented, "This makes two officers confined to quarters. That is if

Captain Langley is still under that restriction."

A wide grin split Nigel's face. "He most certainly is." Helping her from the low seat and cupping his hand beneath her elbow, he assisted her over the uneven terrain. "And snarling like a caged panther. He fancied himself your escort today. I'm sorry if you are disappointed." He didn't look in the least repentant.

Elizabeth shuddered, recalling yesterday's revelations into Langley's character. "Not likely." She swallowed, then asked the question she truly found troubling. "Major, do you believe Lieutenant Toppenham is the murderer?"

"At this point, Miss Mainwarring, my mind remains open regarding everyone."

Chapter Thirteen

A *maidan* is by definition a park ground, and indeed, the Maidan was an oasis of green verdant lawn adorned by a collection of vibrant jewel-hued tropical flowers, as well as the familiar, more sedate pastels of petunias, carnations, and gladiolas waving gently in the breeze drifting off the rushing brown Hooghly River. The small wood bordering the car park and the Maidan itself also provided spectacular splashes of colour in the form of flame of the forest, coral and red silk cotton trees, all in full bloom.

People dotted the park. Some, drinks in hand, threaded between the native servants setting up tables and chairs at the far end of the park near the ghats. Others bowed their heads over a game of croquet; a laughing group of young people halfheartedly played badminton, and several young boys tussled in an energetic game of rugby. "April in Paris" blared from a nearby Victrola, and as Elizabeth watched, a few intrepid couples attempted a foxtrot on a patch of trampled grass.

Nigel flagged a waiter carrying a tray of full champagne glasses, and thus fortified, they joined the group surrounding the Victrola and found them arguing amiably over which record to play next.

"I say," announced a red-haired, freckle-faced officer, "this new jazz music is brilliant! Woodford could make a fortune lending out his American recordings."

"Well, I'm afraid I'm missing the charm, Lieutenant Fairfield." Georgina Smythe scrutinised the record jacket she held of a black man blowing a trumpet for all he was worth. "It's a bit jarring, and I must say, a little *too* earthy for my tastes."

"How does one actually dance to it?" enquired a petite brunette whom Elizabeth remembered from the dance at the Mohd Bagh Club as Amanda Crosshaven, the young wife of the middle-aged District Magistrate.

Captain Henderson smiled at her indulgently through his heavy, dark handlebar mustache. "If one possesses an imagination, Mrs. Crosshaven, anything is possible."

Mrs. Crosshaven's sherry-brown eyes twinkled up at him. He was far younger and better looking than her tedious husband, who apparently derived more entertainment from his cigars and brandy than he did his wife's company. "You are a true visionary, Captain. Why don't you demonstrate your inventiveness? Do please play another of those splendid new songs, Captain Woodford."

Harry softly sung "It Don't Mean a Thing If it Ain't Got That Swing" as he carefully placed the needle in the groove of the black disc, and seizing Fiona by the hand led her in an incomprehensible jumble of steps. The gyrating on the impromptu dance floor attracted a sizeable audience who tapped their feet to the music and clapped for the few brave performing couples.

The next song was a favourite on Top of the Pops, and far more traditional. Nigel set their glasses down on a nearby table and clasped Elizabeth close in his arms for an intimate dance to the romantic strains of "I'm Getting Sentimental Over You." One hand held hers firmly, while the other splayed across her lower back, pressing her closely to a hard-muscled chest that rose and fell with his steady, even breathing. All at once she felt terribly shy and found she could look no higher than the base of his throat, where black curling hairs escaped his linen shirt.

"Elizabeth," he ordered softly. "Look at me."

Elizabeth was intensely aware of him and could feel her breasts swelling and nipples peaking. Still she didn't look up. Blood pooled in her belly producing a drugged, dizzy sensation. Finally, she tipped back her head to find his steady hooded gaze telling her he meant to have her. Even while she met his stare, she felt his pinky finger shockingly fit itself into the cleft of her buttocks.

"Major-*Sahib*." The Indian servant's voice startled them both. "Excuse please, but Colonel Mainwarring wishes a word, sir. Follow me please."

Nigel scowled darkly at the bearer before turning his hot gaze back to Elizabeth. "I won't be long. I promise." Then he was striding off in search of her father. She shivered. That promise had nothing to do with how long he might be absent.

"Miss Mainwarring, may I have the pleasure of this dance?" Lieutenant Fairfield's face was nearly as red as his hair. He smiled in expectation.

"Of course, Lieutenant." Before she knew it, Elizabeth was performing a range of dances to a variety of music, from the old-fashioned ragtime to Harry's favourite Duke Ellington.

Finally she begged relief and retreated to the sidelines to finish her champagne. Nigel had yet to return, and she wasn't sure whether she was sorry or glad. However, she did not have time to dwell on the puzzle as she was joined almost immediately by an out-of-breath Amanda Crosshaven and Captain Henderson.

"Isn't this a jolly good time, Miss Mainwarring? I do so love to dance!" She sipped champagne and darted a flirtatious glance up at Captain Henderson. "Especially with such a willing and creative partner. I say let's—" Amanda stopped mid-sentence, her face dimming as she caught sight of Beryl Tate drawing *her* husband Simon onto the makeshift dance floor. It was a close dance, and Beryl was rubbing herself all over him. Simon in turn made a furtive grasp for Beryl's bottom and chuckled when his hand easily filled with flesh. With a petulant twist of her lips, Amanda wondered what on earth that old slag possessed that she didn't. Smirking at the clear answer (a lot more bottom—that's what!), she declared, "Ronnie dear, do let's find something to replenish our energy. I swear I've never been so famished! Cheerio then, Miss Mainwarring."

Elizabeth shook her head in bemusement, watching the pair stroll in the opposite direction of the food.

"Bloody hot out, is it not, Miss Mainwarring?" Elizabeth turned around to find Canby Tate mopping his damp face with a handkerchief. Stringy strands of hair stretched across his shiny head and the buttons on his short-sleeve plaid shirt strained bravely over his protruding belly. Alas, to little avail, as glimpses of pasty white skin peeked out. It had been amusing witnessing him leave a brothel when she was surrounded by friends. But now, alone, she found him oddly disturbing.

"Good day, Commissioner Tate. Yes, it is quite warm today." It was actually far more pleasant than usual with the refreshing river breeze.

"Expect you'll find it takes some getting accustomed to, as you have just arrived from home."

A couple danced by. It was Tate's wife, laughing as her partner, Mr. Crosshaven, held her by the buttocks. Disgust washed over Tate's portly features, but was gone in an instant. He looked briefly at the sky, then once more to Elizabeth.

"Not a cloud in the sky now, but the monsoons are arriving shortly. Six months of unending rain, Miss Mainwarring. It can take more getting used to than the blistering heat. Your glass is empty, my dear," he said in a quick change of subject. "And so is mine. Let's go in search of refills—I believe the bar is just over there." He nodded, indicating a skirted table several yards distant from the main party and groaning under the weight of a vast supply of liquor bottles, cut crystal glasses, and silver mixing beakers.

"Elizabeth! There you are, dear. You *must* come at once." Emily Stanton threaded her arm through Elizabeth's. "Oh, were you busy?" Her eyes widened innocently. "I had no idea. Do excuse us, Canby. Elizabeth is most particularly needed."

Deputy Commissioner Tate glared at Emily for an instant, then nodded and headed for the bar himself. Emily guided Elizabeth to one of the picnic tables.

"For that rescue, my dear, you may lend me one of your fags. Beryl can be sly and a perfect witch at times, but Canby never fails to bore one to madness! Oh no, dear, not just now." Emily waved her hand in dismissal as Elizabeth opened her silk handbag. "We'll eat first, then enjoy one or two of your marvellous cigarettes. We have an astonishing assortment of food from which to choose. Marjorie does know how to throw a party. She's loath anyone forget her connection to—hmm, can't actually recall. Memories at my age are unpredictable, but someone important at any rate."

Tables were draped in thick white linen, the ends fluttering in the breeze. Platters of seafood, lamb and vegetable tandooris, and curries crowded the trays of egg salad and cucumber sandwiches. More tables bore selections of sliced pawpaw, mango, kiwi, and coconut. The desserts included every sort of cake imaginable, as well as pies and fancy biscuits.

Occasionally Elizabeth hesitated over the native food, and Emily answered questions and made suggestions. A particular favourite she discovered, were tandooris marinated in yogurt, cardamom, and garam masala, served with a ginger chutney.

Finished with their meal, they discovered a few of Emily's friends and joined a chat on politics. Discussing the alarming state of the depression and the trauma social and governmental unrest was causing not just in India, but the rest of the world, proved a little heavy on Elizabeth's stomach, especially after that last bite of pineapple upside-down cake.

"Really, what is one to think when the French president is assassinated by some deranged Russian emigré, and the very next week the Japanese military decides it's time for a new prime minister and murder the one they have out of hand!" the tall, stately silver-haired Thelma Sutton declared in indignation—as if it were a personal affront.

"You'd think attacking and appropriating Manchuria would have kept the Japanese quite busy enough," put in a spritely Ann Newsome. She sipped from a saucer glass, fancying herself naughty for drinking the all-but-taboo pink gin. It wasn't considered at all the thing for ladies. Men, however, drank it with impunity. But the smart ones didn't drink it for long. It exhibited the distressing tendency to rot one's insides. Perhaps she wouldn't drink quite all of it, as she was already feeling just the tiniest bit dizzy.

Lydia Belleville peered at her companions through thick gold wire-rimmed spectacles, a militant look in her eyes. "Yes, and consider the political crises in Austria and the government takeover in Germany, as well as this 'civil disobedience' and self-rule bosh here in India. Yet we ladies are supposed to remain in abysmal ignorance of all these complex and convoluted world affairs. If it amounts to another war, it is our husbands, sons, and brothers who die!"

"Hear, hear," Thelma agreed. "And we who must put everything back to rights after—Emily! You *aren't* going to smoke another of those filthy things, are you? They are positively nauseating!"

"Of course not, Thelma, if you really can't abide it. I do need to stretch my legs a bit after such a feast, and perhaps obtain a fresh gin and tonic. May I borrow your arm to lean on, Elizabeth?"

"Poor Anne. I do worry about her." They were out of earshot now, and Emily shook her head. "A few months ago it was opium, and now she is tippling a little too heavily on that ruinous pink gin. She's feeling her oats, I suppose. She married at a very young age and after almost thirty years was recently widowed. I believe she feels she must flaunt her newfound independence to believe it herself." She paused to light her Dunhill. Inhaling deeply, her eyes closed in enjoyment, she blew out a billow of smoke. "One of life's rarest pleasures anymore."

Elizabeth remembered similar words spoken that morning and decided it was just as well Nigel had apparently disappeared. At this point her will was as weak as water, and she thought herself very lucky if she managed somehow to arrive home without succumbing to his advances. Shaking herself out of that line of thought and focusing again on Emily's conversation, she observed, "Surely pink gin isn't as bad as opium?"

"Don't believe it for a second! It's far more insidious. One smokes one's opium and enjoys a pleasant dream or two. Ingest a glass too much of that pink gin and one simply does not wake up!" Frowning, Emily continued. "I certainly don't believe in that silly prohibition law for which the Americans are so famous—or infamous, I really don't know which—but *something* must be done about that deadly drink."

Thinking of her own mother's death, still so fresh in her memory, Elizabeth murmured, "The death of a loved one affects everyone so differently. Perhaps the lack of perimeters is just what she needs for a time."

Emily nodded. "As long as she doesn't reach too far. We'll keep a close eye on her. Two large gin and tonics, please." They had reached the bar and she spoke to the turbaned attendant.

Sipping from their tall cold glasses, they continued to stroll, arm in arm, through the throng of picnickers.

"Marjorie was extremely lucky to acquire enough help for this do. Today is an important Hindu festival. As long as I've lived in India I simply cannot keep all the Hindu deities straight in my mind. My wretched memory again." She sighed. "Now then, my dear, you must tell me how goes it with your father. I take it he hasn't managed your complete subjugation yet?" She smiled companionably.

Elizabeth stopped to study the lovely violet Karvi flowering prolifically at the edge of the grass. The spicy scent spiralled upward in heady tendrils. "We're not exactly at loggerheads, but . . ." *He's not exactly welcoming either,* she was going to finish. "He's quite civil actually," she began again with hesitation. "I almost feel he is merely tolerating my presence until I tire of my 'Indian adventure' and gad on to New Zealand."

"He *is* known for his taciturn nature," Emily sympathised. "He's several years out of practice as a family man, and I understand that was a role in which he did not thrive."

"My mother did explain the circumstances of their life together, but I thought he might deal better with an adult daughter for whom no responsibility was owed than a dependent child." Elizabeth sighed with resignation and moved on. "I have made it clear I hold no resentments or recriminations against him, that I recognise he and my mother did what they believed best."

"You must be satisfied with the diplomatic distance you share then. Otherwise you are destined for heartache, wishing for a closeness which will never materialise." Emily patted her arm. "But you mustn't let that stop you from standing up to him when you must." Answering Elizabeth's raised eyebrows, she continued. "Your father witnessed you dancing with Nigel, and when he learned Nigel escorted you this morning I truly thought his head in imminent danger of popping off in an explosion of fireworks to rival the more traditional show slated for tonight. He has managed, through one ruse or another, to keep your handsome beau busy for some time."

"He is not my beau!" Elizabeth said with some exasperation. And then, "Do you know everything that happens in Calcutta? Perhaps Nigel should include you in his murder enquiry team."

"As to that, my dear, I am unfortunately in total ignorance." The woman paused, studying her companion. Then, coming to a decision, she said in a neutral tone, "Nigel is a fine man, Elizabeth. You could do far worse. Of course, if you two did make a go of it, the tentative relationship you share with your father is destined to fulminate in a firestorm of bigotry."

"I am aware of my father's unfortunate opinion of Anglo-Indians and Indians themselves. It is amazing an otherwise intelligent man limits himself by allowing the ropes of intolerance to bind him so securely. We shall always differ in this, of course, but you needn't worry about any conflagrations."

Emily drew to a halt, studied Elizabeth for a moment and began walking again. "I'll tell you a story. About a young and handsome British officer and a beautiful young girl. They met on the Indian Riviere while he was on furlough. They fell in love on sight and were inseparable. Two nights before he left to return to his regiment, he bought every man in the officers' mess a drink to announce his intention of marrying. Instead of the uproarious congratulations he expected, silence greeted his declaration. It was assumed he knew, of course. That the girl was an Anglo-Indian. Humiliated and violently angry, he cut her off without a word."

Elizabeth's eyes widened. "How unspeakably cruel."

Emily looked her in the eyes. "The young man felt his lady had betrayed him, made him a laughingstock by leading him on and not informing him of her ancestry." She shrugged. "Oh, he could have married her, resigned from the Army, but he couldn't get past the humiliation of his innocence regarding her race." She paused. "He's never been the same since. And unfortunately he holds grudges. Your father still has the tendency to take himself far more seriously than he ought."

Elizabeth froze midstep, staring. "So that's it." Recovered, she again matched her friend's stride. "It explains so much. How do you *know* all this, Emily?"

"Although India is vast, my dear, the British population manages to keep tabs on each other. If you were to pop down to Bombay I would give you the names of my acquaintances for you to visit for your entrance into society. When you moved on, they would give you the names of their friends at your next destination. After a few years everybody knows everybody else." She sipped her drink, then said, "Don't let him come between you and Nigel if Nigel's truly who you want."

"There is nothing between Nigel and myself." Elizabeth regarded Emily sternly. "Fiona was quite forward in requesting his escort for both of us after my father confined Captain Langley—my previous escort—to his quarters. Then she skulked out this morning with Harry after all, my father in tow."

Emily laughed. "Smart girl. Much better Nigel than that Langley chap."

"Emily," Elizabeth began slowly. "Perhaps there are a few occurrences in Calcutta of which you are not aware. You make Nigel out to be a man of integrity. However, I don't believe such a man stoops to patronising prostitutes." A rosy blush tinted her features when the older woman stopped to stare at her. "It's true. Both Fiona and I witnessed him emerging from what I understand is a very high-priced bordello. We were eating lunch on the lanai of the House of Bengal, across the road."

"Well," Emily finally answered, resuming their walk. "I admit surprise, my dear. Men are typically allowed their peccadilloes, you know. Perhaps the stress of these grisly murder investigations upset his equilibrium. The Commissioner dumped the whole enquiry like rubbish into his lap and told him to solve it. Don't think *too* badly of him, my dear."

"Surely he is assisted by the local police, and Deputy Commissioner Tate must add considerable weight to the team."

"Nigel is head of security and third in the chain of this particular command. He reports to your father, then to the Commissioner. Canby is merely an advisor, as it is completely out of civil authority bounds now. That includes the police force. I understand he has formed an elite crew from his security corps, and they are leaving no stones unturned." Emily placed her empty glass on a standing tray scattered with picnic remains and buzzing bluebottles.

"I don't believe I have met the Commissioner. Is he on holiday?"

"One would think so. No, he is more than likely cowering behind his closed drawing room doors, savouring some quite excellent eighteen-year-old scotch. Sir Clive Harrington was never fond of confrontations, and God knows they would find him aplenty if he stepped outside the safety of his bungalow. He will conveniently wait until these awful killings are solved and then pose for photographers and consent to newspaper interviews, all while taking full credit. He will be everywhere making a nuisance of himself." Emily snorted in disgust.

Smiling, Elizabeth commented, "It's surprising the state of Bengal manages to run itself." She tipped her glass, swallowing the last of her gin and tonic, then nearly choked, startled by a sudden high-pitched shriek.

"WOG BASTARD!"

For an instant the silence was electric. Then, as if on cue, the people ahead parted, affording a clear view of Beryl Tate facing Nigel in, of all places, the centre of the picnic park.

Elizabeth could plainly see Beryl's wild eyes, her mottled features.

Her arm swung with ferocious intent, but Nigel caught her wrist in an uncompromising grip just inches from his face. His lip curled in disgust as he flung loose her hand. Deliberately, he turned his back and walked away.

Beryl stared in furious astonishment at his back. She opened her mouth to hurl more obscenities, but froze when she became aware of the silence and the fact that she was the cynosure of a rapt audience. Her hand flew to her throat in horror, and sobbing she ran in the direction of the car park.

Immediately a buzz of voices rose out of the void. A few of the guests exchanged bewildered looks or hid their shock by sudden hunger or thirst. Most pretended nothing out of the ordinary had taken place. Was it Elizabeth's imagination, or did a number of them glance in her direction, nodding, as if agreeing that, yes indeed, it was she who had arrived with the Major that morning.

"Well." Emily's nose twitched in distaste. "I believe Beryl has finally gone beyond the pale with that repulsive little exhibition. Perhaps Canby can persuade her to go on holiday for a while. Oh dear." Her eyes widened a fraction as she gazed past Elizabeth's shoulder. "It appears your father is having a word with Nigel. A rather cross word."

Elizabeth turned to witness Nigel striding toward the car park himself. Her father stood stiffly staring after him, looking as if he were ready to spit nails. She pressed her fingers to her suddenly throbbing temples and, sighing, asked Emily directions to the loo. An aspirin and a few minutes alone were just the thing.

The old concrete building at the edge of the wood was blessedly cool. Feeling somewhat rejuvenated after taking the aspirin tablet, Elizabeth stood in the doorway a moment. The park was hot and crowded, the soft wind from the river having dwindled to an occasional elusive whiff. Here in the shade of the trees it was quite pleasant, but taking up residence in the loo, no matter how comfortable, was out of the question.

The wood, in all its colourful splendour and cover from the pulsating wrath of the sun, drew her in. Skirting bamboo bushes and ducking under a low-hanging coral tree branch, she entered the hushed realm. She'd not wander far, aware of the dangers of snakes, although she doubted any tigers or panthers lived in so small a wood. No, just far and long enough for some much-desired solitude and coolness. Obviously, her father's temper would have to be dealt with tonight, especially if Nigel reappeared to drive her home. After such an exasperating day, making another pass at her was likely the last thing on his mind. Sighing, Elizabeth realised she might have to leave sooner than expected for New Zealand. It wasn't running away, she told herself. It was self-respect and common sense. Her father was not about to start the ordering of her life at this late stage.

Finding the perfect spot for quiet contemplation, she leaned thankfully against a teak tree with very little underbrush surrounding it. As if welcoming her, a black and yellow butterfly as large as her hand lit on her shoe for the briefest moment before flitting away to a nearby wild orchid. Above, blue sky was visible through a lacey network of branches and vines. Filigrees of golden sunlight trickled down, glinting off dancing particles of dust. Parakeets argued harshly with the more melodious Malabars, and high in the teak tree a woodpecker, ignoring them all, continued its rhythmic tapping. Dust and the smell of rotted vegetation tickled her nose, but a faint, sweet aroma from the flowering trees was still detectable. Already Elizabeth's headache was receding, and closing her eyes, resting her head on the tree, she relaxed and luxuriated in thinking of absolutely nothing for several minutes.

A distant monkey shrieking in alarm brought her instantly alert. A flock of screeching crows set the upper branches of the forest bouncing as they took sudden flight, covering the sky in a temporary black cloud. Hairs prickled on the back of Elizabeth's neck. The forest seemed dimmer now, and peering into the dark reaches of the trees, silent shadows darted, disappeared, re-formed. Foliage rustled stealthily as if someone, something, tried to conceal its movements.

Instinct told Elizabeth she was being watched, and not by an animal. It was past time to return to the party. It was just a few steps through a couple of bushes and around a tree or two. Why, the old loo building was almost visible through the overhang. Gathering her determination, she pushed away from the tree, and as she did so, she became aware of two simultaneous events.

One, a furious crashing of underbrush, as if a herd of cattle was barrelling in—and two, a peculiar wisp of motion just above her head.

The scream sputtered and died in her throat, strangled by her inability to breathe. The kukri missed her head—but it hacked its target in two.

Chapter Fourteen

Nigel stood before her, panting, the long curved blade of his weapon hanging at his side dripping blood. Half of a brown and tan geometric-patterned snake lay at her feet. The other half still wound around the branch just above her head.

"Bloody hell, woman!" He reached to wipe the kukri off in some thick foliage. "Will *this* not teach you to wander off by yourself?"

Shock and terror-driven adrenaline flowed through Elizabeth's system with nowhere to go. Lightheaded and shuddering uncontrollably, she stared dazed at the gory remains of the snake. Finally, she swallowed a great gulp of air.

Nigel swore and replaced his kukri in its battered sheath. Gathering her in his arms, he rubbed her back in a soothing rhythm. "Hush now, it's all over. It can't hurt you now."

Several minutes ticked by, and at last she looked up, hiccupping softly. "I suppose it was one of the deadliest snakes known to man, for which no antidote exists," she said in a small voice.

Nigel's mouth formed a lopsided smile, giving him a boyish look. It was accentuated by the black waves resting on his forehead, loose from his exertions. He no longer resembled the avenging warrior.

"That," he nodded, indicating both parts of the ruined reptile, "was a bamboo pit viper. And yes, they are quite deadly. There are also any number of other types of vipers, as well as pythons and cobra inhabiting this forest. An occasional hyena, wild boar, and monitor lizard break up the monotony. No crocodiles have been spotted recently, however," he added dryly. Regarding her with a stern glint in his eye, he moved his grip to her shoulders. "What in God's name were you thinking to come traipsing in here alone? It's bloody dangerous!"

"It was just a few feet," Elizabeth protested. "Besides, I fancied a bit of privacy. And a cool-off."

"Privacy?" His eyes narrowed, flicking to the shadowy corners of the forest, as if looking for a hidden lover. Suddenly his breathing was harsher and deeper.

"Yes, Major, privacy." She stepped back, craning her neck to look him straight in the eye. "I suffered the damnedest headache, and I wanted out of the sweltering sun and away from the crowd for some solitude. This seemed an ideal solution."

His eyes fell to half mast. So. There was no one else except for him. Galvanised by the untamed possessiveness rocketing through him, Nigel reached out, hauling her close with one hand, while the other tangled itself in her short waves and tilted her head backward. "Yes," he muttered roughly. "Privacy is long overdue."

The sudden, fierce wanting in Nigel's eyes paralysed Elizabeth like a doe caught in the spotlight and left her helplessly waiting for his lips to touch hers.

His kiss was hot, wet, molten. Slowly, her trembling hands crept up his sculpted, muscled chest to fasten around his neck, surrendering, no longer able or even wishing to resist. The rasp of his tongue as it laved and sucked on hers sent a surge of wanton excitement singing through her veins and fire raging along her nerve endings. It had never occurred to her such depth of passion existed. Heat from his hard body permeated hers as she strained closer, lost in his kiss and urgent caresses. He lifted her breasts, weighing them, thumbing her nipples to sharp little points of arousal through the thin material of her dress. His hands moved, insatiable, in a feverish path down her sides, hugging her hips. Cupping her bottom, holding her steady, he rubbed his turgid erection more firmly to the juncture of her thighs. She lost herself, whimpering and squirming in delight, revelling in erotic pleasure.

Something primal, primitive, rose like a wildfire in Nigel at Elizabeth's first eager response. He was starving for the feel of her, the taste of her. God, how he'd dreamed of this. At night he tossed anxiously, haunted by hot, sexual images of her long legs wrapped snugly around his waist, rocking him to orgasm. At dawn he would wake, dripping sweat, unfulfilled and irritable. But she was in his arms now and he kissed her ravenously, plundering her mouth, wanting more, more. Finally her wriggling snapped his tenuous grasp on control, and growling in exultation he bunched up her skirt and slipped hot questing hands into her tiny silk panties.

Elizabeth gasped in shock and broke the kiss as Nigel's fingers splayed over the quivering flesh of her bare buttocks, caressing and probing. He stared down at her, panting, desire rendering his face stark and vulnerable. She gazed back, dazed, aware they were both shaking with excitement. Of their own accord their lips fused again in a voracious frenzy. Her surprise instantly melted into joy as two fingers traced her cleft and, reaching beyond, tunnelled through delicate folds.

He whispered hotly in her ear, "Lift up, love."

Clutching his shoulders Elizabeth did so, as with his other hand he reached under her dress, slid down her flat stomach into the waistband of her panties, and combed through her moist curls. His middle finger extended teasingly over her sensitive nub, meeting two other fingers in a delicious dance of friction that left her in incoherent bliss. Thrilling to the carnal titillation, she spread her legs and allowed him greater access. Ah, it was too much, she thought breathlessly, her legs trembling so violently she was no longer able to stand on her own.

"Not yet, it isn't," he responded raggedly, continuing to tap and tease and rub.

Had she spoken aloud? But her mind went blank because the strange cataclysm building in her core finally burst with the savagery of a force-ten tropical storm, leaving her shuddering and crying out in rapture.

Nigel watched in satisfaction as Elizabeth arched taut as a bow in the culmination of her pleasure, astonished at the fierce tenderness surging through him. What was it about her? Never had a woman defied, infuriated, or driven his blood so hot with lust that all he wanted to do when he saw her was to throw her on the ground and bury himself in her, staking his claim and damning the consequences. Why her? He shook his head, refusing to dwell on riddles, and lowered his lips to swallow her soft cries.

Curiously, they seemed to go on and on and grew increasingly in volume.

Abruptly he realised they weren't coming from Elizabeth. He lifted his head, suddenly alert, listening intently as adrenaline now flowed in alarm instead of passion. Silence. The cries stopped, replaced a moment later by a smashing of undergrowth and an occasional shout.

Elizabeth was still recovering her breath when Nigel let go of her, setting her aside. Confused by a kaleidoscope of emotions and sensations, she restored her clothing to respectability with shaking hands before daring a glance at Nigel. But he was paying her no attention whatsoever. His penetrating gaze was directed behind her, and slowly she turned as the distant sounds reached her ears. She frowned. Some kind of commotion was brewing. She wanted to ignore it, to talk with Nigel. To ask him his intentions, to discover the kind of man he truly was. A man of integrity as Fiona and Emily maintained? Or a Lothario, enjoying respectable women and prostitutes alike? A man she was very much afraid she would fall in love with.

Nigel swore softly as the shouts came in earnest. Taking Elizabeth's hand in a firm grip, he said grimly, "Come on," and set off in the direction of the noise.

He stopped short after a half-dozen strides and, pivoting, cupped her chin in his large hand. "We'll talk later." His voice was warm, intimate. Then he was propelling her through the foliage, following a path only he could see.

Chapter Fifteen

Leaves and blossoms slapped Elizabeth's face and bamboo snagged her stockings and caught her frock, but mercifully there were no more snakes. In less than a minute she and Nigel ducked the last branch and entered a clearing of sorts.

Confusion greeted them. At least a dozen people, mostly men, formed a ring around something on the ground. Some were swearing, gesturing, and arguing with one another, while others gaped saucer-eyed, speechless.

One woman, silently worming her way through the disorder, apparently got more than she bargained for. Her eyes bulged and, letting out a piercing scream, she ran stumbling back to the Maidan. Her absence left a gap of visibility for another woman, who gasped hoarsely into her handkerchief, then crumpled into a heap. For the space of several heartbeats no notice was paid to either one.

Nigel loosed Elizabeth's hand and strode forward, shouldering his way into the centre of the mayhem. Elizabeth hesitated, a niggling feeling of apprehension crawling up her spine and holding her back. Then, almost without volition, the need to know drove her forward.

The blood immediately drained from her face. For a moment she forgot to breathe, and only the resultant lightheadedness induced a sharp intake of air. At once the coppery scent of blood and the acrid odour of urine left her gasping and her stomach rolling.

The gruesome scene took on a surrealistic quality. Her vision tunnelled and grew hazy around the edges, blocking out the people around her. Slowly shaking her head, Elizabeth damned her inquisitiveness, which was responsible for the indelible burning of the unspeakable sight in her memory. Her grandmother's warning echoed loudly in her mind: Curiosity killed the cat. Well, Elizabeth was certainly damaged, but she wasn't dead.

Beryl, on the other hand, was not quite so lucky. She was quite dead. And not from mere curiosity. No, the madman who had wrought this brutal deed was filled with a hate and violence so despicable it defied comprehension.

He'd used her unnaturally. The gory mess smeared on a thick stick tossed near the body attested clearly to the violence inflicted. He'd left her like refuse, her dress thrown about her waist and her legs gaping grotesquely. Bluebottles were already swarming the blood congealing on her thighs. One stocking sagged about a lifeless ankle, the other garroted her throat. Beryl's tongue, thick and black, protruded from blue lips, and blood from a head wound dripped sluggishly into eyes once lively and teasing, now dulled with death and staring sightlessly heavenward.

Suddenly Elizabeth was jostled, snapping her out of her macabre trance. She glanced up, realised she was shaking, and hugged herself. Where was Nigel? Heart racing in rising hysteria, she needed desperately to feel the embrace of his protective arms instead of her own useless ones. Her eyes darted frantically, searching for his familiar form.

But he was out of reach, crouching beside Beryl's head, grimly examining the blackening contusion, lifting the hair out of the way with a car key. She tried calling out to him, but only a croak emerged from her dry throat. Then Major Wight arrived, drowning her meagre effort with his attempt at crowd control.

"Clear off, the lot of you!" he ordered. "This is the scene of a crime. You there! Saunders!" He pushed aside gawking men and hysterical women. "Bloody hell, back off! Any evidence must be preserved!"

Of course, Elizabeth thought distractedly, as the onlookers reluctantly dispersed; they have work to do. Another murder and they must solve it, must find the monster responsible. To steady herself, she breathed deeply and pressed trembling fingers to her temple, grimacing when they came away damp with clammy perspiration. It appeared she was on her own. She wanted to leave. Instantly. She wanted to take refuge in her father's bungalow, to soak in a cool bath, to take several aspirin. And to forget this brutal, insane scene.

Whirling, she slammed into the wall of Captain Woodford's chest. He was not even aware of the contact however, as his normally jovial countenance stared in wide-eyed shock at Beryl's remains.

"What is the meaning of this circus?" Colonel Mainwarring demanded as he marched into the clearing, trailed by several sepoys. "Good God!" He stopped short. Gesturing to the few remaining stragglers with his swagger stick, he spoke curtly to the sepoys.

"Get those people out of here now!" Lip curling in revulsion, he approached the body, coming to a halt behind Nigel. "Hell and the devil, Beryl, what's happened to you?" Rubbing his free hand over his face, he sighed before asking quietly, "What do you make of it, Major?"

"Still quite warm, Colonel." Nigel's voice was matter-of-fact. "Less than an hour. Possibly less than half an hour. This wound"—he indicated the forehead—"occurred very shortly before death. You see it didn't bleed much. Probably a rock or something of the sort. Strangulation appears to be the cause of death. The post mortem will furnish the details. Dr. Stafford can sort that out tonight." He stood, but continued studying the body.

Half an hour? Elizabeth clutched her stomach as it lurched threateningly. Could Beryl have been murdered while she and Nigel . . . ? "No, no!"

Colonel Mainwarring noticed his daughter for the first time. "Elizabeth! Who let you through, for God's sake?" He closed his eyes and pinched the bridge of his nose in exasperation. What in flaming hell was she doing here? It was bad enough *he* was witness to this abomination, let alone an innocent young woman.

Opening his eyes, he noted the audience had departed, leaving four sepoy guards standing at the perimeter of the clearing facing outward. In his peripheral vision, he was aware of Major Wight running a hand through his hair and pacing with a nervous step. He looked to his daughter again, still leaning against Woodford, her face pale and her eyes haunted. What was he to do with her? He wasn't used to playing the father, wasn't sure he wanted to at this stage in his life. And history proved quite clearly he was utterly incapable of dealing with women with any sort of patience or understanding.

Sighing, he said quietly, "Elizabeth, girl, you must forget this, wipe it from your mind. Captain Woodford, escort my daughter home at once."

Nigel flushed, angry with himself. But there was no denying the fact that the longer he waited to collect evidence, the colder the trail. Still, he should be in Harry's place comforting Elizabeth, taking her home. He knew what she was thinking. It was running through his own mind. While he and

Elizabeth had been intent on celebrating life in its finest form, a ceremony of death had played out within a hundred yards. He felt sick himself.

"Yes, sir." Harry saluted and turned to usher Elizabeth out of the wood, but stopped abruptly as their exit was blocked by the portly body of Deputy Commissioner Tate barrelling along the newly made clearing from the Maidan.

The sepoys closed ranks, making an unyielding wall, but the Commissioner rushed them, beating their chests with both fists and loudly demanding entrance. At last managing a glimpse of what was left of his wife, he slid to his knees, dazed and silent. At a nod from the Colonel, a sepoy helped him to his feet, but before Tate could be escorted from the scene, he came back to life, shaking himself out of the soldier's hold and pointing at Nigel.

"You! It was you!" His voice rose in hysteria and his eyes shot maniacal sparks as he worked himself into a frenzy. "You have been after her for months! Dirty blacky-white lusting after a white woman. She wouldn't have you! Wouldn't contaminate herself with the likes of you. Couldn't stand it and took what you wanted anyway. Bastard. Filthy wog bastard!"

A pulse beat steadily in Nigel's temple and his face flushed, but he looked at Tate with a hard glint. He'd be damned if he'd give the insulting allegations the dignity of a reply.

"For God's sake, man! Control yourself!" Colonel Mainwarring's voice cut like a knife. "Remove him," he ordered the soldiers.

"He followed Beryl to the car park! I saw him! It was after she called him a 'wog bastard,'" Tate insisted. "He didn't return to the picnic, did he? He's been missing all this time. Ask him where he's been!" Two sepoys seized an arm apiece, preparing to drag him away, but Tate dug his heels into the dirt of the forest floor. "Go on! Ask him!"

Something in the Deputy Commissioner's voice made the

Colonel pause. He held up a hand, halting the soldiers. Facing Nigel he asked, "Just to clear the slate, Major, did you follow Mrs. Tate to the car park? Where *have* you been all this time. I don't believe I've seen you in a good while."

Nigel's nostrils flared in anger, but otherwise he managed to keep his expression bland.

"Yes, Colonel, I *did* visit the car park. But I did not follow Mrs. Tate. You will recall, immediately after Mrs. Tate so freely expressed her opinion of myself, you requested, rather strongly, I make my presence scarce." He saw Elizabeth start in surprise, but did not pause. "I merely took the opportunity to call out on the communications wireless to check what answers might be available to one or two of my enquiries regarding the recent murders."

Colonel Mainwarring lifted his eyebrows. "Surely it did not take the better part of an hour, Covington-Singh?"

Canby Tate snorted in disbelief. He was calmer now that he was apparently being taken seriously. "Rubbish! You stalked my wife and bloody well killed her!"

"Shut up, Canby, I'm asking the questions. Well, Major? What took so much time?"

Elizabeth stepped forward. "He was with me." As if in warning, a crow overhead cawed, shattering the stunned silence. "He saved me from a snake. A pit viper. He killed it with his kukri. Then w-we took a walk." She faltered a moment under her father's piercing gaze, but gathering her courage and attempting a faint smile, continued gamely. "So you see, he couldn't possibly have killed Mrs. Tate."

"Liar!" The Deputy Commissioner rounded on her. His face was turning maroon as he struggled to free himself from the native soldiers. "You're protecting him. You're lying!"

Nigel snarled and leaped toward Tate, sending his fist in a vicious uppercut to the man's jaw.

Major Wight caught his arm in another back swing. "Not

now, man," he advised urgently. It was a moment before Nigel relented, his eyes still blazing, but he lowered his fist and stepped back.

Tate spat blood, swore at the sight of it and resumed his struggles with new vigour.

Colonel Mainwarring thrust himself between them so that he was nose to nose with Tate. "By God, sir, you will not so insult a daughter of mine, regardless of the strain you are labouring under! Remove him at once!" he ordered the guards, then approached Elizabeth, his face set in anger.

"As for you, young woman, I shall pretend I didn't hear that. And so will both of you." He levelled warning glares at Harry and Major Wight. Pivoting back to Nigel, his tone clipped, he said, "I'll give you one more chance, Covington-Singh. You were not with my daughter, so where were you?"

Nigel's face closed. Red edged his vision, but he managed after a moment to speak without emotion. "It doesn't seem to matter where I was, Colonel. Sir. For your record, however, I did not commit this atrocity. You have my word as an officer." He added dryly, "For what that may be worth to you."

"I told you, Father! He was with me. And I will stand in a court of law and say so." The steely determination in Elizabeth's voice was unmistakable.

Slowly, Colonel Mainwarring studied his daughter, taking in her dishevelment: missing hat, mussed hair, and swollen lips. He'd failed to properly command first his wife, and now his daughter? What kind of a man submitted to such female insubordination?

And now Elizabeth humiliated him by openly consorting with an Anglo-Indian. If the gossips got wind of it, his career was dead in the water. Twice already he'd been passed over for promotion. It didn't matter to him that Covington-Singh was the son of a maharaja. An Indian was an Indian. Inferior. His skin crawled, imagining this eight-anna's filthy brown hands degrading his daughter's body. If she was anything like her mother—like most women—she'd turn her back, blithely doing as she pleased, not giving a damn that it made him look like a fool. Not this time, he vowed, and just for an instant he wobbled on the brink of a precipice, panicked by his sudden unthinkable lack of control over both his daughter and this bloody cock-up of a situation. Control regimented his life, defined him. Without it he was nothing. He teetered dizzily for that instant before regaining himself.

And as he did, inspiration struck like lightning. A very convenient solution, indeed. It really was quite remarkable in solving a multitude of problems. He'd try one last time with Elizabeth, however. His gaze, laden with contempt, raked her appearance.

"You will be shamed if you make such a mistake. For God's sake, have you no self-respect? No pride? He's a bloody Indian. You will be as ruined as the Compton chit. Worse, as you appear to *enjoy* attentions from a darkie." He turned back to Nigel, his lips pressed in growing fury. "And you, sir, shall steer clear of my daughter. If I ever catch you sniffing around her again, not even your"—he paused to snort in scorn—"royal relations will save you from my wrath. Do I make myself clear?"

The red receded at the Colonel's insulting words. Instead, a cold, deadly calm settled over Nigel as he drew himself to his full height, topping his commanding officer by a generous two inches. He looked down his nose a moment before replying with cool disdain.

"Your daughter, Colonel, is of age and may do as she sees fit. If we choose to enjoy each other's company it is nobody's business but ours. And don't make the mistake of overestimating your own importance. The ambitions of my relations run higher than do mine. I choose to hold a tight rein on my family. Their network, particularly the subversive, should not be taken lightly."

Colonel Mainwarring took a step forward, his face working in disbelief. Finally he ground out, "You dare threaten me?"

"Not at all, Colonel," Nigel replied equably. "I'm merely telling you to mind your own business."

"Apparently, my business is teaching you a richly deserved lesson." Colonel Mainwarring tapped his swagger stick against his leg as he paced, circling Beryl's body, a smug smile hovering about his lips. "You have no alibi for the time at which this murder took place. You were seen following Mrs. Tate after she publicly spurned your attentions. I put it to you that you assaulted her and dragged her to this secluded spot. You proceeded to defile her body, and then with vicious deliberation, murdered her." He nodded in malicious satisfaction and spoke to the remaining two sepoys. "Take Major Covington-Singh to a holding cell. At once!"

"You are arresting me for Mrs. Tate's murder?" Nigel was incredulous.

The sepoys stood on either side of Nigel now, ready to conduct him from the forest.

"No, Major, you are not formally under arrest. You are to be held and questioned until I am satisfied with your answers. The evidence will be studied meticulously. We shall see what may come to light with a more appropriate individual in charge of these investigations." Mainwarring's voice was thick with insinuation. "Major Wight, see that this scoundrel is locked up."

"Colonel Mainwarring." Major Wight ceased his nervous pacing and regarded his commanding officer in dismay. "Have you considered the consequences of arresting a son of the Maharaja of Kashmir? Excuse me, sir, but Covington-

Singh may be quite correct in surmising his family could cause you a deal of trouble. Indians are very good at repercussions."

"The Maharaja rules Kashmir by the grace of His Majesty's government." The Colonel's voice dripped contempt. "He will not be allowed to interfere."

"You realise, sir," Wight stressed, "Covington-Singh will likely not stand trial. At the very least this whole fiasco will be hushed up."

"Perhaps," agreed the Colonel, giving Nigel a dismissive glance. "But he'll be cashiered and sent back to Kashmir in disgrace."

Elizabeth watched in disbelief as Nigel marched smartly past her between his guards. "No, Father, you can't do this. I have already told you—"

"I have heard nothing from you, Elizabeth, nor do I intend to. I believe I ordered you, Captain Woodford, to escort my daughter home. Do it now."

The thick, hot air embraced Elizabeth like an unwelcome blanket as she stepped from the coolness of the wood. Shielding her eyes from the late afternoon glare, she was not immediately aware of Fiona until her friend spoke.

"There you are! Thought you'd gone for a Burton! I wish you hadn't told me to stay here, kicking my heels, Harry. It's been most unpleasant not knowing what is going on. This . . . this bully"—she indicated the sepoy sentry standing at attention, "refused me entrance. The talk is wild." She laughed briefly. "Why, according to one of the stories, Beryl Tate is dead, unspeakably mangled by some feral animal. In this small stand of trees? How ridiculous. No one would throw a party when there are dangerous animals wandering about. Now tell me . . . oh dear." Slowly she covered her mouth with a trembling hand. Harry wasn't meeting her eyes and Elizabeth was a mess. Her clothing was somewhat disordered, but one might expect that from brushing by snagging trees. It was her face, pale and drawn, and her eyes: empty, haunted, unseeing. So caught up in her curiosity, Fiona had neglected to notice her friend's distress.

She gathered Elizabeth in her arms and said to Harry in a low voice, "Perhaps you better tell me just exactly what occurred while we make our way to the car."

Elizabeth gently pushed Fiona away. "I'm quite all right. Really, I am." Her smile was crooked. "You might offer me a cigarette, however. I seem to have misplaced my handbag."

Once it was lit, Elizabeth drew deeply on the cigarette, turning the end of it into a glowing orange ball. Striding out into the sunlight she felt the heat beat down on her bowed head. She looked up after a moment with shadowed eyes.

"Believe me, old girl, it is far more unpleasant in there." She nodded, indicating the wood. "Come, let's walk a bit. My father is probably on his way out, and I'm afraid I'm all out of patience with him." She stopped by the loo. "It's true. Beryl is dead. But not by an animal." Throwing her cigarette down, she crushed it viciously beneath her heel. "No, let's not give innocent animals a bad name. That brutal mauling was committed by a monster." Her face twisted. "And the man who fathered me insists Nigel did it!"

Fiona gasped. "This is outrageous! I refuse to believe it. Nigel is a fine man. My intuition said so from the very beginning, and it's seldom wrong. Come," she said decisively and took Elizabeth's arm. "Let's get you home. Harry may fill me in on the way."

"If you don't mind, I'll just pop in here to splash a little cold water on my face first." Elizabeth headed into the loo. "Why don't you light another fag for me while you wait, Harry. In fact, why don't you just give me the entire box?"

"Honestly, Elizabeth, you'll make yourself sick—" Both girls stopped short.

Lydia Belleville sat on the stoop of the old stone building, sobbing softly and dabbing her eyes with the hem of her dress.

"Oh, my dears." She sniffed and regarded them forlornly through the fog of her wire-framed glasses. "It's Anne. Anne Newsome. She—she's inside, in the last cubicle. So much blood. I-I think she's dead!"

Chapter Sixteen

Elizabeth's bedroom door opened and the corner of a tea tray emerged, pushing it back. She was reclining on the bed in a rose-coloured silk nightgown, still damp from her bath.

"Tea and sympathy, Fiona? Thank you. It's very welcome, indeed."

"Rot." Fiona set the laden tray on a low table. She poured a good dose of amber liquid from a green bottle into the teapot, along with a bit of hot water from another pot. "Remy Martin and sweet oblivion." She twisted a lemon rind over the concoction, poured it out and handed the delicate bone china cup and saucer to her friend.

Elizabeth wrinkled her nose as the cognac fumes drifted upward, almost choking her. "Gad, Fi, I doubt I can bring this close enough to actually drink it."

Fiona leaned back in a cushioned wicker chair, sipped from her cup and sighed blissfully. "Don't be silly, darling, take the plunge, as they say. It'll do wonders after today's ordeal." So saying, she took her own advice, liberally, and coming up for air, added, "Good Lord, first a deadly snake—who would have thought such dangerous creatures inhabited that small stand of trees—and in a public park. But we are learning things are not as they might seem in India, aren't we? And secondly, all but witnessing a violent murder." She availed herself of another deep swallow. "Thirdly—why is it these things happen in threes? Two are more than sufficient. Poor Mrs. Newsome."

Elizabeth absently stirred her toddy. "At least she's alive. Unlike Beryl." At last she ventured a sip and immediately coughed. "Good God, Fiona! It might as well be fire! Did you add any water to this brew?" She tried again, and when it didn't cause any adverse effects, she finished the cup and served herself another.

Feeling a warm glow expand in her veins and a pleasant fuzziness blur the hard emotional edges, she pushed aside the mosquito netting and leaned back on her pillows once more.

Fiona frowned and said quietly, "How long will she live, though? She was beaten nearly to death. Her attacker meant her to die, that much is certain. She might have, too, if Harry weren't versed in artificial respiration and we in basic first aid. We ought to send your solicitor a thank-you letter for insisting we take a course in it before leaving for the tropics." She removed the top to the teapot, added a few more drops of hot water and a couple of good slugs of cognac. Shrugging, she repeated the dosage of liquor and refilled both cups.

"According to Dr. Stafford, some coma patients never regain consciousness. Even if she does, there may be enough brain damage to ensure her life is never the same. She might not be able to walk, see, or even talk."

"Father won't say so, but of course it has to be the same monster who killed Beryl. Two violent attacks, one ending in murder, so close and at virtually the same time. Did you see the look on his face? He actually thought he could pin Beryl's murder on Nigel—and now here's another victim popping up! It won't wash and even he's beginning to realise he has painted himself into a very tight corner. Really! Nigel didn't have time for one murder, let alone take a crack at another." Cocking her head to one side, she wondered aloud, "Why does Father think he can browbeat me?"

It was a moment before Fiona answered. "Your mother left because she tired of the way of life he imposed on her. Perhaps he is letting you know that you are welcome only if you live by his rules. Then again"—she reached for the carved mahogany box on Elizabeth's nightstand and extracted a cigarette—"maybe it never occurred otherwise. After all, who doesn't follow his orders?" Her eyes remained on Elizabeth as she lit up and, exhaling casually, commented, "It seems you have experienced an about-face regarding Nigel. Kiss you silly again, did he? Is that why you know he hadn't time for a couple of murders?"

Blushing a becoming rose, Elizabeth deliberately enjoyed a long sip of the fiery cognac. Setting the cup and saucer on the bedside table, she shrugged. "I know because he was busy rescuing me from a pit viper. I underwent the most frightful attack of hysterics. It took some time for me to recover from them. It was all quite terrifying, I assure you."

Fi smiled. "I'm sure he took proper care of you, dear."

Remembering how well indeed Nigel had comforted her with the heat of his body, the exploration of his tongue, the urgency of his hands, Elizabeth felt her face flood again. "Er . . . well, yes." She cleared her throat. "As you see, I'm quite well now."

"Yes," Fiona agreed, her eyes wide with false innocence. "Quite healthy, indeed."

"Oh, do stop it, Fi. Nothing—well, almost nothing happened. The point is, Nigel is innocent. I sincerely hope Father sees sense, releases Nigel and lets him go back to work to find out who *is* responsible.

"You know . . ." She leaned forward in excitement as a new idea dawned. "Mrs. Newsome must have seen something. Or the killer thought she did. Father informed me the previous victims were raped and strangled. Mrs. Newsome was beaten, but she did not appear to have been sexually assaulted. Unlike Beryl and Diana, her underthings were intact and there was no bruising or scratches in the, er, nether regions." She tapped a finger thoughtfully on her bottom lip. "Yes, yes," she murmured, warming to the notion. "Emily told me she was beginning to worry because Anne had been making a habit of drinking that awful pink gin recently and was indulging in it again this afternoon." She stood and began to pace the length of the room. "What if, while Anne was toddling in or out of the loo, she saw or heard something in the woods? Did she investigate? Did she call out? Or might she merely have been standing there in a haze of pink gin, unaware of the circumstances when the killer saw *her?*"

The outer door of the bungalow slammed. The Colonel's angry voice echoed through the halls as he swore at a servant unfortunate enough to have been present. Another crash shook the house as the study door slammed shut. There were a few more muffled bangs and thuds before silence fell.

"I say, old girl, it doesn't sound as if your father enjoyed the best of luck with Nigel. Just as well we'll not be seeing him before breakfast." Fiona squinted at the Remy bottle and said hopefully, "If we consume enough of this, we shan't have to see him even then. In fact, we'll be lucky if we can limp to luncheon."

Elizabeth wasn't listening. She came to an abrupt stop in her pacing and snapped her fingers. "That's it, Fiona, I'm sure it is. If only Anne regains consciousness, we'll know who the murderer is!"

Emptying the cognac bottle, Fiona commented, "It stands to reason. *If* she comes to. *If* she saw anything. Two very big ifs, dear."

"I must tell Nigel. Since Father is in such a foul mood, he must have been forced to let him go. He should be back to his quarters by now. Let's go."

"What!" Fiona blurted, alarmed. Her brimming cup was halfway to her lips. "It's late! I'm sure someone has already thought of this and everything is being taken care of. Besides, we have no idea where he lives, and there will be hell to pay if we take your father's motor. Sit down, dear, and let me pour you another cup of this delicious toddy. Believe me, you will feel like nothing but sleeping afterward. I guarantee it."

"No, Fi, it must be now. It was such a palava this afternoon, everything happening at once. With Nigel under arrest we can't be sure if anyone has seen to it. What if Anne regains consciousness sometime in the night? She must have a guard at her bedside! What if even now it's too late?" She was already pulling on a pair of wide-legged trousers and sliding her feet into the first pair of shoes within reach. "Hurry! We shan't take Father's Stutz. The keys to the household car are on the wall by the kitchen door."

Fiona sighed and looked longingly at her fresh drink. Reluctantly, she set it down and stood. Eyeing Elizabeth's attire doubtfully, she thought herself fortunate in never having undressed. She was never as fashion-conscious as Elizabeth, it was true, but even she drew the line at appearing in public wearing a crimson silk blouse paired with turquoise sequined high-heeled sandals and a mint green canvas handbag. Thank goodness for the black trousers, at least.

Elizabeth nabbed a lavender hat and flew through the doorway. "Come *on*, Fiona!"

They drew to a halt in front of a small bungalow at the end of a well-kept street of bachelor officers' residences. Their directions were furnished by a houseboy disinclined to part with the information.

"Young English ladies do not visit the bachelors' quarters. No, especially at night." He had shaken his head and admonished them. "Not good for miss sahibs' reputations, no."

The girls supposed this was because they might see the neat little dwellings behind the bungalows where some officers kept native mistresses. Quite inconvenient for the officers if visited by their respectable British lady friends or fianceés. It was understood that British women did not visit this part of the cantonment.

Elizabeth slid her moist palms off the steering wheel and cut the ignition. The lights shone brightly at the edges of the tightly drawn curtains of Nigel's bungalow. Now she was here, she was suddenly nervous. She hoped fervently he did not keep a mistress. If he did, she would just have to deal with the heartache and embarrassment it caused in the few minutes it took to relay the critical information he needed. But she would do so alone. She didn't think she could stand Fiona's pity.

Fiona glanced at her. "Shall we?"

"No, Fi. I'll attend to this myself. I shouldn't have dragged you here. You go back. I shall ask Nigel to drive me home."

"Here now, what's this? I'm not leaving you alone," her friend said firmly and reached for the door handle.

Touching Fi's shoulder, Elizabeth stopped her, pleading, "No, Fiona. I'm adamant. Besides, now I'm here, it occurs to me I should also talk to Nigel about another matter. Privately."

Studying Elizabeth's face a moment, Fiona relented, nodding. "I understand." She slid across the seat as Elizabeth exited the car. "Mind, though," she said sternly, "I'm sitting by the blower until you give me a bell. Don't be too late. I don't fancy mucking about your father's foyer all night!"

When the taillights disappeared, Elizabeth took a deep breath of the still muggy air, and spinning on her heel, approached the door.

Her knock was answered by a solemn native in a khaki dhoti and tunic. He surveyed Elizabeth from head to foot, raising his eyebrows. "Memsahib?"

Before she could answer, Nigel called from another room, "Who is it, Ravi? For God's sake get rid of him."

Ravi was already sliding the door closed. "Another time, perhaps. It is inconvenient for the Major-Sahib to entertain at this time. Goodnight, Memsahib."

"No!" Elizabeth wedged her foot between the door and the jamb. "Nigel! I must speak with you immediately! It's extremely urgent."

Unwilling to hurt her, Ravi opened the door and she stepped inside.

A moment later Nigel strode in, drying his jaw with a small towel. He was shirtless and drops of water beaded, glistening in his black chest hair. He wasn't furry like a bear, but there was certainly enough hair to run one's fingers through, yet still appreciate the well-sculpted muscle underneath. Elizabeth felt her pulse accelerate.

Nigel frowned and put the towel around his neck. Reaching for her hand, he drew her forward, settling her in a chair in his small dining room. Studying her, he offered her a wry smile.

"It must be important. I have never witnessed Miss Mainwarring looking anything but perfectly coordinated. Now tell me what brings you to my bungalow so late and alone." He plucked the lavender floppy from her head and placed it on the dining table.

Elizabeth glanced briefly down at herself and started in surprise. "Good Lord! Not very clever of me, but my mind wasn't attending."

"Obviously. Now tell me your news."

Nigel listened intently for several minutes, then stood and left the room. He returned seconds later wearing a uniform shirt, which he was busy buttoning. "Are you sure Mrs. Newsome was not sexually molested?"

"Reasonably. I'd not have noticed the difference if not . . ." Elizabeth cleared her throat and began again. "Had I not attended Diana or witnessed Beryl Tate's body. After determining Mrs. Newsome was alive, Harry carried her outside and began artificial respiration. Fiona and I are trained in first aid. We examined her carefully to ascertain what else needed tending. We cleaned wounds and stopped the bleeding by the time the orderlies arrived. Of course I'm no expert, but I would be willing to wager a large part of my fortune she was intact in that area."

Finished with his fastenings, Nigel turned his back to tuck his shirt into his trousers, his movements swift and decisive. Facing her once more, he asked softly, "Now why, do you think, did no one else pick up on this?"

"I suppose nobody paid close attention. The shock of Beryl being found dead in the middle of a party, *you* of all people arrested, another victim found barely alive, and my father insisting you were guilty of that as well. Details were missed. Wait, I'm coming with you!" He had picked up his motorcar keys and was heading to the door.

He retraced his steps to cup her face tenderly with his large hands. "No you are not. If you are correct in this, the killer may at this moment be at the hospital. I'll have enough on my mind without worrying about your safety, too. If you want to help, call the hospital, tell them—on my orders—no one but her nurse or doctor is allowed access to Mrs. Newsome. Also, telephone Captain Woodford and tell him to meet me there with a dozen men." He kissed her briefly before turning to the door again. "If you need anything, call Ravi. He's out back."

Well, that answered one question. Surely a manservant didn't share an abode with his officer's mistress.

Elizabeth quickly made the necessary calls, and with the wheels finally in motion she felt exhaustion seep into her system. Falling back into her chair, she eyed her lavender floppy in distaste. And then, in dawning horror, she glanced down at her feet. Shuddering, she removed her prized turquoise Mainbochers and set them carefully under the dining table out of sight. They were stunning with the proper gown, but made frightening companions to trousers and a siren-red blouse.

As tired as she was, she couldn't sit still after all. Nigel's bungalow was small with only a sitting room, dining area, bedroom, and tiny kitchen. It was decorated simply but richly. Lush Kashmiri carpets covered the dark wood floors; the mahogany tables and chairs were carved in great detail and the two chesterfields were upholstered in soft, buttery leather. Porcelain planters shaped and painted like tigers, panthers, and lions, filled with hibiscus and jasmine, decorated table tops and window sills. A pair of blue and gold ceramic elephants guarded the entrance to the sitting room where several glass-fronted bookcases lined the walls. Several framed photos and a bronze statuette of a shapely woman with a multitude of arms rested on the mantelpiece above an empty fireplace shielded by a copper fan. Did one actually require a fireplace in India? Just thinking of the extra heat sent her searching for a switch for the idle punka overhead. She found the lever above a large floor model wireless in the corner.

Basking in the soft breeze provided by the mechanical fan, she pulled up a leather ottoman and went to work fiddling with the dials on the wireless. Tuning through a belligerent German voice, a spate of Hindi, and an English melodrama, she settled delightedly on a station broadcasting the Hit Parade from New York. Singing along with

"Grenada," "You're an Old Smoothy" and other favourites, time passed swiftly for her. But when the last hit was spun and Nigel had yet to return, she checked her gold Longines. It was near eleven. She should ring Fiona and tell her to go to bed.

After hanging up, she raided Nigel's drinks table, examining his collection until she came upon a nearly full bottle of eighteen-year-old Glenfiddich. She poured two fingers and briefly passed the generous portion of pale golden liquor under her nose, enjoying the smoky peat aroma before savouring a sip.

"Much longer, old boy," she murmured, "and you'll discover a sizable dent in your best scotch."

Sinking into the cushions of the chesterfield, Elizabeth's thoughts wandered back to Fiona. True to her word, she'd camped by the telephone, braving a chance encounter with the "wounded lion" as she referred to Elizabeth's father. So far he had not ventured forth from his den, much to Fiona's relief, and thus it didn't take much convincing to send her off to her much-needed slumber. In fact, Elizabeth thought, as she swallowed the last of her Glenfiddich, catching some kip wasn't a bad idea. Stretching out comfortably, she closed her eyes.

Nigel closed the door to his bungalow, removed his uniform cap and wearily pushed his hands through his thick, wavy hair. He was dead tired. Hearing soft voices issuing from the wireless, he stepped past the elephants into the sitting room to see Elizabeth sleeping and an empty glass on the low table adjacent to the leather lounger she occupied. As fagged as he was, he felt thrumming excitement course through him at the sight of her waiting for him. In his bungalow. Late in the night.

Slowly he approached her, bent to run his fingers through her bright hair, marvelling at the trust and closeness she must feel to have come to *him* with what was, indeed, vital information. He frowned and drew back, thinking about her father and recalling the events earlier in the evening. The situation at the Maidan rolled from snowball to fast and furious avalanche within minutes of reaching garrison headquarters. He wasn't at all sure how she would take the outcome.

Elizabeth's eyes flew open and they stared at each other for several moments. He was so close she felt his body heat, smelled the spicy patchouli of his aftershave, and, catching her breath, suddenly saw, again, in her mind's eye the intimacy they had shared that afternoon.

Nigel straightened, breaking the brief spell and briskly picking up her glass, enquiring if he might pour her another.

Shaking off the erotic memories and her drowsiness, Elizabeth sat up, stretched and smoothed her hair.

"Perhaps a drop of tea would be best. I'm afraid I've committed the unpardonable sin of mixing '82 cognac and '14 scotch. Oh, not in the same glass, of course," she said in answer to his raised eyebrows. "Fiona medicated us with the better portion of a bottle of Remy earlier. I have a feeling I shall have a head in the morning." She swallowed and continued, "Mrs. Newsome? Is she—"

"Alive, though still in a coma. No new injuries." He fished ice out of a small bucket, dropped it into the drinks he poured and handed one to her. "As it *is* morning, you might just as well enjoy yourself." Sitting down opposite her he added, "Besides, you may be glad of it in a minute or two. Later, if you like"—he managed a crooked smile—"I'll rustle you up a delightfully bold '31 Darjeeling."

Elizabeth sighed, relaxing. "Indeed, what a relief. I didn't realise how tense I was." She frowned in suspicion. "Then, why will I be needing this drink?"

Leaning back, Nigel stretched his legs, crossing them at the ankles. He ignored her question, instead informing her how, after ascertaining Mrs. Newsome's condition, he and his men searched every nook and cranny of the hospital and found nothing unusual. The doctor had confirmed his patient showed no signs of sexual molestation, so they were proceeding on the assumption that Elizabeth was, indeed, correct in her analysis of the situation. Nigel had instituted a twenty-four-hour guard—two at Mrs. Newsome's door and two at the hospital entrance.

He swallowed the last of his scotch and finished with, "Anyone showing undue curiosity in Mrs. Newsome will immediately become a person of intense interest."

"Did the doctor say when we might expect her to regain consciousness?"

"No. Unfortunately, comas present a baffling question mark to the medical profession. They know next to nothing. A theory exists that a coma is the body's way of shutting down to concentrate fully on the healing of a traumatic injury." He shrugged. "Some patients never come to. Some are out for years. And some remember nothing of the time preceding their head wound."

"So, unless someone comes sniffing round, we may never know."

"We *will* know, because I intend to find the bloody swine," Nigel said in a no-nonsense tone as he rose to help himself at the drinks trolley again. This time he didn't bother with the ice. "I do have some leads and am expecting more in the next week or two. Delving through years of records and bins of old newspapers unfortunately takes time." He moved to the fireplace and rested his elbow on the mantel.

"Good heavens, why on earth are you going through rubbish bins?" Elizabeth asked incredulously.

Nigel gave a tight smile. "Definitely not 'rubbish bins,' love. History. This has happened before."

Chapter Seventeen

Elizabeth's hand froze, hovering above the carved wooden box of cigarettes she had been about to select from. "Nigel, what are you talking about?"

"Not déjà vu, I'm afraid." He bent to light her cigarette once she pushed it snugly into its holder. "The other day in the Mohd Bagh Club I overheard one of the civils mention something I thought curious. About the murders of native women seeming to lead to murders of British women. Similar unsolved murders occurred on the island of Barbados back in '14. Two or three natives were killed, followed by two English women. Then the Great War broke out." He sighed and lit a fag himself. "And yesterday, just before I took care of your snake, I'd been out to the wireless receiving some riveting information." He paused, inhaling fully and carefully tapping the ash in a receptacle on the mantel.

"*Nigel*," implored Elizabeth. And then, "I shan't blow the gaff."

He only quirked one eyebrow.

"Right then, I shan't even tell Fiona—not that she has a wagging tongue either. Now *tell* me."

Satisfied, Nigel continued. "It's for your own safety, especially as you have sussed the attempt on Mrs. Newsome's life may not have been planned." He was silent a moment as if gathering his thoughts. A new jazzy tune suddenly blared from the wireless, jarring them both.

"Apparently, the murders are not just similar, but *exactly* like those committed in several locations worldwide."

"My God, Nigel!" Elizabeth's eyes were wide and frightened. Her cigarette forgotten, she reached for the iced scotch she'd ignored until now. After drinking deeply, she commented in awed tones, "This certainly collapses the popular 'native did it' theory. Not that an Indian wouldn't possess the means to travel, of course, but he would be an oddity outside India or England and so commented upon. Even questioned, should any irregularities arise. This means . . . Good God!" Her hand flew to her throat. "It means we might *know* this fiend. Might actually"—she swallowed—"have danced with him, or, or . . . suddenly I feel quite sick," she finished, as her hand shot down to her stomach.

"You see now why you must not even inform Fiona? If you both abruptly shut yourselves away or act strangely, it might tip the killer. I'm counting on you, Elizabeth, not to start peering suspiciously at every Tom, Dick, or Hal. Be your carefree, confident self."

Elizabeth resolutely moved her hand from her stomach to grip the arm of the lounger. It was smooth and warm. She brushed her fingers to and fro on it to concentrate on something other than the parade of images marching through her mind of the male acquaintances made in the last several days.

She forced a weak smile, and folding, or rather clutching, her hands in her lap, said in a determined voice, "Of course. Stiff upper lip and all that rot. Well, then." Someone with whom she had laughed or socialised with was a conscience-less, sodding fiend. And she must smile and go on as if she suspected nothing, nothing at all. "Since you have told me this much, you must see to the rest."

Nigel noted that there was, after all, some of her father in her. He was thankful it was an admirable trait. "Singapore, 1922. Kenya, 1927. This is where mucking about through ancient newspapers and records comes in. All I have to do is find who is currently in Calcutta who was also present in those locales at the times in question. Simple, but it takes time. Time in which more atrocities will occur."

"Was anyone ever apprehended? Were the murders ever connected?"

"As a matter of fact, yes." He closed his eyes for a moment, grimacing as he rubbed his aching neck. "Some poor sod in Singapore was summarily shot. A Eurasian. It didn't seem to matter he possessed an alibi, *and* two more women were killed afterward.

"In answer to your second question: no, not that I am aware of. No reason to, really. As I mentioned, I only veered in that direction after hearing that comment in the club, and proceeded with some preliminaries." He shook his head, puzzled. "The native murders in these countries are usually turned over to the locals to sort out. Accountings are not always kept. Take the killings in the Bustees, for example—sorry, you won't be aware of them as you are so new—"

"To the contrary. Father told me of them."

Nigel nodded. "Consequently, we are in the dark as to the pattern of native murders preceding those of the British women. What *is* clear, is that there is no pattern afterward." He ticked off his fingers. "Two British women in Barbados in as many years. Three in Singapore—unofficially, of course, as the last two took place after the execution—in five years. Two in Kenya in two years."

"He's out of control! Merciful God, the bugger is escalating—two murders, an attempt, and a rape inside a fortnight!"

"Let's not forget the Bustees."

Elizabeth stared at Nigel. "Who is next?"

Nigel stared back grimly, wishing he could reassure her and knowing he was unable to do so. "I seem to recall a lecture in the back of a rug shop. I cannot stress enough the importance of *never* finding yourself alone. If you are vigilant, you will not give this monster the opportunity to catch you unaware."

"Might there be more than one?" Elizabeth asked in a small voice.

"It appears to be the work of one individual, but I am ruling out nothing," he conceded. "The Commissioner had a word with the Viceroy, and he in turn has urged speed and compliance with the other governments involved. We will apprehend this bastard and put him away for bloody good. In the meantime it is vital you go about as normal."

"This is a nightmare." Elizabeth shivered as another thought occurred. "I was rather leaning toward Lieutenant Toppenham, but he was a mere child in 1914."

"Around twelve, I should think. Child killers exist, however. Mental illness, apparently, doesn't bother discriminating in age. You recall the Southwark tragedy back in '22?"

Elizabeth nodded. Two boys, aged ten and twelve, beat two younger children to death as they walked home from school. They were caught in the act, otherwise it might never have been believed. "I was young at the time. It was quite traumatising. But how could a twelve-year-old possess the strength to strangle a full-grown woman? Surely it's impossible."

"By himself, unlikely."

"So we're back to more than one?"

"Not necessarily. Perhaps he witnessed one of the murders. The killer trots off to fight in the War and is killed. The child becomes a man and takes a go at it himself." Nigel shrugged. "Pure speculation until we uncover the truth." Seeing Elizabeth stifle a yawn, he finished briskly, "It *is* quite late. I'll drive you home."

"Not until you tell me what happened after my father hauled you off under guard."

Nigel sighed and ran a hand down his face. His fingertips were still cool from touching the scotch glass. "It wasn't pleasant—for either your father or me."

"I imagine not."

She was going to hear about it anyway. It might as well be from him. Shoving his hands deep in his pockets, he faced her fully, leaning back on the mantel. "The Commissioner called a halt before I'd been in questioning more than a few minutes. In fact, he gifted headquarters with his august presence, sweeping your father out of the room and subjecting him to a verbal shelling." He ignored Elizabeth's gasp and continued, getting it over with. "Sir Clive is very cognisant, if the Colonel is not, of the importance of friendly relations between Kashmir and the British government. Especially now in this climate of political upheaval. He's also aware of the degree of offense my father will take when he learns of this debacle. And he will learn of it, even if *I* do not inform him.

"Already, Sir Clive is busy concocting a public relations scheme to explain away my arrest. Part of the plan includes your father's retirement by year's end—although he is free to present his resignation before then—and my promotion to Lt. Colonel."

"Good Lord, no wonder he slammed into the bungalow and barricaded himself in his study. He will be at such a loss, and furious with it. The Army is his life and always has been. He even lost my mother and me because of it. Well, that and another detail or two." She stared unseeing at the Indian goddess on the mantel, deep in thought. "What will he do now? I don't think he would accept an invitation to live on my sheep station. Then again, his company might drive me to live in the sheds with the sheep." She switched her gaze back to Nigel. "Not that he doesn't deserve reprimand. It was appalling to use a private agenda to arbitrarily arrest you!"

Nigel relaxed at once. He didn't realise how stiff he had become despite his loose repose. She didn't hold the good fortune of a promotion against him while her father received the blunt end of the stick. And it was good fortune, he told himself. He was due an ascension in rank anyway, never mind it was given out of contrition. He still felt slightly soiled.

"Who will take over as Colonel when Father steps down? You are the only Lt. Colonel of this regiment now, are you not?"

He laughed shortly. "By no means. You have not met Lt. Colonel Porter. He is enjoying his annual furlough with his family on a houseboat at Lake Dal. Very near, in fact, to my home in Kashmir. Or Lt. Colonel Melyn. He, er, does not socialise. He emerges from his bungalow for official duty only. Porter is the likely candidate for your father's job, as the brass is disinclined to look favourably on an 'odd duck,' which Melyn is often termed."

"Well, that must indeed be a comfort for you." A small smile of understanding curved Elizabeth's lips as she rose and moved toward the dining table where she'd left her sequined evening sandals. She sat in one of the ladder-back chairs to slip them on. "How disconcerting to rise to the top on another man's back, so to speak."

Watching her buckle her shoes, it struck Nigel like a powerful blow from a polo stick. It hurtled out of nowhere, sending him reeling. By God, he was actually falling in love with this woman. Surprisingly, the idea warmed him and instilled a quiet sense of contentment. And why not? She was undeniably beautiful, courageous, and possessed of a finely honed understanding of honour.

Elizabeth looked up from fastening a glittery strap. He followed her and was standing close. Very close. Staring down at her with smouldering sapphire eyes. Concentrating on her other foot, she remarked, "After all, it might be said you didn't deserve your new command because of the questionable circumstances."

Finished with her shoes, she slowly stood. There wasn't quite an inch of space separating them, and she tingled with the electricity that sparked off their bodies. Tipping her head back, she looked him in the eye, whispering, "I think you prefer to earn your dividends with honest ability and hard work."

His searing gaze lowered to settle on her now trembling lips. "You're an intuitive girl, Elizabeth. So you ought to run for the door now, while you can."

Still not taking her eyes from his, she replied breathlessly, "You would let me go if it was what I truly wished."

"I'm but flesh and blood, and I want you more than I've wanted anything in this life," he murmured, reaching for her at last. She caught the flash of uncertainty in his gaze before it was veiled, and then she knew only the sweet, fiery passion of his kiss.

She was falling, drowning in the conflagration of sensation that flicked up her limbs and rendered them weak. The feeling climbed further still, to spiral and twist low in her abdomen. And when her legs buckled, Nigel caught her behind the knees, picked her up and carried her to the cool, smooth sheets of his bed without breaking contact with her lips.

A warning bell sounded dully in her mind. If she stayed, let him have his way, there was no going back. But would she wish to go back? Happiness had no guarantees in life. Her parents' marriage served as a dreadful example, and as an incentive to experience these exquisite sensations while she might. Besides, her willpower melted with each kiss, with each caress of Nigel's warm fingers. . . .

A baritone serenaded them with "Scotch and Soda" from the wireless in a low, sensual rhythm, crooning about his scotch and a jigger of gin.

What a spell you've got me in . . .

Nigel rose and moved to the bureau to light a taper. The candle sizzled, flickered, threw jumping shadows on the walls and ceiling; and then he was back sitting on the edge of the bed, reaching for the buttons on her scarlet blouse.

Do I feel . . . high . . .

He made short work of her clothing, and stretching languidly, Elizabeth watched him strip out of his uniform, revealing powerful shoulders tapering to hard sculpted thighs. She caught a tantalising glimpse of the thick length of his sex jutting from a patch of black curls before he pressed her to the mattress, and rolling with her, devoured her mouth, her throat, breasts, and belly with hot questing lips. That he tasted of the warm, smoky scotch he'd been drinking was her last lucid thought as her mind emptied, filling with nothing but pure sensation and pleasure. Nigel's hands followed his voracious lips, moulding her, learning her body; and shuddering, she urged him on, allowing him to do anything he wished.

She was perfect. Her curves fit his body as if made for him. She tasted sweet and musky, and Nigel didn't think he'd ever get enough. He'd never wanted a woman—not like this. Blood pounded in his temples and raged to white-hot fever in his veins. This was craziness, madness. God, he must slow down, get hold of himself so he could take her with the finesse of an experienced lover, not the brutality of a rutting animal. Skimming down her body, leaving a trail of fire, he stilled at the apex of her thighs where he tunnelled long fingers through her delicate folds. Separating them, he looked up, his dark eyes glittering. He whispered, "Look at me as I love you, Elizabeth."

Her dazed eyes met his, and then he dipped his head to lick and lave at her sensitive flesh. Elizabeth stiffened as shock registered, but it was gone in an instant, replaced by a roaring in her ears and a quickening of her senses for which she was quite unprepared. Desire coiled and built low in her belly as she panted and whimpered, arching into Nigel's inflaming caresses. She clutched at his hair, desperate to press him closer, her head whipping from side to side on the pillow, nearly incoherent from pleasure, straining for some unknown pinnacle—only to be left bereft when Nigel abruptly pulled away.

Meeting her stunned gaze, Nigel braced shaking hands on either side of Elizabeth's shoulders and slowly sheathed himself in the hot liquid depth of her body. Both caught their breath. She had not known a man before and cried out sharply at his invasion, but he sprinkled her with kisses and whispered encouragement in her ear. She was as tight as a fist and he gritted his teeth in an effort not to lunge mindlessly into her. When she relaxed and moved restlessly he began thrusting in a slow, steady rhythm. In response to his rough instruction, she raised her legs and wrapped them around his waist. He savoured her arousal and enthusiasm, and in return let her feel his weight rocking sinuously in the cradle of her thighs, rubbing his heated body against her belly and breasts.

Elizabeth moaned, feeling heavy and hot and shameless in her enjoyment. First she gripped him tighter to express her urgency, then bucked wildly and writhed against him, thrilling at the fullness and delicious friction created by the pulsating hardness of his erection. Suddenly her climax claimed her without warning, slamming into her like a meteor, erupting in a colourful shower of sparks.

Nigel watched her ecstasy, felt Elizabeth's shuddering contraction and could hold back no longer. Catching her cry in a hot kiss, he grasped her knees, splaying them wide, and with a harsh groan, plunged in, reaching the very core of her. He drove in again and again until finally he exploded, emptying himself into her.

The echo of his harsh shout faded and only their heavy breathing disturbed the silence that followed. It seemed the wireless had tuned off for the night. Stirring at last, Nigel smoothed her hair off her forehead.

"I was rough. I'm sorry," he whispered. "I've never been out of control before."

"Never?" Elizabeth's fingers danced down his perspiration-damp back.

He jerked and shivered, then seized her wrist and stretched it over her head. "No, you imp, never." He was smiling now.

"Hmm," she murmured silkily. "Might that be because I aroused dormant passions in the wild beast?" The fingers of her free hand traced the crevice of his bottom.

Nigel groaned and flexed, hardening inside her. "You are playing a dangerous game, madam. Never having done this before, I assume you are unaware of the consequences of your indiscreet actions." He stilled and continued in a serious tone. "Perhaps we should talk about that. I've compromised you."

"So you have." Elizabeth found she didn't want to discuss it. Even head over heels for him, the idea of Nigel's offering marriage out of a sense of honour filled her with revulsion. If he asked her to marry him, it must be because he loved her.

Rational thought, however, was fast disintegrating as he hardened even more, filling and stretching her. Squirming and arching underneath him, she finished breathlessly, "I do believe, Lt. Colonel, that you best do so again. Just to make sure the job is done properly."

The telephone shrilled, jolting them awake instantly. Nigel's hand shot out, seizing the handset off his nightstand.

"Covington-Singh," he barked crossly.

"Bloody hell! When?" He sat up, brushing impatiently at the lock of hair falling on his forehead. "Why the devil are you just finding out now?"

"I see." Nigel's tone turned forbidding. "No, you needn't. I'll be there." He squinted at his bedside clock. "In thirty minutes. Right."

He rang off and snatched his trousers from the floor, dragging them up his legs. "Ballocks! Of all the . . ." He turned to Elizabeth, who was staring at him with wide, startled eyes, the sheet pulled up over her breasts, and his anger evaporated. "I am sorry, love. A matter of some urgency, I'm afraid. I must drive you home immediately."

"What is it? What's happened, Nigel?"

He picked up a handful of garments from the floor and tossed one to her. It was her red silk blouse, now sadly wrinkled. He shrugged into his shirt.

"Toppenham's done a runner."

Elizabeth gasped, her fingers freezing on her blouse buttons. "Good God! When?"

"There's the difficulty. Apparently his honour guard fell asleep on duty—a very serious offense. I'll find out more when I get to his bungalow." He'd finished dressing and was sorting through her clothing. Wistfully, he passed Elizabeth her silk stockings.

Her hand lingered on his as she took them from him. A blush spread along her cheekbones at his warm gaze travelling over her exposed curves. Why, after all they had done to each other, should she be shy now? Perhaps it had something to do with the fact he was entirely covered, while she remained next to naked. She quickly shook away what were becoming languorous thoughts and returned to the matter at hand.

"If he escaped this afternoon—"

"That makes him the prime suspect, yes. Are you ready? Good, let's go."

They climbed into his Romeo, but did not roar down the street. Nigel kept the car's headlamps off. The last thing he wanted to do was draw attention to the fact he was out driving with the Colonel's daughter near four o'clock in the morning. Fortunately, the moon shone sufficiently to light the trail.

He sniffed the air suspiciously and looked again at the sky. Faint shadows of wafer-thin clouds rode high in the dark blue dome.

"The rains are coming soon now," he said. "Very soon."

An ominous premonition skimmed down his spine, and he shivered.

Chapter Eighteen

The sharp cracks reverberated, causing an ugly stabbing pain to throb in her head. Someone was discharging his damned rifle. Whoever it was, Elizabeth thought uncharitably, ought to be shot himself! Wincing, she groped for her pillow in a clumsy effort to bury herself in it. Where was the bloody thing, anyway?

"Miss-Sahib? Please Miss-Sahib, the Colonel wishes to see you at once in his study! Miss-Sahib?" Nazim's call was strained.

Elizabeth sat up, groggy. Why, it was only her father's butler making all the racket by banging on her door, instead of what had sounded to her very sensitive head like the beginning of a second Great War.

"Yes, all right, Nazim." Her voice was hoarse from lack of sleep. "You may cease attacking my door. I'm quite awake I assure you. Be so good as to inform my father, will you, that I'll be a few minutes dressing."

She felt weak and wondered why her head should smart

so. And then the memories came tumbling one after another like advertising trailers for the films. No wonder! All that cognac Fiona had pressed on her. Of course the scotch at Nigel's bungalow only added the surfeit sloshing about in her bloodstream. Nigel!

Blushing hotly, she remembered what he had done to her in his dark bedroom. What she had done to him as well! Her body was beginning to tingle, especially her breasts and between her legs.

He had made love to her four times. The second time, excruciatingly slow and thorough, the third fast and a little rough, and the final time he'd showed her in meticulous detail just how to please him and how to take a more assertive role. Elizabeth trembled, recalling her boldness. Strangely, she found she wasn't in the least embarrassed. In fact, her head had quit aching, and she was feeling quite gay and thrilled with life.

Smiling, she stood to stretch and then made her way to the sink in the corner. Running some cold water, she washed her face. She must be in love, she thought giddily, blotting her wet features.

She peered into the mirror but could detect no change, except perhaps her eyes sparkled a bit more brilliantly. Didn't love affect one thus? Fill one with an exhilaration for no reason at all? Already all she could think of was how soon she could see Nigel again.

A slamming door somewhere in the house startled her and sent her happy imaginings out the window. Her father was waiting for her. Undoubtedly he wanted to discuss that nasty scene from yesterday. He would likely disown her for her liaison with Nigel. Now a great sadness enveloped her. A relationship with her father meant so much. All her life, she had denied the void of a father, but it *did* matter after all. Nevertheless, she would not let that keep her from Nigel.

But how would Nigel's parents feel about *her?* She certainly wasn't royal or even noble. And perhaps she was rushing the points. Just what did her "liaison" with Nigel mean? Elizabeth had never before allowed a man to make love to her. Of course, the ultra-modern girls maintained it a necessity to "try out" a man or two before one's nuptials. However, she was just old-fashioned enough to believe in not going to her husband shopworn.

And would he even ask her to marry him? Did he even love her? And might last night result in a delicate condition?

Sighing, she replaced her towel on the hook beside the sink. Being in love with Nigel was one thing. The reality of the situation was quite another.

Several minutes later Elizabeth knocked on her father's study door, and, entering at his gruff call, saw that he was pouring the dregs of the Lock Dubh bottle into a none-too-clean glass. Turning to a servant hovering in the hall, she ordered tea brought immediately.

"Good morning, Father," she said brightly. "It seems just a bit cooler today, don't you think?"

Colonel Mainwarring smacked the empty whisky bottle on his desk and rose. He was unshaven and his hair stood on end as if he had been running his fingers through it all night. Bleary green eyes so like her own focused steadily on her.

"I will make this short and to the point, madam. I don't know, and I don't want to know how far it's gone, but you will cease keeping company with that darkie. Is that clear? Dismissed." He tossed back the contents of his glass in one gulp.

"Ah, thank you, Nazim." Elizabeth smiled at the butler as he entered with the tea tray. She was pleased to see a stack of toast there—her father definitely needed something in his stomach besides hooch. "Just set it over here," she said, indicating a low table across from the desk. "Do shut the door behind you, there's a good chap.

"I shall overlook your appalling lack of manners," she

went on dryly, setting a cup of tea before her father. "As it appears you have been sitting up all night, as well as skipping supper and breakfast this morning." She returned to the tray to pour a cup for herself. Her head was beginning to ache again and her stomach growled rudely, demanding sustenance. Ignoring them both, she continued, "However, I will remind you I am *not* one of your subordinates. I am your daughter and I have passed my majority." She looked up from stirring milk into her tea. "And I possess a comfortable independence." Sitting in an overstuffed chair, nonchalantly crossing her legs and sipping from the china cup, Elizabeth braced for the eruption she was sure was imminent.

Her father glowered back at her, not touching the tea. "You have six million pounds so you needn't honour your father, is that it? You are still young enough to need guidance, girl! It's for your own good. Have you any idea how you'll be ruined, seen going about with a wog?" He snorted and shook his head. "No decent Englishman will have you afterward. The stigma will follow you to your grave."

"That is really my lookout, isn't it? Unless you are afraid some of it will rub off?" Elizabeth kept her tone bland, determined not to lose her temper. "If there is an afterward, I seriously doubt I will suffer any shortage of beaux. If nothing else, the world is populated with far more fortune hunters than fortunes. Many would be willing to overlook, shall we say, an 'unfortunate episode' in my extreme youth. I wouldn't be stupid enough to marry one, of course, but they do make excellent escorts and sycophants."

"Just what do you mean 'if there is an afterward'? You are not actually thinking of embarking on any sort of permanent relationship?" His voice was dangerously soft.

"What I am telling you, Father, is that if I choose to accept Nigel's—or any other gentleman's escort—it is none of your concern. I have chosen my own escorts for some years now," she said pointedly. "My reputation"—her voice almost wavered—"remains intact."

"He will never marry you, you know. No, you represent an exotic feather in his cap. A rich English girl, who is also the daughter of his colonel. I'm not saying he doesn't find you attractive, but how he must laugh to make the daughter of a man who despises him fall in love. Eventually he will marry some Indian princess whom his father chooses for him. Forget him, Elizabeth."

Elizabeth was only too afraid her father was correct about the Indian princess. Pushing her empty cup toward the tray, she stood. "Such an allegation is beneath both you and Nigel. But you may set your mind to rest. I am not marrying anyone at this time, Father. However, when I do, it is my fervent hope that you accept my choice gracefully. After all, it is I who shall live with him, not you.

"Now you should get some sleep and a decent meal. Perhaps we shall see one another at supper and enjoy a more pleasant conversation. Good day."

Elizabeth sighed as she closed the study door behind her and with a stoic step made her way to the breakfast room where she observed Fiona bowed over a teacup. A piece of dry toast lay crumbled on a small plate at her elbow. It would be a long while before the girl soothed anyone, including herself, with *that* particular brand of medicine again.

"Not feeling quite the thing this morning, old girl?" Elizabeth sympathised just a bit too smoothly. "Perhaps a wee drop of the hair of the dog to perk you up? I'll just see if I can scare up a fresh bottle of Remy, shall I?"

"No!" Fiona regarded her mournfully, supporting her head in her hands. Her eyes were bloodshot and red-rimmed. Wincing, she answered in a rough voice, "I believe I have consumed quite enough cognac to last me into the next decade. Or the next time, God forbid, I nearly encounter a murder scene." She eyed Elizabeth with a glassy gaze. "How is it *you* are looking so dashing this morning? Green ought never to become someone who polished off at least as many toddies as I did." Her envious look noted the colour in her friend's cheeks and the lack of dark circles under her eyes. Although she was unaware of exactly the time Elizabeth returned, she knew it quite late indeed. So why didn't Elizabeth look exhausted?

Elizabeth glanced down at herself and smiled ruefully. She hadn't actually remembered what she had dragged on to answer her father's summons. It turned out to be a slim-belted, sleeveless, cotton knit frock matched with her mother's cherished carnelian jewellery and camel leather sling backs. One of her favourite ensembles.

Filling her plate at the sideboard with bangers and a soft boiled egg, she replied, "I rather doubt it was quantity, old thing, as opposed to the quality. We only drank a couple of them, but they definitely zinged!" Her eyes twinkled. "Sure you don't want a wee dram?"

"If I weren't a lady, I'd tell you to bugger off. You are really going to eat that? Ugh! Eggs are disgusting after an intimacy with a cognac bottle. Speaking of bottles, was your father at it all night? I saw his study door was still shut fast when I came in." She reached for her Players, thought better of it, and filled her cup instead.

"Everyone always assumes when a woman shuts herself in a room by herself she's indulging in a good cry. When a man does likewise, he is raiding his drinking stock." Elizabeth chewed thoughtfully and swallowed. "In this case, however, it appears you are correct, dear. He was quite, er, squiffy and in a temper with it. Nigel has been promoted to Lt. Colonel and Father is to retire his commission by the end of the year. Also, it seems he has decided whom I shall see and whom I shall shun. Curious, isn't it, after so many years, this sudden fatherly concern over my reputation?" Reflecting again, she added, "Hmm, perhaps, 'concern' is not an appropriate word. Control is more like it, don't you think?"

"Good for Nigel and just as well the old man is in the dark about just who you rushed off to see last night—and particularly the time you returned. Quite late, I gather?"

Elizabeth found herself jabbing at the toast she'd dipped into the soft egg yolk. More colour crept into her face as it broke, but she picked up her fork to fish the bread out gracefully. "Yes, well, it was rather, but as to the exact time I'm afraid I don't recall. I was exhausted and simply dived under the mosquito netting. You really should eat something, you know, or you are likely to sick up sooner rather than later."

"Thank you for the graphics, old thing, but as I'm not keen on breaky at the moment, I believe I shall wait for elevenses, or even luncheon," Fiona finished grumpily. "Besides, you're eating enough for both of us."

"It looks as if this bungalow is populated with temperamental, ailing, hung-over individuals this morning," Elizabeth replied mildly. "Perhaps you might feel a bit better if you ventured out into the fresh air. I fancy visiting Emily. Will you accompany me, or is a car ride more than you can tolerate just now?"

Fi sighed and extracted a silver compact and lip rouge from her handbag. "Soldier on, as they say. Or more to the point," she added dryly, "have sick bag, will travel."

Elizabeth drove her father's old household jalopy and thought wistfully of the sporty blue rag-top cabriolet she'd ordered shipped straight out to New Zealand. Oh well, this old thing *did* get them about.

They found Emily busy in her garden wearing an old canvas smock and a broad-brimmed straw hat. She was attending a lush bed of colourful roses. There was quite a hustle and bustle of Indian bearers carrying crates out of the bungalow and stacking them in the back of an ancient lorry. Seeing Elizabeth and Fiona, Emily rose from her kneeling pad with the help of a servant and greeted them with a wide smile.

"This is an unexpected pleasure! I planned on stopping by in a day or two to wish you the best of luck before I decamped." She peeled off her gardening gloves and motioned them inside. "Come in out of this heat. Contrary to the pother, I've plenty to offer in the way of refreshment as the food is never packed, but left here for distribution among the families of the servants. The rest of the house may be at sixes and sevens, but you will find the kitchen is an oasis of calm."

"But Emily," protested Elizabeth, astonished at the idea of her new friend leaving. With a murderer on the loose and the situation with her father, she needed all the normalcy and support she could gather. "Where are you going?"

"Why, to my plantation in Ceylon, of course." Seeing her distress, Emily frowned. "I always go when the rains start. I'm actually late this year because the rains have usually begun by now. They *are* imminent."

Fiona searched Emily's face. "It has nothing to do with yesterday?"

Emily pursed her lips and averted her gaze to study the heat waves shimmering in the distance, which gave lie to her words regarding the rain. Yet she *had* caught a trace of what might have been a cloud just before dawn. Now the white glare of the sun filled the sky in a blinding brilliance.

"Perhaps," she began, and then meeting the girls' eyes she admitted with sad finality, "yes. The atmosphere here is becoming surreal. I've lived in India all my life, you see, and political strife is a constant in this mysterious land of religion-driven existence. Life here holds a multitude of layers, the depths of which you may not comprehend even after decades spent here. I revel in all the intrigue, really.

"But there is a killer among us. Apparently, an indiscriminate killer. Yesterday one acquaintance of long standing was murdered, and another nearly so and not expected to live. I am an old woman and I want to feel safe."

Even feeling the wave of sad resignation wash through her, Elizabeth found Emily's reasoning impossible to deny. At least they might enjoy a cheerful parting memory.

"Well then, we must take you to luncheon as a going-away present," she offered briskly. "Let's stay in familiar territory and see what savouries the Mohd Bagh Club offers its mid-day patrons. Perhaps some champers might cheer us up. Oh, do be quiet, Fiona," she said when Fi groaned. "If you can't quite face it, leave it for Emily and me. I assure you, we shall appreciate it!"

Emily swiftly changed and freshened up, but insisted her chauffeur drive them in her automobile.

Soon they were seated at a comfortable table in the club's dining room under a wonderfully energetic electric punka and enjoying the merry tinkling of the nearby indoor fountain.

Fiona did partake of the champagne, and all three, feeling a bit homesick and yearning for simpler times, indulged in a truly British meal of roast joint and potatoes with Yorkshire pudding and overdone peas.

Replete, they leaned back in their chairs when the plates were removed and were about to pour tea when they were surprised by several acquaintances, some of whom had gathered around the Victrola the day before.

"I say, jolly good to see you Miss Mainwarring! Er, of course you too, Miss McKay and Mrs. Stanton." Lieutenant Fairfield stammered to halt, blushing and earning a look of annoyance from the very young blonde possessively clutching his arm. He introduced her as Miss Celia Armstrong, just arrived that morning from home.

The blonde beamed up at him, fluttering long fair lashes. "I'm the daughter of his mother's *dearest* friend." She lifted her chin a notch and stretched her lips in a smug smile. "We are staying with dear Johnny and his mother *indefinitely.*"

Georgina Smythe, who was accompanied by Amanda Crosshaven and Captain Henderson, quirked her brow, amused. "I'm sure Johnny and his mother will have you for as long as it takes, dear."

Miss Armstrong flicked Georgina a dark look, but scrutinising her, apparently thought her an old maid of twenty-five or thereabouts; far too old to be considered competition. The stunning blonde in the sage couture dress, however, occupied a different chorus line altogether. And that was exactly what she might have guessed her to be: a cheap chorus girl. If not for the frock, which she was quite certain was the one she had coveted in *Vogue* by some new and coming designer by the name of Cocoa or something chocolately, at any rate. She patted her immaculate bob and enquired, "How long are you here for, Miss Mainwarring? I don't imagine you intend to coop yourself up here for long."

Elizabeth's eyes twinkled, but she replied moderately, "Why would you imagine such a thing, Miss Armstrong? Miss McKay and I intend to remain some time before moving on to my sheep station in New Zealand."

Fiona, looking quite surprised, opened her mouth but shut it precipitously after a sharp glance from her friend.

"Oh, well, a sheep station. To be sure." Celia examined her sunset glo–coloured manicure. Again, no competition. Johnny might drool over this one, but propose—never! Johnny's career was the Army. It was quite laughable to envision him in some outback herding sheep of all things. "One sees why you might prefer the relative sophistication of Calcutta. You must try London sometime. Why, I visited last year and it was simply sublime." Really! Whoever heard of a shepherdess wearing couture? She'd probably never even been to the city. It must be a convincing fake she was wearing.

Mrs. Crosshaven shifted in her chair and exchanged glances with Captain Henderson, who harrumphed and opened his mouth but in the end clamped it shut.

"Celia!" reproved Lieutenant Fairfield. But Celia appeared undaunted.

"What a coincidence, indeed. I was there myself last year, as well. Fancy not running into each other," Elizabeth quipped.

"London *is* a big city." Celia's tone was pitying. "Besides, we wouldn't occupy the same social circles. So there you have it."

Fiona finally lost all control and buried a hiccup of laughter in her teacup.

But Elizabeth was no longer listening. The door to the drinks lounge swung open and revealed Nigel standing alone at the bar. Suddenly she was hot and acutely aware of her racing heart. "Excuse me," she murmured to the assembled party before strolling toward the still swinging door.

"Well!" said Celia huffily, and smoothed her rose linen frock as if something unsavoury had brushed it. "Definitely not the same circles."

Georgina Smythe made a seat on the lip of the fountain, and holding a cigarette out for Captain Henderson to light, commented, "Oh, certainly not." Exhaling a cloud in Celia's direction, she leaned casually back on one hand and, canting her head to one side, a mischievous smile playing about her lips, said lightly, "After all, a millionairess may occupy only the most discerning of circles."

"Millionairess! Oh, you are funning. The owner of a sheep station?"

"Did you not hear of the recent New Zealand oil strike?" Georgina carelessly flipped her ash into the pool. "Well, perhaps those in your circle do not read the newspapers or listen to the BBC. At any rate, it seems Miss Mainwarring's sheep station is positively swimming in delicious and titillatingly scarce black gold."

* * *

Just as Elizabeth slipped through the lounge door, she heard a rather undignified squeak. Glancing over her shoulder she observed Miss Armstrong's wide eyes and the surprised *O* of her mouth. Poor Miss Armstrong. Disillusionment did not prove flattering to her delicate complexion.

Turning back, Elizabeth shivered as Nigel's appraising gaze darkened to black in appreciation and his nostrils flared. Goose bumps raced, prickling her skin as he smiled, his lips curving sensuously under a luxuriant mustache. Suddenly, the world seemed to decelerate and in slow motion she was underneath him again, naked and straining. Touching and tasting his hot, salty skin. Fingers, lost to control, skimming down his back, clutching . . .

Nigel's warm blue gaze watched Elizabeth's approach. She moved gracefully toward him, the green dress hugging her curves, making her emerald eyes glow and setting off the gold shimmer of her sleek finger waves. God, she was beautiful. A fierce need for her sliced through him. A fleeting image teased him, and again he was in his bed seeking entrance to her soft body, feeling the snugness and delighting in' her unbridled response. . . .

"Covington-Singh. It's Lt. Colonel now I hear." Deputy Commissioner Tate's voice snapped both Elizabeth and Nigel smartly to attention. His tone was bitter with resentment and his jaw drawn tight in anger as he placed his topi on the bar. "Am told I owe you an apology for my behaviour yesterday. Consider it done. Was out of my mind with grief." He thumped the bar with his fist and yelled to the bartender, "Here, you, get me a large gin and tonic. Harry by or I'll marrow you bloody!" Wiping his sweaty forehead with a bar serviette, he eyed Elizabeth in some disfavour.

"I must say, I'm surprised to see you in the men's lounge, Miss Mainwarring." His gaze slipped past her to Nigel and back again. "Daresay you weren't informed the fair sex don't wander into this portion of the Mohd Bagh."

Nigel's eyes narrowed and gleamed in irritation. In fact, it was with some surprise Elizabeth noted that Mr. Tate did not expire from the sharp missiles that Nigel seemed to issue.

"None of the other gentlemen present"—there was a slight emphasis on the word *gentlemen*—"has expressed an objection to Miss Mainwarring's presence—"

"It's quite all right. I was just leaving in any case," Elizabeth interrupted stiffly, laying a hand on Nigel's arm. "I am sure you are not feeling yourself today, Mr. Tate. Please accept my condolences on the tragic loss of your dear wife. You will find a large support group in this community to help you through your sorrow. Good day, gentlemen." Her gaze lingered on Nigel for the briefest moment. Then she left, her dress swaying elegantly about her calves.

Canby Tate's speculative gaze followed Elizabeth until she disappeared into the dining room. Then he turned back to the man he hated.

Elizabeth paused inside the dining room to take a deep, calming breath. She felt as if she had just stepped off one of those new motorised whirli-gigs. Divided by the exhilaration of her swift, hot response to Nigel's sizzling gaze and the sheer wrath directed toward Canby Tate and his arrogant, unrepentant apology, she gave herself a mental shake. Not only was it uncharitable to make intolerant judgments when a man had just lost his wife in the most horrific circumstances, but unsettling in the extreme to have nearly made a cake of herself just because the object of her affection merely glanced at her.

It was quite understandable, she admonished herself, that Mr. Tate was affected in the most profound manner by the tragedy of his wife's demise, and could in no way be held accountable for his tactless actions.

Meanwhile, *she* intended to act with the decorum of a worldly heiress and not the silliness of a lovestruck young girl.

It wasn't until she was halfway back to her table that she realised she hadn't asked Nigel about Toppenham.

Chapter Nineteen

A delightful trifle was being handed around as Elizabeth resumed her seat. Although Mrs. Crosshaven, Captain Henderson, and Miss Smythe stayed to partake of the treat, Lieutenant Fairfield and the possessive Miss Armstrong took their leave.

" 'Sweets are ruinous to one's youthful figure! *I* don't intend to begin.' " Amanda imitated Miss Armstrong with an airy wave of her hand. With the other she daintily nibbled a spoonful of the gooey desert.

"Why, that just leaves more for us!" Captain Henderson interjected gallantly. "Besides, one needs a little something to hold skin and bone together. What does a man want with a wraith, I ask you? Can't keep him warm at night. Great God, wouldn't even know she was there! Got to have something to, er, hang on to . . ." He stumbled to a red-faced halt and cleared his throat.

"Captain Henderson, such shocking conversation! Why, you managed to put an old lady to the blush." Emily smiled

mischievously. "I can tell you, though, I admire such senti-
ment in a modern man. These fashion models nowadays are
slender enough to be mistaken for boys. However, I believe
that trend is about to backfire in a large way. I hear Hollywood is now promoting 'blond bombshells' in its films.
Voluptuous girls to augment the sagging sales in tickets, you
understand."

Fiona immediately held out her plate. "That definitely
calls for a second helping, darling!"

As Emily replenished Fiona's plate, Amanda, her gay
mood suddenly deserting her, set down her fork and looked
nervously around the circle.

"We are all laughing now, but I can't help remembering
yesterday. I try so hard to forget, to be cheerful, but it all
comes tumbling back like a tidal wave. The truth is, I'm
frightened. When will it all be over? When may we enjoy
normalcy once more?" She shuddered. "Certainly no love
was lost between Beryl and me, but what an awful, horrid
way to . . ." She clutched convulsively at the linen serviette
covering her lap. "And that shocking episode with the Colonel and the Major. Are any of us safe?"

Elizabeth too, set down her fork, leaning forward with an
earnest mien. "We mustn't allow this fiend to control our
feelings or make us doubt our security! Of course, sensible
precautions are essential, but we cannot live in fear. If we
give in, we shall end as prisoners cowering inside our homes
and let this . . . this savage affect our quality of life! I intend
to go about my normal activities—but never alone. It is critical we use the buddy system at all times."

"Hear, hear!" chimed in Georgina. "We'll stand up to him
and show him for the coward he is, attacking lone women."

Amanda tendered a weak smile. "I am not so brave, I fear.
Unless dear Ronnie—Captain Henderson, that is—or of
course, Mr. Crosshaven escorts me, I believe I shall stay
home."

Captain Henderson glanced surreptitiously around the dining room, giving his handlebar mustache a thoughtful stroke. Then he cleared his throat and confided, "I say. Probably shouldn't tell you this, but . . . well, no reason to keep the women paralysed in fear." Still, he hesitated.

"Don't keep us in suspense now, old chap. Out with it!" Georgina demanded.

"Oh Ronnie, tell us! Is the monster in custody? How could you have not said anything!" Amanda all but jumped with anxiety.

"Steady on, old girl. Nothing too drastic, but it may calm your fears. Two bits of news. Lieutenant Toppenham, er, flew the coop sometime yesterday—or overnight. Apparently his guard either fell asleep or was drugged, and Bob's your uncle, the sodder does a scarper. Massive search out for him as we speak. Find him in no time!"

Amanda gasped, her eyes wide in shock. "How is that supposed to calm our fears? Obviously he's the murderer and he's on the loose! We could be killed in our beds!" A note of hysteria touched her voice.

Georgina leaned over and slipped an arm around Amanda's shoulders. "Hush, dear. We shan't come to any harm. The finest of His Majesty's soldiers are on high alert. Besides, you have a husband to protect you." But she too was shaken, and sent Captain Henderson a disturbed look.

Rather than reassure her, Georgina's words horrified Amanda. Her husband rarely bothered coming home until dawn.

"Toppenham's the rotter, then?" Emily's expression was stark disbelief. "Usually I account myself an excellent judge of character." She shook her head sadly and continued almost as if to herself. "Never thought him the brightest young man, but never, never in my wildest imaginings . . ."

"Is it positive then, Captain? The authorities have proof?"

Fiona suddenly found the trifle lost its charm and shoved aside the uneaten portion in distaste.

The Captain shrugged. "This is all hush-hush, precisely because there *is* no proof yet. Personally, I'm quite confident plenty of proof exists. It just has to be found."

Fiona persisted. "He just may not have cared for the ambiance of his bungalow. Perhaps a scotch too many and he thinks, 'bugger this,' and off he goes for some fun."

"Miss McKay," Captain Henderson said with an indulgent smile, "you must leave the reasoning to the authorities. Everyone may trust Lt. Colonel Covington-Singh's superlative crime-solving abilities." Seeing several eyebrows lift in question, he clarified, "The, er, unfortunate scene Mrs. Crosshaven spoke of a moment ago is, of course, satisfactorily resolved. One must appreciate Tate's state of mind."

"You mentioned two pieces of news, Captain. What is the second?" Elizabeth enquired.

"Not as important as the first, Miss Mainwarring, but interesting just the same." Henderson paused to light cigarettes for Georgina and Amanda, the latter shaking so badly he was forced to grasp her wrist, holding it steady for the flame to catch. Lingering longer than strictly necessary, it was a moment before he turned his attention back to Elizabeth.

"Captain Langley greeted the Lt. Colonel this morning in a most disreputable manner. Apparently, his bedroom door viciously attacked him, blackening his eye. And his shaving razor slipped not once, but a number of times leaving a variety of rakish scratches and one rather deep gash running from temple to chin."

Chapter Twenty

Despite brave words and resolutions, the rounds of parties and soirees waned for several days until everyone, inevitably bored with caution and his or her own company, began venturing out into society once more. In no time the social whirl of Calcutta resembled a frenzied revelry more in tune with the loose post-Great War era than the current staid depression. In a single-minded effort to ignore the recent unpleasantness—native riots and train explosions for the usual political reasons as well as the recent murders and assaults—the majority of the British population consumed hooch as if they might soon find themselves run aground on the same dry shore as the Americans.

Elizabeth chuckled at that thought as she stood alone at one such party, sipping her frothy gin fizz and glancing at the door for the umpteenth time that evening. Instead of Nigel, she saw her hostess, Amanda Crosshaven, approach her, a warm colour in her cheeks and a sparkle in her eyes.

"My dear, you look stunning tonight. That colour suits

you." Amanda admired Elizabeth's clinging bronze gown shot through with metallic gold threads. It was cut low in front and even lower in back. "Quite daring! Now then, who escorted you tonight? Only a cad brings a lady to a party, then abandons her. And so I shall tell him."

"Captain Woodford did double duty tonight." Elizabeth smiled, hoping her disappointment didn't show. Nigel's investigations were keeping him so busy she'd hardly set eyes on him in days.

"He's been doing rather a lot of that recently, hasn't he? Although I did notice you on Lt. Colonel Covington-Singh's arm a time or two this week. Well, this won't do at all. We must find you a beau." Tapping her forefinger on her chin, she contemplated her guests through the blue haze of tobacco smoke hanging in her crowded drawing room.

Several of the guests were arguing over which record to play next at the Victrola, and another group gathered around a game of cards. Someone played the piano and sang, slurring his words and a bit off key, the added verse to "It's a Long Way to Tipperary."

> *That's the wrong way to tickle Mary,*
> *That's the wrong way to kiss!*
> *Don't you know over here, lad,*
> *That they like it best like this!*
> *We didn't know the way to tickle Mary,*
> *But we learned how, over there!*

It didn't take long for more of the inebriated to join in, including Mr. Crosshaven, who had his arm wrapped around a statuesque woman, his eyes pinned to her generous cleavage.

Amanda's lip curled briefly in distaste. Facing Elizabeth again she said, "Captain Barnes is eminently eligible, if not the tiniest bit bashful. And then there's—"

"Thank you, Amanda, but no matchmaking please. I

shan't remain in Calcutta long enough for that sort of thing. Lt. Colonel Covington-Singh, or if he is not available, Captain Woodford shall do nicely."

"Yes, well, Woodford is quite singularly interested in Fiona, and of course, Covington-Singh won't do for a steady sort of escort. So we really must find someone suitable. Now, Captain Barnes isn't precisely dashing, but he possesses a sterling reputation."

Elizabeth frowned. "And why will Nigel not do for an escort, pray?"

Amanda laughed. "Why, people might think he was something besides your escort, silly. Once or twice is perfectly fine, but any more and you've created the most succulent grist for the rumour mill."

"Are Fiona and Harry creating such grist?"

"It's not the same thing, darling, not at all." She stopped a passing waiter and reached for a gin and French from his tray. "I mean, Harry Woodford isn't Indian, is he?"

Elizabeth felt a sudden chill in the stuffy, overheated room. Searching Amanda's face, she asked in a controlled voice, "And that makes a difference, does it?"

Amanda's eyes widened in surprise as she sipped her drink. "Of course, darling, all the difference." Ignoring Elizabeth's glittering eyes and stiffening posture, she glanced at the group gathered around the card table. "It really is too bad about Johnny Fairfield. He'd make you the perfect squire for the time you have left here. He's quite in awe of the daring Miss Mainwarring—even more in awe of Colonel Mainwarring. Why, I'd be willing to wager he'd not even attempt a peck on your cheek at the end of an evening." She sighed. "A dying breed that. But the poor chap is stuck with that cow Celia. Notice the death glares she's shooting at you every time Johnny glances your way. Fancies herself the new 'It Girl' in Calcutta society." Amanda snorted. "As if none of the rest of us possess any SA."

"What's all this about SA?" Captain Henderson asked as he joined them.

Amanda's features lit and she bussed him on the cheek. "Sex appeal, dear boy." Her lips curved seductively. "We were just discussing who had it and who didn't."

Henderson's gaze sizzled as it rested on Amanda. "Astounding what the ladies talk about at parties these days. Speaking of parties, thought you claimed you'd lost the party mood, old girl. Glad to see you in such good spirits again."

"Not so much out of the mood, darling, as not stepping the tiniest inch outside of this bungalow until that nasty murderer is caught! Really, what is taking so long? It's quite tiresome staying home all day. You should come by to cheer me up sometime, Reggie. I could use the company."

"Perhaps not quite the thing. Your husband may object." He stroked his mustache nervously and cleared his throat. "Nothing untoward of course, but—"

"Don't be ridiculous. Simon is never home." Taking a slow sip of her drink and fluttering her eyelashes, she said, "I'd feel ever so much safer with a man about, you know."

"Yes, well, I'll take a look at my schedule, see what I can do. Covington-Singh's got me quite busy these days. So much bumf."

"Bumf! What has paperwork got to do with catching a killer? Why isn't everybody out scouring the . . . the Bustees or the bazaar? *That* is where all of Calcutta's ruffians may be found. No wonder the madman has not been ferreted out yet!"

Henderson ran a finger inside the collar of his lightweight linen shirt. "It's not all glamourous footwork, I'm afraid, m'dear. We must engage in research so we know precisely where *to* look."

Amanda raised her eyebrows. "What sort of 'research'?"

The Captain cleared his throat again. "Not at liberty to

NAME: _____

ADDRESS: _____

_____

_____

TELEPHONE: _____

E-MAIL: _____

_____ I want to pay by credit card.

__ Visa   __ MasterCard   __ Discover

Account Number: _____

Expiration date: _____

SIGNATURE: _____

*Send this form, along with $2.00 shipping
and handling for your FREE books, to:*

Historical Romance Book Club
20 Academy Street
Norwalk, CT 06850-4032

*Or fax (must include credit card
information!) to:* 610.995.9274.
*You can also sign up on the Web
at* www.dorchesterpub.com.

Offer open to residents of the U.S. and
Canada only. Canadian residents, please
call 1.800.481.9191 for pricing information.

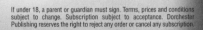

say, dear girl. However, I may tell you we are making progress." He waved his free hand in a dismissive gesture. "Maniac will be in irons before you can say 'Bob's your uncle!' You have my word."

"I say, good luck and KBO, old chap," Harry said as he and Fiona approached.

"KBO?" asked Amanda, her brow furrowed.

"Keep buggering on," supplied Elizabeth before taking a sip of her fizz. "Latest slang, you know."

"Captain Henderson." Fiona spoke over the chuckles. "I just heard an interesting bit of information. Perhaps you might clarify as to whether or not it is rumour. Is it true Rose Durrow was, in fact, not kidnapped as everyone assumed, but out with her beau? A Eurasian beau?"

Henderson finished off his drink, set the glass on a nearby table and shoved his hands in his pockets, where Elizabeth could see them fist. "I'm, er, rather limited in what I may say. I'm afraid I let a tad too much slip in the club the other afternoon. I can say there is no evidence of abduction, so you may all sleep easily in your beds as long as all doors and windows are locked, of course."

"Did Toppenham and Langley supply alibis for that night?" asked Elizabeth.

"As to that, I'm afraid I cannot say."

"Well." Amanda's tone was sardonic. "So much for 'who you know.' Perhaps you may tell us instead if you have rounded up the culprits responsible for all these explosions and riots. No wonder I've not ventured outside! One escapes strangulation only to be trampled in the marketplace or blown to kingdom come while minding one's own business waiting to board the train to Lucknow."

Henderson quirked his brow and asked dryly, "And when, m'dear, was the last time you visited Lucknow? Hadn't heard it is the new popular destination."

"Reggie! That's not the point and you know it. Why, only

the other day those rioting hooligans attacked Mrs. Belleville at the train station. The poor dear is languishing in hospital with a broken leg, sprained wrist, and goodness knows what else."

"No doubt gossip rumoured it she was an innocent by-stander?" the Captain asked wryly.

"No doubt you will gladly inform us of the true circumstances," Elizabeth said, fastening a Dunhill into a holder and presenting it so the Captain might light it.

"Surely, Reggie, you are not implying Mrs. Belleville actually asked for her injuries?" Amanda watched as he lit Elizabeth's cigarette, but relaxed when, as soon as the flame caught, he pocketed his lighter.

"It seems the old girl couldn't resist a captive audience when she heard about the natives covering the tracks with their own bodies. Marched right on out and proceeded to give the poor blighters a piece of her mind. Made it quite clear she didn't believe in an independent India," chimed in Harry, looking pleased to have imparted it.

Captain Henderson took up the story. "Yes, well, you will have noticed it's even warmer than usual these last few days? The poor buggers had been lying there for hours without any water, and er, without relieving themselves. Understandably their tempers were a little, er, uncertain. It soon degenerated into a rather unsophisticated name-calling contest. Some rather nasty epithets went flying back and forth. A few of the natives leaped out of the track pit, and before the sepoys could come to her aid the old girl fell onto the tracks, breaking her leg. The crowd soon dispersed without a shot fired and the trains were up and running again. Colonel Mainwarring had a strict word with her. Don't think she'll be up to another of these, er, capers until India is independent." He shrugged. "Which is arguable, of course. Quite a firecracker is Mrs. Belleville!"

"We must take her some flowers when we next visit the

hospital. Elizabeth and I looked in on Mrs. Newsome yesterday. No change of course," Fiona put in. "By the way, isn't Nigel supposed to drop in tonight? I haven't seen him."

"Highly unlikely he'll be attending tonight, I'm afraid. New batch of intelligence arrived by courier tonight just as I was leaving. Quite curious about it myself, but he ordered us all to toddle off," Henderson remarked.

"I do hope it's something useful. Has the wireless been very forthcoming, Captain?" Elizabeth asked.

"Moderately, Miss Mainwarring, but we expect more. Research unfortunately takes time. When all our contacts have finished supplying information we'll be inundated, I'm sure."

"Enough of this depressing talk now. We're here to enjoy ourselves and so we shall. Reggie dear, Elizabeth will be needing an escort for the next several weeks. Obviously she cannot depend on Nigel for every outing. Are you aware of anyone suitable in your company?"

"You needn't put yourself out, Captain," Elizabeth said quickly as he began stroking his mustache in a considering manner. "I'm quite content as matters stand. Really, all this fuss in these modern times. It's not as if I'm wandering off into some wilderness on my own."

"Not putting myself out at all, Miss Mainwarring, I assure you. Tedious, some social conventions, but it will be a pleasure to keep an eye out for a suitable escort."

Behind Henderson, Simon Crosshaven hit a very sour note in an unfamiliar rendition of "How Deep Is the Ocean," and, wincing, Amanda caustically muttered, "Apparently not deep enough." Then, with a deliberate smile she turned to Captain Henderson. "Reggie dear, you have been promising me for absolutely ages to teach me chaturanga. Did you know"—she addressed the rest of the group—"that chaturanga was the first version of chess? The Indians have been playing it now for about four thousand years. Instead of the usual pieces, elephants, chariots, horses, and foot soldiers make up the game. I picked up the most stunning set in carved onyx and ivory weeks ago in the Chitpore market."

"How intriguing! Do you mind if we sit in on the lesson? Come on, Harry, it might be a charming alternative to Scrabble and backgammon."

"Of course you must join us, Fiona. The study is this way." Amanda left the room without a glance at her husband, who was still leering down the deep bosom of his singing partner.

"Are you coming, Elizabeth?" Fi asked from the doorway.

"I don't think so, dear. I'll mingle for a bit."

"Do retrieve us if you are ready to leave. An early night wouldn't do us any harm," Fiona called, then followed the others to the study.

Elizabeth sighed and crushed out her cigarette. She didn't at all feel like mingling. What she felt like was sitting close to Nigel with her head resting on his shoulder while they sipped cognac and listened to the wireless. When the cognac was finished they'd stand, stretch a little and then walk hand in hand to Nigel's bedroom. . . .

How delightful if life were so simple. Smiling and nodding, she made her way through the crowded drawing room and shadowy dining room to the muggy verandah. Making herself comfortable on a wide cushioned swing at one end, she adjusted the mosquito net and started a gentle to and fro motion.

Much as she desired to repeat a night in Nigel's bed, she knew she mustn't. She might already be pregnant, and the possibility existed that Nigel didn't wish to marry her. If that were the case and she did carry his child, she could always present herself in New Zealand as a widow or even a divorcée. Once so scandalous, divorcées were now quite fashionable. Living a lie would certainly cause her discomfort, but rearing a child without his father was insupportable. The sensations he aroused in her were very nearly irresistible, and glad as she was to have experienced them, she refused to engage in a tawdry affair—even with Nigel. Dared she call his office at this hour?

No! Elizabeth squared her shoulders. Absolutely not. She was not one of those clinging, whining women who confronted a man, begging or even demanding he make an honest woman of her. Raising her chin, she decided to remain the cool, confident, and modern woman and treat Nigel when she saw him with warmth. If he did not wish to marry her, she'd not make a nasty scene. But if he thought himself entitled to the freedom of her body, he had another think coming! Perhaps she should find another escort. No, as an adult she'd not let pique interfere. She'd see this thing through with Nigel first. If only Emily were still here. Emily Stanton was one of the most level-headed people one could hope to meet, and Elizabeth felt an instinctive need for counsel from such a wise friend.

It was peaceful out here, listening to the constant whir of cicadas and the soft buzz of conversation and laughter from the party. The night air was musky with the scents of tropical night-blooming flowers and a trace of pungent Indian spice. Occasionally the music hit a jarring note, but Elizabeth leaned back, enjoying the solitude for several minutes before she became aware of high-pitched giggles and low male chuckles just inside the house. She sat up, about to whisk the netting out of the way and make her presence known when the couple burst out the screen door in a fervent embrace.

Very little light escaped the bungalow, and the swing Elizabeth occupied was swathed in deep shadow. Slowly she sat back again. It seemed inappropriate at this juncture to announce herself, as it appeared to be her host intimately groping the woman he'd been leering at inside. She only hoped they didn't intend to continue their extracurricular activities on her swing. Instead of moving toward her, Simon Crosshaven pushed his partner against a pillar just a few feet from the screen door, yanked the lady's hem so that it was bunched around her waist, and fumbled with his fly.

Oh Lord, I really don't want to see this, Elizabeth thought, squeezing her eyes shut. A muffled scream had them flying open and she watched as the woman struggled with Crosshaven, pushing at his chest and tearing her mouth from his.

"Get off me, you bastard! Damn it!" Finally separating herself from him, the woman rearranged her clothing. "I don't mind a little fun, Simon, but for goodness sake, on your own verandah! A little bit of finesse certainly wouldn't go wide of the mark. I wasn't ready, you know. Or did you even care?"

Simon Crosshaven was panting heavily, fastening his fly. He looked up, an ugly sneer marring his features. "A whore is always ready. I've a mind to take you anyway."

"You really are a nasty bit of work, Simon. I pity your poor wife." The woman curled her lip in contempt. "She's welcome to you." Spinning on her heel, she made for the door, but Crosshaven seized her arm, flinging her against the same pillar and holding her there.

"Don't you ever walk away from me, you bitch. I'll decide when I'm done with you. When I snap my fingers, you come." He backhanded her across the face. "Do I make myself clear?" he demanded, stepping back.

His former flame whimpered, staring up at him in terror. Reaching up to touch the blood on her lip, she sobbed and ran blindly down the steps, disappearing around the corner of the house.

Crosshaven stood, gazing into the darkness of the garden, then fished in his pocket for his handkerchief. He wiped the bright red lip rouge off his mouth and, turning, reentered the bungalow.

Elizabeth took a great lungful of air, not realising she had held her breath. Well. No wonder Amanda seemed to prefer Captain Henderson's company to that of her husband. Deciding it was definitely time to leave, she climbed out of the mosquito netting. If Fi and Harry were still busy with chaturanga lessons, she would summon a taxi or call her father's butler to send her a driver.

Tossing the netting behind her, she stood on her toes and stretched to ease the cramped muscles after sitting in the same position so long. Suddenly she stopped, slowly lowering her arms to her side and backing against the wall of the bungalow.

She felt it again. As if someone were watching her. Twin spots on her shoulders tingled—like eyes boring right through her body. Surveying the 160-degree view of the garden gained nothing. Only a sliver of moon hung in the dark sky. Shadows flitted with the moving tree branches in the slight sultry breeze.

"Is anyone there?" she called. Silence. Did she really expect someone to pop out of the bushes, cheerfully saying, "Just me, getting a bit of exercise wandering around in the black of night and sharing my blood with the charming mosquitoes!"

Might it be an overactive imagination? Elizabeth wondered. After all, her life *had* been a bit of a bish in the last few months. Her mother dying, inheriting a fortune, and now she was in the middle of a love affair *and* a murder investigation. She really must take firm hold of herself with this nonsense.

Moving to the doorway, she froze and then whipped her head round. Cigarette smoke tickled her nostrils. And it came from the garden, not the bungalow. Grasping the balustrade, she leaned over it, attempting to locate the direction of the smoke. It was no use. One more try then.

"Hello? Do you mind lending me a fag? I'm all out, you see. Hello?" The cicadas continued their symphony. Elizabeth shivered. The breeze seemed to become abruptly cool. It was time to go. She hurried to the door, ignoring the tingle on the back of her neck.

"There you are, darling, I was just hunting for you," called Fiona from the drawing room when she saw Elizabeth enter the bungalow. "Harry thought up the most marvellous idea! He suggested attending the cinema tomorrow night. What do you think?"

Elizabeth breathed deeply in relief. Everything was so *normal* inside. Nothing at all sinister. "Brilliant, Fi. It's simply ages since we've indulged in a film. I'm fagged and ready for home."

Fiona yawned. "Another marvellous idea. Let's retrieve Harry from port tasting. I didn't realise it was such a science, but apparently Simon keeps one or two hard-to-find vintages. And as Simon is absent, it might be just as well if we remove Harry before he samples our host right out of his collection."

Chapter Twenty-one

"Really, Elizabeth, we should be heading to Hollywood instead of New Zealand," Fiona lamented dreamily.

Both girls, with Georgina and Harry, had just left the dark cinema auditorium after enjoying *Grand Hotel*—the new smashing success from America.

Elizabeth sighed as they entered the plush red-carpeted lobby. It was several days now since spending that glorious night with Nigel, and she missed him dreadfully. He had called twice on the telephone. The second call, however, was to cancel a date made on the previous call. After investing hours in interrogations with both Langley and Toppenham, it seemed many other details in this case were taking up his time. No news had been released. She was beginning to wonder—just a little—if he might be avoiding her. At least calm prevailed since that horrible day Beryl and Mrs. Newsome were found. Fixing a smile on her face, she listened to Fiona's fantasy.

"Just imagine living next door to Douglas Fairbanks and

meeting those luscious Barrymore brothers at a sparkling poolside party given by some important director or rising starlet. Who knows—we might be 'discovered' and followed everywhere by photographers eager to idolise and idealise us."

Elizabeth laughed, in spite of herself. "Steady on, old girl. It's all make-believe."

"The London reviews say *Grand Hotel* is the most glittering film ever made," Georgina remarked. "But you're right on the mark, Elizabeth, about the make-believe. It's widely rumoured Greta Garbo and Joan Crawford were constantly at each other's throats. So much so, it played havoc with their filming schedules." She grinned. "It must have been vastly amusing to have witnessed the shenanigans from the sidelines. Miss Crawford is said to have substituted glue for Miss Garbo's hair-setting gel, and in return Miss Garbo let loose several snakes in her rival's dressing trailer!"

"Having lived with them for a number of years, I can vouch for the high-spiritedness of the Yanks." Harry laughed. "Not a one of them knows the meaning of 'staid'! I say, that reminds me. We must watch for *Scar Face*! It's causing a roaring scandal in America. It's to do with a gangster named Capone who ruled Chicago with an army of machine gun–toting thugs. Powers that be don't care for Hollywood showing such an irreverence to law and order. Believe it or not, there is now some kind of commission to keep films wholesome."

"State-run filmmaking? Why, that almost smacks of communism," remarked Georgina.

"By no means, old girl. Nothing to do with the government, actually. This commission, I gather, keeps an eye out for, er, raciness, and too much violence. The filmmakers agree to abide by their ratings. So one knows by the mark given if it is suitable to take one's kiddies. One may appreciate the inconvenience of listening to them howl through all the great murder and mayhem scenes! Still," he went on thoughtfully, "it would be interesting to see what all the fuss is about in *Scar Face*." His eyes sparkled. "Imagine, a gang murder or a machine-gun battle on the streets of London!"

Fiona shot him a sharp look. "I'm sure we would just as soon not." Turning to Elizabeth she said in a resigned tone, "I concede, New Zealand it is. I shouldn't do as a blonde anyway." She patted her springy carrot curls.

"You are magnificent as you are. Wouldn't change, er, the tiniest detail," Harry said gallantly while eyeing her bosom. Fingering his upper lip, he added, "Suppose I could grow one of those thin, trendy Barrymore mustaches. I'd make a more dashing escort for my lady fair. Make her feel like a film star." He ended by waggling his brows more like Groucho Marx, making everyone giggle.

A cool evening breeze greeted them outside and, glancing up, Elizabeth noticed a halo embracing the nearly full moon, dulling it and the luster of the normally brilliant stars.

A sudden gust of wind set the fronds of the potted palms in the courtyard to clattering, and shivering she drew her gold silk shawl closer about her shoulders. Threading through the crowd, they gathered under the marquee, where Harry left to fetch his motor so he might collect them at the curb. Reaching into her bag for a cigarette to smoke while they waited for him, Elizabeth saw her gold lighter was missing. Frowning, she thought back to the last time she'd used it. During the film; she was sure of it. It must be under the seat she'd occupied.

"Rot! I've dropped my lighter in the auditorium. I won't be a minute."

"Why not ask an usher to go back for it?" Georgina suggested.

"I'll have found it by the time I've described it to him," Elizabeth called over her shoulder, already retracing her steps.

The lobby was empty now but for an usher sweeping pastry crumbs from the carpet. In the darkened auditorium, the heels of her shoes echoed hollowly in the eerie silence—so different now deserted of the audience that just minutes ago was laughing, snacking, and staring in rapt fascination at the silver screen. Heavy crimson velvet curtains were drawn snugly across it now, and shadows cast by the low footlights on the stage stretched long and narrow to touch the first several rows of chairs.

Was it the fifteenth row in which they had been seated? Or the sixteenth? No, it was the former, she was sure. The third chair in.

Slipping between the rows, she bent, skimming her hand on the dusty floor. Nothing. If only she'd thought to bring a torch. She was leaning over in the next row when she felt a cool blast of air. Looking over her shoulder, she saw the auditorium door remained closed. How strange. There it was again. Some instinct kept her eyes on the stage, and as she watched the heavy curtain rippled in the breeze. Of course, a worker had obviously opened a door back there and was fiddling about with something or other. Dismissing the thought and looking down, she spotted the gold glint of her lighter. Grasping it, her head snapped up in sudden alarm. If someone was working back there, where was his light? If no overhead light existed, surely she'd be able to see the arcing motions of a moving torch? Why was someone sneaking about in the dark?

Aware of her accelerating heart and quickening breaths, she clenched her lighter more tightly in her trembling fingers and straightened.

"Who's there?" Her voice, even to her own ears was hoarse. A stage floorboard creaked loudly in the silence, followed by a shuffling sound and a *whish* as the curtains parted slightly in the corner.

As if in a dream—where the faster one wishes to move,

the more slowly one actually does—she made her way to the end of the row. She was closer to the door than whoever occupied the stage. There was no reason to think she wouldn't reach it first. A peculiar impulse drove her to look over her shoulder as she reached the aisle. Even before glimpsing the shadow lurking in the corner of the stage she felt its evil. She sensed it as a tangible thing, hanging heavy in the air, overwhelming, permeating the furnishings, the very walls.

Fear and revulsion mesmerised her, freezing her for a seeming eternity before the silhouette moved deeper into the darkness. Suddenly utter blackness fell as the dim illumination of the footlights was extinguished. Needing no other prod, Elizabeth sprinted up the dark aisle. The thump of a man jumping from the stage to the auditorium floor added even more speed to her stride.

On her third frantic push she found the door and burst into the lobby. She didn't slow as she raced single-mindedly for the outer doors. Outside she ran straight into Nigel's arms.

"Oh, Nigel!" She found she was trembling violently. Stealing a frantic glance behind her at the cinema entrance, she saw nothing except curious looks from the other film patrons. Drawing deep breaths, she finally managed to stammer, "Nigel, I-I think i-it was *him!* The murderer! In the-the auditorium—"

He frowned, searching her distraught features, then abruptly handed her to Harry. "Take care of her," he murmured before striding into the lobby.

Fiona rushed over, grasping her by the arms. "Oh God, Elizabeth, what's happened?"

When Elizabeth didn't answer and continued to shake, Fiona enfolded her friend in her arms, rocking to and fro. "Did some fiend attack you? My God, you were gone only moments. What are we coming to? Ssh, ssh, it will be fine. Nigel's here. He was on his way home when he spotted us waiting for Harry."

"Memsahib? Your shoe. It was found in the lobby." An Indian cinema employee proffered a black kid mule.

Straightening, Elizabeth extracted herself from Fiona's embrace. "Of course, thank you." Her voice was wobbly and distant. She didn't remember losing it. She slipped it back on her foot, noticing her stocking was twisted and a ladder was creeping up her ankle. Looking up, she found Georgina staring at her. Her face was white and strained.

"Please—can you tell us what occurred?" Reaching into her bag, she extracted a handkerchief and handed it to Elizabeth.

Elizabeth dabbed at her eyes, blew her nose, and haltingly told her story. She was just finishing when Nigel emerged from the cinema.

He shook his head, his face tight. "Nothing. Not a damned thing. Whoever it was is long gone."

"I did not imagine this, Nigel!" Elizabeth's voice rose shrilly.

His face softened and, reaching out, he gently smoothed back a blond wave. "I know you didn't, darling. We found footprints on the dusty stage floor and the door was wide open. The manager tells me no one ever goes back there. No reason to." His gaze was warm and intimate and comforted Elizabeth enormously.

Everyone noted Nigel's intense regard and an abrupt silence descended. Fiona and Harry discreetly looked away, but Georgina raised her eyebrows.

Well, why should the feelings she and Nigel shared remain a secret? There was nothing to be ashamed of. No one need know of the other night, however. That *would* cause a scandal.

"I have sent for patrols," Nigel continued. The whole area will be cordoned off as soon as the sepoys arrive. It will be closely guarded until dawn when we may take a proper look.

"Now, Elizabeth, I need to know exactly who or what you saw." He signalled a cinema employee who hovered in the background holding a small chair. Gratefully she sat down and, when she finished, Nigel squeezed her hand.

"Well done, darling. If it was the murdering bastard, you may have been the only person to have escaped him once he had a victim in his sights."

"If you are done, Lt. Colonel, I should like to take Elizabeth home," Fiona said quietly. Their group was quite alone now, aside from the soldiers standing guard. "She needs rest and quiet after this horrid episode."

Elizabeth tendered her friend a crooked smile. "You are right of course, dear, but I believe I shall skip your brandy toddy this time and settle instead for a nice warm bath."

Chapter Twenty-two

Elizabeth plucked a stray hair from her fashionably thin eyebrows, and sitting back in her dressing chair critically studied her face for any ill effects of last night's ordeal. No black smudges encircled her eyes. No paleness marred the healthy glow of her smooth skin to indicate the sleeplessness of a night spent thrashing and sweating in her bed, reliving the terror of a narrow escape from the grasp of a psychopathic butcher.

And it *had* been him, she had decided. No, she *knew* it. She couldn't explain how, but they had experienced some kind of silent communication between them. Her skin prickled as goose bumps spread, and she shivered. But not with cold. No, it was far too hot for that.

It had been late afternoon when everybody, it seemed, retired to their bedrooms enervated by the heat. Overhead the electric punkas whirred, only sluggishly stirring the sweltering, muggy air. Outside the sun beat mercilessly down on the cracked earth and parched plant life. Even with closed window slats there was no escaping the sultry rays squeezing through, sending narrow dusty beams of gold stretching across her quiet bedroom. A bluebottle buzzed listlessly on the corner of the dressing table and she swiped at it, but missed as it flew out of sight.

Sighing in fatigue, Elizabeth rested her elbows on the dressing table and, cradling her head in her hands, closed her eyes. Immediately she saw the silhouette on the shadowy stage. How did the fiend know anyone had returned to the deserted auditorium? A guess? Perhaps he lay in wait every night. If so, it must not be a successful venture for him. Did he hear her mention she was going back for her lighter? And if so, was it her in particular he was after, or would anybody do? If he wanted *her*, then for goodness sake *why?* Damn it, who was it? And did it have anything to do with the eerie, watched feeling she'd experienced recently?

No! The idea was pure nonsense. It had to be. That spooky feeling was just her overactive imagination. It was merely the strain of this whole ridiculous situation.

Nigel had taken the night's incident seriously, unlike some men who might put it down to female vapours, and escorted her home. Over a sherry he had informed both her and Fiona that he was, indeed, making progress in his hunt for the killer, and made known to them what developments he was at liberty to discuss. But he had not been happy to learn they knew about the latest information concerning Captain Langley.

"I have spoken to Captain Henderson about the small matter of confidentiality when he spoke so freely of Toppenham's scarper. I was not at all ready to release that bit about Langley being roughed up," Nigel had said, leaning back in her father's leather wing chair. "Insisted he'd cut himself shaving and run into a door in the middle of the night because he couldn't see where the devil he was going. Bal-locks. Clearly, he escaped for a few hours. The question is, where did he go and why did he return?"

"He *is* a frightfully cheeky fellow. Perhaps he thinks he may brazen out of almost anything," Fiona had commented.

"He may not be quite so full of himself before long. In fact, he may start singing rather like a canary." Nigel gazed into his sherry with a pensive expression. Coming to a decision, he'd raised his head and said soberly, "A post mortem team is checking underneath Beryl's fingernails. They are looking for skin and blood. If Langley escaped, killed Beryl and scurried back to his bungalow thinking it a perfect alibi, he is severely mistaken."

"If your team does find skin and blood under Beryl's nails, will they know who it belongs to?" Elizabeth wanted to know.

"Not arbitrarily, no. However, if the blood type matches Langley's, it is very strong circumstantial evidence by itself. When the other evidence comes pouring in it should be an open-and-shut case." He leaned forward. "But don't forget we are still looking strongly at Toppenham. *He* didn't re-turn." Shrugging, he continued, "And then again, we may be way off track. It could be anybody. So don't forget not to go anywhere alone." He looked directly at Elizabeth. "Appar-ently even for just a moment to retrieve a cigarette lighter." Draining his sherry he stood, ready to take his leave.

"I've meant to ask, Nigel, how the Comptons are faring." Fiona caught him before he reached the door. "We heard the other day that they are accepting no sympathy calls. They seem to have shut themselves off from the world entirely."

Nigel frowned. "They are in seclusion. The Major and his wife do not even allow the doctor to examine Diana. They insist she has recovered physically and does not wish to see anyone. The Major intends to retire his commission and move his family back to England as soon as may be. The paperwork is on the Colonel's desk."

"How sad for them all." Fiona shook her head.

Elizabeth agreed. "I do wish we could do something for them. Perhaps before they leave, if they are ready to receive, we shall hit upon an idea. Which reminds me, has Mrs. Newsome regained consciousness yet?"

They were in the foyer now, heading for the door, and Nigel turned to gaze down at her. Was he thinking, as she was, that the last time they discussed this they were alone in his bungalow?

He shook his head. "I'm afraid not. The doctor sees no improvement, but cautions us that at this point it could go either way." He flicked a glance at Fiona. "Goodnight then, Fiona. Elizabeth may see me out."

Fiona's lips twitched, trying to hide her smile as she bade them goodnight and departed for her bedroom.

Nigel stared intently down at Elizabeth, filling the doorway with his broad shoulders. She caught a whiff of his patchouli cologne combined with his unique male smell, and she stepped closer to him.

"It's been too long and we need some time together, love." He reached for her, his eyes glinting in the low light leaking from the drawing room. "I've been awake now for over twenty-four hours and I could still spend hours making love to you. Hell, all night," he murmured, tipping his head.

"Lt. Colonel! You have an excellent reason for calling at this time of night, I presume?"

Elizabeth's father materialised behind them in his plaid dressing gown, his hair mussed with sleep, and whiskers beginning to stubble his chin. Even so, he stood straight and raised his eyebrows in an imperious manner.

Nigel raised his head at once, his eyes narrowed. "Good evening, Colonel."

Elizabeth whirled, confronting her father. "Yes, Father, he has excellent reason. I needed him in his official capacity this evening. I was nearly attacked in the auditorium after the film finished and everybody had left. As you see, I managed to escape. Narrowly. We believe it was the murderer."

The Colonel looked sharply from his daughter to Nigel, and approaching them barked, "Is this true?"

Nigel nodded. "Not definitely established, but we believe so, yes."

Colonel Mainwarring eyed his daughter thoroughly before speaking. "Indeed, I am relieved you are unharmed, my dear. As if anyone would dare hurt you." He gifted with her a brief peck on the chin in an uncharacteristic show of fatherly concern. "Now off to bed with you"—he gave her a gentle push—"while I speak with Covington-Singh in my study." Stepping away from her, he tightened the belt of his dressing gown and led Nigel down the hall. "Bloody *cheek* of the sodding bastard. Well, come on then and apprise me of the details."

Elizabeth had stayed awake listening for Nigel's departure, but all too soon, fatigue and nightmares overtook her.

Now, blinking, she sat up in her dressing chair once more and automatically reached for her favourite Max Factor lip rouge. She unscrewed the metal tube and applied the bright scarlet to her generous lips. Red. The colour of blood. Was she ever going to get that last picture of Beryl out of her mind? She shuddered and felt her stomach lurch.

Determined to blot out her unpleasant thoughts, she headed to her closet and searched her wardrobe for something cool to wear. She'd engaged in enough resting and contemplation, and anyway it was nearly the cocktail hour.

Loud voices and scuffling broke the muggy silence outside, but she paid scant attention. She was already thinking of Nigel and where they stood with each other. Surely her father couldn't be right about him? Only a princess would do?

The situation was becoming untenable for her, but he didn't seem too uncomfortable with it. She must find a way of meeting with him, to talk like civilised adults. Perhaps tonight.

Elizabeth was speculating between a navy and white polka dot Lanvin and a bright yellow embroidered Valentina chiffon when Fiona burst in without knocking.

"The Maharani of Kashmir is here—in the drawing room—to see *you*!" Fiona spoke in awed tones. Walking over to the window, she peered between the slats and waved Elizabeth over impatiently. "You must see her motorcar. I've never seen anything like it."

Elizabeth stuffed the two frocks she'd been studying in the closet and hurried to join her friend. The vehicle parked at the curb was indeed unusual. The fact that it was a Humber limousine ragtop itself was out of the ordinary, but it was decorated with garlands of multi-coloured roses, gardenias, and jasmine. And surrounded by eight turbaned guards in scarlet and gold livery.

"She arrived in great fanfare, as well. Didn't you hear the commotion?" Fiona dragged her gaze away from the impressive sight to study her friend.

Elizabeth frowned. "I suppose I did, but my thoughts were elsewhere."

Fiona's eyebrows rose to her hairline. "I'll say. But come, you must ready yourself. Goodness! You have royalty waiting on you!" She rushed to the closet, picking ruthlessly through Elizabeth's expensive wardrobe. Finally she dragged one ensemble free. "This is perfect." She held up the only Worth that Elizabeth owned, a deep rose silk suit shot through with silver thread. Although Worth's designs were, indeed, sumptuous, he tended toward conservatism, and Elizabeth prided herself in being a modern girl.

Fiona grinned. "You wore this when we called upon Lady Aberfoyle to solicit a donation to the orphans' fund."

"Yes. We left with a very generous check, indeed." Elizabeth began donning her stockings, but paused to give Fi a mischievous look. "I don't think she fancied being outdone by a mere oil heiress."

"Yes, well done, old thing." Fiona was rummaging through Elizabeth's jewel box. "Here they are. You must wear these pink pearl hair combs with the matching eardrops and bracelet."

"My, you *are* bossy this afternoon." Fastening her last button, Elizabeth reached for the pearls.

Fiona stood back and crossed her arms. "Well, someone must take charge. You didn't even hear the racket when the Maharani arrived!"

"Of course, dear." Elizabeth took a last glance in the mirror before heading for the door. "Come along then, and let's see what this is all about."

"She called for *you*," Fiona said in horrified tones. "Goodness, I'm not dressed for royalty."

"But you are taking charge, darling, remember!" Elizabeth eyed her friend's simple but elegant white sundress and slipped an arm through hers. "And don't be silly, your frock is charming."

Her Royal Highness, the Maharani of Kashmir, née Lady Vanessa Covington, sat comfortably on the leather settee in the drawing room. Her blue topaz and diamond jewelry was understated and matched her stylish turquoise afternoon suit ideally. Lustrous dark blond tresses streaked with the occasional white hair were drawn into a sleek French twist. Only a few character lines marred her smooth, almost youthful skin. Her startlingly blue eyes sparkled and her mouth widened in a welcoming smile as Elizabeth and Fiona crossed the threshold.

"Ah, Elizabeth, here you are at last." Colonel Mainwarring stood, setting a nearly empty aperitif glass on a side table. He performed introductions and the girls curtsied deeply.

The Maharani inclined her head. "Thank you for entertaining me, Colonel. I shan't take up any more of your time."

He looked startled, but recovered quickly and took his leave, bowing over her hand and shutting the door behind him.

"It's a pleasure to make your acquaintance at last, Miss Mainwarring. You have made quite a stir in this little community, I hear," the Maharani said when the girls had seated themselves on the settee adjacent to hers. "Miss McKay, I wonder—are you a relation perhaps of Lord Reay?"

Blushing, Fiona admitted that indeed she was. "But he was my father's third cousin, Your Royal Highness, and I'm afraid he wouldn't know me if he fell over me."

"Nonsense, I'm sure. Now may I offer you some of my favourite Cinzano?"

At their nod, the Maharani lifted her hand, gesturing to a turbaned and smartly liveried servant. He came forward at once, carefully setting a large teak box, inlaid with ivory and shell, on the low table between them. Lifting the high arched lid, he withdrew one of six cut-glass decanters and detached two small stemmed glasses from inside the top of the box. He served the sweet vermouth with ceremony and retreated to the window in the corner.

"One of the benefits of royalty, my dears. One may bring one's luxuries and not be thought in the least odd. I admit I am used to doing just as I like." She sipped her Cinzano and leaned forward with a conspiratorial air. "Now then, Miss Mainwarring, I understand that we both prefer flying to depending on rail travel in India. Except that I have not yet plucked up sufficient courage to actually pilot the contraptions. But my pilot"—her eyes twinkled—"was far less daring than you. He insisted upon taking the longer route, landing some miles from here at the airfield. Being new to this type of transport, I'm not yet up to barnstorming, but when I feel so intrepid I shall make a point of engaging a woman as my pilot!"

Laughing, Elizabeth replied, "Undoubtedly, ma'am, your aeroplane is in far better shape than mine. I am informed mine will do far better on the rubbish heap than in the sky. After our shaky landing on the parade ground I don't feel adventuresome enough to test the theory."

The Maharani smiled warmly, and afterward came twenty minutes of polite conversation discussing Kashmir as the holiday destination on the sub-continent of India, with its house-boating on Lake Dal in the summer and faultless skiing conditions in the nearby mountains in the winter.

Elizabeth told her visitor with some excitement her plans for taking an active hand in managing both her oil fields and sheep station. The easy conversation ended soberly with comments on current affairs.

"The world is changing, and not all for the better," the Maharani remarked seriously. "Indians fighting each other because of the jealousies between Hindu and Muhammadan. Tensions between Indians and British over home rule, worldwide bank failures, the rise of communism and fascism. And now, of course, these horrible murders right here in Calcutta." Standing, she signalled her servant to gather the box and glasses. "But if we dwelt too heavily on all the doom and gloom of the world we should be very sad creatures, indeed. Now I shall leave you to your supper and evening's entertainment."

She turned back upon reaching the door. "Oh, I almost forgot. The Commissioner is organising a tiger hunt in my honour this Friday. I should be very pleased if you would attend as my guests. You will find it very entertaining, I'm sure. Have you ever ridden atop an elephant? No? Well, it's not nearly so dangerous as flying!"

"We shall look forward to it, ma'am," Elizabeth said.

"Well!" Fiona threw herself onto the settee after watching their guest drive off in her fancy motorcar.

"Indeed!" Elizabeth departed the window and joined her friend on the opposite settee. "What do you suppose brought her here to Calcutta? Is she merely visiting her son, or is it some kind of state occasion, I wonder?"

Fiona studied her friend slyly. "Perhaps she is curious about the object of her son's affection."

Elizabeth looked up, stunned. "Don't be ridiculous, Fiona! As if he informs his parents of any girl in which he may be the least interested. No, come to think of it, it probably has more to do with the scandal of Nigel's brief arrest for Beryl's murder. Did you notice how cool the Maharani was to my father? His parents may be showing the flag, so to speak, but holding the formality of the Maharaja in reserve just yet."

"If that were the sole reason, why then did she call here and specifically ask for you?" Fiona asked smugly.

Elizabeth opened her mouth to retort, but abruptly closed it and blushed. "Perhaps she is merely making the social rounds. Isn't the oil heiress daughter of the regiment's Colonel rather an oddity?" She canted her head to one side. "I didn't know you were related to Lord Reay," she said, changing the subject.

Fiona wrinkled her nose. "Technically, but the connection is so thin it's hardly worth mentioning."

"Still . . ." Elizabeth's tone was wistful. "You may claim a connection to nobility. For all my six million pounds, that is something I cannot do."

Fiona frowned, concerned. Elizabeth never before had been disturbed by the lack of titles in her family tree. So why now?

A moment later realisation dawned, and Fiona stared dumbfounded at her friend. "I don't believe it! I can't believe it. You of all people!"

Elizabeth, startled at her friend's vehemence, shrugged defensively. "I'm afraid you will have to. It's just not there in my family tree. I'm a millionairess, not a magician."

Fiona laughed. "That is not what I mean, you idiot! You are actually afraid you're not good enough for Nigel! The-prince-and-the-commoner rubbish. Now who is being ridiculous? As if he would care, if he loved you."

Spot on. If. Elizabeth nearly flinched at this stinging reminder. Acting the lovelorn maiden suited her not at all. These doubts were exceedingly uncomfortable, and she found she was not yet ready to speak of them—even to Fiona. Her mind racing for some plausible explanation to put Fi off the sensitive subject, she reached for one of her Dunhills and lit it with a wooden match from a box on the table in front of her. She shook out the flame and answered her friend in an indulgent tone.

"A certain fondness has sprung up between Nigel and myself, I will admit, but get a hold of yourself, old girl. Who mentioned love? I do not have to be 'good enough' for anybody, thank you very much. I was just contemplating the romance of tracing one's ancestry to a title of some kind. After all"—she allowed herself a small smile—"titled gentlemen were the movers and shakers in history. Imagine the thrill of knowing one is related to a historical figure."

"Rubbish! But if that's the way you prefer it, I shan't argue. For now." Fiona shot Elizabeth a pointed look, then relented, changing the subject. Thank goodness the situation between her and Harry was far simpler. He was coming to dinner tonight with the Crosshavens. A thrill of anticipation ran through her. "What do you say to dining on the verandah tonight? It seems to be cooling off sufficiently and we may enjoy a spectacular view of the setting sun."

Chapter Twenty-three

Elizabeth watched the blaze of brilliant orange light inch reluctantly into the western horizon. With it went the hot, arid air, and now a cool breeze rippled across her supper guests on the verandah. Loosely clad, turbaned boys left their posts at the ropes of manual punkas as the servants cleared the table and set out the cheese and port.

Simon Crosshaven leaned back in his cushioned cane chair sipping his wine. "I say, fine meal and company," he complimented Elizabeth. "Could almost believe we are living in normal times. It's a shame you and Miss McKay are not witnessing India at her best."

"Bosh." Amanda cut a crumbly slice of Stilton, sliding it onto a cracker. "It's always something in India. Flood, drought, disease, tensions between one faction or another. *That* is normal life in our little home away from home."

"Strange, you don't sound content in your life here, my love. I thought you found enough to keep yourself amused," Simon remarked snidely.

Amanda flushed. "I meant nothing of the sort. Merely, I've yet to experience any tranquility of life in this country. However"—ever so casually, she brushed her short dark hair behind her ears, revealing ruby-and-pearl studs perfectly matching her red and white chiffon dress—"I do find some of the local customs intriguing."

An expression of doubt crossed her husband's features. "I was under the impression that only Indians or women of low moral fibre defiled their bodies in such a manner."

Fiona's eyes lit in admiration. "I say, how daring of you, Amanda! I think it's quite appealing, don't you, Elizabeth?"

"Indeed! I must confess, I've thought about having it done myself. One sees the most stunning creations hanging from the ears of Indian women every day. I'm sure you can relax, Simon, it is only fashion changing yet again. After all, Queen Victoria herself sported pierced ears! How did this business get started anyway, that only fast women pierced their ears?"

"Hrrumph. Next you will all be wanting to pierce your noses or mark your skin with those whorish henna designs like the Indian women, as well." He grumbled, burying his nose in his port glass.

"The world is ever changing." Harry helped himself to more wine from the cut-crystal decanter and grinned, "Just a few years ago we were all gasping in shock at the rising hemlines; a few years before that, at horseless carriages and flying machines. Look at us now."

"Quite." Colonel Mainwarring fished his tobacco out of his trouser pocket and proceeded to fill his pipe. "We even countenance women drivers and aeroplane pilots. Sometimes, I believe, we can be too forward-thinking for our own good."

There was laughter in Elizabeth's voice as she leaned over to light her father's pipe with her gold lighter. "Why, Father, your sense of humour shows itself at last! You must delight us with it more often."

He only eyed her balefully through the curling wisps of smoke, declining to comment.

Amanda looked at her host with uncertainty, not all sure a row wasn't in the offing, and hurried to step into the breach. "Please, Elizabeth, you must enlighten us about the Maharani's visit this afternoon. You only mentioned she called. I'm dying to know the details."

Shrugging, Elizabeth said, "I admit to curiosity myself. I have no idea why she should bother calling on me, but nothing of import was discussed, except her invitation to join her on the tiger hunt on Friday."

Simon stroked his chin and looked at her thoughtfully. "It was her only social call since arriving this morning. Something was meant by it. The Maharani has lived among the Indians too long to do anything without a specific reason." He glanced at the Colonel. "The rumours regarding her arrival—"

Colonel Mainwarring slammed his pipe into the ashtray at his elbow. "I think we all have an inkling why she's chosen this particular time to visit, Crosshaven. Because I bloody well bollixed up. Because I stupidly let personal issues interfere in a murder enquiry. Never mind I believed I was correct at the time." His hands tightened into fists on the table as he struggled to bring himself under control. Finally, his face set in hard lines, he continued in a more subdued voice, but there was an emotional edge to it.

"I'm washed up, you know. I'm to retire by the end of the year. I'm an embarrassment to His Majesty's government in India." His movements weary, he pushed himself away from the table. "You won't mind if I excuse myself early."

"Well," Amanda said, in a falsely bright voice when the screen door closed behind her host, "I'm sure the Colonel will feel more himself after a decent night's sleep. It really doesn't matter why the Maharani is here, after all. What we need is some gaiety this evening. Why don't we toddle over to the club. The Secretary is hosting a Monte Carlo night to raise funds for starving children." She shrugged her shoulder in unconcern. "Or stock market widows, or whatever the current good cause is."

"God forbid you would gamble away my money in a questionable cause," her husband observed dryly.

"Oh shut up, Simon. You needn't come if you insist on one of your sour moods." Amanda turned to her hostess. "It will be great fun, and since it isn't formal we may go just as we are."

Elizabeth had changed her afternoon suit to a clinging gold silk gown, caught at one shoulder and with a string of gold set emeralds streaming down her back. Fiona was slightly more casual and daring in a bold geometric art-deco patterned dinner frock. She swore it was the latest from Milan, but Elizabeth couldn't help wondering why Fiona either possessed exquisite taste in her clothing selections or roared off on peculiar tangents, bent on curdling one's digestion.

"Capital idea. Nothing soothes the psyche like spending lots and lots of money—especially in a good cause." Elizabeth stood. "Let us away to the games."

Green baize–topped tables replaced the usual furniture in the ballroom at the Mohd Bagh Club that evening. Turbaned croupiers spoke in subdued tones as they pushed and pulled chips in the appropriate directions. The roulette wheel spun, and the dice rolled. Doleful cries of disappointment from losers mingled with the smug laughter of the winners.

One card table was particularly lively, surrounded by people two and three deep. In the midst of this crowd sat the Maharani of Kashmir, dressed in a luxurious black beaded evening gown. She looked up from her cards, laughing.

"You must play next, Commissioner. This game is far more entertaining than whist. One has merely to count to twenty-one and poof! One either wins or loses."

Sir Clive Harrington licked his lips nervously. A small man of middle years whose shyness was often mistaken for snobbishness, he was desperately wishing for the solitude of his study and his prized butterfly collection. But he had strict orders from the Viceroy to keep the Maharani happy. The Maharaja was in a smouldering temper over the insult dealt his son, and he was making things distinctly difficult for the British in Kashmir.

"Perhaps the Lady Amarita should play instead, Your Highness. She seems quite eager to try the game." With ceremony, he pulled out a chair vacated by a young officer.

Lady Amarita had travelled with the Maharani from Kashmir. The widow in her early twenties had borne her husband no children and been given back to her father's care. He was a Kashmiri nobleman who desired an alliance with the Maharaja and offered his daughter as wife to the third son. As a widow with no children she was not important enough for the two elder sons, despite her nobility and wealth.

She was dressed in the Western fashion in a crimson satin gown, her long black hair sleeked up in a classic chignon. Kohl outlined her eyes, and gold bangles clasped her wrists and hung from her ears.

Glancing at Nigel standing beside his mother, she asked with a flirtatious curve of her lips, "Perhaps Your Highness would stand here to help me count my cards?"

"Please remember, Amarita, I am not a prince in Calcutta." He moved to stand at her back and did not see her frown.

Amarita was determined to achieve the status of princess— and to reign as one wherever she happened to be. But first she must marry a prince. Hardly a strenuous task, she thought, looking up at Nigel. After all, she knew how to please a man. Her first husband had seen that thoroughly and energetically.

"Well, well, a prince of the blood *and* a millionairess. We certainly have landed in the crème de la crème of society, haven't we, Mummy?"

Elizabeth's view of Nigel abruptly was cut off by Celia Armstrong and a portly, greying woman in a tight dark red gown. Celia herself wore a black gown and an old-fashioned headband with a feather. She struck a dramatic pose as if she were the first glare of fashion and puffed on a cigarette fastened in a long black holder.

Elizabeth switched her attention to the two women before her and resisted the urge to look beyond. There Nigel was bending over a stunning woman of apparent Indian nobility, who smiled enticingly up at him while his mother beamed. Whoever she was, Nigel's mother's approval was palpable. Just as palpable as her disapproval of Elizabeth's father. Nigel had said they must talk. Her heart raced in trepidation. Was he promised to another after all? She almost jumped when Celia spoke again.

"I didn't realise natives were allowed to mingle at one of our clubs," the girl said with a moue of disgust.

"To gain membership one must be put up by five members, Miss Armstrong." The censure in Harry's voice was clear. "I'm afraid only men are accepted as members. The ladies, however, are welcome guests."

"I suppose if the members do not mind, I shall have to accustom myself accordingly," Celia allowed, her tone grudging. "It does seem strange, though. Oh—there you are, Johnny! Over here!" She slipped her hand immediately through his arm upon his arrival, lest he get away. "You promised to teach Mummy and me that silly dice game. People seemed to be winning scads of money, but I didn't understand one bit of it."

Lieutenant Fairfield nodded to the rest of the company and signalled a waiter carrying a tray of brimming champagne flutes. "A stop at the well first, Celia. I'm parched."

"Champers, how delightful," declared Georgina, joining them, and reaching for a glass. "Just the thing after snacking on those exquisite petit-fours in the other room. And do you know"—she favoured Celia with a look of wide-eyed innocence—"my frock still fits me. Plenty of give, in fact. How sad that some increase by eating so much as a piece of lettuce. Fortunately, I've always been able to eat what I like and not worry about such mundane things as growing out of my clothing." A beatific smile on her face, she sipped her champagne.

Celia coloured violently, and her eyes shot daggers, but it was her mother who replied in a haughty tone. "How fortunate indeed for you, Miss Smythe. However, such may not always be the case." Her eyes flicked grimly over Georgina's trim figure. "Now then, John, the dice if you please—and then you may escort me back to your mother's bungalow."

Lieutenant Fairfield rolled his eyes as he set his glass on a nearby table. "Of course, dear Mrs. Armstrong. You will find it quite easy, I assure you."

"That young man may just foil the dragons' plans yet." Georgina's eyes twinkled, following the small party to the dice table across the room.

Harry smiled. "If Johnny possesses an ounce of sense, he will arrange an extended manoeuvre in the thick of the jungle lasting until the middle of the monsoon. It's doubtful those delicate creatures could last through what I hear is not just worse than the forty days and nights of biblical fame, but chock full of plague and pestilence as well. I'll give them ten days before they are scurrying for the first ship for

Europe. Now then, I fancy a Ramos Fizz. Come on Fiona, let's see if that chap making busy behind the bar can make one." He rubbed his hands together in anticipation.

"Is that one of your fancy American cocktails?" Fiona asked dubiously. "They tend to be either so cloudy or so colourful one never knows quite just what is in them. I believe I'll stay with something more straightforward, thank you."

"And miss out on the same delectable recipe served and enjoyed in one of those daringly forbidden American speakeasies?" He waggled his brows at her.

Fiona laughed. "Put so drolly, who could refuse. Lead on, Odysseus."

Harry bowed. "Although there might be a king or two in the family tree, we don't acknowledge them, my dear. No claim to royalty, I'm afraid."

"I only referred to an adventurer who travelled the world, you silly man. We'll leave royalty for others to sort out." She flung Elizabeth a sideways glance before following Captain Woodford to the lounge.

"You may be leaving Fiona behind when you depart for New Zealand, you know," Georgina commented.

Glancing at her friend's departing figure, Elizabeth agreed. "Yes, it did occur to me. I shall miss Fi, of course, but wish for her happiness. I do believe Harry is almost worthy of her."

Georgina's gaze slipped behind Elizabeth. "The next matter to speculate on—will *you* be leaving for New Zealand?"

"What's this, double Dutch?"

Georgina swirled the champagne in her glass and watched the bubbles pop to the surface. "Well," she drawled, "perhaps you should be aware of some of the talk. It concerns you and the new Lt. Colonel."

"Go on," Elizabeth said, her voice sharp.

"Oh, Elizabeth, I've mucked it up. I didn't mean to offend

you. I just thought you might shore up sufficient ammunition, because one of those snide biddies is bound to ambush you sooner or later."

Elizabeth gave her a tight smile. "No, you are right, of course. What are the gossips up to now?"

"They're only jealous, you know. You are young, beautiful, wealthy, and independent, so of course you must be maligned. The gist is that you are gratifying both yourself and the Lt. Colonel in," Georgina's voice lowered, "a *sexual affair*! Isn't it ridiculous? I suppose it started because you verified his whereabouts at the time of Beryl's murder. It's far more interesting to imagine naughtiness than a rescue from a wild and dangerous animal. Why, even your father questioned your time alone with Nigel. Anyway, it's doubly scandalous because Nigel is half Indian—the ultimate sin. You must merely ignore the innuendos."

Elizabeth felt heat creep into her cheeks and heard a buzzing in her ears. Draining her glass, she reached for another from a passing waiter, listening as Georgina continued blithely.

"Now of course, they are saying you are being thrown over in favour of the daughter of some Kashmiri lord, and that the Maharani visited you today to warn you off her son. She brought the dark beauty down especially to make her son's acquaintance, and to impress upon him the importance of the marriage for the sake of strengthening Kashmiri alliances."

"How very interesting." Elizabeth set her fresh glass down deliberately, a militant gleam in her eye. Had Nigel been aware of his father's plans when he made love to her? Or had his mother dumped his duty in his lap and said, *Surprise, dear!* Just what were the Maharani and her son up to?

"Why don't we crush these rumours out of all recognition by wishing the royal couple happy." She headed toward the Maharani's table. "Come on, Georgina, I'll introduce you to Her Royal Highness."

"I say, bravo, bravo, Lady Amarita," Sir Clive was exclaiming as they reached the table.

Lady Amarita clapped her hands in excitement and drew in several chips. "I am only successful because of my lord's instructions." Her voice was prim, but the eyes caressing Nigel were not.

"I cannot take credit for your mathematical abilities, Amarita. And I am *not* a lord. If you cannot bring yourself to call me by my given name, then Lt. Colonel will do." Nigel took her cards and tossed them to the dealer.

"Miss Mainwarring, what a surprise! Are you a gambler, my dear?" the Maharani asked, tossing in her own cards. "Of course you are, or you wouldn't have dropped in tonight. Try your luck at Pontoon. Here, take my chair—I'm afraid my luck has run out."

Nigel's head whipped around, and he sent Elizabeth a frankly admiring look, taking in her clinging gold gown. She ignored him and curtsied to his mother, introducing Georgina.

"Thank you indeed for the offer, ma'am, but roulette is more my style. Pure chance." She shot Nigel an acerbic look. "And no silly rules to forget."

Lady Amarita regarded Elizabeth narrowly. "Chance—and considerable sums of money. One can only pity your future husband, Miss Mainwarring, if you plan also to spend his funds with such abandon." She flicked a sultry glance at Nigel. "I would never dream of inconveniencing my husband so."

"Capital, fortunately, is something my future husband shall not be worried about," Elizabeth answered dryly, glancing conspicuously about the ballroom. "Is your husband here tonight? I am sure he will be thrilled at your winnings."

Amarita flushed and placed a proprietary hand on Nigel's sleeve. "I am currently a widow. However, I don't expect to remain one forever. I am young and of noble blood. My father believes he has found me a suitable mate."

"How fortunate for you both. I certainly wish you happy." Elizabeth's eyes clashed with Nigel's, and the smile froze on her lips.

"Yes, well, nothing is certain yet." The Maharani rose from her chair, waving a hand-painted silk fan in a desultory fashion. "Gaming is thirsty business. Why don't you accompany me to the lounge, Amarita, where we may refresh ourselves with something exotic and cool."

Amarita appeared reluctant, but nodded and followed the Maharani. Their entourage of army officers and civils were not far behind, leaving Nigel and the dealer at the gaming table.

Elizabeth snatched a cigarette from her evening bag and fitted it into a holder. A flame appeared immediately. She grasped Nigel's wrist, holding the blaze steady. She noted his hooded eyes as he flicked out the match.

"I understand congratulations are in order for your upcoming nuptials. I'm sure you will both be very happy." Elizabeth couldn't help the biting tone in her voice.

"Your secret is out, Nigel. Everyone is agog with the news tonight. Any announcement is sure to be anticlimactic," Georgina put in brightly, oblivious to the flowing undercurrents.

Nigel tossed the used match carelessly into an ashtray on the green baize. "I doubt Calcutta is privy to any of my secrets, but I can assure you *that*"—he jerked his head in the direction of the lounge—"is not one of them. Politics must be played at periodically, but not necessarily given into," he added enigmatically.

"If you are not keen on acknowledging the event yet, I shall say no more." Georgina sighed and took the last sip from her glass. "It *is* such a romantic story. Indian girl meets her prince."

Nigel shot her a lopsided smile. "Sounds like you've kissed a frog or two, Georgina."

The woman twirled her empty glass between her fingers and shrugged. "One is taught never to judge a book by its cover, so how else is one to discover whether green slimy scales ooze under a perfectly respectable facade, or the man of one's expectations? Now"—she fixed her gaze on a handsome young officer at the roulette table—"I will feast on stale, bromidic tea towels if *that* is a frog in disguise. If you two will excuse me, my handkerchief is about to fall. I should like to be passing the roulette wheel when that happens."

Elizabeth waited until Georgina was out of earshot before smiling coolly at Nigel. "You are a busy chap. Romancing heiresses, noble ladies, and solving a string of nasty murders. One almost hesitates to ask what's next. But I never was a shrinking violet. Care to enlighten me?" Only her flushed cheeks hinted at her temper.

Nigel rubbed a weary hand over his face. "Christ, what a tangle. One thing you must learn about India: Nothing is as it seems. Indians thrive on intrigue. I was brought up understanding both worlds, which only makes balancing the two more burdensome and very complex to explain."

"I hear your mother has caught on nicely. She paid me an afternoon call today. Apparently the only one since her arrival." Elizabeth's eyes sparked as she reached for the ashtray on the gaming table, pulling it closer to crush out her cigarette. Nigel's warm hand covered the back of hers, stilling its violent stabbing motions. She stared down at their hands, feeling her heart skitter at his touch, and then up at him. That did it. Her armour came crashing down under his warm, tender gaze, leaving her feeling naked and vulnerable.

Blast him.

"I must speak with you." He lowered his voice. "You will agree this isn't the place for uninterrupted conversation. I don't wish to cause gossip or comment, which is rampant at the moment." He smiled briefly. "Meet me in ten minutes just outside the garden door. There is a gazebo outside, secluded enough for privacy." And turning his back, he was gone, threading his way through the throng of gamblers.

Chapter Twenty-four

Elizabeth made a short stop at the roulette wheel, won a modest sum and donated it to the club secretary's charity fund. Making her way to the garden door, she was intercepted by Mrs. Wight.

"There you are, my dear! I heard about your ordeal the other night at the cinema. Dreadful, my dear, dreadful!" She took Elizabeth's hand in hers, bussed her cheek and held her at arm's length. "We mustn't be too careful. You must acquire a bodyguard immediately, if you haven't already. Mine is just there, you see?" She indicated a sepoy standing several feet behind her. "Your father will see to it. By the way, is he in attendance tonight?" Her cheeks coloured becomingly. "He has been working far too assiduously. He needs to get out more. It will do him a world of good. Especially just now."

"No, Mrs. Wight, I'm afraid he wasn't feeling quite the thing and has retired early." Elizabeth caught a glimpse of Nigel slipping through the garden door and was about to take her leave when they were joined by a slender uniformed man with sandy hair greying at the temples. His face, chapped and reddened from a life spent in a harsh climate, cracked into a welcoming grin. With him was a petite woman near his own age. Her golden brown hair was cut short in a shining cap, and she wore an aqua gown several years out of date.

"Derek, Alice, are you returned so early then?" Mrs. Wight positively gushed to the newcomers. "How was Lake Dal? Divine, I'm sure. You must meet the Colonel's daughter. Lt. Colonel Porter and his wife, Mrs. Porter, Miss Elizabeth Mainwarring."

"Enchanted, my dear." Lt. Colonel Porter bowed over Elizabeth's hand in a courtly manner. "You won't remember us, of course, but we made your acquaintance a time or two when you were just a mite in pigtails before you left for school in England. Grown up quite nicely, you have. Image of your mother, to be sure—isn't that so, darling?" He spoke to his wife.

"Indeed so," she said warmly. "She was quite the local beauty. Did she ever recover from the malaria that plagued her so?"

"Oh, I am sorry," Mrs. Porter replied when Elizabeth informed her of the sad news. "We did think of the two of you often over the years." To Mrs. Wight, she said, "Kashmir was indeed delightful, Marjorie, but it was strongly suggested we cut our furlough short in light of recent events. The girls blossomed and didn't wish to leave. Kate and Tess, our daughters," she added for Elizabeth's benefit. "Tess was especially annoyed as she had found a beau." She shrugged with sang-froid. "Try explaining to nineteen- and twenty-year-old girls that love is like a train: There's always another one rattling down the track."

"Ah, but not with the reliable punctuality found in Europe, my darling," remarked Lt. Colonel Porter. "If another train has not arrived in a week or so, perhaps we may invite the young man for a short stay."

"If it will keep Tess indoors, by all means. Thank goodness they are safe at home tonight, otherwise I wouldn't want them a foot out of sight until this wretched murder business is solved. Derek, darling, do find us some champers, will you? Oh, here's a waiter now." She helped herself to a crystal flute from the serving tray and sighed in deep satisfaction after a hefty sip. "Absolutely nothing like champagne, Miss Mainwarring."

"No, indeed. If you will ex—," Elizabeth began.

"Why, it's Bruce!" Mrs. Porter interrupted. "Bruce!" She waved her free hand. "Do come here, you recluse of a man."

A slight-statured officer nodded to Mrs. Porter as he pushed back his chair at a nearby card table. Draining his glass, he stood and pocketed his winnings.

Elizabeth watched him approach and became aware of Mrs. Wight's stiffening posture and Lt. Colonel Porter's effort to maintain expressionless features. Mrs. Porter alone seemed glad to see him and introduced him as Lt. Colonel Melyn.

Melyn was pale for such a tropical climate. His wheat-hued hair was slicked back and provided a marked contrast to his black eyebrows and a full, almost girlish fan of black lashes above colourless eyes. He exchanged only a minimum of courtesies before bowing woodenly and excusing himself. The Porters followed suit, Mrs. Porter opining as she trailed her husband, that "Bruce should really come more often out into society."

Mrs. Wight grimaced in revulsion, watching Lt. Colonel Melyn head for the lounge.

"That man is an offense to the regiment if you should ask me. A more immoral, perverted deviant I never hope to meet. Poor Alice has no idea, and one so hates to disillusion her. Most everyone knows." In answer to Elizabeth's blank expression, she said with some asperity, "He's a pouf! A . . . a . . . well, he is overly fond of men, if you know my meaning, Miss Mainwarring. I shouldn't be at all surprised to find *he* is responsible for these ghastly murders. He and a native in cahoots, most likely. One hears the most frightful stories concerning his private indulgences. Even"—she leaned toward Elizabeth—"violence." She shuddered and glanced at the reassuring presence of her bodyguard.

Elizabeth frowned, remembering Nigel's reference to Melyn as an odd duck. He hadn't seemed concerned that this man might be a suspect. Not wishing to delay her trek to the gazebo any longer, she bade Mrs. Wight goodnight.

"Miss Mainwarring!" the woman called before Elizabeth took two steps. "Just a word, dear." Her eyes darting about the room to be sure no one was in earshot, she continued in a considerably lower voice. "Rumours abound in such small communities as ours, my dear. I feel I should warn you, as I should hate to see you take a wrong step.

"The races are best left to their own. We are all much happier that way—Indians and whites stay to their own societies. Of course," she went on, not noticing Elizabeth's darkening expression, "there are exceptions at the highest levels, as you may be aware, but it doesn't do at all if there is no inherited title involved." She fixed Elizabeth with a pointed look. "And there isn't in this case, my dear. Although peccadilloes are eventually forgiven, outright disregard for the conventions is not. I am afraid he is not for you, Miss Mainwarring. Just think of poor Diana Compton. She is ruined for life and not a bit of it is her fault. The scandal would cripple your father and—"

"Mrs. Wight." Elizabeth's voice was clipped, her eyes cold. She positively thrummed with fury. "My personal life is none of your—or anybody else's—concern. How dare you take me to task. I will choose my own friends, be they white *or* Indian, and be damned to society's approval. Good evening to you."

Mrs. Wight's mouth hung so far open in astonishment, a robin could have flown in and happily made a nest. "But Miss Mainwarring, think of your father—"

"Do not ring *that* guilt bell above my head, madam. My father would be an ineffective man, indeed, if he were incapable of fighting his own battles."

But even in her high temper, Elizabeth noticed heads swinging in her direction, faces clouded with expressions of censure and condemnation as she stalked toward the garden door. She almost felt sorry for them, trapped in their tiny little minds.

The air outside was a little cooler than usual and wonderfully refreshing. Breathing in the familiar heady bouquet of mimosa combined with the faint perception of coriander and cardamom, tempered her frame of mind. A macaque darted out from under the hedgerow and stared at her with bright, inquisitive eyes before clambering up a tamarind tree. Smiling at his antics, she cast about for the gazebo. In the far corner of the garden, some twenty feet from the clubhouse, stood a white-washed six-sided structure, its wide glass windows covered by bamboo blinds. Nigel must have tired of waiting by the door and proceeded to their trysting place.

The dry, stiff grass crunched under her sandals as she made her way cautiously among the shadows. A light wind skittered through the branches of the palm and coral trees, waving them gently and throwing dark shapes across her path. The moon and stars, covered in a veil of cloud, gave only the dimmest light. It was the coming of the dreaded—and anticipated—monsoon. Maybe that helped explain the soaring tempers and native unrest. The Indians were still loudly demanding the killer of their women be brought to justice. Added to their quest for home rule, perhaps what the whole situation needed *was* a good soaking.

A rustle behind the trees and the high squeak of an animal caught in the larger jaws of another sent a shiver down her spine and Elizabeth quickened her steps, feeling suddenly that she, too, was caught in a predator's sights. Shaking off the sensation, she realised it must be Nigel watching her from the gazebo. She sighed deeply in relief and mounted the first of four stairs.

"Nigel?" she called into the inky interior. She was surprised how unnerved she was, and delighted at the prospect of an escort back to the club. She didn't bloody well care if they were seen together. Of far more concern was the possibility of his marriage to someone else. "Nigel, where are you, for goodness sake?"

Silence. With the blinds closed, the gazebo was stark black. And empty. Granted she was a bit late, but a gentleman did not make an assignation and not keep it. Certainly not Nigel. And really, one didn't just tear across a social gathering making a desperate bid for the door. A little tardiness was to be expected in such a situation.

Leaning sideways in the doorway, for some reason hesitant to put her back to that which she could not see, Elizabeth tapped a long scarlet nail to her lip. She'd seen him leave, so where was he? What to do? Wait? For how long? Already her skin crawled. A tree branch scraped noisily on the back portion of the structure, causing her to jump. No, she definitely didn't care for this place, nor for what was becoming a nearly constant impression of being watched.

Lowering her foot to the stair, she came up short with a gasp as a familiar voice said, "Sorry to keep you waiting." Nigel stood less than a foot away at the bottom of the steps. "Not to worry, we have a candle. I'll light it momentarily."

Stifling a scream, Elizabeth leaned back, making room for him as he started up. Brushing by her, he disappeared into the darkness, making his way as if it were daylight to a narrow windowsill to light the stub of a candle. It wasn't enough to illuminate the farthest corners, but it was a distinct improvement. She followed him to the small glowing circle, the tingling thrill of seeing him alone warring with the adrenaline rush of the start he had just given her.

"Good Lord, you nearly took my breath away, popping out of the night so abruptly!"

Nigel shot her a provocative grin. "A compliment, indeed, to steal a girl's breath. Gratifying to discover I possess the knack."

"One would have thought that particular talent apparent. Your intended worships you," Elizabeth commented dryly, her thrill waning at once with the memory of the Indian beauty.

Nigel's eyes narrowed dangerously and his voice hardened. "Once and for all, I am not affianced to Amarita!" His lips drawn in a tight line, he tipped the candle, pouring a drop or two of wax onto the sill and affixed the candle there. Suddenly he stiffened and canted his head toward the window, then relaxed and shook his head. "I'm becoming neurotic, sensing menace everywhere. When waiting for you I spotted someone leaving the club, skirting the shadows in a secretive manner. Unfortunately, I was unable to make out his—or her—identity, but thought a little reconnaissance in order." He gazed beyond Elizabeth to the dim doorway of the gazebo, then back to her. "Nothing. It was probably just a romantic tryst. One might think a murderer on the loose would clamp a lid on the extramarital affairs, however it seems that activity is de rigueur among colonials." He shrugged. "Whoever it was has gone."

Elizabeth's skin pebbled with goose flesh, remembering the feel of a predator's eyes. "Are you sure?"

He nodded. "Reasonably." He gave her a sharp look as she rubbed her arms. It wasn't cold. "Did you see anyone on your way?"

"Only a macaque scampering through the garden." She forced a smile and dropped her arms to her sides. She needn't let him think she was neurotic, as well. Especially not now. It was time for business. Their romance—was that what it was? She didn't know anymore; it appeared love was a very complicated tangle in India.

"So perhaps you will explain this mysterious Indian surreptitiousness you mentioned earlier. I'm all ears." Determined to show an outward calm, even as her pulse raced, Elizabeth coolly extracted a Dunhill from her evening bag, bent to light it from the candle, and inhaling deeply settled herself against the wall.

Nigel ran a distracted hand through his hair. Hell and damnation. What a bollixed snarl. The circumstances involving Amarita and her father required a subtlety and artfulness he found himself losing. Suddenly he was sick and tired of treading the narrow diplomatic line between Indian and British relations. And tonight Sir Clive had displayed the temerity to suggest that now was not the time to pay particular attention to British girls.

"Of course, it is not really my business," the man had said hastily while removing his spectacles and rubbing them with his handkerchief. His movements were jerky, and he darted anxious glances at the Maharani across the room. "But, well, that is to say, such a complication to present matters, you know. Probably better to, er . . . Well, a little more discretion might be appropriate, old boy, eh wot? Hmm, I'll just see that your mother is enjoying herself properly. Oh, and do give your father my best regards, won't you, dear chap?" The Commissioner had inclined his head, relieved at last of conveying what he considered a very delicate communique, before threading his way between the party-goers toward Nigel's mother.

Elizabeth now fixed Nigel with a gimlet eye at his continued silence. "One can almost hear cranks and pullies grinding away in your head," she mused, tapping ash from the tip of her cigarette.

Nigel's expression was wry. "It's all a game, Elizabeth, albeit a carefully played one. The majority of the population in Kashmir is Moslem, while my family is Hindu. Amarita's father is a landowner of some stature, and happens to be a Muhammadan. Such alliances are necessary occasionally to keep power. To reject Ramesh Ali's offer out of hand is to insult him. It must be entertained as a matter of courtesy. If either party takes the other in dislike, the matter ends graciously."

"That presents a problem then, does it not? The lady obviously adores you and it appears you may have a ticklish job informing her that you do not suit. Besides, does your father not wish the match? It sounds terribly important." She turned from the glow of the candle so he would not see the bleakness in her face, and ground the remains of her cigarette with unnecessary force under her heel.

"It is not so important as you might think, just a bloody inconvenience. For one thing, it was decided soon after my birth that I was to hold no state office. For another, my elder brothers have made five advantageous marriages between them. As soon as Amarita realises she will not live as first wife to a Kashmiri prince, but as only wife to a working soldier, she will lose interest rapidly." Nigel lounged against the wall and crossed his arms across his chest.

Elizabeth arched her eyebrows inquiringly and commented, "One might think Amarita glad of the role of only wife. Sharing one's husband must be repugnant."

Nigel's mustache twitched, and she caught the white gleam of his teeth as he replied. "Not to a Moslem or Hindu woman. A man's consequence increases with the number of his wives. The wealthier he is, the more wives he may acquire. The more wives, the more important the first wife. She has the ruling of the household, you see. To be an only wife is to be pitied for wedding a poor man."

Elizabeth shook her head, puzzled. "I must admit the Eastern mode of thinking escapes me entirely."

Although aware that he was half Indian, it hadn't occurred to her it was more than skin deep. How mortifying to think so superficially. So many contrasts that may indeed grow into obstacles, she thought sadly. It was easier to understand why the races kept to themselves.

Trailing her finger thoughtfully through the dust on the window sill, she remarked casually, "I did not realise you were Hindu. Quite silly really, but I just hadn't thought. It must have been a very great change for your mother."

Nigel looked at her meditatively. His answer was sober. "My mother must show respect for the Hindu faith, but there was no need for her to convert. I have spent the majority of my life in England, as per my mother's wish for one British son. I am as familiar with the Anglican Sunday service as I am with Hindu rites. The code I live by is to combine what I consider the best of my two heritages. For example, avoiding beef and celebrating Christmas. But I am as likely to send up a prayer to God as to Shiva."

Yes, perhaps the differences were too steep after all. Then again, perhaps they were moot. She intended to find out. Pushing away from the wall, Elizabeth walked slowly toward him.

"Why did your mother visit me this afternoon? It seems universally agreed that she has something stuffed up her sleeve." She stopped inches from him and gazed directly into his eyes. They were almost black, and she could see herself mirrored there. Did she really look so calm and self-assured?

Nigel was silent, his gaze unreadable. Then he reached out a finger and lifted Elizabeth's chin. "Do you not know then, love?"

"Why don't you tell me, Nigel?"

He grinned. "I told her I'd met someone very special," he whispered, lowering his lips to hers.

His kiss was slow and savouring, and heat flowed through

her like molten lava. Her arms twined languidly around his neck, the tips of her fingers playing in his crisp hair. His hands cupped her face, then slid unhurriedly down her back while his tongue explored the sweet cavern of her mouth. Elizabeth threw back her head, giving greater access, and his mouth left hers to blaze a trail of fire down her throat.

"God, I've missed you, love," Nigel whispered roughly in her ear before tracing hot kisses over the slope of her bare shoulder. She trembled and felt the familiar quickening, but before surrendering she pushed gently on his chest.

"Nigel, wait. I must know plainly what we are to one another," Elizabeth murmured, a catch in her breath. "You have spoken with your mother, but you haven't told me anything! I realise we are special friends, but—"

Nigel's arms dropped like anvils, and he stepped back. He was very still. "What do *you* want, Elizabeth?

Elizabeth felt the blush rising in her cheeks. She wanted him to tell her he was hopelessly in love with her. He hadn't. And she wasn't going begging. Definitely she wasn't about to act like that silly cow, Celia Armstrong, clinging to a man's arm, angling for a marriage proposal. She felt her hands fisting in frustration and turned her back to compose herself. Indeed, this visit to India might be shorter than planned. It nauseated her to indulge in a sordid affair when she was head over heels. Well, at least she knew where she stood—"special," but not quite special enough to marry. Facing him once more, pulse pounding in her temples, she made every effort to smile placidly.

"I've always fancied myself a modern girl, Nigel, but perhaps I am a bit more old-fashioned than I thought. I find the idea of the occasional romantic tryst abhorrent and cheap. I am not quite sure an affair is any nearer my style." A brittle tone entered her voice. "Perhaps if you familiarise me with the rules—but no. I don't think so after all."

He glared at her and when he spoke his voice had a menacing edge.

"How dare you! You think I possess so little honour and no respect for you? A bloody affair?" He nearly spit the words. Abruptly turning, he paced the perimeter of the gazebo once and confronted her.

"Elizabeth, do you truly suppose I wish to initiate a less than respectable offer to you?" He was visibly calmer but his tone was unbelieving. "What we did the other night could result in nothing but marriage. I wired my parents informing them I had met the girl I intend to marry. This requires a deal of public relations, albeit I am of no real importance to the state. Preparations for introductions, parties, etcetera." He became suspicious when he saw the blankness in her face and small *o* of surprise on her lips. His expression shuttered and he asked frigidly, "Or is it that you wish to call off everything between us? No dirty cheechee in your bed after all, is that it?"

"Why, you presumptuous cad!" Red appeared around the fringes of Elizabeth's vision. She felt like screaming, but gave the floor a good stamp with her high-heeled evening sandal instead. Hands on her hips, she exclaimed crossly, "And you have the unmitigated nerve to claim you are not a prince? How dare *you*? To wire your parents of your intentions without a *word* to me? As if I may not have something to say in this matter?" Bloody hell, the man was infuriatingly arrogant! Taking a deep breath to steady herself, she continued in a more composed tone.

"You have not expressed any tender feelings for me, only the cold fact that intimacy must necessitate marriage. Without love, I view such an alliance with an aversion."

The release of anger was quite satisfying after all the uncertainty she'd had regarding his intentions toward her, but now she rather felt like an empty siphon bottle, all the fizz spent. Even if he were to kneel now at her feet espousing undying love, she wasn't sure if she could live with such a high-handed man.

Lifting her chin, she said stiffly, "I believe we have said all that we may. We are quite capable of maintaining civility between us, I'm sure. It will only cause nasty gossip if we do not. Goodnight, Nigel." She headed for the door with a curious heaviness in her chest. It must be her heart breaking.

"God, Elizabeth, I've made an unholy mess out of this," he called in a gruff voice, grasping her arm and swinging her back toward him. "Please let me start over—"

The rasp of a match lighting drew their attention like a shot to the doorway. The portly figure of Deputy Commissioner Tate leaned against the door jamb watching them intently as he brought the flame toward his cigar. His white linen suit was pristine, and the thin strips of his remaining hair were oiled and immaculately pulled across his scalp. The mocking gleam in his eyes shone through the cloud of smoke he exhaled as he gazed pointedly at the closeness of their stance and the fact that Nigel still held Elizabeth's arm.

"Not interrupting anything of importance, I trust?" he drawled. "Devil of a time finding solitude for a smoke."

Nigel dropped his hand, and Elizabeth moved away. What had he heard?

Nigel's eyes smouldered in annoyance and his words were clipped. "A gentleman might announce his presence, Deputy Commissioner."

Tate spat a shred of tobacco on the floor. "Just did." Clamping the cigar between his teeth, he surveyed Elizabeth dispassionately. "I had surmised, Miss Mainwarring, that had you not learned by example, at least your father might educate you as to how things are done in India. Indeed, throughout the Empire. As we are alone"—he flicked Nigel a stony look—"I shall be quite direct: Respectable British girls never cultivate the acquaintances of natives—or Anglo-Indians. To do so leaves them open to insult."

Nigel sprung at Tate, seizing his shirtfront with both hands, lifting him off the floor and slamming him into the wall. The cigar tumbled from Tate's mouth, rolling forgotten into a corner. Nigel's fists dug into the Deputy's throat, colouring his face purple as the man gasped and gurgled for air.

"Fortunately for you," Nigel snarled, "I am too *Anglo* to carve an unarmed man to shreds with my kukri. Insult Miss Mainwarring again, and I will indulge in a more primitive practice my *Indian* half is not above carrying out." He finished with something in Urdu, and the blood drained abruptly from Tate's face, leaving it a sickly grey. Nigel then pulled the Deputy from the wall and threw him nearly the length of the building.

Elizabeth cried out, stunned. Her hand flew to her throat as if her breath, too, were cut off. This was a side of Nigel she had never witnessed, and it left her dazed and rooted to the spot. The snake was one thing . . . but such graphic violence to another man? As she studied the inert form of the Deputy Commissioner, his deliberately disparaging words came floating back and her lips tightened. Well, then. The fisticuffs really hadn't been uncalled for, had they?

Nigel stood in profile to her, breathing heavily. His forehead was glazed in perspiration, and his lips curled in distaste watching Tate, who by now had risen to his knees and was coughing with a savagery that brought up the contents of his stomach.

Elizabeth wrinkled her nose and averted her gaze. "Nigel? Please, let's leave—"

The giggle came from just outside, and for the second time in a quarter hour their attention was drawn to the doorway by unwelcome company. Shoes scraped, climbing the short staircase, and a laughing voice Elizabeth recognised as

Amanda Crosshaven's said, "Don't be silly, Reggie, no one's seen us—*Oh!*" Amanda stopped short on the threshold, causing her companion to bump into her.

"Don't stop now, darling—oh dear, er . . . I say, sorry to intrude." Captain Henderson cleared his throat and stepped away from Amanda. A red stain spread across his features and, at a loss for what to do with his hands, he smoothed back his oiled hair before shoving them deep in his pockets. "The club is bally smoky, don't you know, and Mrs. Crosshaven felt quite lightheaded. Needed fresh air before she fainted on the floor and was crushed underfoot. Thought a short stroll just the thing for her."

"Good gracious!" Amanda had been holding a hand weakly to her head to illustrate her frailty but dropped it like it contained a hot coal at a movement in the corner.

Canby Tate was attempting to heft himself to his feet, but only managed to sit, leaning on the wall. His eyes closed, he groped for his handkerchief, and finally grasping it, held it to his mouth.

"Poor Mr. Tate. Has there been an accident?"

His features inscrutable, Nigel replied coolly, "Mr. Tate fell."

"So unfortunate," Elizabeth put in quickly and made her way to Amanda, linking their arms and guiding the woman outside. "Sheer blackness in there without a candle, you know. It's not at all surprising he tripped. Wasn't the club just blue with smoke tonight? Something should be done about it! Other than opening the doors and letting in the mosquitoes, that is. Oh look," she exclaimed, nodding her head at the gathering on the club's patio. "A number of others are braving the little winged buggers as well."

Behind them, Nigel exited the gazebo. "Come, Captain, I'm sure the Deputy Commissioner wishes to recuperate in privacy."

Captain Henderson directed an uncertain glance to Tate

before following. "Yes, sir, of course. Sir, I may rely on your, er, discretion?"

Nigel flung him a wry look over his shoulder. "Captain, I think the least said the better."

Celia Armstrong watched Elizabeth Mainwarring and Amanda Crosshaven stop to exchange greetings before entering the club. The men behind them didn't bother with courtesies, but immediately disappeared inside. Hmm, something was going on. Amanda was jittery and Elizabeth a bit too bright and friendly. Murder had been etched in the starkly handsome features of the Lt. Colonel, and Henderson looked suspiciously as if he expected to be the victim.

"My, my, how wonderfully juicy!" Celia murmured spitefully to her mother. "Do you suppose the heiress was receiving her conge? Or perhaps it was the other way around."

Her mother sniffed in disdain. "We needn't concern ourselves with their sort, my dear."

"Indeed not," agreed Johnny's mother, Mrs. Fairfield. She was a small woman with a lined face and hair a novel shade of red. "*He* should marry that Indian trollop and go back to Kashmir. For good, I say. It's not right a half-caste should hold rank above subdar-major, royalty or not. The wogs are granted far too many freedoms these days. It's no wonder they are bold enough to demand we quit India.

"As for that heiress person, she must possess no self-respect at all to have dallied with him in the first place. It's time Calcutta was cleaned out for respectable people. *That* is why a murderer is on the loose, you know: too much riffraff about." She shuddered. "That half-caste is responsible for finding this scoundrel. Ha! 'Not necessarily an Indian,' he says. What rot! Everyone knows the native men all want a fair-skinned European woman! We'll all be murdered in our beds before it's over with, mark my words!"

"Quite right, Violet dear," Mrs. Armstrong agreed, nodding regally. "One may only hope the brass realises this before all is lost."

Celia, however, was more interested in gossip. "How do you suppose Mrs. Crosshaven and that Henderson fellow fit in?" she speculated, a malicious gleam in her eye.

"Caught sneaking about, I should think," Mrs. Fairfield said in sour tones. "The girl's a scrapper and Henderson is her latest fling. Crosshaven married beneath him, poor chap. And such a congenial fellow, too."

"Perhaps it is just as well everybody knows each other's secrets, my dear," murmured Mrs. Armstrong smugly to her daughter as they followed their hostess inside. "All the ladies shall know Johnny is spoken for."

Chapter Twenty-five

Fury and adrenaline rushed in, searing his veins like a potent narcotic. It gave him a smouldering glow, an exhilaration. And anticipation. He was trembling with it. He'd hunted and targeted her twice—and failed. But he would win. Right and morality commanded him. She deserved the punishment he planned for her. They all had. Filthy slags. For a British woman to demean herself with a native was against all decency. It was repulsive.

His feverish eyes darted, following the tall slender blonde as she greeted acquaintances and entered the club. Just like she belonged. She didn't. None of them had. He'd shown them.

He could have followed her and no one would have blinked an eye. He angled away from the club instead. There was one more task to accomplish tonight.

One in which he would not fail.

Chapter Twenty-six

The whisky slid down Nigel's throat in a satisfying burn and spread outward in a pleasant numbness. Unfortunately, it wouldn't last long. He gazed longingly at the bottle of twelve-year-old scotch in the bartender's hand but shook his head when offered more. No, he'd already made a bloody cock up of things with Elizabeth, and the sooner the situation was mended the better. Besides, a long night stretched ahead of him.

"I say, old boy, you have that distinctly sour look of one who has tobogganed down Ruin Mountain only to land flat on his arse. Lost a bit of lolly, have you? Know the feeling well. Bloody nuisance being a younger son." Harry drained his glass and set it down. Leaning an elbow on the bar, he eyed Nigel closely and nodded knowingly. "Ahh, *not* lolly then," he commented delicately, intercepting a particularly nasty glare from his friend. "This calls for vast quantities of 'hooch' as the Yanks call it. Allow me the honours." He grinned, patting his trouser pocket. "I have turned into a veritable Midas." Humming happily, he pulled out a wad of rupees. "So sorry, old boy, but it looks as if I got all the luck tonight. Not just in gaming either." He smirked as he counted out notes to pay for the drinks.

"Woodford, shut it," Nigel growled.

Still grinning, Harry said, "I shan't crow about it, then—at least not until you are in a similar position. Won't be long I expect, if you are in such a state. I spied a certain lady entering the loo a moment ago. Suspiciously dewy look about the eyes. Once such emotions surface, it's either the beginning or the end—okay, okay, consider it shut." He stammered to a halt at Nigel's scowl. "In the meantime," he recommended bravely, "take my advice: Get good and rat-arsed, and when you give the damned hangover the old heave-ho, you will find the obvious solution staring you square in the face and you'll wonder why in hell you didn't see it before! Yes, dear fellow." He spoke to the bartender as he approached. "Two large whiskies. The best you keep in stock!"

"Small whiskies," Nigel corrected. "Woodford, I'd like you to attend a strategic briefing at my bungalow in"—he consulted his wristwatch—"two hours, 23:30 sharp. Normally only members of my special investigative murder team take part, but I have a special reason for wanting you present."

Harry regarded Nigel curiously, but waited until the bartender served their neat whiskies and returned to polishing the glassware several feet away. "I'm only a supply officer and a raw one at that. How can I possibly help in your investigation?"

"As a bodyguard and observer. I informed Major Wight your services were needed for my mother's tiger hunt on Friday. Supplies have a way of disappearing on a trek such as this. Your official duty is to secure the safety of my mother's costly delicacies. Trumped up of course, but easily attributed to the peculiarities of royalty." Nigel scrutinised Harry closely, hoping he'd chosen correctly.

Harry swirled his untouched whisky glass in small, tight circles. Without looking up, he said softly, "You had better tell me the rest."

For a long moment Nigel stared at his whisky, then shot it back in one go. "God help me, I think that sick bastard wants Elizabeth next." His fist tightened around the glass. "By God, I'll kill him with my bare hands first." He turned his fierce gaze to Harry. "She is not to know. Jesus, she's frightened enough. That is why I need you."

"Hold on, man!" Harry's head bolted up, his eyes wide. "She needs a professional! Bloody hell, she needs a *dozen* bodyguards."

"Keep your voice down," Nigel demanded sharply. "No obvious guards. I'll not have her terrified. She will not think your constant presence unusual. Believe me, I'll never be far away." He grimaced. "At this point, your proximity shall be far more reassuring than mine."

Harry, feeling a bit overwhelmed, followed Nigel's example, gulping his whisky, shuddering as it stung his throat and hit his belly like a ball of fire. He shoved his empty glass away and frowned at Nigel, puzzled.

"Why do you think the bastard is after Elizabeth? Is Fiona in danger, too?"

"Not for herself, but if she gets in the way, I don't imagine she'll be spared, no," Nigel said with resignation.

Harry's features hardened. "Sodder must blast his way through me first," he said decisively, surveying the room as if he expected the killer to pop out announcing himself. Abruptly he whipped his head back to Nigel.

"What the hell is *he* doing out and about?" he demanded, indicating the entrance to the lounge. Captain Langley stood smiling and nodding to acquaintances. "Isn't he one of your suspects? The bloody cheek!"

A spasm of irritation crossed Nigel's features. "As much as I'd enjoy locking him up and throwing the key into a piranha-filled pool, I can't—at least for now. Unfortunately he is alibied for Beryl's murder and has been disciplined for the un-officer-like conduct that confined him to his quarters. I'm watching him, though. Closely," he assured Harry, his eyes narrowing on Langley.

"Alibied?" Harry's eyebrows melted into his hairline. "Surely you don't believe—"

"Moneylenders," Nigel supplied curtly. "His gambling debt approaches six figures. Yet the concept of quitting escapes the stupid bugger. *Never* borrow from the native moneylenders." He flicked a warning glance at Harry. "Interest tends to accrue at their discretion. Actually, Langley is phenomenally lucky to walk among the living. 'Mercy' is not in their vocabulary. Examples are well set. No, he didn't walk into that door. He was merely reminded a payment was due."

Elizabeth observed the play at the roulette table, her festive mood gone. She'd escaped from Amanda at the first opportunity and wandered toward the capricious, whirling wheel, only to find she lacked the heart to play.

"*Mademoiselle, voulez-vous participer?*" The turbaned croupier gestured toward his table.

Elizabeth shook her head. "*Non.*"

"Of course you must, Miss Mainwarring." Captain Langley appeared at her elbow, smiling down at her. "Here, let me wager for you. I've been rather lucky tonight." He dropped several notes on the table and spoke to the croupier. "Twenty-one red and, er, thirteen black—that should do it."

Good God! How was it he was actually free? Elizabeth's eyes widened in surprise as the wheel clacked into action. She resisted the urge to back away, her skin crawling at the proximity of the man who very possibly had committed several hideous murders. Lifting her chin instead, she said coolly, "Please do not trouble yourself, Captain. I am quite capable of placing my own wagers. I'm simply bored with roulette for now. Goodnight."

"Oh come, come, dear Miss Mainwarring, I assure you I am quite tame—"

"Thirteen black," the croupier's voice interrupted flatly. "Five thousand rupees, monsieur."

"You see, Miss Mainwarring. I cannot lose!" Langley crowed, scooping his winnings into his trouser pocket. "I shall purchase the best champagne and you must share it with me."

"I think not, Captain. We have nothing further to say to each other."

Langley frowned. "Miss Mainwarring, I am indeed sorry you witnessed that vulgar little scene the other day. My only excuse is extreme provocation and the impaired judgment of a trifle too much gin. Still, I am deeply ashamed to have responded to that . . . er, Mrs. Tate's jibes. I am, however, duly disciplined and quite respectable again," he assured her.

Elizabeth ruthlessly suppressed a shiver, observing the scabbed scratches and yellowing bruises prominent on his face. "Indeed, I am glad all is well with you, Captain. Please continue with your celebrations without me. I am just on my way home."

"Miss Mainwarring kindly accepted my offer of escort earlier." Nigel suddenly appeared at her side, cupping her elbow protectively in his large warm hand. He threw Langley a dark look. "If you possess the funds to gamble so freely, I suggest you make payment to your moneylenders. You were incredibly fortunate this time—they ordinarily take body parts instead of a little smashing about."

Langley's features suffused with ugly colour. "My affairs, sir, are tended to quite adequately," he said stiffly. "I wish you a pleasant evening, Miss Mainwarring." He bowed, but shot Nigel a look of resentment before taking his leave.

"No, I'm not mad," Nigel informed Elizabeth before she could utter a word. "Apparently he owes a significant sum to one of the most notorious moneylenders in the Bustees, and was grimly occupied by becoming intimately acquainted with the fists of said lender's thugs the night of the last murder. Considering the lavishness with which he is throwing about his rupees tonight, it is not inconceivable that he may not wake up from his next beating. I hope he was not bothering you?"

Now that Langley was gone, she needed distance from Nigel and pulled her elbow from his possessive grasp. He stood tall and intimidating, and she was keenly aware of his virility and magnetism pulling her closer. No, it would not do to yield to her desire for him. After all, he as good as told her he only intended to marry her because he felt he must.

Steeling herself to remain cool, she stepped back shaking her head. "It was nothing." She glanced at the Captain's retreating form and remarked mildly, "You know at the polo match, the day before she was murdered, Beryl mentioned the possibility of Captain Langley being found facedown in the Hooghly as a result of his debts. She also commented on his, er, penchant for the 'ladies of the evening.' It was a rather coarse scene and the Captain certainly looked angry enough to murder. Are you *quite* sure about his whereabouts that night? He gives me the horrors."

"Sure enough to release him. This was a crime of passion, and whereas he may have been angry enough to murder, I think a more straightforward approach, such as a good clean bash on the head, more his style. I agree, he is a rather unsavoury character." He shrugged. "As I said, his presence may not affect us long."

Elizabeth raised her eyebrows, somewhat taken aback. "How detached you are."

Nigel regarded her with a stern glint. "Langley has dug his own hole and right now is no credit to the Army. If he does live through this he may very well find himself cashiered sooner rather than later. Come, I'll drive you home." He reached for her elbow again:

"No, Nigel, it is not necessary—"

"It *is* necessary. Come." He led her outside, down the entrance stairs to his Alfa Romeo, which was parked at the curb. Opening the passenger door for her, he said, "Don't worry about Fiona. Harry is seeing her home."

The rag top was in place, making for a hot, muggy ride. Unrolling the window, Elizabeth took a deep breath of the thick, tropically scented night air. Nigel was silent until he drew up at her father's bungalow. Clicking off the ignition, he removed his uniform cap, tossed it on the dash and turned to her. Half of his face was shadow and the other half hard and set.

"Elizabeth, apparently we both need a lesson in communication." He bent his head for a moment, took a deep breath and then looked her straight in the eye. "I love you. God, I've tried not to. I've told myself we are wrong for each other, from two different dimensions. The last thing I want you to do is choose between your father and me—but you may have to do so. I want to marry you. Admittedly, I made a mess of it earlier, but you were not exactly forthcoming in telling me your feelings. I never would have compromised you did I not hold such sentiments for you. I am disappointed you should think otherwise. Indeed, I recognise the mistake in speaking to my parents before opportunity arose to talk to you. It *was* high-handed of me. In my defense, it did seem expedient since my mother was due to arrive and I assumed you returned my feelings. You were a virgin, and I don't think I imagined your intense response to my lovemaking. You are too genuine to give yourself lightly in some tawdry affair. I do hope I am not wrong, but there must be no more assumptions between us."

Elizabeth gaped inelegantly as she listened to what she most wanted to hear in all the world. *He loved her.* Hope quivered within her and soon grew stronger, tingling and rushing through her veins. Her thoughts dissolved in chaos. He *said* he loved her, but he was so collected, so matter-of-fact, while she was hot and cold at the same time.

"I wish you would say *something*, as I have just bared my soul to you." Nigel ran a distracted hand through his hair, and for the first time she thought she perceived a shadow of uncertainty in his eyes.

"Yes, well," she managed at last. "I have never received a proposal in so cool a manner before—"

"Cut to the chase, Elizabeth. Do you love me?" he interrupted impatiently.

She blinked at his anxiety. "Oh, Nigel." She felt tears gather in the corners of her eyes. "Yes. Yes, I do. That's why I was so offended when it seemed all you desired was an affair. You are quite correct about our lack of commun—"

He yanked her across the seat into his arms, smoothing her hair back with one hand, pressing her closer with the other and sprinkling kisses along her jaw. "God, Elizabeth, you know how to keep a man on tenterhooks, don't you? Damn it, I love you more than life," he whispered raggedly before his mouth descended on hers, claiming her very soul. His tongue teased and sucked at hers, drawing her inward. Her nipples pebbled and his fingers were plucking at them through the thin silk of her gown, lifting and cupping her breasts. She felt herself falling, aware of nothing but the urgency of the sensations drowning her, until he suddenly lifted his head and set her away from him.

"Damn it to hell, I'll not seduce the woman I love in an automobile!" He threw himself back in his seat, shaking his head as if to clear it. Finally he looked at her and confided in a low, gravelly voice, "I've never told a woman I've loved her before. Forgive me if I don't go about it correctly."

Looking up at him through her thick fringe of lashes and smiling impishly, Elizabeth admitted, "Neither have I. All told, it wasn't *too* bad."

He let out a crack of laughter. "Brat," he said, and then sobered. "I meant it, Elizabeth—I want to marry you. No, don't say anything now." He placed a finger over her mouth, silencing her. "This is a decision you must think about very carefully. Mixed couples are not looked upon favourably in India." He sighed. "It is done, but rarely in our class. Society has always been open to me—as long as I didn't cast glances toward a British girl. We both have been warned off each other. It will not be easy. And there is your father. He will not countenance me as a son-in-law."

Elizabeth's high emotions plummeted as if attached to a boulder in an avalanche. She'd never really moved in society before her inheritance, so the lack wouldn't be terribly missed. Her lips pursed at the memory of the insult offered by Mr. Tate. No, society she could do without if she must. But her father . . . How did she feel about that? If it came to a choice, Nigel won hands down, but she'd rather it didn't come down to a draw. Her father was the only family left to her.

"You see," he said sadly. "It does require thought."

"No, Nigel—"

"Yes, love, it does. You need to realise exactly the sort of marriage you are entering. *I* do." Lifting the handle on the door, he let himself out and strode around the roadster to assist her. He left her at the bungalow door with a peck on the cheek and a heavy heart.

Chapter Twenty-seven

Harry observed the rag-tag crew seated around Nigel's dining table in some trepidation. Three were native officers, their dark skins glowing in the low light. One, a subdar-major, was the highest in native rank, the other two slightly lower, at jemadar. All wore pristine uniforms with the native sashes and turbans. Wicked-looking kukris hung from their belts, and each sported close-cropped beards and mustaches. With very little effort, Harry could imagine any one of them clenching a honed knife in his teeth and the sacred white scarf of the *Thuggee* Kali worshipper pulled tight between his fists. He blinked. Actually they were quite tame compared to the other two dressed in rags, filthy and stinking of the slums, small, cruel eyes darting warily about the room.

He noticed Ravi, Nigel's bearer, threading between the guests serving drinks and distributing ashtrays. A good stiff scotch proved very welcome indeed.

"Now then," Nigel announced, standing at the head of the table. "For Captain Woodford's benefit I shall repeat information with which the lot of you are familiar. Mrs. Tate's murder is a bit of a complication. No obvious suspects were apparent before her killing. Evidence suggested one perpetrator who very possibly may have been active for many years in several locations."

Harry listened, astonished, as Nigel detailed a murder career spanning two decades and thousands of miles.

"It may be that Mrs. Tate was one in a lengthening line of these victims, or she may have been made to appear so. She was . . . promiscuous. Jealousies are a common result of her activities. Our list of suspects is by no means complete, and I am still awaiting intelligence regarding the similar murders committed elsewhere." Twisting a chalkboard around to face his guests, Nigel tapped it with a pointer.

"The list, such as it is."

Harry's eyes nearly popped in shock.

"Yes, Captain, Major Wight *and* Colonel Mainwarring. Many believe Toppenham the obvious choice because of his alleged rape of Miss Compton and his subsequent disappearance. However, my instincts tell me he is not our murderer. He fails to strike me as intelligent enough to remain undetected."

Harry's brow furrowed. "Are you sure you are not prejudiced regarding the Colonel, old boy? It was a rather nasty scene, him accusing *you* of murder. Turnabout fair play?"

Nigel's lips tightened in irritation, and Harry could feel the stares of the native soldiers.

"I hope, Captain, I retain a far sight more professionalism. No, he possessed what is necessary to commit the crime: opportunity and motive. Colonel Mainwarring and Beryl Tate were briefly involved. She enraged and embarrassed him publicly at the polo match the day before she was killed. Which brings me to Major Wight." He shook his head in disgust. "Poor blighter was actually in love with her. I experienced the acute misfortune to witness an episode of *his* jealousy."

The Subdar-Major made a slicing motion with his hand and spoke shortly in Urdu.

"English please, Ashish, as the Captain does not yet speak the native languages." Glancing at Harry, Nigel translated. "Ashish firmly believes we are barking up the wrong tree with the jealous lover theory, and that Beryl's murder was not a copy. I am inclined to agree with him, but we must explore all possibilities."

Feeling distinctly uncomfortable and not at all positive one of the sinister types sitting at the table might not be responsible for a murder or two between them, Harry reached for his Woodbines, fumbling until one finally fell out.

"Afraid you've nearly lost me, old boy. No experience in crime solving, you know." He lit and drew a bit nervously on his fag. "*Is* there some motive for Beryl and the others if not a jealous lover? And, er, sorry old boy for bringing it up, but speaking of jealous lovers, wasn't the tart after you as well?"

Nigel grimaced, and several of the Indians snickered. "If our idea is correct, I am, unfortunately, connected to Beryl's murder—and may be the reason I believe the killer is after Elizabeth," he said soberly.

Harry choked on the smoke he was inhaling. One of the jemadars rose at once and slapped him on the back, but Harry waved him away. Catching his breath, he tossed down a slug of scotch and stared at Nigel. Clearing his throat, he demanded, "What the devil is going on here? How is it you are involved, Covington-Singh?"

"Involuntarily, I assure you." Nigel seated himself at the table and reached for his drink, swirling the amber liquid before partaking of it. "It seems this 'repeat' killer bears a singular hatred for women who 'dally' outside their race.

"One of the Brahmin victims was married to a German, the other was rumoured to be seeing an Englishman. The poor Durrow girl was on her way home from a rendezvous with her secret beau, an Anglo-Indian. Her parents thought her safe in bed, not out sneaking about." He gazed into his glass before looking directly at Harry. "Beryl was not a subtle person and her pursuit of me was no exception. She was a bloody nuisance, and I wanted none of her. However, the murderer may not have known that, as few men tend to turn down a willing woman. Or, perhaps desire on the woman's part is as wrong as any action." Taking a deep breath, Nigel regarded each of them, an ominous glint in his eyes. "Now, I'm very much afraid my particular attentions to Elizabeth Mainwarring have condemned her. Even if I were to back off, the damage is done."

"Good God!" Harry's features slackened in astonishment. "The cinema the other night! That's . . . The blasted bugger already made an attempt! I just thought it a tasteless prank to frighten the ladies. Are you sure you shouldn't inform her, old boy?"

The table shook with the pounding of Nigel's fist. Pushing back from the table, he rose to pace the length of his small dining room. "No! I'll not have her frightened, nor any more confused than she is already." He paused. "There's more. My own mother married an Indian and now she's here in Calcutta. She may also be in harm's way."

"He *will* be apprehended, Colonel," Subdar-Major Ashish assured Nigel fiercely. "The radio and the wires are manned around the clock. Information is arriving soon."

"Even this night," said one of the ruffians in surprisingly unaccented English, "I meet with one who claims to know the identity of this madman."

His companion grunted. "If it is true, you had best hurry if you hope to find the poor bugger still alive."

Nigel nodded to the two men. "Sita, Baji, both of you are assigned as elephant handlers at the tiger hunt. I'll see to it my mother and Miss Mainwarring occupy the same *howda.*"

"I say, Nigel old fellow, won't that be all the more dangerous?" Harry enquired. "Two targets in one basket, so to speak? The killer may not miss such a plum opportunity."

Nigel flung himself back in his chair. When he spoke, he sounded worn out. "Believe me, I've chafed myself raw over that little detail, and after much reflection, I have concluded it is easier to keep a close eye in one place rather than two."

"Once the party reaches the hunting grounds, will they not transfer to horseback?"

"Riders are assigned to stick like glue to both my mother and Elizabeth."

Harry shifted in his chair as an unnerving thought occurred. "I say, how are we to protect the ladies from a long range rifle shot? After all, it is a hunt. Everyone is armed."

"I am fairly confident we shan't need to worry about that eventuality. It's far too impersonal for our man. His proclivities run to rape and hands-on violence. In fact—"

The shrill ringing of the telephone startled everyone, but Nigel recovered instantly, moving like a shot to the small buffet in the corner, seizing the handset. "Covington-Singh."

Nigel's dark blue eyes widened in apparent consternation, then hardened in irritation. "Yes," he said shortly. "The brig—high security. *No one* sees him but me, is that clear?"

He rang off and facing his guests he announced, "It appears Captain Langley is back on the suspect list. He's just been caught at the hospital—clutching a pillow over the head of our only potential witness."

Chapter Twenty-eight

Captain Langley sat nearly doubled over, handcuffed to a wooden chair. Nigel nodded to the guard, who produced a key, slotted it into the lock and opened the cell door, allowing Nigel and Ashish into the dimly lit cell.

Nigel leaned on the wall, folding his arms across his chest. Giving the prisoner a hard look, he demanded, "Well, Langley, what have you to say for yourself?"

Langley neither moved nor spoke. Ashish snatched a fistful of the Captain's hair, jerking back his head. "Answer the Colonel, *sanp. Ek dum!*"

Langley opened his eyes and croaked, "Frightful misunderstanding—"

His face snapped sideways under a vicious backhand from Ashish. "Talk!" the Subdar-Major snarled.

Langley's head swung down and a rivulet of blood dribbled off his chin onto his trousers. He gave a mirthless grunt of laughter. "More than my life's worth, old chum."

Ashish raised his hand again, but Nigel shook his head sharply. He approached Langley, crouching by his chair.

"I assure you, 'old chum,' that right now you are in far more danger from me." Quiet as Nigel's voice was, the menace in it was unmistakable. "Besides . . ." He stood now, looming over Langley. "Whomever you are referring to must find you before he is able to kill you. You tell me what I want to know, and I'm your ticket out of India. Now talk."

"Well now, that's an offer I can't refuse," Langley managed to scrape out with a ghost of humour. "How about lighting me a fag so I may collect my thoughts?"

Nigel extracted one of his own from his silver case and fit it between Langley's lips. Ashish lit it and Langley puffed greedily, clenching it in his teeth as he exhaled. A moment later Ashish knocked the cigarette out of the Captain's mouth, crushing it under his heel.

"Definitely not cricket, old man, I was hardly finished!" Langley protested.

Ashish's fist flew in a brutal right cross to Langley's jaw, leaving him groaning and gasping for air. Nigel bent over him, hands balanced on the arms of the prisoner's chair.

"I am not here to waste time or play games. Start talking or I rescind my offer and when 'they' find you, there won't be much left to kill."

"Right, right." It came out as a gargling sound. Blood spurted from Langley's mouth. Attempting to sit up he gasped out, "Owe thousands, you know that. One of the lending leeches visited me today . . ." He broke off in a fit of coughing. Clearing his throat, he began again. "He said if I, er, took care of the Newsome woman I'd find my debts forgiven. Entire sum. An answer to a prayer. Can't possibly pay the staggering amount I owe him." His eyes were stark with fear. "My life isn't worth a farthing now I've spilled."

"His name!" Nigel growled.

Langley took a deep breath. "Vinayah Ram."

"I know of him, *huzoor,*" Ashish said.

"Excellent. Bring him in."

"There you are, darling! I've scoured the bungalow searching for you." Fiona shut the kitchen door behind her.

Elizabeth swung around from the small window above the sink through which she'd been staring. It was black of course, nothing visible but her reflection. How long had she been standing lost in thought? She shrugged, feeling a bit sheepish, caught in the kitchen in nothing but her silk baby dolls. Fiona still wore her geometric-patterned frock. If it had been merely loud at dinner, it was downright disturbing at half past two in the morning.

"The most unrelenting craving for tea and bikkies came over me," she said with a tight smile.

Fiona eyed her briefly before going to the stove and lighting it. "Well, old thing, if it's tea you want you must first put the kettle on to boil." Bringing the kettle to the sink, she filled it with water and set it on the gas ring. "The biscuit jar is over there, on the table," she said, nodding to it.

"Oh, so it is," Elizabeth said in a listless voice, pulling out a chair and seating herself.

Fiona reached into the cupboard, bringing down cups and saucers. "Perhaps you should tell me just what is troubling you, dear."

Elbows on the kitchen table, Elizabeth rested her jaw in her hands and sighed deeply. "It's not the end of the world, old thing, but close enough to suit me. Nigel proposed this evening."

Fiona gasped and clapped her hands. "But this is wonderful, darling! I knew it would happen, I just knew it! The wedding shall be such fun to—" She broke off abruptly, noticing her friend's distress, and frowned. "You should be delighted,

Elizabeth—I know you are in love with him. Please tell me what is so terribly wrong."

"That's the bloody trouble, Fiona. I'm positively head over heels for him. But we are so different. Did you know he is Hindu?"

Fiona blinked, taken aback. "Well," she replied reasonably, "it didn't prevent his parents' wedding."

"His parents live in rather an isolated society. As a matter of fact, I was informed not once, but *twice* this evening that I shall not be accepted at best, and insulted at worst if I align myself with an Anglo-Indian. Oh, it is all very well mind you, if an inherited title is involved, but without one I am contaminating myself!" Groaning, she buried her face in her hands.

The kettle whistled and Fiona turned to pour the boiling water into the teapot. When she brought the tea things to the table, she seated herself opposite Elizabeth.

"I must say, I'm surprised at you. Since when do you allow society to dictate matters of conscience? Why are you minding the old biddies now?"

"For myself I do not care," Elizabeth burst out, jumping up and pacing the room twice before sitting again. "Nigel is insulted also, and if he marries me his career will go nowhere! He is, he has told me, innately Indian. India is his home. Kashmir holds no future for him, except an occasional visit. We shall be veritable outcasts in Calcutta—or anyplace else in this country. Think of our future children! Very likely they will be treated abominably!"

"It seems to me he is used to these local mores and must have thought long and deeply before asking you to spend your life with him," Fiona said sensibly, pouring out tea and pushing a cup toward Elizabeth. "He's had no choice but to challenge these issues, and obviously believes you are dauntless enough to do likewise. It is probably one of the reasons he fell in love with you." Stirring cream into her tea, she added, "Must you spend all your time in India? You do own property in New Zealand."

"How may one manage an army career spending part of the year out of the country?" Elizabeth asked miserably. Taking the stem of her teaspoon, she traced the floral pattern in the tablecloth with it. At last she looked up. "Perhaps not all is doom and gloom, and together we can brave all this nonsense. I shall be making it more difficult for him, but it is something to think about." She pursed her lips. "Don't forget my father."

"I know how important family is to you since your mum passed away. However formidable it is, you must decide who is more important to you. Who represents your future? You can start a new family," Fiona reminded her. She reached for the biscuit jar, changed her mind and headed for the ice box. Sticking her head in, she sighed in bliss, resting her chin on the door. "We're getting carried away with tea and sympathy when it's hotter than the devil's drawing room at three in the morning! We need something cool and refreshing. Aha, what's this?" Bringing forth a large ceramic bowl, she plucked off the towel and sniffed. Her eyes bright with merriment, Fiona exclaimed, "Why it's ice cream, Elizabeth! Mango ice cream. Ditch the tea, darling, and dig in!"

Nigel tore off his uniform shirt with an irritated yank and threw it on his bedroom floor. He kicked off his boots next, followed by his trousers. Tossing up the mosquito netting, he flung himself into bed, stretched out on his back, pillowing his head on folded arms and continued to simmer—very near the boiling point of frustration.

Regrettably, Vinyah Ram had not proven helpful. Eventually he'd been found—in his home, seated at his kitchen table, his throat cut from ear to ear.

Another bloody dead end.

Sweat rolled down Nigel's torso, dripping into the already damp sheets. It was as muggy as all hell. He could almost smell the rain and knew it to be only a matter of hours now instead of days. He hoped to God it held off until after the blasted tiger hunt. Keeping a close eye on both Elizabeth and his mother wasn't going to be any easier peering through an almost solid curtain of rain.

The punka whirred monotonously overhead, all but useless. *Think man, think.* There must be some clue he was overlooking. At least Mrs. Newsome still lived, albeit in a coma. Small hope, though, at this point, that she might regain consciousness before it was too late. The wireless, manned twenty-four hours a day, was snail slow in remitting any information. A common denominator *must* exist; there were just too many similarities between Barbados, Singapore, and Kenya.

Closing his eyes, forcing himself to relax, Nigel deliberately thought of something pleasant. Laughing emerald eyes, golden wavy hair, plump, firm breasts that fit perfectly in his hands, and long, shapely legs. He sighed. He'd never been in love before, was unfamiliar with the exultation, the euphoria associated with it—and with the gut-wrenching uncertainty of not knowing if one's sentiments were returned. Enough that is, to brave the complications their union would entail.

Bloody hell, what a note to go to sleep on.

Chapter Twenty-nine

Elizabeth leaned back in her cane chair, lethargic, fanning herself and staring up at the sun. It was only newly risen, yet it already pulsated powerfully through a high thin halo of clouds. Not even the crows were awake to argue over morsels of banana and citrus for their breakfast, and the silence echoed, providing a strange sort of atmosphere.

Perspiration trickled between her breasts, and she wished she could trade her linen shirt and twill trousers for shorts and one of those new and daring halter tops. Alas, the relentless sun and vicious mosquitoes would make short work of her.

"Lord, if only I knew how to perform a rain dance, I'd use what little remaining energy I possess to enact it immediately," Fiona grumbled and kicked moodily at her overnight satchel.

Elizabeth gave a short laugh. "Be careful what you wish for, old thing. I understand the monsoon is just as beastly as the heat."

"Well, I shall be perverse and wish for the sun back again." She pulled at a curly tuft of hair. "At least my hair wouldn't frizz so."

Elizabeth glanced at her friend and giggled. "Nonsense, my girl, you could do far worse. You could stick your finger in an electrical socket."

Fiona scowled at her. "Very funny. *You* have received a proposal of marriage—*I* have not. This isn't the ideal environment to advertise the goods, you know. One must make the most of one's attributes if one doesn't wish to die an old maid."

Elizabeth threw back her head, roaring with laughter until tears rolled down her face. Reaching for a handkerchief, she dabbed at her eyes.

"Oh, you needn't worry on that score, dear. Why, wagers are likely being taken even now as to how long it will take Harry to pluck up his courage to pop the question. Besides," she added dryly, her eyes flicking toward her friend's generous chest, "it's highly doubtful your hair is your best attribute."

"Oh, do you really think so?" Fiona's demeanor brightened considerably.

"Absolutely."

"No, silly. I meant Harry proposing, not—well, you know." She looked down almost bashfully. "I'm most frightfully crazy about him."

Elizabeth shot her friend an indulgent smile. "Darling, does he not squire you everywhere, even to the extent of following you about like a besotted puppy? Any number of people have remarked upon the eventuality of nuptials. It's quite the happy buzz." She finished with a frown.

"Elizabeth, please cease your worrying, it will all come out right in the end." When Elizabeth didn't respond, Fiona asked sharply, "You *are* accepting Nigel, are you not? You're not really letting narrow-minded people stop you?"

Still frowning, Elizabeth replied, "I haven't decided, Fiona. I am not the only person affected."

"I think I am acquainted with you better than anyone, my dear, and I know positively that if you decline Nigel, you will be the most miserable creature. Imagine the fabulous double wedding we—"

"Wedding?" Opening the screen door, Colonel Mainwarring stepped onto the verandah. "Whose wedding, may I ask?" He was still wearing his dressing gown, although he had shaved and brushed his thin skirt of grey hair.

"Good morning, Father. Fiona's, but you mustn't say a word because Harry has yet to propose!"

"Getting a bit ahead of yourself, aren't you, miss?" he said dryly.

Fiona exchanged a sharp glance with Elizabeth and sighed. "Merely wishful thinking, sir."

"I'm sure you could manage better. He hasn't a feather to fly with, you know." Reaching into his dressing gown pocket he pulled out his pipe and proceeded to fill it. "Must depend on his officer's salary. His father is finished financing him as the chap has landed arse downwards in every one of his ventures." He lit the tobacco, puffing until he was satisfied with its start. "The father *is* an earl. Irish, though." He stretched up on his toes and took a deep breath of muggy morning air.

Fiona fixed the Colonel with a gimlet eye. "As I am Scottish, sir, we shall be quite equal in second-class citizenship."

Colonel Mainwarring tendered her an abstract sort of glance, and said, "Er, quite, quite."

Trying to keep a straight face, Elizabeth interjected, "I shouldn't worry, Father. I settled a dowry on Fiona months ago. She could marry a pauper and still be quite comfortable."

"Hmm, well, protect it before you marry him, girl. Wouldn't do if he were a fortune hunter." He cleared his throat and examined the tips of his slippers. "Retiring soon and I shan't be here to keep an eye on him for you."

Elizabeth sent her father a sharp look. "What are your plans, Father? Will you go home to England, or live in another part of India?"

The Colonel puffed meditatively on his pipe before answering. "England hasn't been home in years. Doubt I could become accustomed to the cold and damp again, anyway. India will achieve Home Rule. Oh, not in the next year or two to be sure, but soon, at any rate. I shall not care to be here when that occurs. Think there is conflict and violence now!" He snorted. "Just you wait until the wogs take charge. Whole sub-continent will end up in flames in the fight for supremacy between the factions."

Staring into the shimmering heat waves he nodded and ended on a decisive note. "Rented a holiday cottage in the Seychelles years ago. Quite enjoyed it. I shall discover what is available."

"You may always stay as long as you wish at the sheep station, Father," Elizabeth offered.

"Mmm, well . . ." He flicked her a wary glance out the corner of his eye. "We shall see what transpires. I believe your motor is arriving." He nodded in faint amusement to the flashy Humber limousine pulling up in front of the bungalow. "Satchels instead of trunks?" he exclaimed in surprise, noticing the bags for the first time. "Decent tiger shoot lasts at least a week!"

"Imminent rains and pressing duties the Maharani must attend in Kashmir," Elizabeth informed him, picking up her case and bussing him on the cheek. "No females to interrupt the efficient running of your bachelor household for three days! Relish it, Father, for we intend to make up for lost time when we return!"

The *howda* rolled and dipped similar to a balloon basket ascending as the weights are thrown off. It was remarkably spacious and luxurious, affording deeply cushioned silk-

upholstered bench seats built into its sides. Elizabeth and
Fiona sat opposite the Maharani as her honoured guests,
leaving a pouting and severely disappointed Lady Amarita
riding on the following elephant. Their passage through the
jungle was incredibly noisy, with the sepoy pathfinders
shouting to each other as they hacked relentlessly through
the undergrowth, and the *mahout*'s steady conversations
with their elephants. One wondered what might occur if one
of the huge beasts actually answered, Elizabeth mused.

"You must tell us what we might expect, Your Royal Highness, as neither Fiona nor I have partaken of the pleasure of
venturing out on a tiger hunt before." Elizabeth seized her
seat with both hands as the *howda* gave a precarious lurch.

The Maharani made a slight moue as she, too, hung on.
"Never tell, my dears, but I'm not enamoured of these
hunts. Oh, the occasional elephant ride, an exciting race
through the jungle and sleeping out under the stars are all
quite enjoyable, but killing such a noble and handsome
beast I have absolutely no taste for. One cannot refuse the
honour, however."

Elizabeth laughed. "I am relieved, ma'am. I thought it might
be considered irregular if I voiced such an opinion myself."

"At least the two of you are practised in firearms. Goodness, I wouldn't know the trigger from the . . . the long tubu-
lar thing!" Fiona groused.

"The barrel?" supplied Elizabeth.

Fiona waved her hand in a dismissive gesture. "Whatever."

"I shall teach you when we make camp," Elizabeth offered.

Fiona shuddered. "Please don't bother, darling, I'm a lost
cause. No doubt I should shoot myself in the foot."

The Maharani winked at her. "Then that handsome beau
of yours will have to carry you everywhere."

Fiona blushed and said slyly, "Gunshots are *so* painful—
perhaps I may merely arrange a twisted ankle instead."

The Maharani laughed with delight. "Scheming wench," she accused.

With a distracted smile, Elizabeth rotated about to study the long line behind them. "It seems nearly the whole regiment turned out to escort us. I fully realise you are an important personage, ma'am, but isn't this unusual?"

"Actually, yes. I assumed it was because of the escalating violence locally."

Before Elizabeth might reply, Nigel caught up alongside on his horse and shouted up at them, "We're stopping in half an hour for lunch. How are you ladies holding up? Rather like a ship on the ocean, isn't it?"

Elizabeth grinned down at him. "Positioned as you are, darling, you are quite lucky we all boast sea legs!"

"Cheeky girl," Nigel called back, and then made his way up the line.

Elizabeth's expression clouded as he disappeared from sight, all her uncertainty about their union returning.

The Maharani watched with a speculative gleam. "A mother should never admit to having a favourite child," she said carefully. "I suppose it is because I sense we share more in common. All my sons, of course, attended Eton and Oxford, and were successfully reared in the tenets required of every pupil therein—the very British three C's: the Classics, Cold baths, and Cricket.

"However, my two elder sons were aware of their very important future posts in government, and remained Kashmiri and Hindu in nature. I suppose I was selfish, but I desperately desired one child with whom I could be freely British and share similar beliefs. Yet it has been so hard on him, because in truth he belongs to both races. He feels accepted by neither, while his brothers are secure in their berths in life." She let out a dispirited sigh. "It won't be easy for the woman he marries." Shooting Elizabeth a pointed look, she added,

"I do not expect him to remain in India. It will no doubt be best for him to make a fresh start elsewhere."

"But, ma'am," observed Elizabeth, startled, "it was my impression the Indian Army is Nigel's career!"

"Alas, my dear, that may not be so, even though he has not mentioned it to me. The murder accusation damaged his career so badly it is unlikely to recover—even with his promotion. Everybody sees through *that* rather thin veil. Nigel is becoming increasingly discouraged. He seeks promotions on his own, but after this scandal it will be all but impossible."

"And I am partly to blame for it."

The Maharani shook her head in sympathy. "You are not responsible for your father's actions, child."

"In this case I must bear part of the burden, ma'am. My father was aware of an attraction between us, and desperately attempting to keep us apart, sought to discredit Nigel." Elizabeth grimaced. "Poetic justice if ever it existed—my father's narrow-mindedness is now his own downfall."

"Don't let it trouble you, my dear." The Maharani patted Elizabeth's knee. "You must shoulder your own responsibilities—which are not light, I think, at the moment."

Her brow clearing and summoning a brave smile, Elizabeth declared, "Well, I shan't allow them to ruin a perfectly glorious weekend!" She waved at a cloud of mosquitoes hovering in her face. "How lovely if these horrid little creatures might be banished in the same manner."

Bending to rummage through a small hamper at her feet, the Maharani pulled out a handsome blue and gold cloisonné jar and handed it to Elizabeth. "Rub a bit of this on your exposed skin, my dear, and the mosquitoes will avoid you for several hours. My husband's physician makes it up."

Elizabeth unscrewed the lid, taking an experimental sniff. The mellow gingery scent was a pleasant surprise. Dipping her fingers into the cream, she spread it generously on her face, neck, and hands before giving it to Fiona.

Rubbing the last of the concoction into her hands, Elizabeth looked thoughtfully at Nigel's mother. "Ma'am, forgive me for asking such a personal question, but has it been difficult for you, living in a foreign culture? Do you miss England very much?"

"Let us cease this 'ma'am' and 'Royal Highness' nonsense. You two are my honoured guests, so please call me Vanessa. To answer your question, my dear, not so difficult as you might imagine. My father spent years in the diplomatic corps, you see, and I travelled the world with him. I grew up more in 'foreign' cultures than I did in England. My husband, and indeed, most of the ruling class in Kashmir, is educated in England. It does not, however, make any of them British, but it serves to give them a familiar facade. There are the occasional visits to England, but I am always delighted to arrive home again. Fortunately I always adapted easily to change. Even so, a few customs *are* disconcerting." She gave a small laugh. "For example, having two married sons with *five* wives between them! Goodness, I am a grandmother six times over!"

"Do you ever worry about being forced into suttee if your husband dies before you do?" Fiona asked.

"Not at all. It is illegal for one thing. That's not to say it never happens—it does, but rarely. And one can only hope the widow in these instances, performs her sacrifice out of devotion for her deceased husband and not out of intimidation from relatives." She paused to adjust her gossamer silk scarf more securely around her head. "My husband leads a progressive and liberal government. Besides, most of his subjects are actually Muhammadans rather than Hindu."

Elizabeth pinched a pleat in her trousers with great concentration and without looking up asked, "If your husband should pass before you do, Vanessa, will you return to England or remain in Kashmir?"

Vanessa stared at the elephant behind them for some time

before speaking. "The answer to that requires a crystal ball, I'm afraid. The question of moving may not wait until my husband's passing. It is no longer a question of 'if' but *when* India achieves Home Rule. And the fate of Kashmir is directly attached to India." She counted off the possibilities on her fingers.

"HMG pulls out and we succumb to civil war—Hindus anxious to join the newly independent state of India, and/or the Muhammadans insisting on an independent country of their own, which is happening even now here in India.

"Britain stays in Kashmir and we remain as we are.

"Britain pulls out, India is too busy governing itself and leaves us be. Afghanistan ignores us and we remain as we are.

"Afghanistan invades.

"It is a very complicated time for this part of the world, and there are no easy solutions."

Elizabeth nodded sadly. "It seems the whole world is dicky just now. Governments falling, political assassinations right and centre, epidemics of bank closures, the nonsense with Japan and China, and now this mess. Frightfully cowardly of me, but I'm quite relieved to go hibernate in New Zealand!"

"Yes," agreed Vanessa thoughtfully. "One might escape most of the world's bedevilments and remain free to build one's own life according to one's own specifications. How extraordinary."

"If only one may also escape these flying leeches," Fiona commented, her eyes on a mosquito daring the proximity of the ointment meant to repel them.

Vanessa scratched her neck, feeling the familiar bump of a bite. "A perfect world, indeed, my dear."

"Caught the wee besom!" Fiona cried in triumph, slapping herself on the wrist.

"It appears we need more than Dr. Desai's remedies." Vanessa's eyes twinkled. "I say we change over to horses after luncheon and outride the little buggers!"

Chapter Thirty

Transparent yellow and orange flames leaped high in the tall bonfire, sending sparks popping into the chill night air. Elizabeth leaned comfortably back in her folding canvas chair sipping after-supper cognac, enjoying the warm glow of both the crackling fire and the liquor seeping in a lazy flow through her veins. A serenade of crickets whirred, competing with the ragtime beat of "Twentieth Century Blues" resonating from Vanessa's Victrola in the distance and the jocund voices from a game of Charades led by Sir Clive on the other side of the fire. Fiona and Harry were attempting to decipher the Commissioner's comic antics, but Elizabeth was content to relax and watch the activities. They had not managed to outride the mosquitoes that afternoon after all, but the wild gallop through the jungle proved far more exciting than suffering through a stuffy day in a monotonously rocking *howda*.

Nigel had entertained them at tamer moments by pointing out and naming various flora and fauna, surprising Elizabeth with his knowledge. He assured her that a soldier's awareness between the poisonous and the benign made the difference in survival in the jungle.

He regaled them with adventures of the unwary, including a tale of an officer new to India. Out picnicking with companions, he stepped into the woods for a gypsies—failing to take his service revolver. A near fatal mistake, as he soon found himself in the hungry sights of a yellow-eyed panther. His cry alerted his friends, who came crashing through the underbrush, at the last moment sending the big black cat hunting in a more bountiful direction.

They had all listened to Nigel's entertaining stories of the Indo-Aryan roots of India and how these peoples were conquered by the Mogul Empire, which reached its golden age approximately at the time of the construction of the Taj Mahal in the mid-seventeenth century.

Touching on the incongruity of the goddess Kali, he explained that a segment of her followers were peaceful housewives, who left flowers and spices on the altars of her temples as the Goddess of Hearth and Home. Another sect was voracious in its lust for murder. These misguided disciples strangled whole caravans: hundreds of people in a single night, burying them in mass graves. Infiltrated in the previous century, their gruesome activities were at last terminated—to all outward appearances, at least. For decades now, Nigel informed them, rumours hinted at the continuing bloodlust of Kali's faithful. When the gasps subsided, he'd grinned and advised against alarm, with the reminder that they carried all the latest weaponry and plenty of it.

Elizabeth shivered, remembering those ominous words, but consoled herself that Nigel was quite right indeed. An attack on such a heavily armed party, which included the Maharani of Kashmir and the Commissioner of Bengal, was extremely unlikely.

"Not interested in Charades?" A familiar voice interrupted her thoughts.

Startled, Elizabeth looked up at Nigel's tall form, the light of the fire shining on his face and casting his long shadow over her.

"I'm feeling far too lazy after such an energetic day. The fire and the cognac offer an alternative too difficult to resist just now," she murmured, taking another sip and stretching her legs toward the blaze.

He surveyed the opulently expansive movements of her long, slender trouser-clad legs and felt a sultry heat rise in him, making his own trousers uncomfortably tight. A brief glance across the fire told him they'd not be missed.

"Perhaps you'd care to retire?" He stared at her, his dark eyes sparkling with desire.

Elizabeth froze under his hot gaze and then felt a blush creeping into her cheeks. A pleasurable ache grew within her until it became a tight ball of anticipation. Did they dare? Privacy was limited and anyone might walk into her tent. But it might be her last chance to love, and urgency spurred her.

She rose in a languid glide, her eyes steady on his. "Why, yes. I really am quite fatigued. Perhaps you might escort me?"

His scorching gaze raked her body, his eyes doing that which his hands craved, but he dared not touch her where they might be seen and cause comment. Not while they were unmarried. A state which he intended to be brief.

"With utmost pleasure. You are not *too* fatigued, I hope?"

Elizabeth favoured him with a flirtatious sideways glance. "Oh, I imagine I can make the journey to my tent without disgracing myself by falling into an exhausted heap at your feet."

"How gratifying." His voice hummed with promise.

The fire flickered and crackled behind them, and the dark

figures of servants on the last errands of the night darted in
and out of shadows ahead as Nigel and Elizabeth made
their way to her tent. It was a more spacious tent than most,
and a dark, opaque brown. She and Fiona had been surprised
they did not share a tent on an expedition where everyone
else doubled, but now she realised Nigel might be responsible for the circumstance.

Before throwing back the tent flap, Elizabeth peeked over
her shoulder. Satisfied they were not observed, she ducked
in, Nigel on her heels. Feeling her way to the small utilitar-
ian table just inside, she found the box of matches left there
and struck one. Nigel stilled her hand as she reached for the
lantern, pulling a votive from his pocket instead.

"Too much light and we'll put on a show the rest of the
camp won't soon forget," he murmured.

Lighting and placing the tiny candle on the table, he took
her in his arms. He kissed her tenderly at first, but with a
growing rapaciousness when she responded so eagerly. At
last, reluctantly, he unwound her arms from his neck and
slowly peeled away her clothing, his lips trailing fire on her
newly exposed skin. Finished, he lowered her trembling to
the camp bed while he quickly stripped his own garments.

Elizabeth stretched fractiously, tingling where the coarse
bed linen chafed, watching Nigel, waiting in greedy expectation for his touch. She held out her arms to him and saw his
face was set in hard lines and his eyes glowed black with desire. When he joined her, he immediately slid her body atop
his so that his erection lay sandwiched between them, fla-
grant, huge, and throbbing. Almost delirious with this new
voluptuous sensation, Elizabeth clung to Nigel's shoulders,
purring in pleasure and rubbing herself sinuously over his
tumescent heat.

Nigel inhaled sharply in reaction to Elizabeth's erotic
writhing, and without thinking grasped her hips and impaled
her on his rigid staff. God, he thought frantically, she

clenched tighter than a fist and milked him exquisitely. Gritting his teeth, he anchored her solidly in place, and fought with a savage strength against the ferocious urge to climax immediately.

Elizabeth gasped in shocked delight as he surged up inside her, filling her so thoroughly, stretching her so widely that for a moment she was entirely breathless. Sobbing in stunning, sublime pleasure, she wriggled helplessly against his unyielding hold, creating such a sumptuous friction that she cried out in enchantment. Nigel silenced her abruptly by drawing her down and kissing her ravenously, allowing his tongue full rein, plundering and twisting and stabbing.

"Shh," he whispered, panting when he managed to tear his lips from her hers. "You'll bring one of the guards."

Incapable of restraint any longer, he once more spanned her hips tightly in his large hands, pressing them down hard, jerking her avariciously back and forth, up and down, until she was whimpering incoherently in rapture and he was bucking up into her in a frenzy, groaning in overwhelming pleasure.

Elizabeth's climax broke violent and intense, rolling over in wave after wave of ecstasy, and she collapsed onto Nigel's chest, smothering her cries in his damp neck.

Grinding fiercely into her one last time Nigel felt his awesome release, and clenching his jaw he came silently, his whole body shaking.

Elizabeth slipped off Nigel's chest and onto her side on the narrow camp bed in a blush of contentment. Running her fingers through his chest hair, she remarked, "I never knew making love could be quite like this. No wonder it's all the rage to skip the marriage ceremony and proceed straight to bed!"

"It's not always like this. We are extremely fortunate." Nigel also moved onto his side and, spoon fashion, gathered her in his arms.

His chest and leg hair rasped her tender skin, and she could feel his manhood still hot but recumbent in the small of her back.

"Are you ready yet, with your answer?" His breath tickled her ear.

Stiffening, Elizabeth said, "I-I don't know, Nigel . . ."

"You must make up your mind soon, Elizabeth. I will not cheapen our love by indulging in an affair. I want you for my wife. By the time we reach Calcutta again I need your answer."

"Yes, of course," she said, relieved she needn't answer him just yet. "When we reach town . . ." Suddenly he was growing; and wriggling experimentally, she moaned in delight. "Is this a new way?"

Nigel chuckled softly, rubbing himself in the cleft of her buttocks and plucking gently on her nipples with long, nimble fingers.

"Oh, it's not new, sweetheart; it's as old as time. Let's see how you like it, hmm?"

Arching against him, Elizabeth blissfully succumbed to Nigel's very thorough tutorial.

Chapter Thirty-one

Morning brought the mouth-watering aroma of sizzling bacon through the tent flaps, and stretching languidly, Elizabeth opened her eyes, breathing in the full measure of it. Her stomach growled, anticipating a delicious British-Indian breakfast of chutney-eggs, sliced mango, cold buttered toast with marmalade, kippers, and bacon. Sitting up, she noticed her clothing scattered about on the floor. Nigel had left just before dawn, and even alone, the memories of the night before still made her blush as they played out like a film reel in her mind. An extremely naughty film reel.

Surveying the confines of the tent, she noticed the votive had burnt out during the night, leaving a charred black circle in the wooden table, and no sign of Nigel having stayed, except . . . Was it her imagination, or could she actually smell the musky scent of their lovemaking still? Looking down at herself, Elizabeth saw several whorls of Nigel's black body hair sticking to her breasts and mingling with her blond triangle. A thumb-shaped bruise of passion marred her right hip where he had grasped her so demandingly. With a sharp intake of breath she clamped a hand over her mouth in embarrassment. Good God! Had she really done all those wicked things?

But arousal replaced those feelings as she remembered the pleasure Nigel took from her mouth and the excitement when he performed the same service on her. He had said when they were married they would read to each other from the *Kama Sutra* and study—in minute detail—the positions depicted.

She remained silent when he had said that. Oh, what was she to do? She loved him desperately, but the notion of her children being called names such as cheechee or wog was repugnant beyond measure. And she would never forgive herself for ending his career because they dared convention by marrying. But *he* was willing to brave these barriers. Could his mother be correct in assuming Nigel's army career was already over? Life was becoming complicated and taxing indeed. In a perfect world she and Nigel ran away to her sheep station where her father visited occasionally to bounce her children upon his knee and enjoyed an unblemished rapport with Nigel.

Smiling ruefully, she reached for her clothing and began dressing. As if Nigel ever intended to bury himself in some outback New Zealand sheep station! He was a prince and an Army officer even if his career was over. No, she concluded, pulling on her jodhpurs and wrestling with her riding boots; he'd stifle in such a rural spot. Yet if they stayed in India . . . No, it just wasn't acceptable.

Arranging a small mirror on the table so she might see herself adequately to apply just a touch of lip rouge and translucent powder, she noticed the slumberous cast of her green eyes and the bee-stung look of her lips. Oh dear, that would never do. Splashing more tepid water on her face, she discovered it changed nothing. Perhaps it could be passed off as an almost sleepless night (it very nearly had been, come to that). She must make do, she thought, tidying herself. After all, she could hardly use black eyeliner—which served to give the eyes a more open look—as it melted and dripped annoyingly into the eye in this atrocious heat. Ah well, stiff upper lip and all that rot. With a final pat to her hair, she seized her new topi, and was outside striding to the breakfast table in the centre of camp.

"Ah, there you are, Miss Mainwarring. Good morning to you." Sir Clive rose from his place at the breakfast table, bowing in greeting. The table was elegantly set with thick white linen and Royal Doulton china. Lady Amarita, seated next to him, regarded her warily over her teacup. Vanessa waved from the head of the table and resumed her chat with the turbaned Indian sitting next to her.

"Elizabeth, over here, dear," called Fiona, patting the empty seat on her right. "Oh, darling," she sympathised as Elizabeth sat down and reached for the teapot. "You look perfectly ghastly. Did you get no sleep at all? Those tiny camp beds are bally awful, aren't they? So hard and narrow."

Elizabeth grinned, stirring cream into her tea. "Just the type of friend a girl needs. One who continually tells one the truth, regardless. Good morning to you, too, Fiona. By the way, is that extra baggage I see under your eyes, dear girl?"

"Touché." Fiona laughed and passed her a tropical fruit salad made of pawpaw, cantaloup, kiwi, mango, and pineapple. "It wasn't just the bed. I must admit I found the jungle sounds a bit disconcerting—especially after all those horror stories about the goddess Kali that Nigel 'entertained' us with yesterday." She shivered. "I kept imagining panthers and grinning, evil-eyed maniacs with white scarves coming to call."

"Please! Not so loud. Oh, God, I think a fireworks display is exploding inside my head." Georgina, pale and holding unsteady fingertips to her temples, gingerly sat beside Elizabeth, who immediately poured her a cup of tea. The cup shook on its way to Georgina's mouth.

"My dears," Georgina said after a healthy gulp. "Never, *never* attend one of the Maharani's evenings if she's serving champers, playing ragtime, and has invited a positive regiment of young, gorgeous officers, whose *raison de terre* is toasting young ingenues such as myself and dancing the Charleston until dawn. I am positively fagged."

Fiona giggled and slapped a hand over her mouth, earning a scowl from Georgina, while Elizabeth hailed one of the bearers and ordered a small whisky.

"And to think we missed all this fun playing a tame game of Charades. Elizabeth even retired early," Fiona murmured with a wicked smile. "At least we have our heads this morning, and our mouths don't, er, taste as if a company of foot soldiers tramped through it and then used it as a latrine."

"Oh do stifle it, Miss Clean and Sober—oh, *thank* you." Georgina took the proffered whisky from the table waiter and unceremoniously dumped it in a dainty china teacup. Swallowing a portion of it, she closed her eyes and shuddered.

When the liquor hit bottom, she gasped and clutched at her middle. "Oh dear, now my tummy feels rather peculiar."

Elizabeth handed her a thick linen serviette and, glancing about, finally suggested, "Why don't you go stand by that nice bush over there, old girl?"

"Nice bush?" Georgina's tone was surly. "Good Lord, Elizabeth, you speak of it as if it were a custard or a plum pudding. I certainly *will not* stand beside it. Really, how undignified! If I am about to lose my, er, whatevers, I should sprint into the jungle to be private." Her chin raised a defiant notch, she reached for the whisky-laced tea. Sipping a bit more apparently regained her a modicum of composure and she said far more pleasantly, "Anyway, I feel somewhat better now."

"How is everybody this morning? I say, marvellous day, ain't it?" Harry's voice was cheerful as he pulled out a chair across from Fiona and drew up a platter of bacon.

"Must everyone shout this morning?" grumbled Georgina, wincing. "It's a bloody disaster of a day. Do please wipe that cheeky grin from your face, Harry, it hurts just looking at it. Will someone please light me a fag and put me out of my misery?"

Harry raised his eyebrows as he piled a generous portion of bacon onto his plate. "Gad. Arose on the wrong side of the bed, did she?" He tossed Georgina his box of Woodbines. "Afraid you'll have to light it yourself, old girl. Can't abide the filthy things until I've lined my stomach."

Georgina shook one out and held it trembling between her lips while Elizabeth lit it for her. Exhaling, she asked, "What makes you think, old boy, that I ever *reached* bed? I danced all night."

"Er, quite." Helping himself to the eggs, he remarked in an airy voice, "Hear the Maharani brought several cases of an excellent Mumm's '12 champagne along. Should really like to sample some. What do you say, girls? Might we prevail on Her Royal Highness this evening?"

"Bloody hell," groaned Georgina, burying her head in her hands.

Elizabeth tried in vain to smother a peal of laughter that ended in a coughing fit, with Fiona slapping her on the back. Once more in control of herself and wiping her eyes, she said, "That was too bad of you, Harry. By the way, have you seen Nigel yet today?"

Between mouthfuls, Harry informed her that indeed he had. Nigel had ridden out early with a group of scouts to blaze a path or two to see if they might scare up the trail of a tiger.

Finishing his breakfast, Harry placed his knife and fork on his plate, and taking the tea Fiona poured, said, "Oh, yes, mustn't forget. Nigel stipulated clearly you girls were to carry not only a rifle, but a revolver as well." His eyes darted between the three girls. "Take it you lot are all proficient with firearms?"

Laughing, Fiona apprised him of her complete ignorance of anything that went *bang*.

"I'm just along for the ride, darling, I have no intention of shooting anything. Besides"—her brown eyes sparkled—"it would only add to Georgina's misery, wouldn't it, dear?"

Smiling at Fiona as sweetly as her aching head allowed, Georgina said dryly, "So thoughtful of you, dear girl, to trouble yourself with my comfort—or more pertinently, the lack of it." Wrinkling her nose, the woman took a last draw of the Woodbine and crushed it out in a brass ashtray at her elbow. "That was certainly the nastiest fag I have ever had the misfortune of smoking. How do you abide them, Harry?"

Ignoring her and facing Fiona, Harry's gaze narrowed in concern. "Nothing for it, darling, I must at least teach you the rudiments before we leave this morning."

"Absolutely not!" Fiona's voice turned hard. "I have no intention of subjecting myself to a bruised shoulder and ringing ears. Besides, doesn't one need bottles for target practice? Well, I cannot see one of the bloody things at fifty yards let alone hit one."

"Then we shall begin at ten yards with the revolver." Harry's voice was equally hard as he stood. "Have you no idea, you little widget, how defenseless you are without a weapon in the jungle? You can very easily and quickly be separated from your party, and then what will you do, hmm?"

"I shall make certain I am not separated then," Fiona said sulkily after a moment.

Captain Henderson cleared his throat, announcing his presence, and pulled out a chair next to Harry. His expression and voice were grim.

"Quite so, Miss McKay. Any number of wild animals out there would as soon eat you as look at you. Too many varieties of snakes to name, not to mention a handy shot in the air if you become lost. Might save your life, allowing Woodford to show you a thing or two." That said, he tucked into his meal. If he was disappointed that Mrs. Crosshaven was not invited to join the tiger shoot, he showed no evidence of it.

Sighing in defeat, Fiona stood. "I am duly chastised, gentlemen. Lead on, Odysseus dear, and do be careful where you stand, I would deem it an extreme inconvenience if I shot you by mistake." Turning back to Georgina, she offered playfully, "I'd say come and watch the fun, old thing, but you had your share last night!"

"Where," Georgina asked Elizabeth rhetorically, "did you find that little gem?"

Elizabeth laughed softly. "Rare, isn't she? By the way, how experienced are you with firearms?"

"I'm a crack shot. Learned as a girl. Can hit my target with one eye closed, which is just as well considering the way I feel. Never used a knife before, however."

"Most English misses are not skilled with the blade." Lady Amarita paused in passing their end of the table. "It is not surprising. Shooting is a sterile experience, as it is done from a distance and one may remain quite detached. Not so with a dagger. It requires a certain proximity as well as physical strength and a 'suitable character.' To look one's enemy in the eye at close range and know he is vanquished is exhilarating." She shrugged, but her dark eyes glittered. "Of course, it is a bit messier, but what is a little blood? Especially if it belongs to your enemy." A small superior smile played about her mouth. "I wish you good hunting, ladies. I know I shall bag *my* prey."

"A singularly unpleasant woman," remarked Georgina as they watched the young Indian woman take herself off. "Admittedly, my head is a bit muzzy, but somehow I doubt she has 'vanquished' many tigers with her dagger."

Captain Henderson stood and cleared his perpetually dry throat. "I must see to my duties, ladies, so I'll wish you a pleasant morning."

"In fact," Georgina continued when the Captain left, "the Lady Amarita sounded as if she might be issuing a threat." She studied Elizabeth closely. "Now why might she be so disagreeable?"

Elizabeth shot her a jaunty smile and replied, "Perhaps she is cross because she is forbidden the champagne everyone else partook of last night! Now if your head has recovered sufficiently, why don't we look in on Fiona's progress. I wouldn't mind a few rounds myself."

"Why not, indeed," grumbled Georgina. "How can the morning get any worse?"

After an hour of loading, aiming, and shooting, Harry convinced himself that Fiona might indeed be capable of hitting her target—if it was gargantuan and remained stationary. He groaned and shook his head as yet another bullet sheared into the jungle, dozens of yards off its target. Perhaps she might wing the Taj Mahal if she stood close enough. On a clear day.

Not even encouragement from Elizabeth and Georgina helped, and they soon subsided into silence, reluctant to gain Fiona's attention, as one never quite knew when she might depress the trigger by mistake. At one point she had carefully aimed but swung around to reply to a suggestion and gave them all a start as the gun exploded accidentally, the bullet hurtling into the ground only inches from their feet. Afterward the ladies meekly took up the safest stance in the vicinity—directly behind Harry.

Sighing in frustration, Harry finally took the revolver from Fiona's grasp when a bearer sent to find them ran into their clearing. More practise was urgently required, and he could only hope his red-headed sprite, whom he began to recognise as quite possibly the love of his life, evaded danger with the same concentration she gave her shooting lessons—but with significantly better results. Ready or not, the hunt was on.

Elizabeth had veered away from the others at the entrance to the campsite to use the privy before several hours of jolting about on the back of a horse. On her way back, she discovered Nigel leading a horse toward her and saw with some surprise it was a sleek black mare, not the piebald gelding she rode yesterday. When she mentioned it, Nigel replied, "Evidently one of the handlers gave him to another lady, but I think you will be pleased with Sarasvati. She is named for the patron Goddess of Music and Dancing." He gave her an intimate smile and his hands lingered on her waist once he assisted her into the saddle.

Her pulse immediately accelerated, and she could feel her skin heating and tingling through her clothing where he caressed her waist, sliding possessively up her rib cage and down again. Colour stained her cheeks as she returned his gaze and answered, her voice husky, "Indeed, how appropriate. I am sure I shall enjoy riding her."

"Lt. Colonel-Sahib. Her Highness is waiting." Neither of them had noticed the Indian servant approaching, and his voice startled them both.

"Of course." Nigel nodded to the servant and stepped back to mount his stallion.

"We shall ride with my mother, Harry, Fiona, and Georgina. The other guests—including Amarita—will bring up the rear. We ride in small tight groups to avoid separation." Urging his mount to a brisk walk, he reminded her, "Generally we are not so regimented, but there are several of you unused to the jungle. You will find nothing in common here with a fox hunt."

"That is a relief. Although I do belong to a shooting club, I have ridden to hounds only once and didn't possess the heart for it. One defenseless fox against a pack of hunting dogs." At Nigel's raised eyebrows, she answered, her voice rising as he pulled slightly ahead, "I was not an heiress until recently, you know. I wasn't brought up in the 'foxy' set."

"A tiger hunt can be dangerous even for the experienced. Stay close to me today," he tossed over his shoulder, kicking his horse into a fast trot.

Elizabeth eyed the seat of his snug riding trousers with approval. "Not a hardship I assure you, darling," she murmured, and then leaned forward over Sarasvita's neck, encouraging the mare to a faster pace.

Chapter Thirty-two

In the distance, high above the dense teak trees, vultures circled, causing a shiver to tingle down Elizabeth's spine. The hunting party rode hugging the edge of the jungle. This primal, verdant wilderness hardly resembled the tame, blooming Maidan. She reached for her canteen, but the water was warm and unrefreshing.

Twice since luncheon the scouts had signalled a tiger-sighting to the beaters. Elizabeth didn't envy the beaters their dangerous job. They were to surround a tiger and drive it into the open by smashing at the undergrowth with their stout sticks, allowing the Sahibs, sitting securely on their horses, to take aim at the creature. Only, a tiger often managed to elude bullets and mauled or killed before it bounded back into the jungle.

Elizabeth wiped at the beading perspiration on her forehead with the back of a wrist and glanced at the sky. It was clogged in thick, cottony clouds, but the sun gleamed relentlessly through in a stifling, white phosphorescence. The smothering heat was enervating, yet something lurked in the atmosphere, just out of reach, charging the stillness with an expectation of . . . *some*thing.

A dusty, swirling breeze carried a wisp of the conversation between Sir Clive and Vanessa back to her. Only half listening, she stretched her aching muscles and imagined soaking in a cool bath, sipping a large ice-cold gin and tonic.

A sudden clamour brought her fantasy to a startling end when a swarm of parakeets flew squawking out of the trees ahead. An instant later a furor erupted. The beaters yelled, crashing through the undergrowth bordering the trees. Pandemonium continued even as one of the beaters emerged from the tall grass, rushing toward Vanessa and Sir Clive.

"Highness, Excellency-Sahib," he burst out. "Is true this time! I see him with my own eyes! A king of tigers, fit for the Esteemed Wife of an Illustrious Maharaja!" He pointed. "There. You will see him come!"

A thundering and very menacing roar silenced the palava. Adrenaline charged through Elizabeth's veins like an electrical current as she reached for her rifle. She had no desire to shoot the animal, but neither was she about to chance a mauling. Wiping her damp hands on her trousers, she lifted the stock to her shoulder, waiting. In seconds the tiger pounced into the clearing.

He was ferociously beautiful. And at only twenty paces, phenomenally dangerous. With every breath the beast's black stripes brazenly expanded in his orange fur. Amber eyes spewed disdain. He crouched, quivering with pernicious purpose, tail whipping, waiting. . . .

The beater's eyes bulged in terror realising his weaponless vulnerability, and panicking he turned, sprinting in a desperate attempt at escape.

The tiger launched with lightning speed, soaring after

the frightened man, dinner-plate-size paws outstretched, and sharp, vicious teeth gleaming.

Sir Clive wheeled his horse around, and swinging his rifle into action, got off the first shot. But it veered wildly into the jungle.

Harry and Georgina rode into the melee, rifles drawn. Fiona followed, endeavouring without success to control her agitated horse. Already excited by the earsplitting report of gunfire, the proximity of the tiger sent the piebald tumbling over the edge into hysteria—screaming and rearing.

The tiger, enraged and confused by additional turmoil, twisted around, hunching low. With one last deafening roar, he gathered his massive body and sprang at the terrified horse and rider.

"Fiona!" Her gun forgotten, Elizabeth watched in paralysed fear as her friend, losing the desperate battle to maintain her seat, slid off the rearing piebald's back. She made a lucky grasp on the horse's mane as she toppled. But her tenacious grip held her at a precarious angle between the horse's lethal flying hooves and the tiger's ripping claws.

A strange buzzing filled Elizabeth's ears and, as if the world suddenly decelerated, she witnessed in exquisite detail the tiger freeze, jerk convulsively, then fall to the ground with a heavy thud in an orange and black heap.

A moment later a shot rang out, and shaking her head in confusion, she knew that somehow she had reversed the sequence of events. Then, as if a bucket of frigid water poured over her, movement and sound returned to normal.

Georgina seized the piebald's bridle while Harry threw himself off his mount, clenched Fiona around the waist, and pulled her free of the distraught horse.

Amarita rode up in a cloud of dust just as Nigel grimly returned his gun to the holster. He dismounted and strode toward the fallen tiger.

"You are indeed a great hunter, Your Highness." Amarita's eyes glowed in admiration. Stepping to the ground, she leaned over the kill. "Truly a magnificent animal. How courageous you are, my lord!"

Nigel flicked her a disgusted glance. "It is Miss McKay who is courageous. He was not about to attack me. You will notice my bullet is embedded in the back of the head, not between the eyes."

Amarita cast a peevish look at Fiona, but whirled in shock on hearing his last words. "You repudiate the honour of besting so exalted a foe?" She swept out her hand, indicating the body of the tiger.

Out of patience, Nigel snapped, "Shut up, Amarita," and turned his back on her.

Fiona sat up, huddled between Elizabeth and Harry, hiccupping and dabbing her red-rimmed eyes with a crumpled handkerchief. She lifted her face and tried a gamin smile, but it collapsed before it completely formed.

"The nick of time, Nigel." A tremor shook Fiona's voice and her features were ashen. " 'Thank you' is bloody inadequate, but . . ." Her bottom lip began trembling violently and she broke off. Elizabeth pulled her friend close, but stared at Nigel with glassy eyes over Fiona's head as if shell-shocked.

Harry stood, his eyes blazing. Motioning Nigel several feet away, he demanded, "What the bloody hell is the meaning of this, Covington-Singh? Fiona was very nearly killed just now! Which bloody, sodding charlie was in charge of choosing the horses? That scatter-brained gelding isn't used to the explosion of firearms. Damned witless beast has no business on a hunt!"

Nigel's eyes narrowed in speculation as he observed the growing cluster of onlookers surrounding the dead tiger. He wondered exactly the same thing himself. Facing Harry again, he noted the pulse point racing in the other man's throat and the compulsive fisting of the hands kept stiff at his sides.

"We're bloody well about to find out." Nigel's tone was hard. "And we'll start with the Commissioner's equerry."

"Nigel?" Georgina's voice was hushed. He didn't hear her approach, but now she stood at his side holding a leather girth. "It's cut. Fiona's saddle girth has been cut," she said, handing it to him. "Just a little, but there, you see?"

Chapter Thirty-three

Fiona suffered no physical injury but a few sore muscles unused to the strain of hanging on for dear life, swinging and jerking from the mane of a rearing horse. Once she was secured, riding pillion with Harry, and the tiger tied by its limbs to a rail, Nigel urged all speed in returning to camp. Elizabeth rode beside her still-jittery friend, keeping up a steady conversation to distract them both.

The end of a successful tiger shoot required a celebration honouring the marksman, and there were many questions needing answers by then. The girth cut was clean and sliced halfway through, designed to tear completely under continued stress—and Nigel intended to find out who had perpetrated that bit of mischief. And why.

Nigel doubted the incident was connected to the killer he was seeking. No, that killer liked getting his hands dirty, and there was no guarantee Fiona would have been killed. But the potential for serious maiming was unlimited. Now who, Nigel asked himself, would rather cripple than kill?

Was Fiona, indeed, the intended victim? Elizabeth had ridden that gelding yesterday and had expected to do so today. He tightened his hands on the reins in determination. By God, he'd uncover answers tonight.

He questioned the Commissioner's equerry and his staff, but although quite cooperative, they denied Sir Clive's ownership of the piebald. Sir Clive had provided an adequate pool of mounts, but some guests preferred their own horses and boarded them with their host's herd.

After several private interrogations, one very young groom's assistant admitted seeing a servant belonging to one of the guests attending to the piebald. Immediately Nigel sent men out with the description of the man.

The net was closing fast.

The scent of starch and harsh laundry detergent tickled Sister Winifred's nose as she smoothed her patient's sheets and tucked in a stray corner. She glanced at the watch pinned to her bosom. Two hours left on her shift and she could go home—to a blessedly cool bath and her pet mongoose, Reggie. The small affectionate companion was all the attachment she allowed herself in recent years, ever since her husband, peppered in grape shot, bled to death on a rocky, barren battlefield in France in the last hours of the Great War. It was unbearable to love one person so much as she'd loved her Len, and in a heartbeat to lose him forever. No, she sternly admonished herself, she didn't need the rhapsodic highs and miserable lows associated with romantic love anymore. Nothing was worth crawling through that purgatory of recovery again.

Now Winifred busied herself in the worthy profession of nursing. If she yet yearned for a family of her own, she ruthlessly buried such fanciful desires in her vocation. Her patients became her family.

Especially dear Mrs. Newsome. Winifred patted the

woman's dry, nearly lifeless hand. Even though the poor
thing showed no improvement from the day she arrived, she
was extremely lucky to reside in the land of the living. And
not just from the first attack, but a second one in this very
room. Winifred herself had caught the despicable cad and
screamed like an Irish banshee, alerting everyone in the
ward who was not profoundly deaf.

Clicking her tongue in memory of the blackguard's behaviour, she crossed the room to draw the curtains against
the late afternoon heat. No one knew precisely if Mrs. Newsome could actually experience discomfort in her present
state, but there was no reason to assume not.

Casting a last look about the room before departing,
Winifred spied a few dead flowers in her patient's arrangement on the nightstand.

She was plucking out the last of the dead foliage when a
movement in her peripheral vision stunned her into momentary immobility—and then sent her running for the door.

Inside Fiona's tent, Elizabeth handed her friend two aspirin
and a tall, cool glass of water.

"Take these, dear, and try to relax. Get some rest. I shan't
leave you." Picking up the latest issue of *HELLO* magazine,
she settled into a folding chair.

Fiona lay back on the bed and closed her eyes. "I do wish
I were brave and clever enough to say you needn't stay, but
the fact is, I'm glad of the company. I don't think I shall ever
forget those wickedly gleaming teeth aiming straight for my
throat. Nor that saddle suddenly slipping out from under me,
and my grip loosening on the horse's mane." She frowned,
bewildered. "Who cut my saddle girth and for God's sake,
why? What on earth have I done to acquire such a vicious
enemy? Are you sure it wasn't just normal wear and tear?"

"Quite sure, dear." Elizabeth pursed her lips, angry all
over again. "The tear was precise and placed in a spot guar-

anteed to wear quickly. Nigel is looking into it as we speak and with Harry hounding him like a bulldog, we shan't be long in obtaining answers."

"Yes, well, there *is* a maniacal murderer still lurking about, contrary to all Nigel's assiduous efforts." Fiona's tone was rueful. Jerking into an upright position, she said sharply, "You don't suppose it was he who attempted—"

Elizabeth sat forward, eyes blazing. "No!" she asserted with more force than strictly necessary. "It can't be. He strangles women, remember?" Sitting back again, she gripped the arms of her chair until her knuckles showed white, but presented a calm facade to Fiona.

"This is all likely some stupid one-upmanship among the grooms—you know, one trying to make another look bad. It may even be politically motivated. One less of the undesirable faction working in the Commissioner's stable and all that rot. Now do try to relax."

Fiona sighed and closed her eyes again. "You are quite correct, I'm sure. I'll never understand all this Indian intrigue. Certainly they thrive on it. I'll indulge in a wee nap then and be ready for the do tonight."

"Don't fash. No one expects your attendance after your ordeal this afternoon."

"Indeed, I must," Fiona replied drowsily. "Nigel saved my life and this party honours him."

Elizabeth watched her friend drift into sleep but did not relax herself. She'd made lighter of the situation than she believed to be the case. In truth she was scared witless. Rolling the magazine, her hands slick with nervous perspiration, she saw again the horrifying image of Fiona suspended, utterly helpless between an attacking tiger and her terrified horse. And shuddering, she remembered her own inability to aim and fire her rifle; instead sitting atop her mount in paralysed impotence. Why? Her gun was positioned at her shoulder, ready to fire—and yet she'd done nothing! But everyone present did exactly the same. Only Nigel, cool and competent, raised his weapon and fired.

Fiona slept deeply now, and Elizabeth tossed the crumpled magazine onto the camp table. Filled with uneasiness, she wondered about that girth and about a hunt horse that shied at the sound of gunfire. She herself had ridden that gelding yesterday. Had the girth been tampered with then?

"How is she?" Harry stood in the tent entrance, his features etched in worry.

Elizabeth looked up, startled. "I would be very surprised if she didn't suffer from nightmares. Probably will for some time. I'm staying with her tonight," she whispered. "Any news?"

He frowned and his eyes smouldered. "No. When I find the sodding bastard who did this, I will bloody well tear him limb from bloody limb. Then I'll feed his damned entrails to the monkeys."

Elizabeth smiled in understanding. "Do allow me a go, won't you? I promise not to inflict too much damage before you do your bit."

Harry dragged a hand down his face and offered her a ghost of a smile. "Suppose you'd best have first go or there'll be nothing left!" He gazed at Fiona, and shaking his head, murmured, "Wasn't supposed to be her."

Elizabeth sat up straighter. "What did you say?"

Harry's eyes widened, then he winced. "Flaming, blo—" He broke off, raking a hand through his hair. "Right boffin, I am. I'm arse about face now."

"Harry, what are you talking about? Blow the gaff!"

Harry reached for a camp chair and, sitting down, pinched the bridge of his nose between forefinger and thumb. After a moment, he let his hand drop and looked directly at Elizabeth.

"You weren't to know. Nigel will be furious. Yes, yes," he said when Elizabeth frowned and opened her mouth to speak. "I'm getting there. May not live to see another sunrise, but . . ." He took a deep breath. "Apparently, this murdering sod takes exception to, er, women who dally with Indians. You see what this means, old girl?"

Elizabeth's pulse accelerated and her hands grew damp again. "Go on."

"You alibied Nigel, and now the gossip about your involvement with him is rampant. Of course, there's Nigel's mother, too. Both of you are prime targets. And this tiger hunt complicates protecting the two of you. Puts you in rather a spot of bother, old girl."

Elizabeth shot out of her seat, staring at Harry. "He *knew* this? Nigel knows I'm in danger and neglected to inform me? Does the Maharani know?" Her voice, low but intense, drew a moan from the sleeping Fiona.

Harry gave Fiona a sharp glance, then returned his attention to Elizabeth. "Nigel didn't want you frightened. He was adamant about that. If you think about it, it stands to reason that we can better protect you if you remain in ignorance. Believe me, you are surrounded by bodyguards. Eye contact with them could easily tip off our man. Or an inadvertent word to your—to anyone might prove fatal."

The furrow in Elizabeth's brow deepened as she dropped back in her chair. "My . . . what, Harry?"

Harry rolled his eyes and shrank in his chair. "Nothing, old girl, nothing at all. Must be prudent against careless words, is all."

"Don't you 'old girl' me, Harry. You came this far, tell me the rest." But Harry refused to look at her, and suddenly the answer hit her in the belly like a steel toed boot. "Oh my God. You meant my father. *Why?*"

Harry swallowed, and still not looking at her, recounted Nigel's details.

"Of all the idiotic notions," Elizabeth exclaimed when he finished. "My father may be narrow-minded, controlling, and bad-tempered, but he is no murderer. If Nigel and his team wish to catch this killer, they should be rowing their boat up another stream. And so I shall ruddy well tell him."

"Elizabeth." Harry half rose, but sat back down. "Nigel cares a great deal for you. This is his responsibility. If anything were to happen to you or his mother . . ." He broke off with an anxious glance toward Fiona and looked back at Elizabeth with stricken eyes. "He can't afford to ignore possibilities."

Outside Fiona's tent, Elizabeth shivered and cast an uncertain glance about the camp in spite of herself. She could feel the gooseflesh rippling her skin, remembering the attempted attack at the cinema—not to mention the many occurrences she could swear someone was watching her. Perhaps Harry and Nigel were correct. *Knowing* the full score could be far worse than merely suspecting.

And then she saw Nigel—striding toward Lady Amarita's tent, his face as dark as a thundercloud.

Chapter Thirty-four

Lt. Colonel Porter was annoyed. Bloody, damned annoyed.

Abruptly he ceased pacing the crowded confines of the Comptons' drawing room and pinned his gaze on Diana Compton's old ayah, Meenu, standing before him head bowed and wringing her wrinkled brown hands. Mrs. Compton had retired in hysterics to her bedroom and Major Compton leaned against the drinks cabinet, tipping the last of a large gin and tonic down his throat.

"How long since Miss Diana disappeared, woman? Did she run off or was she abducted? Speak up! We haven't all bloody evening!"

"The bitch isn't talking, Derek. I've tried everything but thumbscrews already." Compton's voice was slurred. He reached for the gin bottle again, poured a good measure but neglected to add tonic this round.

Porter threw him an irritated glance. "Perhaps we'll just try a different tack, shall we." Removing his uniform cap, and setting it on a photograph-strewn table, he hooked his

ankle around the leg of a ladder-back chair, pulling it toward
him. Sitting in it backwards, resting his arms on the top
rung, he scrutinised his subject. What besides torture might
induce Meenu to spill her secret? Bloody hell if he knew—
as officer in charge of logistics, ask him to supply the whole
regiment and transport the lot of them to point B from point
A—but Colonel Mainwarring had seen fit to delegate this
chore to him since the absent Covington-Singh was off directing that thrice-damned tiger shoot.

Locking herself in her room several days before, Diana
had refused to see anybody but her old ayah. Deeming it
time to end Diana's self-imposed isolation, her parents had
broken the lock on her bedroom door when she failed to answer their calls—and found the room empty. When confronted, the ayah, who ostensibly had served Diana's meals
and otherwise cared for her, clammed up.

Now, to loosen her tongue. The obvious answer, he supposed, was to find her vulnerability. Apparently, it was Diana. Feeling more in control of the situation, Porter sat up a
bit straighter.

"Are you aware of how much danger Miss Diana is in,
Meenu? We must find her without delay."

The old ayah raised her watery brown eyes. "No! No danger," she insisted.

"I'm afraid there is plenty. Even if a murderer weren't on
the loose, a young British girl alone will not survive long.
Think of the thugs, gangs of thieves, and ponces just waiting
for such a juicy plum to fall into their hands." Porter ignored
Compton's muttered expletive and the loud bang of his high-
ball glass slamming onto the drinks cabinet. "Come now, tell
me what's happened with your mistress."

The ayah jumped at the explosive sound of the glass striking solid wood, and glanced nervously at her employer. He
stood leaning over the cabinet, his pale, strained features partially obscured by several locks of hair fallen loose from his

stiff styling pomade. Turning back to Lt. Colonel Porter, alarm blooming in her cheeks, the ayah sounded less positive.

"No, Miss Diana is *safe!*" Meenu clasped her chest. "I know she is safe. I promised her I would not tell."

So she'd left of her own free will. Some progress at least. Porter nodded encouragement.

"No doubt Miss Diana told you she would be safe, but what does a naive young girl who has never been on her own know about it? Her parents are worried sick, woman! How might you feel right now if you did not know where she was, hmm? The longer it takes to find her, the worse the odds are of finding her alive. For the child's own good, you must reveal her whereabouts!"

Before Meenu could reply, Major Compton flung his glass across the room, where it crashed against the inlaid tiles of the fireplace. In two short strides he pounced on the old Indian woman, seizing her frail throat in his fists.

"Tell me, you damned harridan! Where is my daughter?"

"Bloody hell!" swore Porter, springing from his chair. He wedged himself between Compton and the ayah, pushing them apart. Shoving Meenu onto the settee, he dragged Compton by his shirt lapels to a corner of the room.

"Control yourself, man!" Porter shook the distraught father for emphasis and then let him loose. "We'll get sod all if you kill her or send her into a faint." He was panting from his exertions and took a moment to regain his breath. "How long do you *think* she's been missing? Have you any idea?"

Compton breathed deeply and dragged a hand down his face. "Perhaps a week."

"Good God, man! Have you run mad? Not checked in on your daughter in a week! The poor girl is heinously assaulted and left to languish in solitude? Unbelievable!" Porter stepped back and swatted an overstuffed leather lounger with his swagger stick in exasperation. He paced the length of the room. He'd never allow his daughters to withdraw from life in similar circumstance. By God, he'd not abandon them!

"What do you bloody know about it?" Major Compton spit out bitterly, his face stark in grief. "My flesh and blood, my defenseless daughter was raped! *Raped,* damn you! I couldn't protect her. I wasn't there. Have you any idea how inadequate I feel?" He pounded the wall with his fist. "Do you realise how anxious I am to crush that craven bastard's throat? Christ, I get hard thinking about it! And what can I bloody do? *Nothing!* Nothing but watch my daughter curl into the fetal position in her bed and listen to her whimpers." He collapsed in a delicately wrought walnut chair and buried his face in his hands.

Several moments passed before he sat up at last, the fight drained out of him. His brown eyes swam with tears, but none toppled over the ragged red rims. "When my wife isn't hysterical, she stares at me in accusation and I am crushed with the guilt of not keeping my child safe.

"I'm frightened, Derek," he admitted. "I'm damned good at wielding a kukri, I'm a crack shot, and I may certainly go several rounds with my fives, but it means nothing if I'm impotent in protecting my family. If only it had been *me.* Now my poor girl must carry this with her for her entire life. I wish I could give her that strength, but I cannot. She must find it from within.

"So when she asked for seclusion in an effort to come to terms with herself, I agreed. She needs all the support her mother and I can give. Now she is missing, and I've failed her again." His grasp on the arms of his chair tightened until his knuckles whitened.

God in Heaven, Porter thought, what am I to say to that? There but for You, go I? Clearing his throat, he muttered instead, "Sorry, old chap. Indeed, frustrating situation, should have thought before I spoke. Now, then." He paused, dreading asking the next question. "You don't think she might . . . she wouldn't . . . harm herself—"

"Never, Major-Sahib!" Meenu cried indignantly. "Miss Diana would never do this! She is young and beautiful with everything to live for!"

"Then hell and damnation, woman, tell where she is!" demanded Lt. Colonel Porter.

Major Compton looked at Meenu, his eyes now dry and narrowed in a dangerous glint. "You are of the Vaishya Caste, are you not?"

"Yes, sahib." The ayah nodded proudly. Most of the Compton servants were of the servant class. As Vaishya, Meenu was middle class.

Compton spoke slowly and with deliberation. "If you do not tell me immediately where I may find my daughter, I shall order the untouchables of this household to empty the contents of their latrine over your head."

It was truly a despicable ploy, one which might very well damage the Major's relationship with the sepoys under his command, but Porter understood Compton's desperation.

Meenu gasped in shock. "No, sahib, you mustn't. Purification will take months! I shall never retain my caste!" She rose from the settee and backed toward the door, her eyes darting wildly between the officers.

"Balaji!" Compton called for his major-domo, who appeared at once in the doorway, blocking Meenu's exit. "Inform the dung squad to scoop out their latrine." His eyes cut back to Meenu. "We've discovered a new use for it."

Balaji's gaze widened in shock, but he bowed and closed the drawing-room door, effectively cutting off Meenu's escape.

"No! Please, Major-Sahib, do not do this, I beg of you!" A note of hysteria tinged Meenu's voice. Holding out trembling hands, she beseeched him, "It is wrong to contaminate me with such filth. I do not deserve it. I have served your daughter with loyalty all these years."

"And I do not deserve the anguish I have suffered since I discovered my daughter missing. Now tell me where she's gone."

The old ayah gripped her hands together hard, as if to draw courage. Then she sat down on the settee and told him.

"Holy God!" sputtered Lt. Colonel Porter, his craggy jaw agape.

Compton stared at Meenu, dazed. A bomb might have detonated and he'd not have blinked. Slowly he shook his head.

"No," he said with a hitch in his voice. "My daughter wouldn't do that."

Nigel pulled back the tent flap with a livid jerk. He could feel his pulse thudding in his temple as he ducked, entering the dim interior. It took only a moment for his eyes to adjust from the overcast sky outside and narrow on the figure *en deshabille* reclining on the floor, sipping fruit juice.

Forgoing a camp bed, Amarita lounged amid several large tasselled pillows, wearing only a short silk shift and several pieces of heavy silver jewelry. Her eyes widened fractionally at his abrupt entrance, but she recovered smoothly, sitting up and clapping her hands, dismissing the two maidservants hovering over her.

"Out, both of you," Nigel thundered. "At once."

As one, the two young Indian girls jumped at Nigel's biting tone, and without a glance at their mistress, fled outside.

Amarita lifted a hand in welcome, her bracelets jingling. "My lord, I—"

Nigel cut her off, "Stow it, Amarita." He tapped his swagger stick against his leg in irritation and noticed her gaze fastening on it in sudden alarm. He seldom carried it, but was so angry he found he needed the distraction of keeping his hands busy or he just might do something he regretted.

"You bloody well deserve it and worse, madam, but no, I shall not strike you." He glared at her as if daring her to tempt him to go against his word. "You could have killed a woman today; you are bloody lucky I don't publicly horse-whip you!"

Amarita quickly manoeuvred into a kneeling position and, clasping her hands demurely together under her chin, gazed at him with wide, innocent eyes.

"My lord Nigel, you are upset with me, but I do not understand why. I assure you I would never annoy you, yet it appears I have." A frown marred her smooth, dark brow. "You believe I have *killed* a person? I have not! And I have done nothing to merit horsewhipping."

Nigel curled his lip in contempt. "Get up, Amarita. Your dirty little secret is out of the bag. The virtuous facade you so vainly wear hasn't only cracked—it's crumbled to dust. The groom fell over himself confessing his part in your horse-switching scheme. Apparently, instilling loyalty is not your forte."

Amarita stood, her movements choppy, and seizing her chuddah settled it on her head. When she faced Nigel, her eyes flashed in fury. "I do not understand of what I am accused. I *do*, however, understand the insult you offer me. If my father learns of this slanderous attack upon my character, he will be righteously offended. Is it your intention to acquire an enemy in the person of the Great and Powerful Lord Ramesh Ali? I think not. I shall accept your apology and you may leave." She lifted her chin a proud notch.

Nigel's laugh dripped disdain. "And just what, I wonder, will the Great and Powerful Lord Ramesh Ali do with his daughter when faced with proof of her murder attempt on an honoured guest of the Maharani of Kashmir? As a man and head of his household, he wears *your* dishonour. Murder is strictly against your Muslim doctrine, and the most shameless disgrace you may bring upon your house. Your father is a progressive man, I hear. So he may not kill you—outright. He may choose any number of punishments: stoning,—"

"No one is dead! It is *not* attempted murder! Oh—" Her eyes bulged in shock and she clapped a hand over her mouth.

"No," Nigel snarled. "No one is dead, no thanks to you. Only by divine providence—Allah's, Shiva's, or God's—is Fiona McKay alive!"

Hands on her hips, Amarita glared back at Nigel. "The red-hair! Pah!" She kicked at the silk pillows scattered on the floor. "She is insignificant. She was not supposed—"

In an instant Nigel was on her, seizing her arm, pulling her close so she could not escape his penetrating gaze. "Now we're making progress," he said silkily. "And just who *was* supposed to fall from that horse?" He knew, of course, but the admission must come from her lips.

Amarita did not attempt to break his hold but took a silent, impassive stance, sticking out her chin in defiance. Grasping her free arm as well, he shook her, making her aware he meant business.

"Roughness appeals to you, Amarita? I don't care for it myself, but one of my men suffers no such scruples. Ashish is without a benevolent bone in his body when it comes to concluding his job. Isn't it so much easier just to tell me?"

She gave him a sharp kick in the shin with her slipper-shod foot and twisted out of his hold.

He released her and she stood before him, glowing with animosity. "It was a stupid, stupid mistake. Not my planning—which was brilliant, if I do say. It was stupid to choose that imbecilic excuse for a groom to help me.

"No, that witless beast wasn't intended for the red-headed cow." Her lips turning up in a parody of a smile, she spewed out her next words with a malicious glee. "It was that blond harlot! Your strumpet! A crippled female holds the attention of no man, except for pity. While you were blinded by her

English blond insipidness you did not see me. I am born to make a prince a fine wife and bear many sons." She flicked a hand in contemptuous dismissal. "Your English slag is far too frail to take a large man with any pleasure for long. She will soon grow tired of your virile demands upon her body. And her fertility is dubious with such narrow hips." She caressed her own generous hips. "See what you deny in favour of that banal, blond—"

"Enough! Even if your father were not informed of your debacle, he'd not find you another husband—unless he paid a fortune for the poor, ill-fated sod." He shook his head in mock sorrow. "Apparently, your first husband cocked up his toes just to escape you."

Amarita snorted. "If you tell my father, you will look a fool! It is my word against yours. I am the daughter of his loins. Why should he believe you instead of me?" A calculating gleam entered her eyes. "And I will also tell him you beat me! You have now made an enemy of my father. Ha! You will wish you had not spurned me for some puny English girl!"

Nigel's fist tightened on his swagger stick again, feeling the anger-laced adrenaline throbbing through his veins. He couldn't afford to think of Elizabeth's near escape lest his temper burst forth in all its volcanic glory. Taking a deep breath, he spoke with cold deliberation.

"Only a vindictive and narcissistic shrew would consider creating a political incident of this magnitude over a petty jealousy. Do you actually imagine Lord Ramesh incapable of seeing through your lies? You value yourself too highly and forget your co-conspirator." He saw her lips tremble as she no doubt contemplated the truth of his statement, and the possible punishments Lord Ramesh might devise for his unruly daughter.

Amarita whirled away from him, hiding eyes suddenly full of tears. To be sent home without the royal husband for whom she longed was disgrace enough, but to arrive at her father's palace in bonds, accused of an attempted murder!

"I do not wish to shame a loyal subject of my father's with the cowardly and cruel behaviour of his daughter."

Amarita turned back to him, unmindful of her tears, hope burgeoning in her swimming eyes.

"Enough political strife exists in this sub-continent to give every man, woman, and child living here a bellyache to last years.

"Apologise to Miss McKay. Add a generous gift or two—you can well afford it. Retire from society as soon as we arrive in Calcutta and make immediate arrangements to return home. I never want to hear another peep out of you—is that understood?"

Amarita lowered herself to the pile of cushions and gathered her legs to her chest, resting her chin on her knees. An aura of defeat weighed heavily about her. Risking a glance at Nigel, she asked, "Will you tell the Maharani?"

"She knows."

"Oh, well, you quite have me, don't you, my lord?" Acid spiked Amarita's tone. "My father is likely to banish me to the seraglio as a useless female: barren from a first husband and incapable of enticing the prince he desired as a second son-in-law. No doubt I shall die as the widow I am."

"Madam, you nearly killed a woman, and escaping with your life and limbs intact you are worried about your marital state?" Nigel shook his head. "If Captain Woodford succeeded in his plans, he'd beat you to mush before he upended you in a drum of hot tar, and finish off by sprinkling you with copious goose feathers. Definitely unhealthy in this climate. And no, he knows nothing—yet. So keep the hell out of his way—and mine—and keep a low, in fact invisible, profile until you leave for Kashmir."

Amarita watched Nigel stride out of her tent. She and submission didn't even enjoy a nodding acquaintance. But the

only alternatives were returning to her father in shame—
quite unacceptable—or swallowing poison.

And poison *did* have the distressing tendency of inducing
one to spew one's insides quite uncontrollably, and turn
one's complexion a most uncomplimentary shade of
purplish-black. She touched her smooth, flawless cheek. No,
that wouldn't do at all.

Elizabeth was waiting for Nigel outside Amarita's tent, her
arms folded across her chest and her foot tapping the dusty
ground.

"What's this nonsense about my father being a murder
suspect, Nigel?" she demanded without preamble.

Nigel gritted his teeth. Damn Harry and his big mouth.

Chapter Thirty-five

Amarita spared a cold glance at Elizabeth and Fiona and tossed her head as she rode trotting past them, flanked by several fierce-looking sepoys.

Fiona looked back just as glacially and nudged her chestnut gelding with her knee, indicating a move to the right, making room for the group to pass. "Definitely no remorse from that quarter," she grumbled.

Elizabeth merely elevated her pencil thin eyebrows, surveying Amarita from head to toe, as if she found her insignificant, and murmured, "I'd like to give the stupid cow a jolly good slap across her smug face."

When Amarita moved out of earshot, Elizabeth sent her friend a crafty smile. "As it happens, fate holds an appropriate future for her. Nigel informs me the only mischief she'll conjure from now on will be in the seraglio. Surrounded by women for the rest of her life. No husband for her, especially not a prince."

Fiona snorted. "Something to be said for vengeance

served cold, after all. Never thought I possessed such a capacity for vindictiveness, but then, no one ever tried to kill or maim me before. Or terrorise me so." She directed a sober look over her shoulder at their bodyguards, and then to Elizabeth. "And you were meant to be the victim, all because she desired a prince for a husband. I hope she's shut away forever." She paused. "Did you give Nigel your answer, dear girl?"

Elizabeth felt a sudden prickling spread from her middle out to her fingertips. Her hands were suddenly slick inside her riding gloves. Touching her heels to her mount's side, she broke into a canter. A gust of humid air whipped her topi off her head, sending it in a frenzied roll behind her. No sun filtered through the dense bruise-coloured clouds, and the jungle seemed even darker than usual. And silent. No crows or parrots screaming, no chattering monkeys, or distant roar of jungle cats, only the *clop* of horses' hooves on the dry ground, the creak of the supply wagons, and the occasional shouts from their party.

At last Elizabeth reined in and Fi plunged to a halt beside her, one hand clutching her own topi and concern etching her features.

"He requires an answer by tonight," Elizabeth said, looking straight ahead. "I shan't marry him, Fiona. It won't work." She gave a mirthless laugh. "Although I mentioned my chat with him about my father and Amarita, there's something I didn't tell you." She finally met her friend's eyes. "Sir Clive saw us together in close conversation and took it upon himself to 'rescue' me. He made it clear—in all politeness, of course—that we shouldn't do as a couple. Too much social turmoil now, you know, not the political thing to do. He even insinuated to me that Nigel wouldn't be long in Calcutta."

Fiona stared at her in disbelief. "What the bloody hell are you on about, Elizabeth? You two are in love! Of all the ridiculous notions, 'will not work' my skinny backside! Nothing works if no effort isn't put into it, for goodness sake!" Fi snatched off her topi and tore out the tangled straps. "You will have observed by now," she said dryly, "that life is not perfect—and so it shouldn't be, for with no irregular turns we'd be bloody bored, indeed. I want no more of this nonsense, Elizabeth. Snap out of this pet and marry the man!" She slammed the topi back on her head, wrenching the straps into place and tying them.

"I am firm in my decision, Fiona." Elizabeth regarded her friend grimly. "I must be sensible for the sake of my future children. Where would they belong? Look at what Nigel has suffered. No, I don't wish to discuss it further."

"Codswallup! Your children will belong anywhere they wish to. It's a shame such shallow people exist, darling, but will you kowtow to them, or live life on your own terms? If you wish to change things, you must help to make one world rather than contribute to the making of several hostile ones. Come, what is life without a spanner or two?"

"Nigel and I cannot change the world."

"Perhaps not. But you *can* live to your own standards, do what *you* believe to be right. I've known you since leading strings, Elizabeth, and I know you have backbone. Use it."

"I've lost the damn thing then!" Elizabeth lashed out. Instantly contrite, she said, "Oh, I *am* sorry, Fi. Please, I cannot discuss this now. I'm numb and not keen on speaking to Nigel. He'll be . . . disappointed, and I think, angry." She rubbed a restless hand under her damp collar, wishing it were tomorrow when she could plan her voyage to New Zealand. The sooner out of India the better. "I think—"

"I'm derelict in my duties, ladies!" Harry called out, interrupting Elizabeth as he rode in, joining them. "Supposed to be keeping an eye on the two of you, but here I am gadding about. I say, juicy bit of news!" Leaning toward them in a confidential manner, he murmured, "It's rather hush-hush, worse luck, but you needn't fear any more snipped girths. Amarita—"

Fiona cleared her throat. "We know, dear."

Harry's eyes widened in surprise, then he grimaced. "Piece of rotten luck, Kashmiri politics. Personally, I'm gagging to see how far the slag will stretch on the rack."

Fiona laughed in delight. "I do love a bloodthirsty man!"

Elizabeth saw the warmth gather in Harry's eyes, and then Nigel rode in.

"No time for stopping, I'm afraid." His voice rose over the increasing wind, and he nodded to the southwest where black clouds bloomed. "The monsoons are arriving with a vengeance, and this storm may very well break over southern Bengal instead of Burma. If so, Calcutta will receive the brunt of it."

As if concurring with him, a low rumble reverberated several miles to the south.

"Elizabeth, where is your topi? Thought you knew the danger of going hatless in this climate, even when the sun is hiding. Here, take mine—I'm not so vulnerable as you are." Nigel removed his own topi, fixing it on her head.

Elizabeth could smell his musky patchouli scent as he leaned over her, and she was back in her camp bed, underneath his naked body, straining. . . .

Mumbling a thank-you, she abruptly averted her eyes from his hungry regard.

Nigel's burning expression melted into a frown, but he swung his stallion around, preparing to gallop up the line. "Haste is imperative," he shouted. "When this volley hits, flash flooding is a very real danger. Stay with the ladies, Harry." Calling up the line, he issued orders in Urdu, then addressed Harry again.

"Pass the supply bearers quickly. If we're hit, those chaps are instructed to cut the supplies off the pack horses and gallop for their lives—as we all will." With one more curious

glance at Elizabeth, he bent low over his stallion, riding hell
for leather up the column.

Elizabeth securely fastened Nigel's topi, closing her eyes
as she breathed in his scent once more. Perhaps she might
forget to return it, and pack it away in a trunk to take out now
and again when she felt especially lonely living on her rural
sheep station.

"Come on, Elizabeth old girl, we must 'scram' as the
Yanks say," Harry urged.

Elizabeth's eyes snapped open and she pressed her mare
forward. The wind was brisk, but it was the occasional vigorous gusts that slowed their progress. Bowing her head in
an attempt to escape the flying dust, Elizabeth gave up at
last, stopping to rifle her saddle bag in search of a kerchief
to tie about her lower face. She could feel the individual
grains of sand beating into her clothing and stinging the
back of her neck.

Fi halted with her, doing the same with a square of dark
pink silk, and Harry, having nothing with which to cover his
face, spit out a mouthful of dust.

Wiping his mouth with the back of his hand, he shouted,
"Let's go!"

Another severe blast hit, and both girls had to steady their
jibbing horses.

"Will we make it do you think, Harry?" Fiona lowered her
kerchief just enough to speak.

Harry merely regarded her grimly and motioned them
forward.

"The devil you say!" Colonel Mainwarring surged to his
feet, throwing his pipe in a brass ashtray and striding round
to the front of his desk. The veins in his neck stood out in
livid ridges and his eyes bulged in incredulity as he stared at
his secretary.

Lieutenant Fairfield stood red-faced before him. "Yes, sir.

He simply walked in and surrendered himself. He's waiting in the outer office under guard."

"Well don't just stand there! Bring him in—and get Porter here on the double. And Covington-Singh, when he condescends to show himself."

Bloody hell, if this didn't beat all! Perhaps, Mainwarring thought, he needn't retire after all, if he received the credit for arresting the "Bengal Killer," as the press had now dubbed the local murderer.

Snorting in ironic amusement, the Colonel leaned backward on his desk and folded his arms across his chest. All the work Covington-Singh contributed to this investigation and the killer hands himself over on the proverbial silver platter to the wog's arch rival. *Ha! So much for you, Covington-Singh*—I've *got him*!

Lieutenant Toppenham entered the Colonel's office, his uniform pristine, uniform cap correctly under his arm, and flanked by two sepoys.

Standing to attention, he said, "Reporting for duty—and reprimand, Colonel Mainwarring."

Celia Armstrong stumbled into regimental headquarters, one hand holding on to her hat, the other grasping the doorjamb as a *whoosh* of muggy wind blasted her from behind. Really, how undignified for the future wife of the Colonel's secretary to arrive at headquarters looking as if she'd skipped through a child's sandbox. Fortunately, the outer office appeared deserted.

Glancing at her new Timex wristwatch, she saw that it was just after 6 P.M. Well, no wonder, everyone had likely departed for home—except her Johnny. Celia had called the club and dropped by his bungalow, but the inconvenient man had not called in at either location as yet, so that left only one place for a dedicated young officer on his way up the regimental ladder. Johnny's mother, Mrs. Fairfield, had as-

sured Celia her son was destined for great things. Well, of
course. After all, he was destined to marry her, wasn't he?
Celia's mouth lifted in a smug slant as she smoothed her pale
linen suit. Wouldn't her old schoolfriends just tear at their
hair when she sent them her betrothal announcement. Yes,
she could see it now:

*Young Calcutta Socialite to Marry Capt. J. Fairfield of
the 1st Rangpur Foot, Bengal, Indian Army.*

The promotion to captain was certainly imminent, and
soon after, major. Why, eventually Johnny might serve as a
full colonel in charge of the whole regiment! While her former classmates were smothering under the yoke of medioc-
rity, with husbands working in such unimaginative and
nowhere occupations as accountants and factory supervi-
sors, *her* future husband served as an officer stationed in an
exotic locale. And if war broke out, think of all that lovely
potential for promotion!

"Celia, what the hell are you doing here?" Johnny Fairfield hissed.

Celia blinked in surprise. What could Johnny be up to
eavesdropping at the Colonel's partially opened door?

"Language, Johnny! I'm shocked you should forget yourself so in a lady's presence." Smiling archly, she said, "Even
if that lady is me." Could it be he might be so comfortable
with her that he had just spoken naturally? She tingled all
over, imagining again the black print of their engagement
announcement.

But Johnny had turned his back on her, his nose stuck in
the door opening. He waved his hand behind him in a cutting
motion.

Celia sniffed and pushed out her chin defiantly. "I certainly did not come here to be treated in this dismissive and
insulting manner, Lieutenant Johnny Fairfield!"

Johnny abruptly shut the door and resumed his chair,
dragging agitated fingers through his reddish locks. "I'm

sorry, Celia. It was indeed inexcusable of me to treat you with such disrespect, but what *are* you doing here?"

Mollified, if only slightly, Celia seated herself, even though he had not invited her to do so, in a straight back chair, her hands folded primly in her lap.

"I only came, Johnny dear, to remind you to escort me to the Hunt Gala this evening." She leaned forward, excited. "Your mama procured the invitations. Anybody who is *anybody* is attending. Your mama also purchased a divine gown for me! I'm just dying to wear it!" *Eat your heart out, Miss Mainwarring. Let's see Johnny even* glance *in your direction while I'm in lavender satin and lace!* "Perhaps we might enjoy a quiet supper, just the two of us, in the club's dining room before the event? And don't bother with your stuffy old uniform, darling, wear that fashionable Prince of Wales suit. It gives you such an air of sophistication and genteel refinement. In fact—"

Colonel Mainwarring's voice boomed, nearly shaking the walls of regimental headquarters and startling Celia into silence. His choice of words were, for the most part, foreign to Celia's limited vocabulary of obscenity. For the part she did understand, she felt the flush of embarrassment spread on her cheeks and down her throat.

"Well!" she managed at last. "The Colonel must be ignorant of my presence, or I'm sure he'd never so much as mutter those words under his breath."

Johnny massaged his temples. "Celia," he began slowly, as if he addressed a child. "The Colonel is absorbed in a critical meeting just now. He is oblivious to anything outside his office. I suggest you leave before any violence breaks out."

"Violence!" Celia shot to her feet, holding a dramatic hand to her throat. "Oh, my goodness. Johnny, what is going on? Are we—are we going to war?"

Johnny sighed deeply and closed his eyes momentarily. "Of course not. But it is a rather a dicey situation, you see— Lieutenant Toppenham just turned himself in."

Celia's eyes widened not quite so much because a suspected killer was now safely confined, but more importantly, because *she* would be the first to spread the news!

"Oh, jolly good show! How wonderful, darling. We shall all feel safe again with the killer behind bars. I'm off to inform both our mamas. How thrilling!" Running as fast as her high heels allowed, she barrelled through headquarters nearly knocking down a sepoy as she did so.

Johnny Fairfield watched Celia's departure in relief. God, he'd end up in Bedlam— or the bloody frogs' Foreign Legion if he actually married the whiny, tattle-mongering little witch. Turning quickly, he opened the Colonel's office door just wide enough to hear the proceedings. Something damned peculiar was unfolding, and as the old man's secretary, it was his job to be informed. Even if the old man had forgotten to ask him to sit in.

Colonel Mainwarring paced the generous area of his office, then whipped about, confronting Toppenham.

"Do you realise, Toppenham, you are wanted on a charge of murder? Desertion is the least of your problems."

Toppenham's eyes nearly popped from his face. "Murmurder, sir? B-but sir, I assure y-you, I haven't murdered anyone! Gr-granted my behaviour has not befitted an officer, but . . . I didn't kill anyone!"

"Beryl Tate was found murdered in the most hideous manner on the day you went missing, Lieutenant! What have you to say to *that?* And before you boast an alibi, you'd best make sodding sure of it. Not that it will make any difference." He paused, squeezing the bridge of his nose. "Bloody wogs will have a field day with an Englishman under arrest for one of these God-awful murders. But an officer in the Indian Army! We'll drown in scandal like billy-oh."

Hearing a step behind him, Johnny swung around to find a subdar-major proffering a folded piece of stationary. Opening it, he felt his heart rate accelerate and adrenaline speed through his veins. He tore into Mainwarring's office without knocking, but ground to a halt at Toppenham's words.

"Colonel Mainwarring, I *do* have an alibi. My wife. I eloped with Miss Compton that afternoon!"

Chapter Thirty-six

Elizabeth riffled listlessly through her extravagant wardrobe, pulling out one evening gown after another until she finally settled on a dramatic Valentina for which she had paid a truly exorbitant sum. The emerald silk chiffon slid in a sensuous ripple through her fingers and hundreds of diamantés winked and sparkled when she held it up to the mirror. It was strapless and clung to the body, falling in a luxurious swirl to the floor. It was the poshest gown she owned. But it wouldn't make her feel any better. That wouldn't happen until she was safe on her sheep station and deep into her resolution to forget Nigel. But God knew how long that might take. Maybe never.

Well, one step at a time. First she must inform him of her decision. She took a deep breath. She did not look forward to telling him tonight. Then, first thing in the morning she must book passage to New Zealand.

Sliding up the side zip of her gown and slipping on matching diamanté-studded high-heel sandals, she switched her attention to her hair. It was still a little damp from her bath, but it would dry quickly. She efficiently applied powder, mascara, and eyeliner. Screwing off the tops of several lip rouges, she finally selected Max Factor's Bronze Sugar and automatically reached for her favourite Arpège, but hesitated over the tall, gracefully curved crystal stopper. No. From now on Arpège would remind her of Calcutta. And Nigel. She'd not wear it again.

Instead, she chose a small cobalt bottle, applying the contents to her wrists and the hollow of her throat. The heady, spicy scent of Evening In Paris surrounded her. She clipped a gold and diamond band to her wrist, and was fastening a cascade of diamonds to her ears when the window pane rattled violently from a particularly vehement gust of wind.

There was a banana tree outside her window, and she could see in the dusk its fronds whipping to and fro, slapping the glass. The black clouds were overhead now.

The lamp on her cosmetics table flickered, went out, and came back on only grudgingly. Seizing the emerald envelope evening bag in one hand, Elizabeth slowly reached out, turning off the lamp with the other. A shiver slithered down her spine, giving her a distinct feeling of foreboding. It must be the stormy atmosphere, she thought, heading for the door.

In the drawing room she found Fiona squinting through the window, a doubtful furrow marring her brow, and Nazim tidying the drinks table.

"Nazim, do you know the whereabouts of my father? I take it he has not returned home?"

Nazim bowed. "I believe, Miss-Sahib, he must still occupy regimental headquarters."

"He hasn't sent word then?" Elizabeth persisted, agitated. She shouldn't let the storm affect her so, she told herself. "Is this usual, for him to stay so late?"

Nazim shrugged philosophically. "It happens, Miss-Sahib." Clapping his hands sharply, he called out in rapid

Urdu. "I have summoned your macs, Miss-Sahibs. You will need them. The monsoons come tonight."

When Elizabeth and Fiona arrived at the Mohd Bagh Club, it was already crowded, and the dance band was tuning up on the stage. White party lights were strung in the potted palms, and each table boasted a flickering candle.

Elizabeth grasped a flute of champagne from the tray of a passing waiter and scanned the ballroom for Nigel. Might as well dispense with the unpleasantness straight away.

Fiona, following Elizabeth's anxious gaze, frowned and attempted to plead with her one last time.

"Elizabeth, I wish you wouldn't end it—"

"I must," Elizabeth insisted. "If you don't fancy watching me, go find Harry. He'll be thrilled to see you. He's barely let you out of his sight since that awful accident."

Fiona snorted. "Accident, my skinny backside!"

"There you are, my dears." Amanda Crosshaven's eyes sparkled in the low lighting, and happiness seemed to glow from every pore. "I see the hunt was extremely successful. The beast's skin is on display in the men's lounge." With a conspirator's wink, she added, "Just for tonight the ladies are allowed into the men's inner sanctum. Makes one feel so fast!" Her eyes slid away momentarily. "Speaking of fast, you must be among the first to share my secret."

Finally distracted, Elizabeth grinned and demanded, "Out with it, old girl. We're dying of curiosity!"

Amanda smiled widely. "I found the gumption at last to ask Simon for a divorce. He agreed!"

"Goodness," murmured Elizabeth in surprise. She remembered vividly the scene on the Crosshavens' verandah, but infidelities were so common, couples seldom divorced over them. "I had no idea."

"Well, everybody else did," Amanda said dryly and sipped her champagne. "Bugger's incapable of keeping his damn fly closed. Don't mean to air the dirty laundry, but it's common knowledge. It's almost respectable nowadays to be a young divorcée. But I shan't remain one long." Dipping a finger in her champagne, she moistened the rim of her glass and looked up at them saucily from beneath her lashes. "Reggie has filled out the bumf to retire his commission. We shall return to England, and he to a position in his family's shipping business. Import and export, you know."

"Are both he and Simon here tonight?" Fiona asked uneasily.

"Reggie is arriving soon." Waving a dismissive hand, Amanda added, "Simon, for all I know or care, is with his latest mistress, or 'languishing' at the most expensive cathouse, fondling the newest girl, and sucking on a hookah. He shan't spoil the party fun tonight. Likely he's only too glad to be rid of me. Wives can be dreadfully inconvenient, you know, when you wish to bring home your latest paramour. I give him three months before he is asked for his resignation."

"State officials not keen on him then?" Elizabeth asked, mildly curious.

"Fiona, darling, I must speak with you." Harry appeared, nodding to Elizabeth and Amanda. "Hope you don't mind, ladies." He clasped Fiona's hand and guided her to a more secluded spot several feet distant.

Amanda watched them with a dreamy expression. "I'm in sympathy with all young couples in love, and those two definitely adore each other." Facing Elizabeth again, her features tightened. "To answer your question bluntly: No. Although men are allowed an abundant share of foibles, Simon's increasing activity in the opium dens is raising eyebrows. That, and the women. I understand one of Simon's curb crawlers complained of his rough treatment within earshot of an 'elevated personage.' Oh Lord, turn the other way, it's Miss Butter Wouldn't Melt In My Mouth—Oh hello, Celia. Didn't know you were attending tonight."

Celia Armstrong's gaze narrowed in envy on Elizabeth's gown, but cleared, leaving a smug smile playing about her mouth.

"I recall seeing you in green, Miss Mainwarring, upon every occasion I meet you. It seems, well, such a common inclination for one of your social stature."

"While you invariably favour customs popular in the last decade, Miss Armstrong." Usually content to slough off the biddies with a casual flick of her dry wit, Elizabeth found her temper running a short fuse this evening. Tense with the trepidation of her imminent meeting with Nigel, angry with herself for being so, and now this little cat experimenting with her needle claws. Giving Celia a pointed look, Elizabeth added airily, "You really needn't bind your breasts anymore, you know. The young boy look is history. Voluptuous bombshells are now all the rage. Perhaps endeavours in another direction might bring you up to snuff in that area."

Amanda nearly choked on her champagne, while Celia turned an alarming shade of red.

"I do *not*—" Breaking off abruptly, Celia glared nastily at Elizabeth, jutted out her chin and changed the subject. "Tell me, have you two *fashionable* ladies heard the latest news? I thought not." Nodding to the stage where the Club Secretary, a tall, broad-chested man, prepared the public address system, she said, "I heard it firsthand myself. In fact, it was I who informed management and insisted upon the announcement."

With a toss of her head, she was gone, threading her way between the party-goers. No doubt intent on inflicting herself upon poor Johnny Fairfield, Elizabeth thought.

Looking over her shoulder to check on Fiona, she caught her breath. Harry slipped a tiny .32-caliber revolver into Fiona's evening bag and Fiona shoved it back at him, violently shaking her head. As Elizabeth watched, Harry grasped Fiona's shoulders and spoke earnestly to her, apparently convincing her to keep it, because she relented, taking back the bag in a cautious grip.

Now what does that mean? she thought. But the Club Secretary's amplified announcement distracted her.

"Ladies and gentlemen, I must have your attention for a short moment to impart glad news: The 'Bengal Killer' turned himself in to the authorities early this evening!"

Chapter Thirty-seven

After several initial gasps, the audience buzzed in delighted surprise.

"Who is it?"

"Who gave himself up?"

"Lieutenant Toppenham! Miss Celia Armstrong must receive credit for bearing these happy tidings, as she heard his confession with her very own ears!"

Celia, extremely pleased with the positive attention, smiled sunnily and nodded as if accepting homage.

Someone shouted, "Hip, hip, hoorah! Hip, hip, hoorah!" and before long the whole crowd had taken up the chant. And then Harry bounded onto the stage. He spoke in the Secretary's ear, who nodded and handed him the microphone.

Harry bowed to the Maharani. "As the lucky blighter who killed the tiger hasn't yet arrived, I'm stealing his thunder with a joyous announcement of my own." He favoured the audience with a silly grin and placed a hand over his heart. "You see before you, ladies and gents, the happiest man in the world! Miss Fiona McKay has consented to become my wife." Blowing a kiss to Fiona, who blushed furiously, he jumped to the floor amid many back-slaps and much cheering.

Elizabeth rushed to her friend and, laughing, hugged her. "How lovely for you, darling! I know you'll be delirious. You couldn't possibly have found a better man!"

"Oh, Elizabeth, I'm so happy! I'm actually to be *married*. I do love him so!" Pulling a handkerchief from her deep bodice, Fiona dabbed at her eyes. "How silly of me, I'm crying like a child, but I can't seem to stop. You truly won't mind me not accompanying you to New Zealand?" She wiped the last of her tears and replaced the handkerchief.

"Oh, you are a bufflehead, old thing. Of course I shall miss you, but I'm certainly not cranky because you're marrying Harry instead of coming with me to my sheep station!"

Amanda bussed Fiona's cheek in congratulation. "This certainly has been a most memorable day, my dear. A huge beast of a Bengal tiger is killed, a murderer is caught, I'm to divorce, and you to marry! Felicitations, my dear. There's Reggie just arriving, so do excuse me." Winking as she left, Amanda murmured, "May not be too far behind you, old girl."

Georgina arrived and squeezed Fiona's fingers. "It *is* a perfect world tonight, isn't it, Fiona dear, aside from the raging wind outside. Congratulations, my dear. No one deserves wedded bliss more than you. Well, there is myself, but unlike you, I haven't brought any candidates up to scratch yet, so you may throw your bouquet directly to me, if you please."

Fiona chuckled. "You may be forced to tackle Elizabeth, as I planned on tossing it to her."

Georgina surveyed Elizabeth with a calculating eye. "You shan't stand a chance, my dear, unless you buff up. I'm in excellent physical health myself, I assure you. Even belonged to the Women's League of Health and Beauty for a month or two." She shuddered delicately. "All that gadding about in black underwear—they called those strips of cloth shorts—and white satin shirts in public. I favour performing my calisthenics in private, thank you very much, and in a much more relaxed costume. So—I'm giving you fair warning, my girl—that bouquet is *mine!*"

"I leave you two to fight it out. Harry is calling me." After a step or two, Fiona pivoted back with a mischievous smile. "Do try not to come to blows. I absolutely forbid bruises and lacerations as accessories for my bridesmaids!"

Elizabeth watched Harry slip an arm around Fiona's waist and introduce her to several officers, and she suddenly felt very lonely. "It's too bad Emily is not here. She thought so much of both Fiona and Harry. I wonder how she's doing in Ceylon."

"Receiving the brunt of the monsoon, I shouldn't doubt. I understand it always moves in from the southwest, so I imagine she's already supervising the placement of sand sacks in the event of a flood," Georgina said, and glanced out the window uneasily.

Elizabeth followed her gaze, but the glass merely reflected the ballroom, with its gay throng of people and scores of burning gold pinpoints of candles and twinkling party lights.

Dragging her gaze from the window, Georgina enquired, "So, shall you traipse off to New Zealand by yourself now?"

"I suppose I shall." Elizabeth smiled wanly. "I had planned to procure tickets for the first ship out there in the morning. Now I must wait for a wedding date to be set."

Georgina was surprised. "Really? I had heard . . . well, rumours. Which," she went on hastily, seeing Elizabeth's mouth tighten and temper spark in her eyes, "of course, one must take with a grain or two of salt. Still"—she couldn't resist pressing the issue—"where there's smoke, one generally expects at least a smoulder."

"Dismiss the very thought, Georgina." Elizabeth's voice rang with a definite finality.

"Hmm, if you say so, of course."

Suddenly the club shook as a turbulent gust of wind hit the building. The walls groaned under the stress, and an air current whistled through the ballroom, extinguishing several candles. Elizabeth felt it blow up her gown, and she shivered. The hair on the back of her neck stood on end and her scalp prickled.

A brilliant white flash glimmered in the windows, lighting the landscape as if it were noon. Outside, tamarind trees bent double against the onslaught of the tempest, teaks and palms thrashed wildly, and orchid and bougainvillaea blossoms whirled like multi-coloured snowflakes.

A deafening crack of thunder followed almost immediately, sending the crystal chandelier frolicking.

"God in heaven!" Georgina gasped in fright. Lifting a shaking hand to smooth her static, crackling hair, she said, "Excuse me, dear girl, I must sally forth in search of two— no, three fingers of brandy, or even that horrid pink gin. I *hate* storms. Which is to say, of course, that I'm frightened like bloody, bleeding hell of them. After a generous slug of hooch, I believe I shall find a tall, handsome protective man who is willing to convince me everything is going to be fine." She shivered again. "Since speed is of the essence, tall and handsome are not necessarily required. How quickly one's standards tend to evaporate in times of privation," she trailed off as she made her way to the bar.

Another flicker of brightness startled Elizabeth, but she saw it was only the flash of a camera as a photographer clicked a snapshot of Fiona and Harry. They smiled, posing for another as a ginger-haired officer broke from the group surrounding them and leapt onto the stage.

Fishing a harmonica out of his pocket, he put it to his mouth, blew a few test notes, and then spoke into the microphone. At first Elizabeth thought the poor man garbled around a mouthful of marbles, but then recognised his speech as a thick Glaswegian accent. There was a short ap-

plause, so either *some* people actually understood him, or
they were just being polite. Shunning amplification, he
played his instrument quite melodiously for several minutes
before breaking into song. Ironically, when singing, his
words were quite clear. It was a jolly strain, beckoning
everyone to join in.

> *I've been a wild rover for many's a year*
> *And I've spent all me money on whisky and beer!*
> *There's girls that I've kissed—oh a dozen or more,*
> *But who's keepin' score?*
> *But it's no, nay, never*
> *No, nay, never, no more*
> *And I'll play the wild rover*
> *No, never, no more!*

A laughing, clapping circle formed around the happy couple, and Harry swung Fiona in his arms, careening wildly
about the dance floor.

> *I've travelled all over, through city and town*
> *Ah, the prices go up and the whisky goes down!*
> *In all my wild rovin' just one thing was wrong:*
> *The nights were too short and the days were too long!*
> *It's no, nay, never*
> *No, nay, never, no more*
> *And I'll play the wild rover*
> *No, never, no more!*

> *There's corn in the jug now and grapes on the vine*
> *Aye, and lassies whose kisses are sweeter than wine!*
> *I've counted all the girls I've fallen in love*
> *Just as easy as countin' the stars up above!*
> *But it's no, nay, never*
> *No, nay, never, no more*

And I'll play the wild rover
No, never, no more!

The Scot proved a born showman, leaning into the audience, gesturing and cavorting about the stage. He was a small, slight man, but his voice rang out loudly, rich in its baritone.

For now I can hear them,
The wedding bells chime!
Aye, and one bonny lassie who's gonna be mine!
Last night I was with her
Last night I was free!
And these are the last words she said to me:
It's no, nay, never
No, nay, never, no more
And you'll play the wild rover
No, never, no more!

The crowd went wild in approval and Fiona and Harry collapsed laughing in each other's arms. Elizabeth felt tears prickle her eyes. She really *was* very happy for Fi, but thinking of what could never be hers was overwhelming. Suddenly the lively throng closed in on her, and draining the last of her champagne, she headed for the ladies' loo to compose herself, managing a brave smile as she progressed through the party-goers.

As the loo door swung shut behind her, Elizabeth heard the smooth baritone begging "Lassie, Come and Dance With Me!" That would keep everyone busy for several minutes. Running cool water over her wrists did calm her, but she was still in no mood to return to the ballroom and wandered aimlessly down the hall away from the revelry, until she came upon the French doors leading to the secluded garden where Nigel had first kissed her. Leaning her forehead on the smooth window, she felt the wind seep in around the panes, thick and muggy. Another crack of thunder and almost instantly a flash of lighting. This time she saw the jagged bolt—angry, threatening, and very close.

The reel wound down, and out of the hush a ballad, haunting and sad, filled the ballroom and overflowed sweetly through the separating doors.

Closing her eyes, Elizabeth listened intently, the poignant tale of unfulfilled love penetrating her heart and awakening her. She'd heard the tune "The Miles to Dundee" before but had never paid heed to the words.

It was a mournful tale of a love lost forever. An old man recounted meeting a young and lovely lass in his youth on a stormy winter day, of walking with her to Dundee, and falling hopelessly in love with her. But having nothing to offer her, he'd bravely kissed her upon arriving in the city, and left her. Now he was ancient, lamenting the barrenness of a life spent without the joys of love, and he admonished repeatedly to never let go if your love was pure and true.

Suddenly her eyes were swimming. Oh God, was she truly willing to lose the love of her life because she possessed so little mind of her own, to blindly follow the dictates of a few narrow-minded people?

The tears overflowed, cascading down her face. Maybe it was something else altogether. Something she'd hidden so deeply inside herself because it felt safe, consigning it to lie lost in some dark, bottomless hole. To actually face it meant taking it out and examining it. And that in turn meant heartache.

Hadn't she learned that one invariably lost what one loved most? She'd lost one after another: her father, a home with two parents, and finally the anchor of her life, her mother.

Her father, by not giving her the enthusiastic welcome she had craved, had unwittingly given her the opportunity to achieve the goal she needed most to realise—facing the fact that she must be her own anchor. And hadn't Nigel expected that very strength by asking her to marry him, knowing full well just what they were up against?

She pulled a silk handkerchief from her envelope bag and wiped away her tears. By God, they *could* make a life together! It would be hard for their children, but she and Nigel would give them the stability and strength to hold their heads high over the pettiness. Besides, the Maharani had told her Nigel's Army career was over. New Zealand would offer a fresh start.

Yes! Adrenaline rushed like an effervescent in her veins, and clapping her hands in sheer triumph, she started to rush back to the ballroom, but the sounds of merriment stopped her short. Fiona was savouring her own happiness, and she would not intrude.

Nigel had yet to arrive, so she reached for the latch of the French door, but it flew open in the wind with barely a touch. Even sheltered, the small garden was gusty, but she reveled in it, twirling and holding out her arms in what might have resembled obeisance to some dark storm god. The static air cleansed and rejuvenated, and now the decision made, Elizabeth felt ready to conquer the world.

"A rain dance is hardly necessary at this point, Miss Mainwarring."

Chapter Thirty-eight

Elizabeth stumbled to a halt at the mocking voice.

Canby Tate stood just outside the French doors. He bit off the end of a cigar and spit it on the ground just missing her toes.

Still slightly dizzy, she managed what she thought an authentically haughty stare. "Coming upon people unawares seems to give you some satisfaction, Mr. Tate."

He clamped the cigar in the corner of his mouth. "Oh, you have no idea just how much I depend on the unawareness of our small community, Miss Mainwarring." Extracting a box of matches from his pocket, he rattled it idly.

The club lighting blinked and then extinguished completely. Elizabeth frowned as uneasiness segued into downright creepiness. Something didn't seem quite on. Abruptly the wind stilled. The shrubs and trees quit waving, her evening gown no longer fluttered about her ankles, and the muggy atmosphere weighed like an anvil on her head. Tate lit a match and puffed vigorously on his cigar so the end of it glowed in the gloomy, isolated garden.

"I'll leave you to your smoke, Mr. Tate." Elizabeth stepped around him, but he caught her wrist in a crushing grip.

"Not just yet, Miss Mainwarring. We have business," Tate remarked calmly.

"Deputy Commissioner, let me loose! At once!" Elizabeth attempted pulling her arm out of his grasp, but he held it firmly. "You are hurting me, Mr. Tate!" A drop of moisture hit her face.

Tate only chuckled and wrenched her around to face him. "Miss Mainwarring, you don't yet know what pain is, but you will. Oh yes, you will. Like the others, you will get precisely what you deserve. You bints cannot be satisfied with one of your own kind. No, slags like you and my wife, you pant after the darkies. Filthy habit." He snorted in disgust. "But not one you'll have for long, I guarantee that, by God."

Fear raced down Elizabeth's spine, tingling into her extremities, almost paralysing in its potency. She stared at him horrified, nearly allowing the numbness to take over. Another drop of rain landed on her cheek, and another, and another. She shook the wetness from her eyes and tried again to free herself.

"Mr. Tate, obviously you are not yourself. You must still be feeling the shock of your wife's death. I know all too well we sometimes commit inappropriate acts while under the influence of grief."

Tate laughed. "Relieve yourself of the notion, m'girl. Grief, my arse. Can't think when I so thoroughly enjoyed myself." He laughed again, but his eyes were flat, dead. "Her surprise was priceless! Stupid bloody cow actually thought begging might save her worthless life." He pulled Elizabeth close as another crack of thunder rumbled and lightning lit

the sky. Excitement now sparked in his eyes, and she caught
the sickly sweet scent of opium on his clothing. "Not after
she's had a wog's johnnie shoved inside her. If it hadn't happened already, it was bound to soon enough, even if
Covington-Singh did refuse her. She'd have gone sniffing
after another one, and not many men refused Beryl. Everybody bonged the bitch except me. And her tastes remained
stagnant, while mine evolved. I find I require a little something extra."

"You? *You* killed Beryl? Your own wife!" Elizabeth strained
backward, frantic to escape his hold. She had *seen* Beryl. Her
stomach rolled.

"Well, stone the crows," he said, his voice thick with sar-
casm.

The rain was coming down now in earnest, splattering
the leaves and bouncing off the dry ground. Water dripped
from Elizabeth's hair, down her shoulders, soaking her
gown and making it cling. She took a sharp intake of air
and smelled damp earth and foliage. It reminded her of the
odour of decay.

"And damn near succeeded in blaming it on your beau. If
that little ploy had worked, it might have saved your life. As
it is . . ." He shrugged, and spit out the doused cigar.

Something inside her snapped and she struggled violently,
kicking his shins, attempting to bite the hand holding her so
securely. The impact of his backhanded strike snapped her
head sideways. The pain nearly blinded her and left her
limp, with her soaked hair smeared across her face, trailing
in the blood dripping from her mouth.

"Why?" she whispered brokenly. "Why?"

Tate panted and water ran in rivulets down his face. "To
keep the British British, of course! Why do you think there
are so many cheechees about? Because women possess no
discrimination! They hold a certain responsibility as the
bearers of life. Once infected with unsuitable seed or the

vessels of such, they are unfit to carry life and must be eliminated."

"You can't possibly kill every female who isn't British!"

"Ha! There's wishful thinking for you. No, but I may humbly do my part."

"But I saw you exiting an Indian bordello!"

Tate's mouth stretched in an ugly parody of a smile. "I wouldn't dream of contaminating myself with the flesh of an Indian whore. I did mention indulgences in certain 'tastes.' Pain, m'dear, is unsurpassed as an aphrodisiac: feeling the weight of a metal-tipped whip in my hand, tearing open the smooth skin of a darkie whore, watching her blood running in rivers down her legs. I allow her one gut-curdling scream before I stuff a rag soaked in her own blood into her mouth. Very expensive, but so satisfying. Now"—he wiped the rain from his eyes—"I fancy a short walk. Come along," he said, jerking Elizabeth into step with him.

Elizabeth opened her mouth to scream, and was relieved to find she could. She half-expected to manage only the hoarse croak common in nightmares. Unfortunately, several staccato cracks of thunder drowned her shrieks. Undaunted, she continued to screech and wrestle wildly, impeding Tate's progress. He stopped and, seizing a handful of her dripping hair, yanked back her head and squeezed the vulnerable arch of her throat with his free hand.

Nearly fainting from lack of air, Elizabeth ceased her struggles, and Tate was able to drag her more easily toward the gazebo. She desperately gasped for air and cast one last despairing glance toward the clubhouse.

A dim wavering light shone through the windows, shadows danced, and as if far in the distance she heard a deep male voice raised in song. Something about rain . . .

Chapter Thirty-nine

Nigel and half a dozen sepoys burst into the Mohd Bagh Club ballroom a second before darkness claimed it. Few candles survived the blast of wind Nigel and his men let in, but it was more his loud arrival than the loss of electricity that quieted the celebrating crowd.

The band leader took one look at Nigel's fierce expression in the flickering light and ran a finger across his throat, signaling silence to the players. One by one, with the occasional sour note, the instruments fumbled to a halt.

Sir Clive stepped forward, glass raised in tribute. "I say, three cheers for the man who brought down that monster of a Bengal tiger!"

"Hip, hip, hoorah! Hip, hip, hoorah!"

Nigel nodded impatiently to Sir Clive and scanned the room for Elizabeth. His mother, he saw, was safely surrounded by her ever-present entourage, but of Elizabeth there was no sign. He signalled to his men, indicating they should fan out.

The Maharani beckoned him as the second rendition of "For He's the Jolly Good Fellow" broke out that evening. It was imperative he find Elizabeth without causing a widespread panic. He endured slap on the back after slap on the back, making his way to his mother. Congratulations slipped in one ear and out the other.

"Excellent job, old boy!"

"Damned good show, sir!"

"Trophy to be proud of, Covington-Singh!"

"Congratulations, sir." Captain Henderson saluted him.

"Get that band playing again, Henderson," Nigel ordered. "And keep Sir Clive out of my way, I don't care how you do it!"

Henderson blinked. "Yes, sir, er, at once, sir!"

"What a night, old chap!" Harry walloped him and seized his hand, pumping it violently. "Killed the damned tiger, saved Fiona, and caught the bloody sod of a murderer! Well done, old boy! You may drink to me, as well, you know! Fiona has made me the happiest of men. We're to be married!"

"We need to find Elizabeth, *now.* I believe she's in danger, and I need your help." His gaze darted about, finding Fiona. He nodded toward her. "Tell one of your friends to keep her busy while we look for Elizabeth. We do *not* need hysterical women."

Harry immediately sobered. "What in blazes goes on, old chap?"

"I've just come from the hospital. Mrs. Newsome recovered from her coma and informed me whom she saw murder Beryl Tate," he replied, seizing Harry's arm, leading him from the room to the hallway toward the loos. If Elizabeth was not in the ballroom, likely she'd slipped out to the loo.

"Of course, old boy, everybody knows. That toffy-nosed cow, Celia Armstrong, browbeat the Club Secretary into making the announcement. She heard Toppenham confess to all."

Nigel snorted. "Obviously she didn't stay long enough. Oh, he blew the gaff, all right and tight, but he didn't murder anyone. No, we're looking for Deputy Commissioner Canby Tate himself."

"You'd better take this then, son." The Maharani had caught up with them, and as Nigel watched, she discreetly lifted her gown, plucking a tiny Remington Over and Under derringer from the top of her stocking. "I never did like that man, the obvious prejudice of his claim against you notwithstanding. No, take it," she insisted, when he tried to refuse. "Your father taught me that one might gain the upper hand by doing the unexpected. Your service revolver and kukri are in plain sight. Why don't you slip this little pepper shot in the back of your trousers." When she saw it tucked properly in place, she said, "I believe I did see Elizabeth come this way, so why don't I check the ladies' for you before I toddle back to the party and keep everyone out of your hair, dear boy?"

Nigel barked orders to one of the two sepoys following them to fetch torches on the double and, striking a match, held it high to provide the needed light to guide them down the corridor.

The Maharani stuck her head into the dark ladies' room, calling for Elizabeth, but received no response.

Noticing the French doors ajar, Nigel swore roundly. "She's outside," he said, stepping out into the pouring rain.

Fiona swung to a halt as the song ended, and she stepped back from her partner, clapping her hands. Another young man bowed before her and took her in his arms for the next reel. Indeed, she was enjoying the time of her life, but she'd rather be doing it with Harry.

MacGregor—or the Singing Scotsman, as he was now dubbed—bent from the stage gazing directly at her as he sang Stewart and Grant's composition about a girl from Glasgow town being queen of the city and the fairest of all. . . .

How strange. Fiona watched as Harry, Nigel, the Maharani, and two sepoys left the room. Reeling across the floor, she noted several more sepoys stationed at various spots. They hadn't been there before Nigel arrived. Elizabeth was missing, too. Something was happening and she intended to find out just what.

Wrenching herself from her dance partner's arms with an abrupt apology, Fiona hurried for the same door Harry had taken. "The Girl from Glasgow Town" continued behind her:

> *Let it rain, let it pour, she said she'll be mine*
> *The sun's gonna shine in my heart forever more!*

"You should have listened to well-meaning advice, Miss Mainwarring." Tate stopped for a brief rest, panting now from the exertion of dragging her.

A jagged bolt of lightning flashed behind him and thunder boomed like a hundred cannon. The heavens lashed and peppered them with sharp needles of rain. Elizabeth could see, courtesy of the lightning, that they stood only a few feet from the garden gazebo. Tate pulled her toward the steps, but her diamanté-studded evening sandal tangled firmly in a bamboo thicket at the base of the stairs. Tate mumbled a few filthy words, and let loose of her throat to force free the affected ankle.

As soon as he let go, Elizabeth jack-knifed into action, levering herself upward, fisting up the long skirts of her dress. Her fight lasted all of two seconds, until the force of Tate's tackle sent them both tumbling to the ground.

"Bitch!" he spat in her ear. He ground her face into the soggy grass until she began to gag, and then tugged her head up by the hair when she felt the black edges of unconsciousness closing in.

"Try anything like that again, and you'll sodding well regret it!" He hauled them both upright and fumbled for a moment.

Something sharp pierced the underside of her chin. Blood, warm and slick trickled down her throat, across her chest, and into the bodice of her gown. Closing her eyes, Elizabeth forced herself to remain still. Any movement might cause the knife to plunge deeper. As it was, her violent trembling might cause the point to sink in.

Finally he pulled the knife—no, it wasn't a knife—away half an inch. Lightning glinted off the ice pick, and somehow that frightened her even more.

"Now then, you filthy wog lover, we're about to enjoy a little sojourn in this gazebo." He chuckled. "Well, I'll enjoy myself at any rate. I doubt you'll have much fun."

Still holding the pick, he covered her mouth with his other hand, pinching her nose, effectively cutting off her air again.

"I can make this fast or slow. It all depends upon you," he said pleasantly. "If you prove uncooperative, and I must admit, most of your kind have been remarkably insubordinate, you will discover how many truly sensitive spots exist on your body. Oh, I'm sure you think your lover has found them all with his lips, but I shall find one or two more with my little friend here." He waggled the ice pick for emphasis and removed his hand from her nose and mouth.

Panic surged through Elizabeth like an electrical current, as she gasped, choking for air. Her vision darkened and dull yellow dots danced before her eyes. Tate already had her halfway up the gazebo steps, and she knew if he succeeded in dragging her inside, she'd never live to see the morning.

Desperately she manoeuvred the edge of a step between her bare heel and her sandal, and positioned her other foot over the toe of that sandal, holding it down. It was a feeble attempt, but it did slow him down.

"Tate! Let her go! Step aside at once!" God, was that really Nigel's voice? Elizabeth nearly fainted in relief, but gathered her wits and immediately began struggling again.

Tate started in surprise just enough for Elizabeth to slip from his grasp, but he recovered with frightening speed, pulling her full length in front of him and positioning the ice pick again at her throat.

"I've got the advantage on you, Covington-Singh," he shouted, peering through the shadows and pouring rain. "I'm sure you possess a firearm—ah, so you do." The garden lit once more. "I, on the other hand, have a bulletproof shield. Well, not precisely bulletproof, but the slag will stop the little buggers quite effectively. Just toss that revolver over here. Woodford's as well."

"Harm her, Tate, and you'll beg for death." Nigel's voice sounded raw as he and Harry tossed Tate their weapons.

Tate laughed and, shuffling a few paces, Elizabeth in tow, he bent and picked up both revolvers. He pocketed the ice pick, tucked one gun into his trousers, and pressed the other to Elizabeth's temple. "Don't think so, old boy. Even your exalted father can't keep you from being cashiered and tried for murder. Such a disgrace. HMG would never stand for the cock up—you might even find your throat cut in a dark alley. Yes, you're far too important to stand trial.

"No, I'll tell you how this ends—"

"You perverted *bastard!*" Colonel Mainwarring stalked out of the darkness behind Nigel, his service revolver drawn and aimed at Tate. Elizabeth closed her eyes briefly. It might as well be aimed at her since her body covered Tate's. Her father looked crazed. The tendons in his throat stood out in livid ridges and his hand shook holding the gun. "Touch my daughter, you—" Spittle flew from his mouth and he stopped, swallowed and regained control of himself. "I'll slice open your putrefied gut"—he walked slowly toward them—"and string out your intestines while you watch—"

The shot was deafening, so close to her ear, the jolt of it reverberating up Tate's arm and into Elizabeth. And then she saw her father lying on the ground in the pouring rain, red blossoming his chest.

"You see I do mean business, gentlemen," growled Tate. "Back off." He flicked a contemptuous look at Mainwarring. "Serves the sod right. He sampled my slag of a wife, as well."

While Tate crowed over the Colonel, Nigel signalled to the sepoys behind him, who had melted into the shadows before Tate had caught sight of them.

"You have a hostage and weapons, Tate, but how do you propose to make an escape? Even if you kill all of us, you'll be caught. And hanged. So why don't you drop the gun and give up?" Nigel called through the beating rain.

Tate's hold tightened on Elizabeth. "I think not. It's only a few miles to Burma, and I have contacts. I'll keep your doxy for insurance all the way. And you'll give me free passage because if you fail, her death will make Beryl's look like a tea party."

Nigel looked at Elizabeth. *Courage,* his eyes said. "What guarantee do you offer to release her unharmed if I set up transportation for you?"

Tate let loose a nasty chuckle. "None. But if you don't arrange it, you know she dies. Now let's get things moving, shall we?" He nodded to Harry. "You, bring a car round with a full tank of petrol." Directing a sharp look to Nigel, he reiterated, "No one stops me, remember that."

Elizabeth risked a glance at her father. The ground was too dry to soak up the heavy fall of rain, and he was lying in a growing pool of water. He was so still, she wasn't sure he was breathing.

"Please," she croaked, her throat raw and swollen from near strangulation. "My f-father needs h-help!"

"Not if I did a decent job—what the—?"

It was over so quickly Elizabeth hardly knew what happened. She heard a popping sound, a high shrill curse, and a slam hitting the gazebo behind them, as if someone had thrown an ax.

Tate twisted away instantly to discover the source, and another explosion rent the air. Tate's hold on her slackened and dropped as he crumpled to the ground, a neat hole piercing his forehead. His eyes stared up sightlessly into the rain spattering his face. A trickle of blood leaked from the black hole.

Nigel threw down the .32-calibre and ran to Elizabeth. He scooped her up in a tight embrace, and she found herself sobbing and shaking. Wrapping her arms around his neck, she clung with all the strength she could muster. "Nigel, oh God, Nigel—my father?"

"I'm sure he'll be fine. I don't think Tate's bullet hit anything vital." He glanced over his shoulder at the Colonel, but blocked her view of him. "The medics are seeing to him, taking him to hospital."

Elizabeth closed her eyes, breathing as deeply as her raw throat allowed, determined to calm herself. She pushed gently from Nigel's embrace. Her body, she found, wasn't as strong as her mind, because she stumbled on legs not yet ready to stand on their own. Nigel caught her and swore when he saw blood mingling with the rain dribbling down her neck. Water streamed off his uniform cap, and he removed it, fitting it on her sodden hair. It dropped low over her eyebrows, but it at least sheltered her face. In only a moment his hair was plastered to his head.

"I must see him. He risked his life for me." But her father was strapped to a gurney and borne at a run toward the clubhouse by orderlies. Harry sprinted forward.

"They tell me it's little more than a scratch. It hit high in the right shoulder. Risk of infection, of course, as far as they can tell now. But it appears a clean shot. No messy fragments." Even at close quarters he shouted to make himself heard over the pounding rain.

"Come, let's get inside and dry off." Nigel noticed that Elizabeth's gown was heavy and dragging in the mud. Lifting her in his arms, he started for the clubhouse. Speaking loudly to Harry over her head, he said, "For God's sake, as well as everybody else's, Harry, keep your firearms well out of your future wife's reach! She might have killed Elizabeth instead of merely hitting the gazebo! Sadistic bastards I can handle, but God save me from amateurs with guns who may only hit the broad side of an elephant."

"I do beg your pardon." They had reached the clubhouse and a dripping Fiona waited for them inside, blowing imaginary smoke from the barrel of her tiny pistol. "There was absolutely no danger of me accidentally killing Elizabeth. I knew if I aimed right for her I'd miss widely. All I intended to do was distract Tate, and so I did." She shrugged and with a moue of distaste dropped the pistol into her evening bag. "And likely I'd miss the elephant entirely, but thank you for the compliment, Nigel."

Chapter Forty

Twenty-four hours later, Elizabeth shivered in her silk dressing gown and turned from the dark, rain-splashed drawing room window. Fiona sat on the settee, similarly attired, leaning on Harry. Her father was seated across from them, his right arm in a sling and his slippered feet resting on the table in between. Nigel stood by the fireplace, his hands shoved into his pockets. Nazim busied himself serving refreshments from a silver tray on the sideboard.

She and Fiona were lucky to have slept all day after staying up most of the previous night. Nigel and Harry enjoyed no such luck and looked exhausted. The shot had gone straight through her father's shoulder, thank goodness, and was of no lasting injury. If no infection set in he could look forward to six weeks with his arm in a sling.

Sitting beside her father, she accepted a cup and saucer from Nazim before he left, quietly shutting the door behind him.

The hot honey and lemon soothed her injured throat and Elizabeth concentrated on relaxing. She'd seen Tate dead, but still found it hard to keep still, not to glance constantly over her shoulder and touch the scab under her chin. At least the electrical power had been restored.

Colonel Mainwarring noted his daughter's trembling fingers and rose to unlock his liquor cabinet. Holding one bottle after another up to the light to check the volume of contents, he set his meagre supply of three nearly empty bottles on the low table between the settees, inviting everyone to help themselves.

Elizabeth added a dollup of Loch Dubh to her drink and Fiona lifted her eyebrows.

"Isn't that sacrilege, darling? Thought you only drank whisky of that calibre neat. Sure you want to pass up the Remy?"

Elizabeth rolled her eyes. "Yes," she said firmly. "I never plan to even take a *whiff* of that stuff again! You quite succeeded in doing me in with your Remy toddies, my girl!"

"Yes, well, I certainly hope you never *need* one that badly again." She sipped her cognac toddy and sighed blissfully.

Elizabeth set down her cup and saucer and leaned back on the settee. "Now then, what happened after Mrs. Newsome regained consciousness early last evening, and *why* did Mr. Tate murder his wife and want to kill me, as well?"

"Covington-Singh was reporting at HQ when the message from the hospital came in." The Colonel rose and moved to stand behind Elizabeth, one hand resting reassuringly on her shoulder. "A bollixed scene it was too, with Toppenham turning himself in and insisting he'd merely eloped, not committed murder."

Elizabeth twisted around, facing her father. "But Fi and I

saw Diana after that cad assaulted her! How could she marry such a beast?"

"As to that." Mainwarring cleared his throat. "It seems they were enjoying themselves and went farther than intended. Afterwards Diana asked how soon they might be married—just the sort of thing a young, and er, innocent girl might ask. Toppenham admitted he turned a bit fidgety, pulled up his trousers and scarpered. Before she finished tidying herself an Indian groom happened along. Word was bound to get out, and she panicked. Knowing her reputation was ruined anyway, she screamed, scratched herself, tore her clothing, and in general put on a believable show.

"When Toppenham came to his senses, he realised he must save Diana from the scandal, even if it meant disgrace for himself. So off he goes out his window straight to Diana's, and persuades her to elope with him. It was her idea to swear her old nanny to secrecy to avoid any search parties sent out after them. They'd planned to return in two days, but didn't include a train derailment in their plans. They spent the last several days sweating like pigs and kicking their heels in a flea-infested hostel in Lucknow."

"I'm sure they'll be happy," Elizabeth remarked dryly. "It seems they are quite suited to one another."

"Perhaps they are at that. Covington-Singh can tell you more about Tate than I, as he compiled the research."

Nigel drained the single finger of cognac he'd poured himself, and filled Fiona and the Colonel in on the background of the previous murders.

"But *why* did he kill?" Fiona asked.

"Apparently, Tate's sister ran off with a man of mixed race on the island of Barbados. After impregnating her, the cad abandoned her—went back to his wife, in fact. Tate, humiliated in island society, refused to take in his sister and her darkish infant. Not long after, baby and mother were found dead, and Tate took himself off to a civil post in Singapore.

"But the real stroke of luck came in the form of Mrs. Newsome. Dr. Stafford found it remarkable she could remember anything of that day, let alone the moments before that bastard beat her." He shrugged and set his empty glass on the mantel among the carved ivory pieces. "Colonel Mainwarring took several soldiers to Tate's residence and I headed to the club and Elizabeth."

"When I think of how close it came, my dear . . ." The Colonel shook his head. "Never such a hellish journey as between Tate's bungalow and the club in that god-awful storm." Pressing his lips in a tight line, he lifted his scotch glass and discovered it empty. He made his way to his liquor cabinet again, and reaching into the farthest corner, brought forth a sealed bottle of eighteen-year-old whisky. Regarding his daughter through narrowed eyes, he said dryly, "I seem to have gone through three times as much hooch since you honoured me with your presence, my dear." Working out the cork, he splashed out a measure for everyone.

"Why, you make me out a lush, father! I've hardly touched your liquor supply."

The Colonel tossed back his whisky. "Not you, my dear. Me." He set his glass down and reached again for the bottle. "The endless worries of fatherhood."

"Well"—Elizabeth glanced shyly at Nigel, who regarded her steadily—"your worries on that account are nearly over. I'm marrying Nigel, you know."

"Yes, I was afraid of that." Mainwarring threw back another shot. Defeat etched his features and he grasped the bottle again, but only to return it to the cabinet.

"We shall make our home far from the nasty politics of India. I believe the wilds of New Zealand a perfect location. Please say yes, Nigel. I would live in India if you asked it of me, but I'd rather not. New Zealand is a new world for both of us. Let's start out fresh?"

Nigel held out his arms and she flew into them.

Burying his face in her bright hair, he said, "Anyplace you are, my love, is home."

Epilogue

The screen door banged shut behind Elizabeth as she walked out onto the verandah of the newly erected house at the edge of the sheep station. Hers and Nigel's. It was early evening and the sun was about to set. With summer in full bloom, the foliage was ripe and colourful. How strange to experience two summers in one year. Thankfully New Zealand summers were not as torrid as the Indian ones.

She stood gazing out at the land she shared with Nigel. The soft, green sloping landscape stretched as far as she could see. Life was good. The post had delivered a letter from Fiona today. She and Harry expected their first child in July. Perhaps when Harry was eligible for leave they might visit. Elizabeth fervently hoped so, for she'd never again set foot in India.

Her father had retired to the Seychelles, and surprised her

with regular letters. He had his own life and even courted a local widow.

Elizabeth turned, about to re-enter the house, but stopped when she heard the music. Nigel came out and pulled her back against his chest. Closing her eyes, she swayed with him to the tune playing on the Victrola. She was no longer alone.

Without a dream in my heart
Without a love of my own. . . .

Glossary

Berk: annoying person

Billy-oh: very much, strongly

Bint: whore

Blow the gaff: spill the beans

Bish: cock-up

Boffin: genius

Bosh: nonsense

Bumf: paperwork

Codswallup: hogwash

Cow: woman, bitch

Diamanté: rhinestone

Dicky: unsound

Ek dum: at once

Gin and French: martini

Give us bell: telephone call

Gone for a Burton: absent for some time

Gypsies' or Gypsies' kiss: urinate

Harry by: hurry up

HMG: His Majesty's Government

Huzoor: honourific term

Jammy: lucky

Kerb crawler: prostitute

Lolly: money

Marrow: hit

North of Watford: beyond civilization

Palava: commotion

Pawpaw: Papaya

Ponce: pimp

Pontoon: Blackjack

Sanp: snake

Scarper: run away

Screaming abdabs: the terrors

Slag: whore

Spanner: wrench

Stone the crows: statement of surprise

Suss: guess, discover

Squiffy: drunk

Toffy-nosed: uppity

EVELYN ROGERS
More Than You Know

Toni Cavender was the toast of Hollywood. But when a sleazy producer is found brutally murdered, the paparazzi who once worshipped Toni are calling her the prime suspect. As a high-profile trial gets under way, Toni herself finds it hard to separate fact from fiction.

When an unmarked car tries to force Toni off a cliffside road on a black, wet night, the desperate movie star hires detective Damon Bradley to find the truth. Someone is out to destroy her. Someone who knows the lies she's told . . . even the startling reality that lying in Damon's arms, she feels like the woman she was destined to be. Yet Toni can trust no one. For she has learned that hidden in the heart of every man and woman is . . . *More Than You Know*.

No More Lies
SUSAN SQUIRES

Dr. Holland Banks is head of the Century Psychiatric Hospital and president of the Schizophrenia Research Foundation . . . but is she going insane? The rest of the world seems to be. There's a sniper on the loose, she's being stalked, her father is conducting deadly experiments, and she's begun to hear voices: other people's thoughts. But a man was just admitted to her hospital—one who searched her out, whose touch can make her voices subside. Is he crazy, too, or a solution to her fears? A labyrinth of conspiracy is rising around her, and Holland's life is about to change forever. Very soon there will be . . . *No More Lies*.

A Kiss TO DIE FOR
CLAUDIA DAIN

Women are dying. Pretty women, lonely women, women who give their hearts to a man who promises happily ever after, but delivers death.

He steams into Abilene on the locomotive, a loner with a legend attached to his name. Jack Skull claims he is tracking a murderer, but Anne feels as if he is pursuing *her*. It seems every time she turns around, she comes face to face with his piercing blue eyes.

Though she's sworn matrimony is not for her, somehow she finds herself saying "I do." When Jack takes her in his arms and lowers his lips to hers, reason flies out the window, and she can well believe his will be a kiss to die for.
